THE
NAZI'S
WIFE

THE
NAZI'S
WIFE

Peter Watson

GRAFTON BOOKS
A Division of the Collins Publishing Group

LONDON GLASGOW
TORONTO SYDNEY AUCKLAND

Grafton Books
A Division of the Collins Publishing Group
8 Grafton Street, London W1X 3LA

Published by Grafton Books 1986

British Library Cataloguing in Publication Data
Watson, Peter
The Nazi's wife.
I. Title
823'.914[F]   PR6073.A87/

ISBN 0-246-13022-9

Printed in Great Britain by
St Edmundsbury Press, Bury St Edmunds, Suffolk

For Kathrine

CONTENTS

Author's Note

The central encounter in this story actually took place in Salzburg in the aftermath of World War Two. The rest is fiction.

THE
NAZI'S
WIFE

PROLOGUE

PROLOGUE

LIKE the skin on black plums, her dark eyes had red in them. That is memory number one. She shouldered her way into the room where I was waiting, barley-blond hair splashing about her head in wild yellow twists. But it is memory number two that counts. In her arms she was nursing a dozen fresh hen's eggs—I can picture the shells now, rasping together, patchworked like pepper. In 1946, let me tell you, fresh eggs in Europe were scarcer than Winston Churchill's cigars and worth their weight in nylon stockings. So at first those eggs eclipsed Konstanze's striking looks; they advertised what a composed, clever, calculating character she was.

Konstanze. Nowadays, I suppose, that name is regarded as old-fashioned, plain and stuffy. But at that time, when a ragged Europe was enjoying the first peacetime spring anyone could remember, the name was appealing and popular—alive, attractive, optimistic even, in that it implied durability after a period when so many relationships had been cut cruelly short.

I met three Konstanze's that year, either in Germany or Austria, where my military duties took me. There was Konstanze Steyr, a nurse from Mainz: she had the smallest—and yet the most disconcerting—cast in her brown eyes. It made her look as though she was always about to laugh or cry, one could never be sure which. There was Konstanze Faller, a bookbinder from Augsburg, who had the longest fingers and who bound for my thirtieth birthday a first edition of James Joyce's *Ulysses* in the colors of Ireland—gold on the outside, in honor of the fire in

Jameson's whiskey, and black endpapers, out of respect for Guinness stout. Third, there was Konstanze von Zell.

As she elbowed her way into the room—in her own home, I should stress—I stood up and introduced myself. "Mrs. von Zell. Good morning. I am Walter Wolff—Lieutenant, United States Army, art recovery unit. You can guess why I am here."

She had been smiling as she passed through the doorway, chatting to her small son, who struggled with the rest of the shopping some paces behind her. The instant she saw me, however, the smile vanished, the motherly tenderness dropped from her eyes and all expression was wiped clean. She had stopped in her stride, too, when she had seen me but her son was busy with his load of vegetables, matches and milk, so that he now collided with the backs of his mother's legs. I smiled as the matches fell to the floor, but not Konstanze. Those eyes were sharp as shrapnel.

She took in my uniform, the pipe, unlit in my hand, probably the fact that I spoke German with a Heidelberg accent. She may have registered that I was much the same age as she, a bit taller, a lot darker. Or she may simply have been waiting, for effect.

I watched, puzzled, as she worked her jaws together, coughed gently and, from where I was standing, seemed to swirl her tongue inside her mouth. I knew that she had once suffered from TB. These contortions only made me more conscious of her looks, so I was completely thrown when she parted her lips in a wet, faintly erotic pout and disgorged a knob of gummy spittle onto the lapel of my tunic.

The house where this . . . encounter took place was in Mondsee, a small town about twenty kilometers east of Salzburg, in Austria. It was the first time I had ever been there. In those days the town was a spruce collection of wooden houses and shops, gaily colored in greens, reds and purples. There was a superb baroque church, sand and cream on the outside, black and gold inside and, since Mondsee was on the lakeshore, there were scores of boat sheds and spindly piers, home for hundreds of ducks. That day Mondsee sparkled in the spring sunshine and, for what seemed the first time in living memory, the Austrian air felt warm to the touch. Throughout Europe the prospect of the months of sun and peace ahead was intoxicating.

I had not been a lieutenant for very long. In real life, or "civvy street" as our British colleagues used to say, I was a professor of art history at Berkeley, near San Francisco in California. I specialized in religious art and architecture and that is why, toward the end of the war, I had been assigned to the art recovery unit. Its real name was the Monuments, Fine Arts and Archives Commission, but that was such a mouthful we all called it the ARU. Our job in the ARU was to recover missing works of art that had been looted by leading Nazis. Konstanze was not a leading Nazi but she *was* the wife of one of them and, if what I had been told was true, this beautiful woman held the key to a sensational and politically important recovery.

Spittle would not put me off. Calmly—one might almost say phlegmatically—I took out a handkerchief and wiped myself dry.

Konstanze's husband, Rudolf von Zell, had been Martin Bormann's right-hand man during the war. He had also been commissioned by Hitler himself to take charge of the Führer's unique collection of gold coins, looted from monasteries in Austria and worth millions of dollars. It had taken generations of monks to collect the coins. The collection contained every denomination in every currency known to exist and was irreplaceable.

After Germany's victory in the war these coins were to have formed part of the Führermuseum, in Linz, Austria, to be exhibited alongside old master paintings, also looted, fabulous tapestries, ancient and exotic weapons and an opera house dedicated to Anton Bruckner, one of Hitler's favorite Austrian composers and someone who, like himself, hailed from near Linz.

But no sooner had Hitler committed suicide, in the spring of 1945, than von Zell disappeared, and the coins with him. Worse, Eisenhower was worried that the coins were being melted down, destroying the collection, and the gold used to pay for leading Nazis, like Bormann, Mengele and Eichmann, to be ferried to safety in South America. We already had evidence that a secret conduit, running from south Germany or Austria, via Switzerland and France to northern Spain, was in place, and renegade Germans being passed along it. Von Zell knew all the leading Nazis who were missing and was a superb organizer. So more than art was at stake. My job, and the reason I was in Mondsee that day, was to interrogate Mrs. von Zell—Konstanze—so that she would reveal to us where her husband was hiding out.

Easier said than done. Konstanze von Zell was as strong and as clever as she was beautiful, as those eggs in her arms served to remind me. By the time I arrived in Mondsee, she had already disposed of three earlier interrogators, professional men trained in all manner of persuasive techniques. She had convinced each in turn that she didn't know where her husband was, that she hadn't heard from him in months, that he really was missing, might already be in South America for all she knew, or even dead.

I, however, had one advantage over the other interrogators who had preceded me. I knew that Konstanze was lying.

PART ONE
WALTER

CHAPTER ONE

1

I can only explain why I knew Konstanze was lying by going back to the very beginning. And *that*, I suppose, was the day I drove from Nuremberg to Frankfurt feeling just a little too pleased with myself. In Nuremberg I had recovered an entire collection of things which, I knew, would make all my colleagues emerald with envy. In an air-raid shelter, eight floors down, in the center of the city, I had located nothing less than the Crown Jewels of the Holy Roman Empire, removed from Vienna in 1938. The collection included the Golden Scepter, the Imperial Sword, the Imperial Cloak, studded with diamonds, the Imperial Orb and Charlemagne's crown itself, in all its eleventh-century glory, with raw sapphires, rubies, amethysts and tipped with a jeweled cross. I could talk about nothing else and, if the story I am about to relate had not intervened, I would no doubt be talking about it still.

Frank Wren, my commanding officer, had congratulated me warmly on the phone when I had told him about the coup, and promptly relayed the facts to the press. Although I hadn't seen the stories, I knew I had made the papers in England, New York and France, as well as Germany and Austria. For a day I was famous. Like many people, I had learned to drink seriously during the war, and as I drove my jeep too fast between Nuremberg and our headquarters in Frankfurt, I was looking forward to a celebratory glass or two of Wren's wine. *His* job in real life was as a professor of classics at Harvard and he was a good deal smoother than I, a real New Englander. Tall and laconic, with that fine blond hair which, mysteriously, always stays in place, he wore a discreet blond mustache and the confident gentleness that comes from being raised among well-paid servants. And he always kept a stock of red Bordeaux, which, like the British, he referred to as claret.

It didn't work out as I hoped. "Walter, I have some bad news and I have some good news," Wren called out as I stepped into his office around five that afternoon. "The bad news is that I am requisitioning your jeep; I need it for someone more important." Who could be more important than me? I wondered humorously. I was the man who had just restored the dignity of the Holy Roman Empire, single-handed. "The good news is parked just under that window."

Our headquarters in those days were rather more sumptuous than they should have been. We were billeted in offices on the second floor of a building which had once belonged to the electrical giant I. G. Farben, and which, obligingly, the RAF had failed to bomb. The construction was made of pure white stone with lots of runnels and buttresses and that made it look rather like the bottom tier of an enormous wedding cake around a central courtyard. It was this courtyard which Frank Wren's office overlooked.

I stepped over to the window and peered out. Underneath were a row of bicycles, a wheelbarrow and a lawnmower. Wren had a sense of humor for there was also a dark blue 1938 BMW convertible about a hundred yards away.

He chuckled. "It's the one work of art *I* was allowed to loot. It used to belong to an SS man who's missing. I hope your legs aren't too long for it."

"It's beautiful," I said. And it was: a long low hood, shiny chrome radiator, those sweeping mud guards that you hardly see any more, a cream-colored leather top, what looked like a proper walnut dashboard and huge headlamps, each one about a foot across. All it lacked was Zelda Fitzgerald in the passenger seat.

But Wren never did anything without good reason, so I asked calmly, "Where am I going in it?"

"Aha!" he purred, pleased that his trap had worked. "Salzburg. Ever been?"

I shook my head.

"A beautiful city. Pretty river, dramatic gorge, baroque churches galore, snowy mountains, Mozart, of course, and saibling—a lake trout you *must* try. Lucky man."

"There has to be a catch."

He waved me toward a chair by his desk and held up a sheet of paper which I could see was a long telegram. "This is from my opposite number in Salzburg, a Major Hobel. Down there they call it the von Zell affair. If you can sort this one out, you might just get a medal. Three interrogators have failed already. Even Ike himself is interested in the outcome."

In this manner I was introduced to the events which were to have such a profound effect on my life. At the time, which was late March, our intelligence people were just getting wind of stirrings in the Nazi underground to the effect that the conduit set up in the months following the end of the war was now active and that some leading characters who, until then, had been lying low, were now on the move, bound for safety in South America.

"If von Zell *is* running this conduit, and has melted the coins down to pay for it, then he has virtually unlimited funds. All sorts of people could get away. You can see why our side is so worried." Wren handed me a sheaf of documents. "Eisenhower has signed your orders personally, giving you all sorts of power, should you need it."

I looked down at the papers. Sure enough, the signature on the bottom of each sheet was General Eisenhower's, a bold, flowing hand, in fountain-pen ink. I still have those orders, framed, here in my bedroom. Next to Konstanze's picture.

"Why me?"

"The Crown Jewels. The general read the newspapers."

Flattering. But it also meant I'd be watched. That there would be no room for failure. I would live to regret the notoriety which the Crown Jewels affair had brought me.

"When do I start?" I was still hoping to taste some of Wren's claret.

He inspected his watch. "In your new car, it's an eight- or nine-hour drive to Salzburg. I told them you'd travel overnight and report to Hobel some time tomorrow morning."

Terrific. But I was not exactly bashful in those days, not backward in coming forward, as our British colleagues used to say. "I was hoping I might have earned a glass or two of your Château Croque-Monsieur, sir. A celebration."

Wren's eyes sparkled wickedly. He stood up and walked to the window. "There *is* a claret known as Château Croque-Micholte, Wolff." He looked at me sideways. "I have a case or two and delicious it is. But Croque-Monsieur, I believe, is a sandwich. Sorry." He grinned as I hurried out, blushing despite myself.

I filled the BMW with gas from the depot and drove back to my quarters, still smarting. I would never be as smooth as Wren. At that time I had rooms with someone named Maurice Ghent, another art recovery type, an Englishman from Cambridge and an expert on Italian paintings. We lived in Offenbach, just outside Frankfurt, in the top half of a large, rambling house surrounded by conifers. The bottom half of the house was uninhabited but we shared the place with three squirrels —red ones, which are rare now but were less so then. One had a black smudge on its upper lip so we had named him Adolf. The other two, naturally, became Hermann and Eva.

After a day baking in the sun, the conifers gave off a sweet tang which permeated the house as I climbed the stairs. I let myself in with the key we kept hidden in a German SS helmet we had found in the attic of the house. The helmet was the only bone of contention between Maurice and me. SS helmets were quite rare and we both wanted to take it home as a souvenir. Sooner or later we would fight over it. As I opened the door I heard the panicky rustle of squirrel feet escaping through the hole underneath the washbasin in the kitchen.

There was a note from Maurice propped against the mantelshelf: "Congrats. on HRE Crown Jewels," he had scrawled. "Shall be in Vienna for a few days or weeks, staying at the Palace Hotel. People at the Kunsthistorisches Museum have discovered yet more things missing. Phone me—sorry, call me—if you get the chance. Join me if, by some miracle, you get leave. I can get opera tickets and that gives a man, even you, sex appeal in Vienna." It was signed "M" but there was a postscript. "Dear boy, have a good look at Hermann next time he comes over to eat our shirts. I'm no biologist but I'm sure he's pregnant."

Grinning, I packed fresh socks and underwear, and took some chocolate, cigarettes and nylons from a little store which Maurice and I kept in the house; in our line they often proved useful "gifts" when people were not being quite as cooperative as they might. There was a little whiskey left, two gulps of which swamped the memory of Wren's Château Croque-whatever, and I took the rest to the bathroom, where I soaked myself for half an hour or more amid clouds of steam.

It was nearly dark when I left the key in the helmet and went back out to the car. Being March, the air was already cooling, although the smack of the conifers still hovered in the air, promising yet warmer days ahead.

I put up the convertible's top, relishing my luck. I might have an all-night drive in front of me but the BMW was practically brand new. There were fewer than 10,000 kilometers on the clock and, once I was behind the wheel, my nostrils were swept with the smells of new leather and polish. The gear lever slid around in its box with smooth yet positive efficiency, like an elbow or a shoulder joint.

At that time, in Europe, the roads at night were just as busy as in daytime, the only difference being that most of the traffic was army trucks, shaking the ground as they wound along in convoy. There was also a great deal of hitchhiking—soldiers rejoining their units at the last minute or civilians traveling around looking for work. A BMW was a luxury most of them had never known, so just before I joined the main autobahn outside Frankfurt, I stopped to pick up two figures holding a board with "München" written on it. As I drew alongside them my heart sank, for I noticed how small they were and concluded they must be Italians. I didn't speak the language very well in those days and a six-hour journey in such company was not a pleasing prospect. I disliked Mussolini's Italy almost as much as I loathed Hitler's Germany. I was just about to accelerate off into the darkness when I noticed that one of the "Italians" had long hair, very long hair. They were both wearing trousers but they were women. That was quite different. I stopped the car.

The one with long hair spoke in German. "Anywhere toward Munich will help, sir." Despite the "sir," she wore a proud, rather arrogant expression on her face, which had high cheekbones, a pointed chin and a slightly crooked nose. But sensuous lips that never quite closed—an alluring if not a classically attractive face. She also had what, in the darkness, looked like an enormous bosom. As she leaned forward to talk to me, her breasts hung, beneath her white shirt, round and smooth and impossible to hide. She saw my eyes stray involuntarily from her face, and a strand of embarrassed contempt slid across her features.

"I am going to Salzburg," I said quickly. "Via Munich. Please, get in."

She turned and said something to her companion that I didn't catch. Then she got in the front with me. The other girl, who had severely cropped blond hair and was as flat as the first girl was big, clambered into the back with their luggage, which, I noticed, wasn't much. Perfume was hard to come by in Germany in those days, but as the girls got into the car, the BMW filled with the unmistakable odor of women, sweet, warm and, in some indefinable way, *cleaner* than it had been.

The blonde in the back introduced herself as Elisabetta and her companion as Inge. She had a much deeper voice and, as the journey progressed, showed herself as the more dominant of the two. Inge, or more probably Inge's bosom, got them the lifts but then Elisabetta took over.

They were, it transpired, art students at Munich University who had just been north to see some medieval paintings that had recently been excavated at a church in Lübeck. They were, naturally, very interested when I told them I was with the ARU, and, as it happens, they had read about my recovery of the Holy Roman Crown Jewels. Inge's field was medieval painting—which is why they had been to Lübeck—but Elisabetta, like me, was interested more in architecture, churches and monasteries mainly.

Inge and Elisabetta are not central to my story, but I enjoy recalling our encounter. Our joint interest in art led all three of us into bed together the next morning in Munich—the only time I have enjoyed the favors of two women or of lesbians. And, I also mention them because of something Elisabetta said that night in the car, something that was to prove vital much later on.

Our escapade made me arrive very late in Salzburg and got me off on the wrong footing with my new commanding officer, Major Maximilian Hobel.

2

THE major could have been more welcoming, though, in fairness to him, I didn't exactly hurry to report. To begin with, I was feeling pretty happy about my good luck in meeting Inge and Elisabetta. I was also aching with hunger, lovemaking having taken the place that day of breakfast. And it was, in any case, such a golden day when I parked my car on the Franz Josef Quay, overlooking the Salzach River, and so close to lunchtime, that I sauntered in the sun across the cathedral square to where I could see a small brasserie. There I tasted my first saibling, the fish recommended by Frank Wren, and sank three, or maybe it was four, glasses of beer. So, by the time I strolled into the local offices of the recovery unit, across the river on Schwartzstrasse, it must have been 2:30 in the afternoon and I suspect there was beer on my breath.

"I expected you this morning, Wolff!" Hobel squealed. "First thing. What happened? Just because you've been written about in the newspapers doesn't mean you can come and go as you please. I repeat—what happened?"

If I had told him the truth I doubt whether it would have improved the situation. Hobel was a small man, in all senses. He was bald and fat and, as if that was not already horrible enough, he had a squeaky voice and viscous, bulging eyes that seemed dangerously big for their sockets. I quickly realized that Hobel was the type of person who was happy only when he was unhappy. Nothing could please him, certainly not the kind of morning I had just spent with Inge and Elisabetta. I made up a story.

"I was stopped by the police, sir. The German police."

He sucked in air, like a puzzled goose.

"Yessir. Because of my car. I have a fairly new BMW, a convertible. Major Wren gave it to me yesterday—temporarily, of course, until he can get another jeep for me. But it's an unusual model and, as I say, fairly new. It used to belong to an SS officer who has disappeared so it's perhaps not surprising that the police thought I had stolen it. Anyway, I was stopped near Ingolstadt and it took hours to convince them that the car really did belong to me."

It was extraordinary how, once you were embarked on a lie, it took on a life of its own. You didn't have to make it up; it was as if it was there, waiting to be uncovered, like the smooth sculptures embedded in one of Michelangelo's rough pieces of stone.

Hobel was looking at me in a strange way, staring fixedly, as if I had just told him Hitler was alive, after all, and living happily ever after with Eva Braun in South America.

"You . . . have . . . a BMW . . ." he choked. "A brand-new . . . convertible. All to yourself." It was clear that it would not be easy to get on the right side of Maximilian Hobel. He had taken a dislike to me from the moment he set eyes on me, and over the next few weeks nothing I did pleased him. I soon gave up trying.

Still, while he was busy being jealous about my good fortune with the BMW, at least he seemed to have accepted my excuse for being so late. It was not mentioned again.

He pressed a button on his desk and a woman sergeant stuck her head around the door.

"Lucy, tell Lieutenant Hartt to step in, please."

The commander looked back to me. "You'll share an office with Hartt. There's a desk in his room that you can use and he is the officer most familiar with the von Zell affair." I judged his accent as somewhere out Chicago way. He lifted his feet onto the desk between us. "They say you're a crack interrogator, Wolff. You'd better be. Mrs. von Zell is one tough lady. She's been interrogated three times already and there's been no progress. The last guy came back convinced that she has no idea where her old man is. It's a mess." Hobel uncrossed and recrossed his legs, loosening his tie at the same time. "I understand General Eisenhower is personally interested in this case?"

I nodded. "He signed my orders."

"Well, it's not Ike you have to worry about, wonder boy. It's flabby Maxy Hobel, right here in this room. I'm not a professor of this, or a doctor of that, I'm a soldier, Wolff, a professional soldier. I don't have a smart job to go back to, now that the war is over, like you and your fancy friends. I shall stay in the Army and hope for another war. But not, God forbid, as a major. And, if I don't make colonel fairly soon, I never will. Which is where you come in. I wanted this case all to myself . . . a little rough stuff with Mrs. von Zell or her son and this Nazi would appear in no time." Hobel clicked his fingers and kicked over a mugful of pencils on his desk. "A pushover. That's the way to deal with Nazi scum. That's what they understand. But no. The general read about you in the paper, how you had 'persuaded' a couple of old men in Nuremberg to tell you about those crummy jewels. And now my promotion depends on you. Well, I want results—fast! You—we—are going to bust this case. We are going to find von Zell, recover these damn precious coins—if there are any left—and everybody is going to hear about it. You can keep all the medals you earn; I just want a promotion, and I'm going to get it. We'll be winding up here soon, so this is my last chance. I give you fair warning, Wolff—as long as you are making progress, you'll get my support, but the minute you run into sand, I drop you and go my own way."

How long this onslaught might have continued, God only knows. Fortunately, it was interrupted by the arrival of Hartt. Here at last was someone I could warm to. Samuel Hartt was tall, around six-two, thickly built and slow-moving, with bunches of prematurely silver hair sprouting from his scalp. He wore gold-rimmed eyeglasses that always seemed about to fall off his nose. When I was a boy I always imagined that God looked like Sammy Hartt.

Hartt was a legend in the Army and I had been looking forward to meeting him. He was Jewish, extremely learned, spoke all sorts of languages and had a fine sense of history. As an American Jew he felt he had to abandon his job in the family publishing firm and enlist in the anti-Nazi cause. But—and this is what had made him famous—he also knew, from his reading of history, that there was money to be made from wars, that the people who stayed quietly at home, besides leading safer lives, often profiteered from the more predictable economic changes that took place during war. When he joined the Army, Hartt had therefore made sure he was posted to communications where he could get his hands on the wire machines. Wherever he was stationed he formed two alliances, two sets of contacts. One set was comprised of the journalists who were at the front, wherever the fighting happened to be. These contacts ensured that he kept in direct touch with the way the war was going. He knew what was censored and what wasn't. The second set were army types in New York who were well placed to talk on his behalf to stockbrokers in Wall Street.

He had started in a small way at first, buying shares in railroads and cinemas. But he had been right: the railroads had been necessary to move things around and cinemas were popular, before television, as carriers of visual news. They prospered and Hartt made money. This profit, so the legend ran, was plowed back into shipyards and canning as it became clear just how long the war would last. He made more money. So much so that the people around him, even his superior officers, began to pay attention to what he was doing. Soon he was playing the stock market with the paychecks of entire companies. He had his setbacks, as when he moved into bricks just before the battle of Berlin. This struggle had delayed the end of the war by some considerable time and shares in all industries that might have been expected to pick up after the cessation of hostilities had suffered heavy losses. But, in general, Hartt did even better at the end of the war than earlier. He foresaw the official report in October 1944 which predicted heavy control of exports and imports for a while in postwar Europe and kept out of those industries. In a particular stroke of genius he foresaw the decline of natural rubber and the development of chemical synthetics, stimulated by the war effort. He had stayed out of the vogue for concrete ships (a disaster) but had bought into paper, anticipating the enormous growth of bureaucracy, and into a British currency-printing firm, anticipating the demand for bank notes.

The irony was that Hartt, though a millionaire back home, was still only a lieutenant.

Without waiting to be introduced, he extended his hand and smiled. "Welcome to Salzburg and congratulations on the Crown Jewels recovery. A great piece of work."

After Hobel's welcome I was grateful for that. "Thank you," I said. "I understand we shall be working together."

The major chipped in. "Sammy, I've explained that you know more about the von Zells than anyone, and I've also explained that I want results fast." He addressed me. "You're supposed to be the interrogator, Wolff. But Sammy here is the fixer. He knows his way around Austria better than you know the smell of your own sweat and almost as well as he knows Wall Street. The government, the railways, the economy, who was who in the war—he knows it all. So use him. He can save you time." He turned back to Hartt. "Where's the file, Sammy? The sooner Wolff sees it, and gets on with the job, the better." No first names where I was concerned.

"It's on my desk, sir. All ready."

Hobel scraped back his chair and stood up. "Do you have *any* plans yet, Wolff? Ever been involved in anything similar?"

I shrugged. "Let me read the file before I answer that." I walked to the door and opened it. Hartt and I saluted and he closed it behind us. He rolled his eyes at me but, being the diplomat he was, said nothing. Instead he led the way down a short corridor.

I recall that the Salzburg offices were in an old clinic building—a new one had been erected a few years before, farther out of town. So there was an elevator, originally intended for invalids too sick to walk, but which was, in those days, something of a luxury for ordinary workers. The smell of surgical spirit, or whatever it is that hospitals smell of, percolated through the entire building. It came as no real surprise, therefore, to find that Hartt and I shared an office that had been a small operating theater. It was a green room, not large, with a window which looked through into a small cubicle, presumably what once had been the preop room where the surgeons washed or the students observed. Above us, against the ceiling, were a number of very large, extremely bright chrome lights, reminiscent of the headlamps I had on my car. Underneath the lights, where the operating table would have been, were two desks, back to back.

A thick, potato-colored folder lay on one of the desks. Hartt waved me to the other.

"Practicalities first—oh, and may I call you Walter? . . . Good. You have rooms at the Goldener Hirsch Hotel. It's one of the nicest here, discreet, with an excellent restaurant and very central. We have an arrangement with them so leave the paying to me, then you can settle up later. You get your gas for the car from the commissary of the military government, quoting our number, which is here." He handed me a slip of paper with twelve digits typed on it. "Don't lose that, whatever you do. It will also help you make collect calls to this office when you are traveling around. Next, if you are here, mess night is Wednesday, tonight. Worth attending since the food is good and the wine better still. The liquor is plentiful both before and after, and it's the best way to catch up on all the news. If you want to go tonight, I'll pick you up at the hotel and introduce you to everyone."

"Fine," I said. "I'd love to. Thanks."

He pushed the potato-colored folder across. "You must know you are

the fourth person on this case. The others have all failed miserably and
have run into a brick wall with this von Zell woman. She's obviously a
real toughie—either that or she really doesn't know where her husband
is. Don't ask me, I've never met her. Anyway, look through this stuff,
then we can talk again about how you want to proceed. I've got some
chores to do this afternoon, so I'll leave you to the preliminaries for a
bit."

Before he disappeared he brought me some coffee. Hartt had a fetish I
immediately loved him for: he hated mugs. Everyone had mugs in the
Army, for coffee, tea, chocolate. All, that is, except Sammy and then me.
He thought cups and saucers much more civilized and so did I. To this
day I never use mugs if I can possibly help it.

Sammy left and I opened the folder, unbuttoning my tunic. There was
quite a bit to go through: typed reports in English, copies of letters in
German, official receipts, photographs. But Hartt or someone else had
pieced together the main documents in chronological order and I had no
trouble following the details of the story I was to come to know so well.

3

IT appeared, from what I read, that the gold coins—two thousand and
more of them—had been "collected" during the war from a number of
Austrian monasteries, beautiful, baroque sites such as Kremsmünster,
Klosterneuburg, Hohenfurth, St. Florian and Wilhering. Names I was
familiar with from my history books, but places I had yet to visit. The
coins, as I said earlier, had been selected by Hitler's art experts to form
the nucleus of the coin collection in his projected Führermuseum in
Linz.

They had been assembled over the centuries by patient monks who
were more interested in the historical importance and the artistic quali-
ties of the coins than any intrinsic value they might have because they
were gold. The collection included a five-sequin piece of Pope Clement
VII, dated 1525 and very rare; there was a *Grossone* of Alessandro de'

Medici, engraved by Benvenuto Cellini; gold *excelentes* of Ferdinand and Isabella of Spain; a gold unicorn of James III of Scotland dated 1486, and a *guiennois* of the Black Prince. There were Venetian *oselles*, Portuguese *marabotins di ouro, shaufthalers* from the Tyrol and Carinthia, quintuple *ducats* from Hungary and Geneva *sol d'ors*. There were early papal *danarii* from the eighth century, gold *rijders* from Holland, *portugalösers* from Denmark and *Royal d'ors* of Louis IX.

These were some of the rarer coins which, I read, were virtually irreplaceable. But in all I learned that there were thirty-two cases of coins, a numismatic library of books and manuscripts and twelve folders of documents, correspondence and catalogs. All vanished into thin air.

Together with all the other works of art which were to have been incorporated into Hitler's spectacular museum, the gold coins had found a wartime place of refuge in the salt mine at Alt Aussee. This mine was deep, and therefore safe. Also, by a miraculous accident, the atmosphere inside the mine was perfect for the preservation of paintings. And it was from this mine that the coins had disappeared a few days before the arrival of the Allied forces in Austria.

The details of the removal of the treasure from the salt mine and its subsequent travels, so far as they were known, had been investigated by the first interrogator, a Lieutenant Falcon. His report was at the top of Hartt's file. Falcon had established that the coins had been removed from Alt Aussee on April 30, 1945 by Dr. Rupprecht Hohenberg and Dr. Hans Edelmann, curators at the mine. Hohenberg and Edelmann had acted on the orders of Dr. Rudolf von Zell, who, I read, held two positions. He was chief of the collection of coins and armor for the Führermuseum, and also ministerial adviser in the Party Chancellery, where he was Martin Bormann's right-hand man. He was so grand that he had no fewer than four secretaries.

I could see then why "our side," as Wren put it, was so worried about the fate of the coins. At that point Bormann's disappearance was one of the biggest mysteries of the ending of the war, and if he did indeed have unlimited funds at his disposal, then our chances of catching him were very remote.

Hartt had a coffee machine in the little cubicle adjoining our office and I refilled my cup.

From Alt Aussee, I read, the coins had been taken to Berchtesgaden, where they had arrived the same day and been handed over to von Zell.

He had an office there, not far from Hitler's own living quarters. From Berchtesgaden, the file showed, von Zell had taken the coins to Bad Reichenhall and it was there that they had last been seen in his possession on or about May 6. According to Hohenberg and Edelmann, it had been von Zell's intention to take the treasure to the southern Tyrol, where he could hide out. But the rapid Allied advance made that impossible and, after May 6, neither the coins nor von Zell had been seen again.

A further interrogation of Hohenberg and Edelmann had revealed the reason for the theft of the coins. With Hitler dead, Bormann had become the natural figure around which fugitive Nazis might rally. The coins provided a convenient gold reserve, an adaptable liquid asset. They were no longer regarded as works of art. This interrogation had also established that when von Zell had traveled from Berchtesgaden to Bad Reichenhall with the coins he had driven in a Mercedes 170. This, too, had vanished.

It was also Falcon who had first established that von Zell's wife, Konstanze, was living in Mondsee, a small town near Salzburg, with their son, Dieter, aged seven. When she had first been interrogated, Mrs. von Zell had said that she had seen her husband in mid-March 1945, when she had gone to a mountain hut near the Ober-Salzburg in order to be near him during the last days of the Third Reich. However, she maintained that she had in fact seen him but twice in two weeks at that time because he had been so busy moving art treasures. She next saw her husband, she said, a month later, in April, when he took her and Dieter to Krimml, on the Salzach River. There they had stayed under a false name, von Haltern. Finally, Mrs. von Zell admitted receiving a visit from her husband on May 9, 1945, three days *after* the coins disappeared. But she insisted she had not seen or heard from him since that day. She said that her husband had told her he intended to make his way north, to visit his mother living in Worms, but, as far as she knew, the elder Mrs. von Zell had not heard from her son either.

Lieutenant Falcon had done a reasonably efficient job, considering he was the first man on the scene. He had added a concluding paragraph to his report in which he said that he believed Mrs. von Zell's story, that she had not seen or heard from her husband for nearly a year. He had written, "The fact that von Zell told Hohenberg and Edelmann that he intended to move south, and yet gave his wife the impression that he was going north suggests that he was deliberately trying to obscure his real path. What this is we can only guess, but without a proper, trustworthy sighting, tracking him down will be very difficult, if not impossible. If he does go abroad, or is there already, then conceivably, in a few months or a couple of years, he may seek to contact his wife. That is a little late for our purposes. I suggest we abandon this case and devote our energies to problems more likely to be resolved."

That had been in June of 1945, before there had been much evidence of an active Nazi underground. A few months later, in September–October, another investigator had examined the case. Major A. P. Wordsworth had visited Mondsee and concentrated his attentions on the boy, Dieter. The boy had cried easily, being just seven, after all, but he, too, had denied seeing his father. Wordsworth had taken away a number of photographs and documents, letters mainly, but to little purpose. He also concluded that von Zell had not been in touch with his family since their meeting on May 9 and that neither Mrs. von Zell nor Dieter knew where he was.

The third interrogation had taken place in January 1946, barely two months before I came on the scene. This coincided with a series of scares that several leading Nazis had made it safely to South America and that the underground conduit, ironically modeled on the one developed by the French resistance to move their people from Switzerland to Spain and Lisbon, was working far too well. The idea that this conduit was financed by von Zell's gold naturally sparked our side into action once again and a monuments man was dispatched to Mondsee.

This time Captain Ernst Kretch was rather tougher than either Falcon or Wordsworth had been. There was no question, of course, of using any physical methods of persuasion on a civilian woman and child, but nonetheless Kretch did try force of a kind. He had established that both Mrs. von Zell and her son suffered from TB and needed to visit the doctor frequently. This was the time when the world was learning with horror about the atrocities carried out by the Russians toward the end of the war, things like the Katyn massacre and the mass slaughter of Yugoslavs. Kretch had therefore informed Mrs. von Zell that, unless she revealed the whereabouts of her husband, he would turn her and her son over to the Russians in Berlin. He said they wanted to trace her husband for their own purposes and were prepared to be far more brutal than the Americans. And she would have no access to a doctor.

It was a total bluff on Kretch's part, but he carried it through to the extent of forcing Mrs. von Zell to pack a few things and accompanying him to the railway station in Munich, where she was to be put on a train for Berlin. He had hoped she might crack at the last minute, but she didn't.

Kretch wrote that he had arrived at the station deliberately early, so that their wait for the Berlin train would be that much longer and more harrowing. Mrs. von Zell, he had written, had been well-dressed that day in a heavy coat with a fine pair of leather boots. She had never once spoken to him of her own accord. He noticed, he said, that it was as if she had two selves: a strong, fierce presence, with a clipped voice, which she reserved for him; and a much softer, looser side to her nature, which she kept for her son.

As the Berlin train had arrived, there was a moment when—what with the noise and the steam and the people—she had disappeared, out of his sight, and could have made a run for it. But no, as the steam cleared, she stood, just staring at Kretch, her face filled with hatred. Then, when he had at last to admit it was a bluff, she had not smiled or shown relief in any way. And all she said was: "Please take us home." So Kretch's ploy was exposed and he, too, reached the conclusion that Mrs. von Zell did not know where her husband was.

That was as far as the investigation had gone. I picked my way through some of the other pieces of paper—letters in German giving examples of von Zell's handwriting, lists of addresses of the people mentioned in the reports, a few photographs. The von Zells certainly made an attractive couple. He had a rather round face, clean-shaven, with smooth and shiny dark hair, swept straight back. There was what appeared to be a dueling scar on his left cheek. She was even more impressive: a full head of blond hair, shoulder length, a strong nose with a narrow bridge, a wide but firm mouth. She was very attractive, but she looked every inch the tough nut she had proved to be.

I put the two photographs before me on the desk and studied them, sipping my coffee. There was no doubt that Kretch's failed bluff made things infinitely more difficult for me. If Konstanze von Zell didn't know where her husband was, then she didn't know where her husband was. No matter how clever my interrogation, it would fail. But if she did, if she had been dissembling all along, then her resistance would have grown stronger each time she successfully saw off her interrogators. And, after Kretch's failed gambit, that resistance must have increased tenfold.

So, my first tactic, I decided that day, was to avoid Mrs. von Zell completely, or, in any case, until I was more certain of my ground and all other avenues of inquiry had been exhausted.

I looked at the photographs again. I thought it interesting that none of the other interrogators had considered it at all relevant to investigate the von Zells' relationship. The war had destroyed many marriages. Men away from home—particularly men on important jobs—had taken mistresses who, over the years, had become something more. Wives left at home had taken lovers, men who, in many cases, had become the fathers of their children. In its way enforced separation may have destroyed as much as blitz bombing. Absence only rarely makes the heart grow fonder —as I knew, because it had happened to me.

Sitting there, in that makeshift office, I thought of my own wife, all those miles away in California. We shared a small house, but we had part of the bayshore to ourselves and we could even see the Golden Gate bridge from our bedroom. We should have been content. Yet when I left to go to the war, after just eleven months of marriage, it was obvious that we had made a mistake. We had married quickly—I did most things too quickly in those days. We had enjoyed a wild, six-month-long sexual romp, then it had stopped. I was an academic, in both the best and the worst senses. I was good at my job, had studied art history under Panofsky in Hamburg and Berenson in Italy. So, as a professor, I had an "interesting" career rather than a well-paid one, and I was happy in myself, a quality which, I have learned, many women find more attractive than good looks. But, as an academic, I lived too often inside my head for my wife's taste. I tended to think things rather than do them. I cared for my wife but didn't show it. It didn't occur to me to show it; I knew how I felt and that was that. It never crossed my mind that, if I didn't show it, to her that was tantamount to saying I didn't feel anything. Now we had been separated nearly three years; we hardly wrote and I suspected that she missed me as little as I missed her. I figured we would divorce as soon as I returned.

I stood up to loosen my limbs and went through into the cubicle. This room, unlike ours, had a window on the street. As I looked out I noticed a marked contrast between the old city itself, its roofs shining splendidly in the afternoon sun, and the people moving about in the streets below.

Neither their clothes nor their faces appeared yet to have fully recovered from the war; even their weary, pinched expressions looked as though they had been manufactured under conditions of austerity when other, happier materials had been in short supply.

Were the von Zells in love still? I asked myself, shifting my gaze to the discreet splendor of the cathedral. Was that why she protected him? Or had the war destroyed their marriage, as it had contributed to the decay of my own and so many others? If so, then she might well not know where her one-time lover and husband had gone.

In front of me and slightly to the right, the elaborate, curly black spire which rose above the Franziskamerkirche seemed almost to scratch the sky. As I watched the birds circle about its topmost digit, I worked out my plan of campaign in more detail. No one had achieved very much by confronting Mrs. von Zell head on. Therefore, I would use a different ploy. Some seemingly less important leads had not been followed up and I would start with those. There was von Zell's mother in Worms. There was von Zell's last job, before the collapse, in the Party Chancellery in Munich. He must have had secretaries who, if they could be traced, might tell me about their boss's habits—for instance, whether or not he had a mistress. If he had a mistress he might be in touch with her still. And there was the last address he had lived at in Berchtesgaden. He may have let something slip to his landlord, or he may have made enemies locally who might just remember something significant. All the while, though, I would keep myself alert for details that told me something about the von Zells' relationship. Then, if I did have to face the wife, I might have some information that would turn the tables.

My approach did not promise the rapid results that Maxy Hobel craved. But it was obvious I would get only one crack at Mrs. von Zell. I had to be properly prepared. Three interrogators had already failed. If I succeeded I would have earned the damn medal everyone kept talking about. I decided to set out the next day for Worms.

I was just putting the papers back into the folder when Hartt returned. He offered to escort me to the Goldener Hirsch to make sure that everything was as it should be. On the way he was full of admiration for the BMW, pleased as punch that we could drive around town with the top down. Watching the dowdy Austrians stare at us from the pavements, or from their bicycles, he suddenly said, "Cars. Everybody is going to want one of these, once the world is on its feet again. If you

have any spare cash, you could do worse than invest in automobiles."
Such advice may seem blindingly obvious now. But in 1946, in a Europe
that was still on its knees—remember Austria had been invaded in 1938
—it was not at all obvious to me. Hardly anyone had private cars in
Europe.

As we crossed the bridge back to the cathedral side of the river, Hartt,
or Sammy, as he insisted I call him, showed himself to be extremely
knowledgeable about cars. Or so I thought. He used words like cam
shaft, differential, tappets and power-to-weight ratio with what appeared
to be an easy familiarity. I listened, impressed. In fact, I was to learn that
Samuel Hartt, who was not what you would call a good-looking man, had
solved one of life's little secrets to perfection. Instead of reading regular
books, like the rest of us, Sammy read encyclopedias. He wasn't interested in plots or characterization, in feelings or happy endings. He was
interested in facts. Sammy had made it his business in life to learn
several paragraphs on any subject you cared to name. Be it cars, horse
racing, the French novel, pasta or religious history, he was never at a loss.
His encyclopedias gave him a smattering of the right jargon, the right
names to drop, a couple of funny anecdotes with which to salt his obser-
vations. And, in a sense, it made him irresistible. Whenever he met
someone new, man or woman, Sammy quickly winkled out their special
interests and, for a short while, was able to talk with them as if he was an
equal. However, once this person was launched on their favorite topic,
Sammy would withdraw and allow them to shine. It was a very clever
form of flattery and it made him extremely popular with men and far
more successful with women than he might otherwise have been had his
looks been his only asset. He certainly charmed me very quickly.

It didn't take him long to see that, although I liked driving cars, what
went on under the hood was as mysterious to me as von Zell's current
whereabouts, and he tried other subjects. He hit the jackpot with Venice; I was mad about the place and I yacked happily all the way to the
hotel.

All was fine at the Goldener Hirsch—they were expecting me and the
room was ready—so Sammy left me to rest for a while, to shower and
change. Drinks in the mess at 7:30; dinner at eight.

And what a curious dinner it turned out to be. The mess was in a
small castle back across the river, not too far from our offices, the Schloss
Mirabell, I think it was called. They have concerts there these days, I'm

told. The walls were lined with tapestries showing hunting scenes, and I remember the ceilings were a brilliant white with carvings in the cornices. They reminded me somewhat of Venice.

Sammy looked after me, made sure I had a drink and then introduced me to the military governor of the area, a Colonel Mortimer Rowe, who was tall and formal, cold almost, an American version of one of those unsympathetic army types you find in Kipling. Stiff and ungiving, with a bearing like a statue. Hobel was there, drinking morosely, I thought, as if he already had a start on the rest of us. Was he a secret lush? I wondered if that was the real reason he hadn't made it to colonel just yet. I tried to ignore him.

That was made easier, all of a sudden, by a commotion. Just before the rumpus blew up I had noticed a small, rather Jewish-looking officer who was the only person not in mess uniform. It took me a while to realize that he was the cause of all the bother.

It soon became apparent that there were elements in the mess who objected to this man not being suitably clad. A thick-set, blond-haired major was rocking back and forth on his feet and barking at another man, roughly the same age and exactly the same rank. I caught only the end of what he was saying.

". . . if he's your guest, George, I can't believe he wasn't told what to wear for tonight and that the dress rules are strictly observed. The rest of us stick by them; we're proud of them, for chrissake. Why not you?"

George, whoever he was, appeared a little uneasy but nowhere near as much as I would have been under the circumstances. He was a touch taller than the other man, with black wavy hair, not unlike that of the young Laurence Olivier. "I've told you twice, Harry, for goodness' sake. The old man said it's all right, just this once. Now, stop it. Please."

Just then dinner was announced and I suppose I would have forgotten about this exchange except for the fact that the Jewish-looking officer was placed next to me at the table. Sammy was opposite and he kicked off before the soup plates had even been set in front of us, dredging something up from volume Aa—Art.

"They say you are an architect in real life, major?"

The man nodded, holding his glass forward for Sammy to fill it.

"Tell me," Sammy went on, "who would you say produces the best buildings—religious architects, civic ones, or the professional boys who do it just for the money?"

It was not exactly the most subtle way of changing the conversation. In fact, it sounded exactly like what it was—something Sammy had picked out of an encyclopedia. Nonetheless, the major was visibly relieved to have something else to concentrate on, so we were all very grateful. I noticed several disapproving looks still snaking down the table from where Harry and his camp were seated but we in our group managed to turn our backs on them.

It turned out that the visitor was not, in fact, a practicing architect but the architectural correspondent for a New York newspaper. He was therefore knowledgeable and opinionated and in no time Sammy was able to retreat safely, his "ignition function," as he called it, complete. Now he would listen, so that the next time he needed a spat of architecture, he would be even better informed.

Architecture was—is—my field, however, and so I was able to keep up with the major for a good deal longer than Sammy. We introduced ourselves and swapped cards. His name was Saul Wolfert and we spent what turned out to be a most enjoyable dinner discussing what we thought were the world's great buildings. It was a relief to get away from army, army, army, and, as sometimes happens, we erected an invisible cocoon around ourselves which, aided by roast lamb, flown in from America, a 1934 claret and local pastries for dessert, kept us apart from the affairs of the rest of the mess until the toasts obliged us to stand.

Wolfert refused to say what he did in the Army, so I naturally assumed he was in some sort of intelligence unit. As I knew from my own experience with the von Zell case, there were plenty of fugitive Nazis in hiding, as well as secret Nazi sympathizers in influential positions throughout Germany and Austria. He was probably involved in searching them out.

In any event he was much more forthcoming about the buildings I should see, if my duties allowed, in Austria. He didn't anticipate any difficulty, though, for when I told him about my hunt for the gold coins and von Zell, his face broadened into a sparkling smile. It turned out that the monasteries from which the gold had been taken, and where I would almost certainly need to visit, were among the most stunning examples of baroque architecture in the whole of Europe, indeed, throughout the world. He said he envied me my job, and this I thought a curious remark. To me, intelligence work was probably the most interesting army specialty of all.

After the toasts we soon adjourned for brandy and cigars. I smoked a lot in those days, especially a pipe, and though this adjournment was generally meant to be a device to help people move around and change companions, Wolfert and I, as relative outsiders, tacitly agreed to stick together.

We located a couple of armchairs in an out-of-the-way corner but were unfortunate in settling ourselves into them only moments ahead of Harry and one of his cronies, who, unknown to us, had been heading directly for the same seats. As may be imagined, this provoked a fresh round of rudeness, so raw in fact that I was amazed Wolfert did not assault Harry. But good manners can work wonders.

Eventually the others moved off and we both gulped at our drinks and sought refuge in the elaborate ritual required to ignite large cigars. Even so, once I had mine lit, I felt it necessary to say, "I am sorry for all the embarrassment you are being made to feel this evening. Especially as we were supposed to be fighting anti-Semites."

He looked at me fiercely and, for a moment, I thought he was going to reproach me for raising the subject. Then he leaned forward and hissed, in a quiet way so as not to be overheard, "Thank you, Walter. But I am not in the least embarrassed, not really. What I am is very, very, *very* angry. Angry with Colonel Rowe, angry with George Held, but most of all livid with myself."

"Why? And what about that Harry character—aren't you furious at him?"

Wolfert sipped his brandy, swirling the glass balloon in his hand. He shook his head. "Let me try this on you. When I refused to tell you what job I do, what did you conclude?"

"That you are in intelligence."

He smiled again, but this time he nodded. "That's what you were meant to think. And not just you, but this whole mess."

"You mean it's not true?"

"Not by a long way."

"I don't understand." I stared at him, my cigar smoking diffidently between my fingers. "What's going on?"

He downed a long swig of brandy before replying. "I shouldn't really tell you but, since I don't have a hide like a rhinoceros, and since you're going away tomorrow, I'll risk it. But, please, keep it to yourself. Everyone else will find out soon enough." His cigar had gone out. He now held it to a flame, twirling it so that it would scorch evenly. "I am a military policeman. A sort of detective in uniform."

I went very still inside. "And?"

"I came here today to arrest George Held."

"What for?"

He drew on the cigar. "Murder."

"What!" But it was a whisper, there was no breath in my voice, as if I had been punched in the chest.

Now that he had decided to tell his story, Wolfert was more relaxed. He leaned forward, keeping his voice down. "It happened a few months ago. During the push north last spring, Held's unit was billeted for a short while in Florence. He visited a whore there, a girl called Regina Passetto, though her name is not really important. As I say, Held wasn't in Florence for very long, but long enough to find out that Miss Passetto had given him a disease of one sort or another. Unfortunately, instead of going to the doctor straightaway, he paid her another visit—only this time he beat her and she fell down some stairs—you know how dark those Italian buildings can be, and how hard the stone staircases are. She hit her head and was killed. Held ran off, his unit pulled out hours later and it has taken me until now to find him." He was enjoying his cigar more than the brandy and paused to tap away the stubble of ash that had built up. "All I had to go on was a description, a knowledge of the units in Florence at the time and a few years in this business, which proves to you that, in some things, people don't change. The poor girl in Florence, the one who 'fell' down the stairs, was a . . . shall we say a 'specialist.' Uniforms, mainly. Nurses, schoolgirls, Nazis even. Comical in its way. In the last few weeks it has been my rather grubby duty to uncover these types of specialists in Munich, in Augsburg, Frankfurt, Vienna, Linz, and now Salzburg—yes, Salzburg," he repeated quickly, as he saw the look of astonishment on my face. "You'd be surprised at how widespread these 'services' are. And Held hasn't changed. Probably, he can't. I only had to tell the girls why I wanted to find him and they fell over themselves to help. I was there when he arrived last night. Interrogated him in the bedroom, with all the uniforms hanging around." He sank the last of his brandy. "He confessed after ten minutes. You will know the scenario. He was, I think, relieved someone had caught up with him."

A mess waiter had seen that our glasses were empty and arrived with a decanter to refill them. Wolfert didn't continue until the man was again out of earshot.

"When I turned up this afternoon, the colonel was horrified, of course. Moreover, he likes Held and wanted to avoid gossip, for the time being at least. He insisted Held attend mess the night before leaving since it would be out of character for him not to, and questions would be asked. It was the colonel's idea that I come tonight, as Held's 'guest.' I had to come of course; just in case he tried to make a run for it. It was the colonel's idea also that I refuse to disclose what I do. Why I agreed to that I don't know, except maybe that I was causing so much bother in the first place that I didn't want to deny Held what will almost certainly be his last mess night. The colonel was cunning, that's what makes me angry. No one has told any lies tonight, but we have managed to give the impression, which you picked up, that I have some important hush-hush job and that 'old George' here is involved in it with me. That's why I have no mess uniform handy; we should have been halfway to Vienna by now, where my headquarters are located. But, having agreed to attend this dinner, I couldn't really respond to all that aggression by telling the truth, could I? I should have overruled the colonel and insisted that Held and I leave immediately, this afternoon. That's why I was so furious with myself." He picked up his new brandy from the table and sat farther back in the armchair. "End of story."

Amazing. It was an extraordinary story, but for me what was most astonishing was the calmness with which Wolfert had responded all evening to such nasty provocation. It wasn't just his uniform, or lack of it. There was anti-Semitism in that hostility. He knew it as well as I did, but chose to ignore it.

I looked around the room. Held was part of a group listening to an army story—long, convoluted and probably wicked—and he was listening easily, as if he was not irked in the slightest by his conscience. I was not then what you would call a moral person particularly but I can remember finding Held's arrogance distasteful. I found the behavior of Colonel Rowe difficult to stomach also. Still, it was none of my business. I looked back at Wolfert, who had followed my gaze, and raised my glass to him. He nodded. We changed the subject and the rest of the evening passed quietly. I didn't see Sammy or Hobel again, and I avoided Rowe.

CHAPTER TWO

1

I set out early the next day for Worms in brilliant sunshine. The hotel breakfast of cheese, salami and fresh coffee, which had probably been stolen from somewhere, scraped the cobwebs from my brain after the two large brandies of the night before. Outside the city the foothills of the Alps were just beginning to be brushed with the powder of blue gentian and, with the top of the car down, the flowers and the smell of wet grass were galvanizing. I decided to pick up no one, but instead to try out the BMW, to push her as fast as she would go. On the autobahn I eased her over the 100 kmh mark (60 mph and dangerously fast in those days). I sailed past convoy after convoy and was rewarded by many an admiring hoot from envious army truck drivers.

The first thing I discovered in Worms was that the von Zell town house had been bombed and everyone had moved out. The address I had for Christina von Zell was Schlossgasse 2 and there was little left of that. It *had* been a smart neighborhood once, at the beginning of the war, but unfortunately it was too close to a factory making explosives. This time the RAF had made no mistake; even the trees lining the streets had been scorched dead by incendiary devices.

It took me an hour or so but, around lunchtime, I located the *Einwohnermeldeamt,* the local offices of the military governor, and from that I was able to establish that the elder Mrs. von Zell had moved to

her country residence at Gut "Wiesenmühle" in Kriegsheim, near Mon-
sheim, twenty kilometers to the west. I broke for a beer and sandwich at
an inn on the road in between and was at Gut "Wiesenmühle" by
midafternoon.

A large brown and black structure, the von Zell house was surrounded
by three hundred acres of arable land—what looked like barley mainly.
The sight of this economic activity reminded me to call Sammy later
that day. If he was making any investments I wanted to be in on the act.

I had taken the precaution of bringing von Zell's photograph with me
and so I prowled the farm buildings and outhouses first. If he *was* hiding
out there, von Zell would have less chance of being warned of my arrival
than if I had announced myself straightaway at the big house. The farm
appeared to employ about half a dozen people, most of them young,
poorly educated laborers and they seemed genuine when they failed to
respond to the photograph I showed them. Only one person recognized
the face and that was the farm manager, a podgy man with ruddy cheeks
called Johann Heine. And he said he had not seen "Herr Rudi" for years.
I believed him.

And so I called at the main house. Mrs. von Zell was in, a sturdy
woman of medium height with lush, pike-gray hair pulled straight back.
Her dark velvet dress was high-necked and, it struck me, somewhat old-
fashioned. I cannot say she was welcoming, but then neither was she
cold. She had the grace to offer me some tea and I accepted. The cups, I
remember, were of bone china with blue butterflies, and were brought in
by a maid. Despite the warmth of the day and the welcome sun outside,
the room where we drank the tea was dark and cool, with an open log fire
in the grate.

With my experience of accomplished Nazi liars, I watched her carefully when I told her why I had come, but it was obvious to me that she
had nothing, and no one, to hide. She seemed genuinely anxious for
news.

"No, Lieutenant, I haven't seen him," she said quietly, "not for a year
or more." She leaned forward to refill my teacup. "Naturally, I wouldn't
tell you if he *was* hiding out here, but that's silly; he is not. However, I
will say this. It is not like Rudi to lose touch. He was always a good son,
attentive, in fact a little too forceful in his attentions at times, inviting
me to visit them when I knew that Konstanze would rather have been
alone. Basically a very considerate and kind son. From what you tell me,

it seems that he must be in some difficulty. Either that or he has been captured already and you don't know about it."

"Then he would surely have contacted his wife?"

"He would have tried, certainly. But would the Allies have allowed him to? Would the Russians? I must pray every night that he will return to us soon."

At this remark I suddenly noticed what, stupidly, I had overlooked before. The room boasted several crucifixes and pictures of the Virgin.

"The von Zells are Catholics?"

"But of course." Of course, it had been in the file.

"I, too, am a Catholic. From Waldangelloch, near Heidelberg." I had lapsed, totally, at university, but I didn't include that.

"And you left Germany?" Was there a hint of reproach in the way she framed her question?

"I left Hitler's Germany, Mrs. von Zell. In 1936."

"Yes . . ." She faltered. "You had great foresight . . . in 1936 Hitler seemed to promise so much. To make Germany . . . first, again. Rudi thought so; he was so . . . so *patriotic*. By the time all that racial business started . . . it was too late." She looked down, into her cup, embarrassed.

I said nothing. I had noticed how, in Germany in the past months, memories had already begun to alter, as shame, guilt or embarrassment had distorted what had gone on. The "racial business," as Christina von Zell put it, had started long before 1936, but now was not the time to contradict her. I wanted her cooperation. I looked back at the walls.

"Mrs. von Zell, I see you have many family photographs. Do you, by any chance, have a family album? And may I see it?"

She didn't want to help me but her reflexes gave her away. She glanced across to a pair of double doors on the far side of the room. There *was* an album and it was through those doors.

I followed her gaze. "Shall I get it, or will you?"

She gave me a thin smile and got up.

She brought it from the next room, which, to judge from the books lining the walls, was a library. The album was a big brown, rather horrid and heavy book, ornate, with the word *"Photographie"* carved out of the leather. She sat next to me while I leafed through it. There were the usual school photos—sports day, prize giving, camp. There were pictures of von Zell's father, with stiff collar and mustache, who had died quite young in 1929. There were wedding photos, von Zell in his first Nazi uniforms, Dieter being christened.

And there was what I had hoped there would be—pictures of von Zell at university, several of them; in academic gowns, with scarves and drinking mugs, in running shorts, on bicycles. And—my luck was holding—one other face, apart from von Zell's, kept cropping up. This was a blond young man, taller than Rudi, with a long, bony nose and a wide, curling, aristocratic mouth. A real lady killer.

"Who is that?"

Mrs. von Zell searched on the mantelshelf for her eyeglasses. Then she sat down next to me again. "Oh yes, a lovely boy, Rudi's closest friend. A beautiful skier."

"His name?"

She thought for a moment. "Was it Eric . . . or Ernst? I'm sure it was Eric. He was growing a mustache, a fine yellow mustache, the last time I saw him."

"And his other name? Eric what?"

"Oh yes, I'm sorry. Von Haltern. He came from a good family, farmers, I think, or wine growers. He and Rudi met at university, in Berlin. They were very close and always kept in touch. They joined the Army together."

"Where did the von Haltern's live, Mrs. von Zell? Can you remember?" I was gentle but insistent.

She took off her eyeglasses. She seemed to find it easier to think that way. "Near Koblenz. The family had such a lovely castle a few kilometers outside—the Schlosshaltern. I was invited once, one Christmas—they were Catholics too. But Rudi went all the time—at least until 193—" Suddenly she stopped herself. "You don't mean . . . ? You think . . . ? But . . . if he was there, hiding . . . surely he would have written . . . or sent word to me in some way?" She was upset at what she might have done. "Have I given him away?"

"He may have thought it too dangerous to contact you, ma'am." I got up to leave. Now she had finally figured what I was after, more questions would be pointless. "But I promise you," I added, feeling as I often did on these occasions, more than a little two-faced, "if he *is* there and I find him, I will make sure that you hear either from him or from me. So that you know he is alive and safe."

"You will?" A minute before she had been resentful because she thought I had tricked her, as indeed I had; but now her son's safety came first and she was ready to respond to any help I might offer. "Shall you go there immediately? When can you let me know?"

"Yes, I shall go now. It is about eighty or ninety kilometers. I can get there tonight, quite easily. You should hear very soon."

She came to the door with me. As she shook my hand she said, "War changes people, Lieutenant. It makes small people big, and rich people poor. But do you think it makes honest people thieves? Rudi would not steal those coins."

"Hitler was a thief. And Göring."

"But they had no breeding, Lieutenant. That's why they were so interested in genetics."

An old woman's logic, neat but little more. I bowed slightly and took my leave. She remained standing at the door as I drove off.

The sun had weakened by the time I crossed the Rhine and turned north. The light was beginning to go and the river, wide and slow to my right, was a muddy cream color, a cold sheet of liquid sand and concrete sluiced from a factory upstream. I couldn't help but smile to myself as I nosed the car forward on the narrow river road. I had the top up now, for the March days didn't hold the heat once the sun started to sink. The old album trick had worked again. It had never failed to amaze me, since I had been taught it at the psychological warfare school in Fort Bragg, North Carolina. People were only too eager to show off their pictures and never considered your real reason for asking. Not until it was too late.

Von Zell might not be at Koblenz, of course. But the file showed that he had made use of von Haltern's name when he had hid his family in Krimml. That surely told us that the name meant *something* to him. That could be relevant later.

Sadly, there were no art students, or girls of any kind, for me to pick up that evening. I had to make do with a catering corps corporal from Boston who was heading north to see his girlfriend in Dusseldorf. It was fully dark when I dropped him at the southern outskirts of Koblenz, at a large truck stop where he could get another lift. I then aimed for the center of the city. In most cities the railway station is well posted and there helpful people can always direct you to the main police station. Police stations generally have good maps, as did the one in Koblenz, so it didn't take me more than forty minutes to find directions to the

Schlosshaltern. As I moved around Koblenz I could see it was a not unattractive city, with fortifications overlooking the Rhine and some fine tree-lined boulevards on the opposite bank.

When I got there I found that the *Schloss* had been badly damaged by bombing. Two of its five white turrets were reduced to a rubble of stones and chunks of plaster. The castle was not so much at the top of the Rhine gorge as set into the side of it; the approach road sloped a couple of hundred feet upward, arriving at an imposing wooden gate studded with iron spikes. A thin long garden stretched beyond the *Schloss* but such was the dark that I could see no more. Lights came from some of the windows, but in general the building had the feel of somewhere abandoned. But that, I thought, might make it a better place for von Zell to hide.

I didn't knock on the gate immediately. Instead, I just sat in the car for a while, listening. There *was* movement in the castle; I could see shadows and hear noises. But no one came to the door set into the gate, nor did I see anyone at the windows. My arrival, it seemed, had gone unobserved.

There were no dogs, or sudden movements, no sign of anyone making a run for it, and when I finally banged on the gate, it took a full two minutes for someone to answer. I knew, because I counted; I was obsessive about things like that. Eventually the gate was pulled back laboriously by a man in his fifties. His hair was still dark but thinning rapidly. Yet, he was slim, a man who kept himself in fine fettle.

I introduced myself, showing him my orders signed by Eisenhower. I asked, "And is there anyone else here, besides you?"

"Only my wife, Annemarie. She is upstairs." He spoke with what I judged to be a southern, a Bavarian accent. They were, he said, joint housekeepers.

"When is the family expected back?"

He shrugged. "They've been gone since the bombing. Who knows?"

"What do you mean?"

"Eric was killed here. Now the Baroness can't bear the *Schloss*. They are all living in Hamburg."

"When . . . how . . . did Eric die?"

The housekeeper looked up at the smashed towers. "Eric's bedroom was up there. A bomb hit the side of the gorge in late '44. The top of the castle was blown away—Eric with it."

So von Haltern had been dead already some months before von Zell
used his name. That didn't mean he wasn't here, hiding.

"How many of the family are in Hamburg?"

"The Baroness, her daughter, who was widowed early in the war, and
Mrs. von Haltern's niece from Augsburg. Her husband is in a camp in
England, shot down over Coventry."

So they took in friends.

I explained that my orders empowered me to search the castle. The
housekeeper made no attempt to resist, but simply stepped aside to allow
me through the gate.

Inside was a cavernous stone hall, vaulted and poorly lit. Several strap-
ping pictures lined the walls, with those lugubrious frames reserved for
ancestors. Uninviting wooden benches were flanked by spindly, wrought-
iron tripods which had once held flowers or cathedral-sized candles but
were empty now. It all felt like a crypt.

At the far end of the hall some stone stairs disappeared upward,
through an arch and toward a light; it was in this direction that the
housekeeper led me. It was already obvious that the castle was too big for
me alone to search properly. If von Zell *was* here he would have no
problem moving around, avoiding me for hours on end if need be. I
would just have to look for signs, for clues that he was, or had been, here.

The stairs, when we reached the top of them, opened onto a living
room with acres of flowered carpet, a fireplace the size of a proscenium
arch and three tall windows that must have given spectacular views of
the Rhine in the right kind of daylight. In normal times this must have
been the formal hub of the house. The pictures in this room were more
numerous and smaller, more intimate: equestrian paintings, men with
beards and medals, that sort of thing. The fire in the grate was out and
sheets were drawn over the sofas. There were no flowers, but also no
dust. The housekeepers were either conscientious or afraid the family
might come back at any minute. The room felt cold and there was no
lingering smell of stale cigarette smoke—no one had been here for some
days at least. Through this main room lay the dining room. Here, too,
sheets had been thrown over the furniture; the sideboards were bare and
the candlesticks put away. Pride of place on the wall went to a rather
new-looking picture of the entire family. I recognized Eric, his sister, her
husband, presumably, the two parents, some dogs.

Beyond the dining room a small, rather steep staircase led down, I assumed, to the kitchen.

"We'll look there later," I said. "Let's go upstairs."

The next floor was altogether more intimate and lived in and I realized that, even when the family *was* here, the lower floors were probably rarely used. This next floor contained a library, stacked with books in carefully carved wooden shelves, some leather armchairs and sofas, many soft electric lights, a small fireplace which *had* recently seen a fire and all the paraphernalia of such a heartwarming retreat: photographs, tubs of bulbs, magazines, boxes of pencils, stacks of paper, knickknacks. This was a room I had to return to and examine in more detail.

On this same floor was another, smaller, dining room, with space for no more than eight people. There was a bathroom and a music room with a piano and, of all things, a harp. Obviously, everyday life went on in these rooms when the family had no visitors.

From then on it no longer made sense to talk of floors. The bedrooms of the castle receded into the towers and turrets, or were scattered, apparently at random, among the numerous gables and eaves. By my count, and, as I have said, I was obsessive about such things, there were eighteen bedrooms, not counting the two destroyed turrets. Most of them had not been slept in for years—not, I suspected, since the war began.

Nor was there any sign of a hurried departure from these rooms. The housekeeper and his wife used two—one as a bedroom and one as their own living room—but, those apart, there genuinely was no sign of life.

It was the same in the kitchens downstairs. Supper had been laid for two and a breakfast tray—also for two—was already set out. The wine cellar, the boiler room, the washroom were all as they should have been, or so it seemed to me. In the billiard room there was a wooden cover on the table and this time there *was* dust on the cues in the rack. I could not believe that von Zell—or anyone for that matter—was in hiding in the *Schloss*.

I asked the housekeeper to show me back up to the library and to leave me there for an hour. I suggested that he and his wife enjoy their supper and that he then come back for me. He was easily persuaded and disappeared.

I slumped into one of the big leather armchairs and tried not to think about food. All I'd had that day was a light breakfast and a sandwich for lunch. I should have eaten something at the truck stop where I had dropped off the corporal, but I hadn't. I took out the pipe that I carried with me in those days; it gave me something to do with my jaw.

I didn't know what I was looking for in the library; I just hoped I would pick up something useful by rummaging around. In the months I had been attached to the art recovery unit I had found it endlessly fascinating, if a little macabre, to delve into the private papers of former Nazis. And chilling too. There was something . . . *unnatural* almost about the way men who in their military lives took part willingly in the most unimaginable atrocities and yet at home seemed to be exemplary husbands and fathers. It suggested something unnerving about human nature, that human beings are capable of sustaining, and indeed flourishing, with the most awful division in their lives, so that we are all, if you like, as split inside as the most warped schizophrenic. It was something I didn't want to think about. It suggested that the very existence of the Nazis, the fact that they could happen, was a warning to all of us about our deeper, hidden nature. The fact that Hitler had dredged up something that should have been left undisturbed made me loathe him and his cronies more than ever.

I examined the books on the shelves: they were mainly literary works —many German authors, of course, but English and American too. I noticed with interest that this family had made no attempt to hide Jewish books. There was a complete set of Proust and Freud's *Introductory Lectures*. The von Halterns, it appeared, were civilized and not anti-Semitic.

The photographs in the room turned out to be of little use: lots of people I didn't recognize and a few of Eric, who, it seemed, had never married.

I did, however, find something to interest me among a pile of magazines on one of the tables. It was an old edition of *Words & Wine*, a curious magazine that existed in Germany in the thirties and which was mainly devoted to literary affairs but also carried articles about drink, presumably on the basis that writers tend also to be drinkers. The issue I picked up contained an article on "The Wines of Austria" and the authors were Eric von Haltern and Rudolf von Zell. It was not a long article but it contained a lot of local references and, to me, appeared authoritative, being devoted to a history of the Sylvaner grape, a native, so I read, of Austria. The article also argued the merits of the three grape-growing areas of the country—Weinviertel, Wachau and Styria, concluding that, in the opinion of the authors, Wachau was the best.

I went through the article a second time and then sat thinking. Published in 1939, the piece had probably been written some time before that. Nonetheless, such was its detail that the article carried the implication, for me, that von Haltern and von Zell knew Austria extremely well; possibly they had good friends in the wine regions.

As I sucked away at my pipe a possible scenario began to form in my mind. Von Zell had used von Haltern's name before, as an alias, that much we knew for certain. Von Haltern was dead but his papers and documents might have survived the bomb that killed him. Was it possible, I asked myself, that von Zell might, just might, have taken Eric's identity *permanently* and be living under his name in Austria, working in the vineyard of a friend he had found while researching the article for *Words & Wine?* He knew about grapes, after all, so he would not appear out of place.

There were other things to be said for this plan, the more I thought about it. Wachau was one of the nearest wine-growing areas to Germany and, indeed, to Mondsee, where von Zell's wife was living. The conduit, to Spain and Portugal, had to begin somewhere in south Germany or western Austria so that might point to the Wachau also. Another thing struck me. If von Haltern and von Zell had done the research for their wine article together, in say 1938 or even a little earlier, people whose acquaintance they had made might not have remembered who was von Haltern and who was von Zell. So, if von Zell had turned up at one of those vineyards after the war, and found some winegrowers sympathetic to him, they might genuinely believe he *was* Eric von Haltern.

I looked around the room again. Now that I was, so to speak, primed, I began to notice a number of things that reflected von Haltern's interest in wine: there were plenty of books on the subject, a small collection of corkscrews on one of the bookshelves, pamphlets on corks, bottles of various shapes. I had not a shred of direct evidence to support my Austrian vineyard theory, but as I took in the odds and ends scattered around the library, the wine paraphernalia, the cleverer the idea seemed to me and the more convinced I became.

It was too much of a long shot to investigate myself but it was something Maurice Ghent or Saul Wolfert could organize from Vienna, which was much closer to the Wachau.

Maurice or Saul? I was just weighing the options when the house-keeper reappeared. I knocked out my pipe into the fireplace and got to my feet.

"Which hotel do you suggest I stay at in Koblenz?" I asked. It was a little past nine.

The warm scent of good food clung to him, reminding me how raven-ous I was. "The Mosel is the most comfortable, and not too expensive. It's by the Market Bridge."

He was right. The Mosel was very comfortable and, more to the point, boasted a restaurant that was still open when I arrived at about ten o'clock.

Since I was so famished, and the restaurant was about to close, dinner came first, and by the time I was through with that, it was too late to get Sammy, Maurice *or* Saul on the phone, as I wanted to do. The next morning I was up at 5:30, so my calls had to wait again until much later.

I left the Mosel too early for breakfast and parked the BMW along the road leading from the Schlosshaltern just before dawn. Once more I was starving and I hadn't shaved, but I had to double-check that the *Schloss* really was clear. I judged that if I had been mistaken the night before, and von Zell *was* there, he would move on next day as soon as it was light. He would be prudent and would not risk my coming back.

Dawn was at 6:17. We tended to know that sort of thing in the Army in those days. It was cool, with a skein of river mist drawn over the road and adjoining fields, as if it were caught up in the branches of the low trees. But you could tell the mist would go as soon as the sun gathered muscle. It seemed much more than forty-eight hours since I had enjoyed a similar but less lonely dawn with Inge and Elisabetta.

For an hour or so, nothing moved at the *Schloss*. Then, around seven, the housekeeper came out and walked across to what I now realized were stables. I sat up and focused my binoculars. But I was disappointed: he merely released two chestnut-colored ponies into a paddock which, in the dark of the night before, I had not noticed. They trotted about, sneezing steam into the cold morning air. The housekeeper returned to the *Schloss* and I imagined the breakfast tray I had seen laid the night before now loaded with hot bread and jams and boiling coffee.

Another hour—8:30 nearly—and the housekeeper's wife appeared on a bicycle. She had placed what looked like a leather shopping bag in the basket on the front and was presumably headed for Koblenz. She rode by the BMW without turning her head.

I waited two more hours, until just after the housekeeper's wife had returned, riding much more slowly now that the groceries were weighing her down. If von Zell didn't show soon I had to assume that he wasn't hiding in the *Schloss*.

By eleven the sun had burned off the mist and the countryside was cheering up minute by minute. My stomach was beginning to complain again that it had been neglected for too long. When the church on the other side of the river sounded the hour, I gave up. Von Zell wasn't there. I switched on the ignition, started the engine and headed the BMW back to the Mosel for some hot soup, sausage and, if they would allow me the use of a bathroom, a shave.

2

AFTER my shave food came first—and not simply because I was pinched with hunger. For some reason I have always found it easier to think while eating by myself. Whether it is the raised level of blood sugar in my veins or else the marriage of mustard with a hot sausage, I can never be sure, but once I have a beer at my elbow and something savory in front of me my mind clears amazingly.

First, I decided against calling Saul Wolfert, just yet anyway. Maurice was a friend as well as an old colleague and was not unused to looking for Nazis in hiding, whereas Wolfert had experience at finding U.S. Army types. I could rely on Maurice to do as I asked, whereas Wolfert was still a relative stranger and, by now, might have all sorts of other things to do. Perhaps, at a later stage, if Maurice got nowhere, I would call on Saul. But not until. That was my first mistake.

Maurice, when I got through to him, was his usual bantering, Noël Coward self. "Well, if it isn't the famous Professor Wolff himself. I have *all* your clippings, dear boy, from the Vienna papers. You better have some children quickly, and then some grandchildren, so you can show off to them. You're a hero here, dear boy. And your picture is in all the rags. I've even met girls who claim to think you are good-looking. Apparently you look like Gregory Peck, whoever *he* is."

"Yes, yes, Maurice." It was flattering and I couldn't help smiling. But I was embarrassed too. "How are you?"

"A little under the weather this morning, to be totally candid. I tell you, Walter, the coffee bars here are most misleading. All they seem to serve is brandy."

"I feel sorry for you, Maurice, I really do."

"Well, the war *is* over, dear boy. Can't work all the time. And the uniform seems to go down so well here, Walter. With the girls, I mean."

"What about the Kunsthistorisches? Aren't you supposed to be helping them?"

"Of course, of course. All in good time. Who do you think I was getting this hangover with? Boden, senior curator. And a brandy connoisseur, if last night is anything to go by. I dread to think what *his* head is like today."

I was clearly missing all the fun. "Sorry to be so dull, Maurice, but I need your help."

"Of course you do, dear boy. Of course you do. One second while I refill my coffee cup." He shouted to someone for "reinforcements"— everyone was "dear boy" to Maurice. Then he was back. "Now, Walter, you have my *full* attention."

As I related my story to him, he made loud appreciative noises, as Noël Coward would probably have done, a bit like an old queen. But Maurice was shrewd and I did not need to spell out my conclusions—he was there ahead of me.

"So you think this character, Rudi von what's-it, is hiding out in the Wachau with false papers—correction, with real papers but someone else's, right?"

"Right," I said. "I think he may be living as Eric von Haltern."

"You've no idea how many vineyards we are going to have to search, I suppose?"

"Sorry, no."

"So we don't know how many men we will need?"

"Not yet. Perhaps you could take advice, or make a quick reconnaissance yourself."

"Hhhhmmmnn." I could hear him swallowing his coffee, deliberating.

Then, being the friend he was, and not just a disinterested or competitive colleague: "Okay, dear boy. We'll do what we can. In between brandies, of course."

I told him I would eventually make my way back to Salzburg, after one or two other sorties I had planned, and that I would call him from there.

"Salzburg?" he sang the word as if the "burg" part had all five vowels in it. "Isn't that where S. Hartt, Esq., is stationed?"

I confessed it was, and that I was sharing an office, or at least an operating theater, with the great man.

"Splendid! Splendid! An opportunity for sport, dear boy."

My heart sank. "Sport" was Maurice's shorthand for a gamble. He was a great gambler, and a not unsuccessful one. Fortunately, I had managed to steer clear of his craze so far.

"Have you any spare cash, dear boy? This is an opportunity not to be missed."

I was cagey but also surprised. It was unlike Maurice to want to borrow money. Not his style at all. And in any case he was a clever gambler—he didn't usually need money.

"I have a little saved, Maurice. If you're short, I could maybe—"

"Borrow money, dear boy! Who *do* you think I am—one of Mr. Stalin's socialists? No, no, no. I am afraid I took a thousand dollars off one of your compatriots only the other night, some poor Midwesterner who thought that only cowboys could play poker. Now I have all this cash sloshing around in my wallet and it's about as useful as a nun in a submarine. No, no, no. As they say in your Navy, dear boy, 'Now hear this.'

"Next time you talk to Hartt, ask him to settle my thousand dollars on something he thinks is worth it. Doesn't matter what, I'll trust him. He's the whiz kid, after all. And here's the sport. If *you* have a thousand dollars you can spare, get him to do the same for you. From then on it's a race."

"What do you mean?"

"We'll settle on an end point, a closing date—since we are both academics, let's say the end of the academic year, May 31. Two months from now, approximately. Whoever has the shares which are worth the most on that day wins."

"Wins what?"

"Whatever you like, dear boy. Make a suggestion."

I thought. Here was a chance to avoid a fight. "The SS helmet in the flat."

"Done." He cackled triumphantly. Too late, I realized he had trapped me at last into a gamble, however small. "Let me know what shares Hartt gives me. I don't mind what they are so long as he favors them. And tell him my check will be in the mail tonight. I know that's a joke phrase to you Americans. But as you are aware, Walter, I cannot bring myself to joke about money."

A thousand dollars was a great deal then and not what it is now, which is not a lot. Furthermore, if I should divorce my wife, I had no idea what sort of financial arrangement we would come to. On the other hand, I did have a bit of money saved, I had no children and I had a job to go back to in California. Sammy was a genius on the stock market, there was no doubt about that, and I would be lying if I said that the sort of risk Maurice proposed had not crossed my mind from the moment I had first met Hartt. So I decided I would pit my thousand against Maurice's. With luck both shares would rise so that whoever lost the helmet would at least have won something.

"Walter? Hi, where are you?" Hartt was as friendly as Hobel would have been cold.

"Koblenz."

"In God's name, why?"

I told him.

"Okay. So what now?"

"I'm going to have the vineyards in the Wachau checked by a colleague in Vienna. And I'm hoping Henry de Jaeger, in Hamburg, will pay a visit on the Baroness von Haltern for me. You can tell all this to Hobel if he asks."

"Got that. What do you want me to do?"

"Spend two thousand dollars on Wall Street."

"Come again."

"You heard me, Sammy." I explained about the bet. "They say in Frankfurt that you are a millionaire already. We'd like to ride on your coattails. You said the other day that auto company shares were worth investing in. Buy a thousand dollars of those for me. I'll trust your judgment. Then choose something for Maurice. He'll go with what you decide for him too."

There was a chuckle down the line.

"Why are you laughing?"

His voice gurgled again. "It's a good thing I'm not superstitious, or I might think you could read my mind. I've got a line through to New York at this very moment. As soon as the market opens, I'm moving five grand myself into Metropolitan Motors. You want to join me?"

"Yes, please," I said quickly. "A grand."

"Sure you've got the nerve?"

"Don't know. This is the first time I've tried it."

"Shares go down, you know, as well as up."

"Yes, but I'm told the ones you back usually go up. And quite quickly. I'll take the risk. So will Maurice. Choose something for him that you can buy with a round one thousand dollars. That way it's clear who is winning the bet."

Silence at the other end. Was Sammy having second thoughts? No.

"Paper. That's what we'll put your friend into. America has lots of space for trees to make paper. And after wars you get huge bureaucracies forming, and socialist governments. They have one in Britain already. They always gobble up paper. And people are going to make babies now the war is over—lots of them. So there will be a boom in education, and schools and colleges are even better than governments at eating paper. Yes, tell your friend I'll try to get him into Confederate Paper Mills—a thousand you say? Okay. I'll confirm it next time we talk. But don't blame me if you are both destitute this time next week."

"Thanks, Sammy. You'll get our money in a day or so." New York came through on the other line and we hung up without even discussing in detail what he should tell Hobel. I sipped the remains of the cold coffee I had taken with me to the phone and twiddled the gold ring on my finger. I had always wanted to know if making money on Wall Street was as easy as it often seemed from reading the newspapers. Now I was about to find out.

Henry de Jaeger, whom I called next, was an excruciatingly polite man from Louisiana; he was of French extraction and had been on the same intelligence course as me at Fort Bragg in 1942. I didn't like Henry but I knew he was good—very good—at his job. Tall, he was a mixture of the boyish—smooth skin, a deferential, diffident manner, floppy hair falling down his face—and a killer. He had hard eyes that shone like glazed quince, hands built like tarantulas, with long-jointed fingers covered in black hairs, and the crudest, most cancerous tongue I had ever encountered.

"Yessir," he sang in that plantation lilt of his, when I finally tracked him down in his office and explained what I wanted. "Be happy to oblige." Dutifully, he took notes without query as I described the situation. "Got that, got that." He didn't ask how I was or what I had been doing since last we met. When I had finished, he simply asked, "And what shall we do with this shithead Nazi if we find him? Dip his cock in cooking fat?"

Down the line I winced. "No, Henry. I hate Nazis just as much as you do. But just hold him and let me know. I'll fly up."

"Yessir," he said, an obedient boy again.

I had done all I could, for the time being, with the first lead I had extracted from the von Zell file. Now for the second one.

That meant Munich, where, I had learned from the documents, von Zell's senior secretary now lived. That afternoon I found myself on the same road I had been on twenty-four hours earlier but headed in the opposite direction. It was sunny now, though not as warm as I had expected. However, provided I kept the collar of my greatcoat up around my ears I did not need to put up the top of the car. Just outside Darmstadt I picked up a very pretty girl, but though she laughed at my jokes and even agreed to share my pipe, she got out near Heidenheim and I arrived in Munich alone.

I found a room at the Bayerischerhof, but since it was now nearly ten o'clock, the restaurant was closed. As usual, in situations like that, the railway station came up trumps. The brasserie was open, serving three types of hot sausage and jugs of beer.

As I undressed that night I wondered about my money working for me all those thousands of kilometers away in Wall Street. Would it, in time, make me a rich man?

3

THE next day I had the early hours to myself. My plan was to call on Frieda Breker, von Zell's principal secretary, in the evening. I reasoned that she probably had another job now and that at night she would be tired, less resistant.

As it had been a couple of days since I had enjoyed a full meal at the proper time, I decided that day to treat myself to a lavish lunch. There was a restaurant, with a terrace, overlooking the river and, provided I kept my coat on, it was warm enough to eat outside. Lamb seemed safest, roasted with potatoes and parsnips—unusual now but common then—fried in a skillet and larded with garlic and oil. The only red wine available was Austrian and that in full bottles. So I drank too much but enjoyed it.

In the afternoon I visited the Alta Pinakothek, Munich's famous art gallery, with its extensive range of Dürers. I called at the main police station to use their map to locate Frieda Breker's apartment. Then it was back to the Bayerischerhof for a snooze. I didn't know it then but that proved to be a lucky move.

It was already a little past 7:30 before I rapped on Frieda Breker's door. I had left it that late so as to be sure she was home. The flat was in a large apartment block with a curved front on one of the main boulevards leading out of the city and overlooking some playing fields. The building had seen better days, with its huge tubs for plants that were now empty and neglected and a reception desk in the main lobby that had been shoved against a wall and forgotten. Spent light bulbs had not been replaced, nor cracked glass repaired. A lot of Europe would be like that for years to come.

It was no surprise, therefore, to find that the elevator did not work and that I had to climb the stairs to the fourth floor.

Whoever was inside took a long time answering my knock, but that may have been because the apartment was so big. I could hear voices—women's voices—and then footsteps approaching the door.

"Who is it?" a voice asked through the wood.

"Lieutenant Wolff," I replied. "U.S. Army. I would like to speak to Fräulein Breker, please."

There was a rattle of chains and bolts and then the door swung back to reveal a statuesque blond woman wearing a flowered dress and very high-heeled shoes, as was the fashion in those days.

"Fräulein Breker?"

She nodded. Speaking in German, I introduced myself again and said that I would like to ask her some questions about her former employer, Rudolf von Zell. "May I come in?"

Often, this was a tricky moment but not this time. She stood back to reveal a long, narrow passage. I led the way along it. Painted a sort of shiny chocolate, it was as dingy as an air-raid shelter but it opened out, at the end, into a much cheerier room, large and gaudy, and containing, to my astonishment, three other gorgeous women. It was their voices I had heard from outside the flat, but now, as I appeared ahead, they fell silent. Not one of them was less than five foot six, and I love tall women. As Fräulein Breker, speaking from behind, introduced me, I instinctively took out my American cigarettes and began handing them around.

My expression, however, must have remained one of astonishment as Frieda Breker continued to speak. For it emerged that the three other girls had *all* worked for von Zell. I now recalled that paragraph in the file which said he was grand enough to merit four secretaries. After von Zell had disappeared, and the war had ended, I was told, the girls had decided to stick together and set up house: they knew each other well, got on, employment and housing were not easy to come by and, this way, they could afford to live provided two or three of them had jobs, supporting the others. And it was fun.

They had all accepted my offer of cigarettes enthusiastically and I was offered a chair and a glass of beer.

I couldn't believe my luck. Tracking down the four girls, had they been living separately, as I had imagined, could easily have taken me two or three weeks. Neither Hobel nor General Eisenhower would have liked that. But now I could get this part of the investigation over in one night. I was in no hurry, however; the girls were far too attractive for that.

I had not arrived empty-handed. For Fräulein Breker I had with me the one thing that was, if anything, more potent as a gift than American cigarettes—nylon stockings. She was delighted with them and thanked me extravagantly, pressing the stockings to her cheeks to feel the smooth sheen. I confessed that I had more in the car and the girls forced me to fetch them immediately. When I came back I handed them out and was rewarded with a big kiss from each thrilled girl. My beer glass had been refilled and the girls had lit up again from the pack that I had left on the table.

Would I like some supper? Frieda Breker asked. The others all pressed me to say yes, so what else could I do but stay? I didn't know how we were to get from dinner to the interrogation, but I didn't worry. For the time being I just let events take their course.

In my honor the girls decided to make it a party. They disappeared, to return in their finest clothes, what they had left of their makeup, which was in very short supply in those days, and, of course, their nylons.

"We must have some music, too," said one of the girls, going to the piano. "And, since you wish to inquire after Dr. von Zell, we shall play some of his music." It emerged that, because von Zell had vanished so quickly, he had left behind a great many things, among them his sheet music, which the girls had taken. The piano player—Pauline, with long hair, verging on red—began by playing a very sad Schubert piano sonata. It was clearly something she had played before and was known to the other girls, for they promptly fell silent. Another sonata followed, then two impromptus. By this time Fräulein Breker had made the table ready.

"Enough Schubert," said Frieda, after the second impromptu was finished. She motioned to one of the other girls. "Margaretta will play some von Zell after supper."

"Von Zell composed?" I said with some surprise.

Margaretta smiled. "Oh no. But he discovered, when he met his wife —she was a music publisher at one time—that there was once an Austrian composer also called von Zell who had studied with Mozart. His works are still played."

Pauline took up the story. "Zell is a place in Austria, but Dr. von Zell was from Worms and he was one of those Germans who have always been interested in the greater Germany—you know, pieces of Switzerland, Czechoslovakia, France and, of course, Hapsburg Austria. Dr. von Zell made a point of acquainting himself with the Austrian composers—

Schubert, Mozart, Haydn, Bruckner—even Schoenberg, whom none of us liked."

And he was the same with Austrian wines, I thought to myself.

The supper was meager but, for all of us I think, huge fun, certainly to begin with. It was ages since they had had a man to dine there and what man could fail to enjoy the company of four such bonny women? It was difficult for me to believe that they had all once worked for the Nazi high command. We ate cheese, bread, a hot soup with vegetables and dumplings in it and there was a pastry to follow. Plenty of beer but no coffee. We lingered over the pastries and I handed around more cigarettes.

One thing of particular interest had attracted my attention during the meal. This was the habit they all shared of referring to their former boss as Herr Doktor von Zell. This, I thought, implied respect for him and an absence of familiarity. Had any of them been more familiar in private? Well, that was what I was there to find out.

I tapped the bowl of my pipe on the table. "Ladies," I said, smiling, "it has been a great pleasure to share your table. Soup and cheese never tasted so good." The girls applauded and stamped their feet, and one or two blew me kisses. I held up my hand for silence. "But I came here to do a job and the information I need is important, so important that I am afraid I must question each one of you separately."

More stamping of feet and laughter as the girls pretended to misunderstand my motives. I held up my hand again.

"Sorry, ladies, but I must be serious for a moment. I have to ask you questions in such a way that you cannot compare stories." The girls exchanged glances at this. In stressing my seriousness, I was stepping across some invisible boundary; the mood of the party was changing.

Sensing this, I added hurriedly, "No, it is not that I don't trust you, or anything like that. But it *is* important that I find Dr. von Zell as quickly as possible." I stressed the "Dr."

"But how are you going to do that, Lieutenant? There are four of us and only one of you?" It was Frieda Breker speaking. "What is to stop three of us from comparing notes while you are in another room with the fourth?"

She had a point but I had thought ahead of her. "Because I shall not question you here." Now I had their attention. "I am arresting you and taking you to jail."

Disbelief and horror spread in equal measure across the four faces. I could see them thinking, as one woman, Was this a way for me to repay their hospitality?

It was not, and I smiled reassuringly. "Please, ladies, don't be alarmed. It is merely a friendly arrest so that we can get this over with quickly. Please think. We've had a lovely dinner but I am not fooling when I say that my job of tracking down Dr. von Zell is important—and urgent. Any one of you may know something that could prove vital. I love all of you but I need to know what you know. So, as I say, please think. The only place I can make absolutely sure that you can't compare stories is if you are safely locked up in a police station, each of you in a cell all to yourself. Extravagant, I know, but I'm going to have to do it. And the only way I can get you into those cells is by arresting you, each lovely one of you."

I took out my orders. "Look, I have the authority of General Eisenhower himself. Does that convince you that the information I want is important?"

No one said anything and my orders remained on the table, untouched. They believed me—or maybe they weren't interested.

Margaretta went to the piano, sorted through the sheets of music and held up a thin booklet.

"This is the von Zell," she said and sat down on the stool.

It was, thankfully, a bright, cheerful piece, with a brisk tempo and a series of loud, deep chords. She was shrewd, Margaretta, and the lively mood of the party was more or less restored by this, with the other girls tapping the table in time. When I handed around more cigarettes they were accepted enthusiastically. Then, when the music stopped, the girls —cigarettes jutting from their lips like the white guns of a tropical flotilla—left the table as it was and clambered into their coats. A caretaker, or night watchman, was standing by the entrance to the apartments, savoring what was probably *his* last cigarette of the day, and he watched in mute amazement as first one, and then all the other girls squeezed themselves into my car, wedging their shiny, nylon-coated legs wherever they would fit, amid giggles and shrieks of pleasure at the prospect of a ride with the top down.

It was 11:00 when we left the apartment block and, since I could not drive too fast with all that flesh in the car, it was another twenty minutes before we arrived downtown. I realize that, nowadays, an army man could not just turn up at a police station late at night and commandeer a few cells. But in 1946 that is exactly the sort of thing you could do. Germany had been a totalitarian country for years and years, which meant that people were used to arbitrary power, to being ordered around. And there was still, after all, a military government in the area, run by Americans. With Eisenhower's orders in my pocket, I was a more powerful man than I have ever been, before or since, which is probably just as well.

The police station, when I found it again, was crawling with activity even at that late hour. It was a six-story building in a sort of yellow stone and had those metal-framed windows that gave it the aspect of a middle-aged, plain, frumpish stenographer. Buildings often remind me of people.

Yellow light came from almost all the windows and on the marble steps leading up to the main entranceway stood a knot of people like a wedding group waiting for the photographer. They could have been anything: police, criminals, journalists, drunks, judges.

Everyone turned to look as the girls disembarked noisily and clattered up the steps and into the building. In German I asked for the station officer. After a couple of minutes a fat, red-haired man stepped out of an office at the back of the room and came forward. He eyed the girls.

"Yes?" he said to me. I noticed that he needed a shave but you couldn't tell until you were close. Blonds and redheads were lucky in that way. No matter how well I shaved, I looked swarthy again by lunchtime.

I showed him my orders, drawing his attention to the general's signature. "I need some cell space, urgently," I said. "I must interrogate these girls as quickly as possible—tonight. And I must see each of them separately, so they cannot compare stories."

He turned back to the girls, inspecting them one by one. Pauline shivered under his look.

"What have they done?"

"Nothing. But one or more of them may have some information I need. It really is urgent." Was he going to be difficult?

"What sort of information?"

"Sorry, I can't tell you." I waved the orders at him again. I didn't want to tell him I was Nazi hunting. In those days you could never be too careful; there were still a lot of secret sympathizers around in all sorts of guises. In 1946 Germany still made my flesh creep.

But the station officer didn't like my approach. He wanted to know what I was up to, and if I wasn't going to be cooperative, neither was he. He gave me a hard look.

"This is a busy station, Lieutenant. There's no free space."

The girls were looking at me now, curious as to the delay. They had to see I had some real authority or the interrogations would be that much more difficult. That's one reason I opted for the police station rather than trying to make do with Frieda Breker's flat. In real cells, whether they had been properly arrested or not, they would feel much more intimidated and, a not unimportant thing, much more uncomfortable physically. However, I judged that arguing with the redheaded captain would only make things more difficult. I turned so that my body was between him and the girls.

"Are you a married man, Captain?"

He looked at me sideways, suspicious. But he nodded his head.

"I bet you don't see a lot of her, eh? Not in this job. You're right—I can see that it is a busy station and that you have a heavy responsibility."

"The hours are long," he said gruffly, not giving yet. His tone implied that, in Germany just then, a lot of people were forced to work long hours.

I lowered my voice so he had to lean toward me to hear. "In my car outside I have three pairs of nylons. They would make a gift for your wife, I think, on those nights when you arrive home late?" I made it a question. "All women like nylons."

He looked at me again, this time turning his head fully in my direction. I recognized with relief the series of expressions with which I had long ago grown familiar. His first look said that he couldn't be bought in that way, and not to think that he could. The second look was a kind of startled realization that, yes indeed, his wife *would* be delighted with some nylons. And the third look was a kind of lost expression, as he realized that, like anyone else, he *could* be bought. But he would like to save face if he could and I knew that now was the time to give him a graceful way out.

"You drive a hard bargain, Captain," I lied. "But I also have a carton of American cigarettes; you could give your men a decent smoke."

It usually worked. The wonderful thing about nylons and cigarettes was that they weren't big enough, as "gifts," to be seen as bribes, as real corruption. The captain would get more than anyone else but that was only his due, he would tell himself, as the ranking officer. Even so, he might give one of his sergeants a pair of nylons for *his* wife. That would make him feel less guilty, spread it more thinly.

I pressed him. "If you give the order, we can go out to my car together."

He spoke quietly to one of his sergeants. "How many prisoners tonight, Hans?"

"Fourteen, sir."

"Anything serious?"

Hans inspected a large book on the reception counter. "Four drunks, two drunken prostitutes, two soldiers in a fight—we're waiting for the military police to collect them—and, oh yes, a robber caught redhanded, shinnying over a factory wall. The remainder are all vagrants."

The captain thought. "Leave the robber by himself, and the two whores, and the two soldiers. That's three cells. Split the other nine into three groups of three and put them in the new wing." He looked back at me. "We have ten cells; that leaves four for you. But the sooner I can have them back the better—if I should get a sudden rush, it could be embarrassing."

"Right," I said, making briskly for the door. To the girls I called out, "I'll be right back, my lovelies, I promise. Don't move."

I opened the door so that the captain could sit in my car. Then I dipped into the trunk and took out the nylons and the cigarettes. Maurice and I had evolved what we thought was the perfect transaction of this kind. The nylons in all our packets were identical, but some were sealed in red wrappers and others in white. I handed the captain one of each. "The red ones were made in California, in Hollywood, and the white in New York. Take your pick." It wasn't true, but sometimes people balked at the last moment and wouldn't accept the "gifts." We had found that offering them a "choice" at this late stage took their minds off any objections or reservations they might have. Choosing red or white seemed to make acceptance less of a sin, as if they themselves had needed to employ some skill in obtaining the goods.

The captain took two packets of red and one of white and I handed over a carton of two hundred cigarettes, king size. We got out of the car together, after he had stuffed the nylons inside his uniform, and went back into the station.

The girls were led down a flight of stone steps to the basement of the building, into a plain gray corridor with a series of white steel doors. It struck me as cold and clinical enough to resemble what you would find if you could shrink enough to crawl inside the cells of a brain: colorless, tidy, efficient space. It was all very forbidding and, for my purposes, perfect. One by one the girls were shown into the cells, each room with white-painted brick walls, a safety light, a table, two chairs and nothing else.

I had been observing the girls throughout the evening and, unobtrusively, trying to sort out how to approach the interrogations. In general, of course, what I wanted was any information that would lead to von Zell, but in practice I guessed that it would boil down to one thing: whether or not he had—or had had—a mistress, either among these girls or someone else.

In my experience a man's secretary was always the first suspect in the search for a mistress and von Zell had had four. If none of these women had slept with him, then one of them *must* at least know if he had a mistress. Over the years that sort of thing is impossible to hide. My guess was that, if von Zell did have someone, he would have been in touch with her recently. Her identity was, therefore, all-important.

When the last of the girls had been deposited in the cells, the captain turned and gave me the keys. He looked at his watch.

"Nearly midnight. It's unlikely we'll get very busy tonight, but you never know. The station brasserie closes at two and there's sometimes a bit of trouble then. If you could be through by that time, it might avoid problems. . . ."

I nodded and he retired back upstairs.

I started where my instincts told me to—not with Fräulein Breker, the senior secretary, but with Margaretta—Margaretta Posse was her full name. She was the better-looking of the two pianists and I reasoned that these two facts, as musician and good-looker, made her the most likely contender.

As I entered her cell she was sitting not on one of the chairs but on the table, swinging her legs backward and forward. She looked like a large teenager.

"This needn't take very long, Margaretta," I said, "but there are one or two things I have to be clear about." She nodded and smiled and got off the table to sit on a chair opposite me. I placed a pack of cigarettes between us and sat down myself.

"You are probably the prettiest of the four secretaries, Margaretta, and of course you play piano so well. Were you ever von Zell's mistress?"

Crude, but it appeared to have worked. For a while Margaretta stared at me, surprised and shocked. Eventually she blinked.

"Oh no," she stammered. "He was—is—a most charming man; we all liked him, but not . . . not in *that* way. At least as far as I was concerned, he was not really my type. And I . . . I'm sure I was not his type." She threw a puzzled glance in my direction. "Wasn't he happy with his wife? I thought he was." She put her hand to her neck and massaged it lightly, closed her eyes and sighed, as if to herself. She was thinking back, but to what?

I let the silence continue for a while. Then I shifted forward in my seat and opened the cigarettes. I half-offered them to her, my hand being outstretched but cradling the cigarettes on my side.

"Tell me, Margaretta . . . that sigh . . . is it a happy memory? Or a sad one? What happened?"

Her hand was still on her neck but not moving now. She looked down. I held out the cigarettes properly.

Absently, she took one and held it tentatively to her lips. I got up out of my chair and went around the table to light it for her. I sat on the edge of the table, near her, looking down.

"What happened, Margaretta? It might be important."

She sucked on her cigarette and inhaled deeply, shaking her head. "It wasn't important. Not at all." Nevertheless, she had remembered it.

I said nothing. She was smoking greedily and usually that was a good sign. I lit my pipe, taking my eyes off her to do so. The pipe was useful for that, it sometimes eased the pressure. Margaretta took another cigarette, this time lighting it herself. Again, she sucked in ravenously.

"Once, in 1943, I think, we were working late. Two of us girls and Dr. von Zell. On those occasions, to show his appreciation that we were working such long hours, he would open the door between his room and the large office outside where we all worked, and at eight o'clock he would switch on the radio in his office for the concert; it was his way of sharing something with us. We would all listen together.

"Well, this particular night was a Thursday, that I remember very well, and the symphony was by Bruckner. It was at the time when Hitler wanted his museum to go ahead as planned in Linz and the opera house was to be dedicated to Bruckner, rather as Bayreuth is dedicated to Wagner. You understand?"

I nodded. I hated Wagner, he'd offered too much inspiration to the Nazis.

"A lot of Bruckner was being played just then, I suppose because he was one of Hitler's favorites. He had lived near Linz for a while. Anyway, I remember it was Bruckner's Seventh Symphony they were playing that evening, the long one. The music was loud, passionate, typical Bruckner, swelling then dying, rising then falling. Pauline, who was the other girl there that night, left after the first movement but I stayed on to finish what I was doing. So there was just the doctor and me. The music continued to ebb and flow, to fill the room at one moment, and then retreat the next. I think I was supposed to be filing some records in connection with Marshall Göring's paintings but I found myself listening to the music instead. I got up and walked around, trying to recapture my concentration . . . and then I noticed that, inside his office, Dr. von Zell had unloosened his tie and taken his boots off. He was leaning back in his chair with his eyes closed, just listening.

"The music had reached that point where the whole orchestra is straining, squeezing rapid bursts of thunder from every direction." She looked up at me and smiled. "You know how it is sometimes with music, it gives you a cold sensation along your spine. As if champagne bubbles have spilled inside your vertebrae. That happened to me then; I can remember it so well. And, of course, I was keyed up—we had been on the go all day, since seven in the morning. Suddenly, suddenly I felt a huge desire to make love." She paused, embarrassed now, avoiding my eye. "To be made love to. I went into Dr. von Zell's room. I had taken off my shoes so he didn't hear me come in, what with the strength of the music.

"He looked rather boyish, with his tie undone. His hair was mussed and, with his eyes closed, he looked almost vulnerable, not at all the tough, controlled Nazi leader. I can remember it *so* well now. As I moved into his room, the feeling I had, the sexual feeling, became even stronger, there was such a mixture of manly smells about him—the leather from his boots, some kind of cologne from his hair, even the ink of his fountain pen. And still he didn't hear me. The Bruckner had changed now and lush loops of strings filled his office.

"And then I must have stepped in front of the lamp for a shadow was thrown across his face. That was when he opened his eyes. I must have looked pretty strange, creeping into his room like that without my shoes and, I think, holding my neck just like this, where the music affected me."

So *that's* why she had massaged herself.

"But, if he was surprised, he didn't show it. He remained calm, calmer than me. He spoke softly and said something like, 'Yes, Margaretta, what is it?'

"At first I didn't reply. I couldn't. I just stood there, rubbing my neck. He didn't make it any easier, for he closed his eyes again. I had to search for something to say—something, well, you know, appropriate. Simple and not embarrassing."

It was dreadfully uncomfortable on the edge of the table but I didn't dare move, it might break the spell. My pipe had gone out but I left it. It was now past midnight, very quiet outside, and there was nothing to disturb Margaretta or stop her reliving the episode all over again.

"I think . . . I think that . . . in the end I said something like, 'The Bruckner is very moving. The sound seems to *foam* in places.' I remember I used the word 'foam' deliberately. I wanted to suggest . . . For a long time Dr. von Zell continued to sit with his eyes closed. I remember that I couldn't see him breathing. Then his eyelids opened. 'My dear,' he said, his tone friendly, easy but ever so slightly reproachful, 'Do you know why I have my eyes closed, as I listen to the music?' I stood in front of him and shook my head.

" 'If I close my eyes and concentrate, and the music relaxes me enough, I can see my house in Mondsee. It's a wooden house with a black roof and a balcony. There's a broken shutter on the first floor and the lake is less than fifty meters away. We have a bathing hut and a boathouse. In that house, Margaretta, in a room with a rocking chair, is my wife, Konstanze. At this hour our son will be in bed. Konstanze is also listening to this music. Her eyes will be closed, too, for she is trying to imagine me, here.

" 'Every Thursday and Sunday we listen to the radio concerts together in this way. Although we are miles apart this is one way we can be together.' The music had faded by now, as Bruckner has a habit of doing, and the sound of my breathing seemed to fill the office. He picked up a pen or a ruler, I forget which, and began tapping his desk, trying to break the mood. 'Why don't you go home now,' he said in a whisper. 'We have an early start tomorrow.'

"After what he had told me, I only wanted him more, but I knew it was hopeless and that I had to leave. As I crossed back through the door to the outer office, he called out, 'Margaretta.' It was still a whisper, confidential. I half-turned, looking back over my shoulder. 'Thank you,' he said."

Briskly, she lit a third cigarette, snapping visibly out of her reverie.

"I can't speak for the others, Lieutenant, but I was never Dr. von Zell's mistress, although I did try that once. He and his wife must have been very fond of one another, to spend their nights listening to the same concert when they were miles apart. After I learned that, I grew to envy them."

I was fascinated by Margaretta's story, but disappointed. It was always wrong to prejudge information collected in interrogations—the most unlikely facts sometimes turned out to be crucial. But it began to seem as if my grand plan to trace von Zell's mistress might be misconceived.

"Tell me one other thing, Margaretta, please."

"Yes?"

"Who handled Dr. von Zell's mail? Who opened his letters, who read them? How was the work organized in the office?"

Margaretta was relieved to be on less emotional ground. She answered readily this time.

"Well, of course, Frieda was his principal secretary, so she saw everything. His number two was the thin, very tall girl sitting next to you at dinner, Delia Hotter. She was also the secretarial link with Bormann's private office, so she would have seen everything that came from there. That leaves Pauline Kletter—she was in charge of the material for the Führermuseum."

"And you?"

"I was the archivist. I filed everything, not just letters but anything Dr. von Zell told me to—books, newspaper articles, photographs, anything and everything. I also had to read everything so that, from time to time, I could act as a kind of rapid reference system. I was a bit of a researcher too. When Bormann wanted Dr. von Zell to find something out, it was usually me who had to locate the experts who could provide the answers."

"So what was the hierarchy in the office? Frieda Breker was the highest but what happened then?"

"Delia, as I told you, then Pauline, because the Führermuseum was so close to Hitler's heart. Then me. But, in a sense, I was more of an outsider than the others, being less of a straight secretary and more of a researcher."

"And that, I take it, means Frieda saw most of Dr. von Zell?"

Margaretta nodded.

"And then?"

"Probably Delia, because she was always talking to Bormann's people."

"Did any one girl stay late more than the others? Did any one job require that?"

Margaretta thought. "We all had to work late quite often. There *was* a war on, after all. Frieda, of course, was there till all hours." Something occurred to her. "On the other hand, it was Delia who had to phone Dr. von Zell at home when Bormann came on the line, and when he was with Hitler anything might happen. It was nothing for the two men to stay up talking and planning until three or four in the morning. If Hitler wanted something fast, it was Bormann's job to fix it. Often that meant us. Bormann, or his office, would call. If Dr. von Zell wasn't there, Delia took the call. If Delia wasn't in the office, she was called at home, no matter what time it was. It was her job to know where Dr. von Zell was at all times. So Delia may have had the most continuous relationship with him, if that's what you're after."

It was. "Thank you very much, Margaretta," I said briskly, getting to my feet. "That's been a great help, most illuminating. You will be released soon, I promise. Here, have another cigarette." And I went out.

Three cells along was Delia Hotter. She was indeed tall and thin, five ten at least, almost as tall as me. On the other hand, unlike many thin women, she had a sizable bust, a combination I have always found virtually irresistible. As I let myself in, she had her legs crossed and looked remarkably composed, considering the circumstances.

I thought a less direct approach might be better this time. I picked up the spare chair and swiveled it, so I could sit leaning against its back. I smiled.

"Just a few questions, Delia. I hope you will be able to help me."

"If I can, Lieutenant, if I can." She uncrossed and recrossed her legs, drawing attention to them. Teasing.

"Tell me, Delia, did you ever meet Martin Bormann? I believe you handled liaison between his office and Dr. von Zell's."

"Yes, I was the link to Bormann. I met him several times and, although I didn't really like him, he could on occasion be most charming. He was, don't forget, very powerful. He had a principal secretary, Amalie, and I got to know her best."

"I understand Bormann would call Dr. von Zell at all hours?"

"Oh yes. He called quite regularly at four in the morning. That was nothing."

"How did you know Bormann called at that hour?"

"Dr. von Zell would tell me the next day. Or, when Amalie couldn't find the doctor, she would call me. It was my job then to find him."

"How often did that happen?"

She thought. "I would say . . . once every two, maybe three, weeks."

Now came the crux. I tried to make it sound casual. "And if Dr. von Zell couldn't be found by Bormann, by Amalie, where was he? Usually."

Delia gave me a sharp look, a scowl that insinuated, better than any words, what she thought of men who took supper off poor girls, bought their affections with nylons, then kept them up late with intrusive questions. But she had accepted the stockings, had already enjoyed their effect. She was reluctant, but she continued to cooperate.

"Dr. von Zell's first love, after his wife, was music. Then came wine. But he had an interest in art, too, and was, in the early years of the war, helping to organize Hitler's art collection for the Führermuseum, planned for Linz. Initially, the doctor was placed in charge of coins and armor, but as the war started to turn against Germany he found himself in an awkward position. As a Nazi he naturally wanted Germany to win and he took pride in the idea of a collection of uniquely beautiful things. Some Nazis, however, when events began to go sour, took a very"—she hesitated—"well, I suppose the word is *sick,* attitude to the collections.

"Dr. von Zell's particular thorn in his side was a certain Gauleiter Eigruber, who lived in Linz. Eigruber was a fanatical Nazi and took it upon himself to prevent the Allies from ever finding out about the Alt Aussee salt mine, which, as you must know, was where most of the art intended for Linz was hidden. Eigruber had even managed to smuggle some explosives into the mine disguised as packages of paintings and antiques. If the collapse did come, he wanted to blow up the lot, destroying any evidence that the Nazis had commandeered art. Eigruber was the gauleiter in charge of that whole area of Austria, and Dr. von Zell was in charge of the art at Alt Aussee. So, in a sense, the salt mine had two commanding officers who had different policies should the collapse come.

"Eigruber had his own men in the mine, of course, people who did the smuggling. But the doctor had his people, too, and they knew when Eigruber's 'specials,' as they were called, arrived. The explosives were never touched by the men in the mine, but Dr. von Zell was always alerted as soon as possible. That's when he would disappear."

This was a new side to von Zell and I was fascinated. I pressed a cigarette on Delia and filled my pipe.

"The doctor would leave our offices sometime between eleven and midnight, when there was no one around to observe him. He would drive himself, alone, to Alt Aussee, which was about eighty kilometers away. Once there, he would search all suspect packages, remove the explosives and replace them with Plasticine. Then he would throw the dynamite, or whatever it was, into one of the many lakes between Alt Aussee and Berchtesgaden. It's a mountainous road, so it would take him most of the night, especially in wintertime.

"He was worried that Eigruber, like many fanatics, was a law unto himself. Even after Hitler issued a directive, stipulating that the mine should *not* be blown up, whatever the circumstances, the doctor still kept an eye on Eigruber. He didn't trust him. The nighttime sorties continued until the very end, even while the attempt was being made to block up the mine, which was Hitler's idea. It proved very difficult to make an effective blockade and Dr. von Zell feared that Eigruber might get his way in the end."

Delia stood up to stretch her lovely legs, her story finished.

I was familiar with the Alt Aussee mine, of course, and had often wondered whether the Germans had ever considered destroying it. I never imagined that von Zell was the man who had saved countless works of art. If I wasn't careful I would begin to like him, which was not the plan at all. A nice Nazi? No—not in 1946.

I smiled at Delia. She was off guard, surely, after so long a story. And it was now coming up to one o'clock. Time for shock tactics.

"Were you ever von Zell's mistress, Delia?"

But I was the one who got the surprise. Delia burst out laughing and coughing and very nearly choked on her cigarette. It was some time before she could reply.

"Is *that* what all this is about? No, Lieutenant, I wasn't. No, no, no. We all thought about it, of course, especially when we were first recruited for his office. He was an attractive man, tall, dark, and that dueling scar on his cheek was very dashing. He was living miles from his wife. And I think Margaretta once propositioned him late at night; at least, that's what she told us, silly girl. But none of us did—go to bed with him, I mean. He was very much in love with his wife. She would send him long love letters, according to what Frieda told us, and he would apparently do the same. In fact, although they were older than us, we all came to envy them—they seemed so rock-solid together, so sure of each other despite what was happening all over Europe." Delia turned to look at me and her look wore more than a hint of defiance. "It was lovely."

She sat down again, a smile—no, a smirk—warping her face. She was still amused that I should have harbored such thoughts about her and von Zell. The tables had been turned in some mysterious way so that I felt I was the one under observation. It was time to move on.

I got up. "Thank you, Delia, you've been more help than you know" —a weak attempt to regain control. "I'm afraid I'll have to keep you here for a short while longer. Then I will ferry you all back to the apartment." She just nodded, her smirk refusing to disappear.

Pauline Kletter had dark hair, which fringed her face, large brown eyes and muscular legs with big calves. She was clad in a blue woolen knit dress, with a navy raincoat on top. She tapped the table impatiently with one hand while the other remained tucked away in her raincoat pocket. She did not look happy.

"I am sorry to have kept you waiting," I said, sensing she might be more difficult than the previous two. "This won't take longer than is absolutely necessary."

She said nothing but stopped tapping the table.

Out came my cigarettes; she leaned forward for me to light hers for her. I fiddled with my pipe. All the signals she was sending out were cold ones; she had been waiting in that cell for close to an hour, so I couldn't really blame her. But that meant a less direct, more conversational approach was called for.

"Pauline, how would you describe Rudolf von Zell? What sort of man is he?"

She continued smoking, inhaling the smoke and expelling it through her nostrils. Then she shrugged. "A good man, I think. A good German. He was efficient, tactful, very practical. He had strong feelings, I think, but working with Bormann he learned to sit on them. He gave the impression of being wise."

She paused, so I said, "Give me an example of what you mean."

She took her hand from her raincoat. It had a handkerchief in it and with this she wiped her nose. She must have had a slight spring cold. "Yes . . . I think it happened in 1942. There was an idea Bormann had which he managed to sell to Hitler. They were all very much against organized religion in those days and so in many cases they ordered the confiscation of church property—relics, jewelry, books, art. The rule was supposed to run right across Germany, which I suppose it did; but it was especially strong in Austria because there were so many Catholics. Bormann was particularly against the churches and the monasteries in Austria because they had so much art.

"We started receiving details of paintings, carved sculptures, altarpieces, manuscripts and other things, like coins, which had been taken from ecclesiastical centers—Kremsmünster, Göttweig, St. Florian, all sorts of places. Not only that, the monks attached to some of the monasteries were ordered out into the world. Their cloisters were closed and they were forced to get ordinary jobs. Humiliating for them. Dr. von Zell was a devout Catholic—I'm not sure whether Bormann or Hitler knew that, for he never paraded his religion, but if they did know, they pretended they didn't. He, of course, hated what was happening but couldn't do anything to stop it, not openly anyway. It was Bormann's idea and had Hitler's enthusiastic support.

"Then one day the doctor called me into his office and asked me to close the door. He swore me to secrecy and asked me to find out how many monks had been displaced in Austria, and from which monasteries. That was all. It took about a week, but in the end I found that about two hundred and fifty monks, Benedictines mainly, had been moved. Kremsmünster had been the worst hit; all the monks were gone from there and the monastery was being used as a warehouse for art; later its contents were moved up to the mine at Alt Aussee.

"A few days later Dr. von Zell went to see Kremsmünster for himself.

It was only a hundred and forty kilometers away but he was gone three nights." The handkerchief came out again.

"I never found out where he had been, or what he had done, until a couple of years later. Then, out of the blue, a crate of wine was delivered to our office just before Christmas. It was Austrian wine, from the Wachau region the doctor said, and he gave me three bottles as a Christmas gift. He said I had earned them. 'Earned' was the word he used, so I asked him what he meant. That was when he called me into his office a second time.

"The door was closed and we both sat down—quite an event in itself. 'Pauline, my dear,' he said, 'I couldn't tell you before—it was too dangerous. But now time has elapsed, things are . . . very different and the war will soon be over. . . . You remember those monks—the Benedictines—who were forced to leave their monasteries? The ones Bormann didn't like and who were made to get jobs?' I nodded. I remembered only too well.

" 'As you probably know, Pauline, I am a Catholic. Not an especially good one perhaps but I do take it seriously. I also know a few things about wine, Austrian wine included. Now you may know this and you may not . . . but monks are often very familiar with wine-making too. Dom Perignon is well known, as are the Carthusians who hold the secret formula for Chartreuse. But their influence is much wider than that, my dear, and dates back many centuries.' He had started to smile as he said this for he could see I was puzzled; what on earth was he talking about? He raised his hand, as if to say, 'All will become clear in a moment.'

" 'In this job, in the last few years, Pauline, I have had to learn to be a fixer, an entrepreneur, an impresario of sorts, someone who can put two and two together and make five. Well, that's what I did this time, except that I didn't do it for the Party but for the Catholic Church.

" 'The displaced monks were looking for work, and some of my friends who ran vineyards in Austria were short of labor, since all the young men from the villages were away fighting. I was able to place most of the monks in a few days. It was work they knew, in the fields, not too far from the monasteries they had been forced out of, and, most important, they could stay together, more or less, and carry on with their worship. When the war ends and the young men return to their jobs in the Wachau, then, with luck, the monks will be able to move back to their monasteries.

" 'Meanwhile, they have sent this case as a "Thank you" for Christmas and, since you helped in the research, part of the gift is yours.' "

Pauline wiped the fringe off her face and put her other hand in the pocket of her raincoat. She huddled her shoulders together as if the mention of Christmas had made her cold. "That's the kind of thing I meant, Lieutenant. The doctor made no fuss; he just made up his mind to do something, worked out how and if it could be done, then did it."

Not for the first time that night, my pipe had gone out. I had been listening too hard to notice. Vineyards, Austrian vineyards of the Wachau, had cropped up again.

"One question, Pauline. Did Dr. von Zell mention the names of any vineyards? Or the names of his friends?"

"That's two questions, Lieutenant. But it makes no difference. He was too careful to do that. The war was ending, but not yet over."

"Were there no labels on the bottles?"

"No. That would have been risky, too, and in wartime there were more important things to do with paper and ink than print wine labels. The bottles were green with long stems."

Terrific. Virtually all German and Austrian wines came in bottles like that. Scraping the barrel now, I said, "And what did the wine taste like?" That might be a clue.

"Sorry, I didn't drink it. The war was on, Germany was losing and Christmas presents were hard to come by. I gave mine away. I'm not a great wine drinker anyway."

Shit! I said to myself, thinking of Henry de Jaeger's tongue. A wine label could have saved me a lot of trouble in tracking down von Zell. Still, Pauline had been most helpful in corroborating my vineyard hunch, so I told myself to be grateful.

I scraped back the chair and got up, repeating my litany. "Thank you, Pauline. Not long now; I just have to talk to Frieda, then you may all go. It's late, I know."

"May I have another cigarette?"

She was still hunched in the same position, a strange figure, I thought. Less beautiful, physically, than the others but more self-possessed, and that made her, probably, the heartbreaker of the quartet. More attractive to me, certainly. I lit her cigarette, pulled on it myself, then placed it between her lips. She didn't move.

Frieda Breker was wrapped in what looked like a length of purple curtain which was in fact, I later learned, a modish coat. The belt, made of the same material, went around her waist twice. But no shrinking violet was she.

"I normally come *first*, Lieutenant. Not last."

Oh God. The textbooks on interrogation all said that the later it got, the less resistant captives were supposed to become. But, I suspect, that worked only for men. Women, it seemed, just got more difficult as the night wore on.

"Yes, Frieda, I know. But look at it from my point of view. All the other girls are strong characters—you must be even more so, to have been Dr. von Zell's number one. I had to lay the groundwork before facing you." I wasn't too good at being unctuous, and Fräulein Breker wouldn't have held down the job she had had without some ability to cut through bullshit of the kind I had just thrown her. But she seemed to accept it, for all she said was, "And I need a smoke and some coffee, quick."

"The coffee will have to wait, I'm afraid. Cigarettes I can do."

I gave her the pack, another attempt to recognize her rank, and struggled with my pipe.

"Frieda, I originally came here to see whether Dr. von Zell had, or still has, a mistress. Someone he might have kept in touch with. I even thought that you, or one of the other girls, might be that mistress."

What sounded like a jeep slithered to a halt out in the street, above our heads. Heavily shod feet scraped the floor and skipped up the steps into the station. The military police had come to collect the two drunken soldiers.

Frieda had unloosened the belt to her coat, as if she needed space to smoke. The brilliant red of her dress, underneath the purple, reminded me of a rhododendron.

"Lieutenant," she said heavily, in the manner of a mother trying to impress on a small son that she has seen it all before, "I worked for Dr. von Zell from September 1939, the same month as the war with England started, and, let me tell you, for every week that he spent away from his wife, the doctor received one letter. Every week he wrote one letter back. What is more, I have met Mrs. von Zell. Konstanze is strong and loyal, a Catholic, Lieutenant. She is also very beautiful. We all went to Krimml one day to look at the waterfalls. I remember there was a film crew there, making a movie. The director was an Italian—tall, gray hair.

Italian men go gray so much better than anyone else, I think. He noticed Konstanze as we all walked by and he shouted after us. In no time we were surrounded by the crew. The director stared at Konstanze, and then beamed at Dr. von Zell, congratulating him on how beautiful his wife was. He said that he wanted Konstanze in his movie—really. Just like that. He wanted her to stand, as she was, then and there, so he could get her in a particular shot, to break up the flow of the camera movement. We all laughed and Mrs. von Zell was very embarrassed. But the Italian was very persuasive; and in any case the crew which surrounded us wouldn't move until she had agreed. So into the movie she went. She is *that* beautiful, Lieutenant. They have a lovely boy, Dieter. They both play the piano and used to send each other music. They would also send books they had read and liked. All this while there was a war on. Does that answer your question?"

My pipe was being difficult. Above us we heard the boots again, moving more slowly now that they were dragging prisoners with them. The jeep barked to life and zipped off out of earshot.

"Did you know that Margaretta once made a pass at the doctor?"

"Of course. She told me the next day."

"Did you know about the Eigruber affair? At Alt Aussee."

"Not everything, not the things that Dr. von Zell thought it was unsafe for me to know. But I knew he used to go there, late at night. And I knew why."

"And what about the monk business?"

"Of course I knew. He was away from his office for three days and three nights. Someone had to cover for him—I helped him work out his alibi, so to speak. We pretended he was looking at other mines, rivals to the Alt Aussee one. Then, when he came back, he dictated his report to me, since he thought it was too risky for Pauline."

I had finally persuaded my pipe to work. The tobacco was sweet, a bit too sweet for me. I preferred drier leaves, but in war we had to make do. And I was better off than most.

It looked as though some of the other girls had their own private areas with von Zell, but Frieda Breker had apparently known his movements at all times—he was too important. So, I decided, she would certainly have known if he had a mistress. I was inclined to believe her when she said, adamantly, that he was too much in love with his wife to think of going off with anyone else, but . . . one could never be too sure. I tried a different tack.

"Tell me about the end, Frieda. When everyone evacuated the office."

Briefly, a look of exhausted annoyance swept across Frieda's face and I realized that she—that all the girls—were much more tired than I thought. Then I remembered that I had slept during the afternoon, whereas most of them had worked all day. I still felt fine, though my beard was beginning to show and I could feel how coarse my chin was becoming each time I took my pipe from my lips.

"Not long, I promise," I said. "Just tell me about the end, Frieda, please . . . then we can all go home and get some sleep. I know you have to be up early for work tomorrow."

She threw back her head and stared up at the white ceiling. Slowly, the events of a year ago were recalled.

"Everything, I suppose, started to go crazy on the last day of April. I remember well because it was just before my birthday, May 3. . . . Early that morning two curators from Alt Aussee arrived, Dr. Schedelmann and Dr. Rupprecht. They seemed very anxious and they had brought with them a case of gold coins. There were about two thousand of them and the coins had originally been intended for the Führermuseum because they were rare art, or something like that. But, at that time, apparently, Hitler wanted the coins for use as a currency reserve in case he had to retreat somewhere; things were obviously going extremely badly for Germany.

"That, as I say, was the thirtieth of April. The next day, May 1, we—the doctor and us four girls—all moved our office from Berchtesgaden to Arthurhaus. I had known about this in advance but the other secretaries didn't. Arthurhaus was a tiny town on the other side of the Hagen Gebirge, the big mountain south of Berchtesgaden. It was always kept ready as a place of retreat—it was in Austria and in the mountains proper. Dr. von Zell was quite a good skier, and, should the worst ever happen, he felt he could . . . well, escape . . . over the snow."

Frieda stumbled over her words because she realized, too late, that she had talked herself into giving something—she wasn't sure what—away. She now realized that she had no choice but to go on. As Maurice used to say, in for a penny, in for a pound.

"The plan was for the doctor to meet up at Arthurhaus with Martin Bormann and then the two of them, later, would rendezvous with Hitler.

But of course it was on that day . . . that terrible day"—and she pulled her coat back around her with a shiver—"that we learned Hitler had killed himself.

"That changed everything, of course, and, for a day or two, I'm not sure the doctor knew what to do. We stayed in Arthurhaus, awaiting news, then we heard that Bormann had withdrawn into the mountains. Later that same day the doctor was driven off and even I didn't know to where, I promise. He was gone overnight, then called the next day to say he wasn't coming back. I talked to him. He seemed very sad and asked to speak to each of the girls, in turn, to thank them. He told us to go back to our homes, to our parents, that things would be chaotic for a while. He told us that he was going away and that he would never see us again."

She was no longer speaking at the ceiling but looking levelly at me.

"I know Germany lost, Lieutenant, and that no one is really interested in how the losers *feel*. But it was a sad time. We had been a contented group—no one is deliriously happy in wartime are they?—doing what we felt was important work. Now it was breaking up. That, I think, is why we agreed to stay together. We all did go home to our families for a week or so, but we had decided to live together in Munich and that's what we did. None of us had boyfriends we cared enough about to stay down south. So we set up house in the apartment where you found us tonight. And no one has heard from Dr. von Zell since."

On the whole I believed Frieda's story; it was the right blend of chaos and detail.

"Just a couple more things, Frieda, then we can all go home. First, when the office was in Berchtesgaden, where did the doctor stay? Was he in lodgings or a hotel?"

"Lodgings. He didn't like hotels. Not good for security, he said."

"And the address?"

"Well, the road was Inzellstrasse but the number I'm less sure about . . . 37 or 47, I think. It was one of the few private houses in the town with a phone."

"And can you remember the landlord's name?"

She shook her head. "Sorry."

"Did the doctor ever say where he might go after Arthurhaus? Either for the short while your office was based there or before, when you and he were discussing it in secret?"

"Nothing specific. He was very cagey in matters like that; he kept secrets well. I think he did say once that, if he could, he would like to remain in Austria."

"Does the name von Haltern mean anything to you?"

It was perverse, no doubt. But one of the satisfactions of being an interrogator was the effect one could produce in others by the insertion of the right question at the right time.

For a brief moment I thought that Frieda had set fire to herself. As her hand had slumped, the cigarette had fallen from her fingers and it landed in her lap, shedding ash everywhere. A mare's tail of blue smoke immediately rose from her coat, where the stub scorched the purple. She batted it out with her hand. It was the best reaction I had produced all night.

"How . . . who told you about that?" It was almost a sob. "I was certain none of the other girls knew."

"Don't worry, Frieda," I said. "It wasn't one of your girls. I found out another way. You tell me what you know."

But she was worried, and unconvinced by my attempt at reassurance. She bought time, dusting the ash from her coat and inspecting the burn mark. Her cigarette stub had gone out and she fussed, relighting it.

"Frieda," I said. *"Please.* It's very late. I visited Dr. von Zell's mother, near Worms. She told me about the von Halterns, and how close the doctor was to Eric. I even visited the Schlosshaltern in Koblenz and found that the family had moved to Hamburg after the bombing. None of the other girls so much as mentioned von Haltern's name, please believe me. Your reaction just now proves that the name means something to you. Tell me what you know."

Our eyes met. Worms, Koblenz, Hamburg. Frieda knew now just how serious I was about this whole business. What she didn't know was how well informed I was, whether or not I was already aware of everything she knew and whether I was just testing her. Even if I didn't know, she could see that I was a formidable adversary who would not give up. She would be here all night, if need be, until I got the information I was after. I wouldn't be put off, and how long we remained in these cells was entirely up to her.

She gave in.

"About two years ago, a bit less, after the English and Americans invaded France, I learned that a good friend of Dr. von Zell's had been killed in an air raid. I was with the doctor when he received the news; it was in a letter from his wife. He was upset, very upset. He didn't do any more work that day, and he even had a drink with his lunch, something he *never* did normally.

"Well, although it was sad, I didn't pay too much heed that day since, after all, we all lost people we knew. But the doctor was no better the next day, or the day after that. In fact, for a short while he went to pieces. The man who had died, Eric von Haltern, had obviously been a special friend, almost like a brother, I suppose. They had been friends at university, and I gather their families were close."

She had paused. Maybe she was reluctant to go on, to tell me more. But I had been right about the cells. They were stark, forbidding. While she paused there was no other sound, either outside or from anywhere else in the building. I said nothing and let the silence work on her. Nothing I could say would make the situation more intimidating. She was alone now. All sorts of things must have been going through her mind, about betrayal, maybe. But then von Zell had looked after himself first, in Arthurhaus. She no longer owed him anything. Slowly, I offered her another cigarette. I moved at a pace intended to imply that *I* had all night.

"He recovered, of course, he was a strong man, but at the same time he was never *quite* the same again. In fact, it was from then that he began to take precautions against Germany losing the war. Up until then he had thought nothing of it, or at least done nothing about it. But that's the effect Eric's death had on him. We all thought of the doctor as a good man but he was, nonetheless, a prominent Nazi. If Germany were to lose the war, it would be awkward for him."

I smiled at her use of the word "awkward." That was putting it mildly.

She pulled on her cigarette, trying to convince herself that she was calm. She was unhappy giving away so many details, but, like the others, she had never seen the inside of a jail before, not firsthand. She hated the effect it had on her more than she hated me. I had seen the reaction before—a human being, decent but unfairly cornered. I didn't like the situation myself very much, but then the Nazis had done the same or worse with our side often enough.

I wound my watch.

"The doctor managed to get Eric von Haltern's passport, and had his own picture put in it. He opened a bank account in von Haltern's name and paid money into it. He got business cards printed."

"What bank?"

"The South Bavarian Bank."

"And what did the business cards say?"

"Baron Eric von Haltern, Wine Merchant."

"And how come you know all this, Frieda? Surely it's the kind of thing the doctor would have kept to himself?"

"Someone had to sign the bank references. Someone the bank knew and he trusted."

It was all falling into place. The hunch I had conceived that night at the Schlosshaltern looked like it was paying off. Von Zell was in the Wachau, using von Haltern's name and working in the wine business.

Frieda did not look well. The war had been over for a year, but she had liked her wartime boss and tonight she had, just possibly, betrayed him. It hadn't taken too much trickery on my part, and it hadn't taken long. Interrogations went like that sometimes, often in fact. People usually give away more than they expect to. People who have never been interrogated invariably imagine that, short of torture, they would give nothing away. But it is amazing what a bit of discomfort, a little isolation and a few seeds of doubt will do. If you smoke, the craving for a cigarette in such circumstances can be very nearly overwhelming. And the reaction is always the same: people don't know why but they feel bruised, as if they had been in a bad road accident and were the only one to have survived; they feel winded, shaky and—yes—guilty. They feel empty, barren.

I said no more but got up and opened the door. Leaving it wide, I opened all the others. The girls appeared, weary from the late hour, jaded with the confinement. Frieda Breker was the last, and the others immediately noticed the change in her and glanced suspiciously at me. I smiled, trying to reassure them, but they were cowed, afraid to question Frieda in public. The gaiety of the earlier part of the evening was quite gone.

We went upstairs, where there was no sign of the redheaded captain, and out into the cold night. No laughter as the girls fitted themselves into the car, a more difficult task now than before, because the cold meant that we had to put up the top. No one spoke as we covered the distance back to the apartment block. Frieda, who got out first, led the way into the darkened lobby area without looking back. I was rewarded with a thin smile from Margaretta and Delia made a weak joke, saying she hoped I would take her somewhere with better music on our next date. But it was a painful moment after such fun earlier on.

I saluted and said nothing. Upstairs, the dinner things remained for them to clear away. After Frieda had talked to them, they would not want to see or think of me again.

4

I'LL say this for the Bayerischerhof: considering the fact that the war had been over barely a year, and that many foodstuffs were still rationed throughout Europe, the hotel kitchen managed to come up with some damn good coffee. Really strong. I remember because when I surfaced, around midmorning the next day, I was still feeling very guilty about the effect I had produced on Frieda Breker. I tried telling myself that I was only doing my job, that such things must be expected after great wars . . . but it didn't work, and as I winced with each gulp of the black, bitter coffee, I imagined how she must be feeling in the bright light of daytime.

I took a quick look at the newspaper—Kaltenbrunner's trial was in full swing at Nuremberg—and then put a call through to Hartt.

"Flowers?" he gasped, when I told him my request. "Why on earth do you need flowers?"

"To send to a lady. You can't get them here, not at the moment. Not at this time of year."

"No can do, friend. Sorry, but your heart is your own affair. And don't let Hobel find out you're enjoying yourself on his time—he'll butcher you."

I explained about Frieda Breker. "So you see, Sammy, I did treat her badly. And we may need her again. A bunch of flowers—daffodils even —would help."

"Hmmmn . . . I see your point, I think. But I don't dare put 'flowers' in the log, eh? Let's just say 'bribe'; it sounds more . . . underhanded."

"Thanks, Sammy. Now, am I a rich man today, or a poor one?"

"Aaah." He sounded a bit embarrassed and my insides subsided. "I did warn you, Walter, that shares go down as well as up."

"How much, Sammy, how much?"

"I put a thousand on for you, like you asked. Two hundred and twenty-two shares at four dollars and fifty cents. And at the close of business last night they were worth . . . let's see, I just have to work it out."

He was delaying. "Sammy!" I could just imagine him, pushing those gold-rimmed spectacles back up his nose. "Sammy!"

"Nine hundred and fifty-two dollars and thirty-eight cents. A drop of twenty-one cents a share, I'm afraid."

"Down forty-eight! In a day?"

"Yeah . . . a lot, eh? I lost five times that, remember."

"Why so much?"

"Not certain, but I'm hoping to find out some time today."

I felt sick. In those days $48 was nearly a week's pay. I had just given it away. "What do you advise?"

"Hold on, at least until we know the full score. If there's that much movement, something must be going on and we might just stand to win if the early indications have it wrong and we hold our nerve."

I dared hardly ask the next question. "What about Confederate Paper? Did you manage to get Maurice onto that?"

"Oh yes, no problem. Two hundred shares at a round five dollars each."

He was playing with me, goddamn it. "And, Sammy? And?"

"Sure you want to hear?"

"Sure." That word had at least six *s*'s the way I hissed it.

"Up seven cents. Your friend is today worth one thousand dollars plus two hundred times seven cents. Making a grand total of one thousand and fourteen dollars."

Shit! I had learned to swear in the war as well as to drink. I wished now I had never listened to Maurice or put through the call to Sammy. His news, coming on top of my guilt feelings about Frieda Breker, got the day off to a lousy start.

"All right, Sammy," I bleated. "Do what you think is best. I'll try to call tonight."

Next I spoke to Maurice in Vienna. He depressed me too. Not only was it his superior airs at being $60 ahead of me already but, it turned out, he hadn't even started to look for von Zell.

"I'm sorry, dear boy, but immediately after I spoke to you something else came up, something that simply *had* to take priority. But don't worry, we'll start on it today, I promise."

"I know you'll think me pushy, Maurice, but can you *please* get people —as many as you can spare—down to the Wachau region today, ready to start the search tomorrow." I explained what Frieda Breker had told me, how it confirmed my hunch.

"Brilliant, dear boy. But if you are that certain, why aren't you coming over here yourself?"

"You can do it just as well as me, Maurice. And besides, I have one other lead to check here, or at least in Berchtesgaden. I don't want to come all the way to Vienna, then have to come back here."

"And what about the bank, dear boy? What was it—the South Bavarian Bank? Have you thought of that?"

"Yes, but you know what banks are. Masters of delay. It could take me three days to get the information out of them if they want to be awkward. And if Frieda Breker is feeling guilty enough this morning, she just might try to warn von Zell. I can't risk the delay—that's why it's important you dispatch someone to the area as soon as possible. You do see that, don't you, Maurice?"

"Of course. It shall be done. You have my word—now don't be tiresome."

It is 150 kilometers from Munich to Berchtesgaden, and in those days it took the best part of three hours, even if you went direct. But there was also a slower, and more luscious, road, which followed the meanderings and the oxbows of the River Inn, slack and sluggish, below Mühldorf, Jettenbach and Wasserburg. I saw plenty of hitchhikers but I still hadn't shaken off my crabby mood, so I kept very much to myself.

I arrived at about 4:30 in the afternoon. Though the day had been sunny, it had never been really warm, and by now the air had a distinct chill to it. Berchtesgaden I found to be a leafy town built on a slope, with the Watzmann and the Hochkönig providing, in the middle distance, a peaceful, white and blue panorama. Lights were beginning to flicker on all over the landscape as the sun went down.

Inzellstrasse, when I found it, was a long, quiet street, stretching up the mountainside toward the majestic Hagen Gebirge, now nearly lost in the dusk. There were no streetlamps and the mature trees that lined the roadway—cherries, I think—restricted what daylight there was left, making my search for number 37—or 47—that much harder.

In fact, I needn't have worried. The road was a dead end, petering out as the slope of the mountain became too severe. And there was no problem over the number: 47 didn't exist. Number 37, a large red chalet-type house with a black roof, was the last building on the street. It was typically alpine, with small windows and large, heavy shutters, and a deep basement where boots, skis, crates of beer, sleds and garden tools lay scattered around. The main door was slightly raised, on a ledge or balcony, also made of wood. It was a house that spent half its year under snow.

I turned my car around before getting out, while I could still see. Then I walked along the short path and knocked on the door. Curiously, the first thing I remember noticing about the woman who opened it was that she wore no rings. She was, I judged, about twenty-five or twenty-six, probably not a war widow but rather one of those who had her man taken from her by the war—otherwise, she would have been married and a mother long ago.

"Yes?" she said. Then, looking over my shoulder and without waiting for me to reply, "What a lovely car you have."

I smiled. The woman spoke with an Austrian accent and was very pretty. She was what I call a butter-and-banana blond: some strands were pale, others a deeper, creamier strain of ivory. She had English skin, pale with patches of red, and a twill of fine blond hair across her face which glinted in parts as it was caught by the last rays of the sun. She had on a blue smock which accentuated, rather than hid, her figure.

"Fräulein . . . ?" I said, saluting. Saluting, I had found, was more useful in peacetime than in war. Civilians were far more impressed by it than other soldiers.

"Stempel," she answered in a friendly, open way. "Alessandra Stempel."

Introducing myself, I took off my hat and gloves and explained why I had come. We shook hands. "I need to trace Dr. Rudolf von Zell, who, I believe, once stayed here. When the war ended he disappeared with a large collection of rare and very valuable gold coins; they were unique, and worth millions of dollars." I paused before adding, "They were stolen from monasteries in your country."

She flashed me a sharp glower. "You guessed . . . I . . . am an Austrian? You have an American uniform, Lieutenant, but a German accent. Are you really a *Yank?*"

I explained my background, which appeared to reassure her, for she invited me to sit on a bench on the balcony of the house, where we could look south and west to the Hagen Gebirge and catch the very last of the day's light. I kept my coat firmly buttoned and even put my gloves back on, I found it so cold; but she seemed not to notice.

"Von Zell did live here, then?"

"Oh yes, for more than a year. We liked him—he was nice—for a German."

"When did he leave?"

She thought for a moment. "It must have been at the time Hitler died. That day or soon after."

"Did he say where he was going?"

"Nnnnno—I don't think so."

"Did he leave anything behind?"

"Not really. A pair of shoes, maybe, some music books. And some wine. But I am afraid we drank that."

Wine again. I looked at my watch. It was almost six. Surely Maurice would have had a man in the Wachau by now.

"Fräulein Stempel, this may sound odd, but do you know . . . how Dr. von Zell came by that wine? Did he buy it here in Berchtesgaden?"

"No—at least I'm pretty sure that he didn't. I have the impression that he brought it home from the office. There were no labels on the bottles, nothing on the box, so I can't be sure."

"I don't suppose you know what wine it was that you drank?"

"Is that important?"

"It might be."

"Let me think." She tugged at a tuft of her blond hair and placed the ends in her mouth, probably a habit she had developed as a young girl. "He did say something about the wine when he first brought it home. What was it?" She frowned, puckering her face like a pixy, her bottom lip flexed over the upper one. "What was it . . . ?" She sucked on her hair again. "Well, I remember one thing," she said, straightening up. "I remember him saying, when he first brought it home, and we had a bottle to celebrate, that we should be proud of it—yes, that's the word he used. He said we should be proud of it because, like us, it was Austrian." She pouted again. "But there was something *else* he said—what was it?"

The sun had gone now and the dusk was gathering around us fast. The color had vanished from the trees and more and more lights glowed in the distance. She shivered.

"It was . . . something . . . something about religion . . . I remember thinking it was an odd thing to say. I'm sorry," she said with a shrug. "I don't think I can remember, after all."

It didn't matter. She had given me an idea, something I should have thought of before. "Fräulein Stempel," I said. "May I use your phone?"

"But of course. Let's go in anyway. It's cold now."

Inside, the house was built more like a Viking or a Scandinavian barn than an alpine chalet. The ground floor was occupied by an enormous room that was kitchen, living room, library and dining room all in one. The kitchen and dining area, however, were divided off from the rest, and from a log hearth, by a staircase that came halfway across the room, opposite the main door. The stairs led to a gallery—bedrooms and bathrooms—and a farther, smaller staircase led into the eaves, high, high up. Shadows, deep red from the fire, poked like long cleats into the peaks of the roof.

The phone was in the kitchen area. I fished out my piece of paper with the magic numbers on it and put a call through to Vienna. Fräulein Stempel perched herself on a tall stool and took two apples from a bowl, handing one to me.

"Dear boy," said Maurice, just a touch exasperated that here I was on the line again so soon. "*Do* trust me. I have a man on his way to the Wachau right now, even as we speak. We shall have some news for you tomorrow, I hope."

"I do trust you, Maurice, of course I do. It's just that I think I have some more information. Tell him to concentrate on vineyards run by Catholics—von Zell is a Catholic himself. And, since he must start somewhere, tell him to find out in which vineyard the Benedictine monks from the abbey at Kremsmünster, who were expelled during the war, worked. Von Zell is the man who arranged for the monks to work in the region so he knows the owners of that—or those—vineyards very well."

"Splendid, dear boy. It shall be done. Keep up the good work. Incidentally, I think I am about to rival you in the newspaper headlines. I've been given a tip about those Italian old masters that were stolen from the Kunsthistorisches here in '43. Fourteen of them. Would you be jealous if they turned up?"

"As a jackdaw," I said, smiling into the phone.

"Good lad," he said. "I'm glad you know your place. Now call me tomorrow, will you? About this time. With luck we shall have some news for you." And we hung up.

I bit on my apple.

"If I were you, I know where I'd look," said the girl, munching her apple.

"Oh yes?"

She nodded, chewing. "Rudi was a good skier. Very good."

I noticed that, unlike the secretaries, she used von Zell's first name.

She flicked her head toward the far end of the house and toward the mountains. "Twice, on weekends, he went up there—and stayed away for two days. There is a whole network of alpine huts up there—six that I know of. It's flat on top, you know; you don't need ski lifts or anything like that. A good skier could last out indefinitely, moving from one to the other, so as not to attract too much attention."

"What would he do for food?"

"Easy, if he had a few friends. They could go skiing on weekends and leave it for him. They have fires in the huts, there's plenty of wood and kindling. Easy enough to melt the snow to make coffee."

"Did von Zell have any friends?"

She shrugged, throwing her apple core into the hearth. "He must have had Nazi friends, in his position. And people who sympathized with the Party. There would be no problem."

What she said made me uncomfortable. You know how it is when you have a nicely worked out theory. The last thing you want is a new one. So far, I had allowed myself to be persuaded that my hunch about von Zell and the vineyards was correct. I was convinced inside that he had done just as I suspected. But I knew, too, that one of the reasons I was convinced by the vineyard theory was because I was pleased with my cleverness at working it out: I *wanted* my theory to be correct. But this Stempel girl's idea made sense too. I remembered what Frieda Breker had said: that, from Berchtesgaden, von Zell had gone to Arthurhaus, which, I now recalled, was on the other side of the *same* mountain, the Hagen Gebirge. So if, in the months preceding the end of the war, he had made arrangements to live in hiding high in the mountains, what better cover than to leave, or appear to leave, Berchtesgaden and then to return, in a manner of speaking. No one would think of looking in the very area he appeared to have run away from. I also remembered that, in the file back at the office, I had read that the von Zells had stayed in a mountain hut just prior to the German collapse in 1945. Another thought struck me. The conduit, ferrying fugitive Nazis to Spain or Portugal, might easily use the mountain routes. Skiing was faster than walking or bicycling and there were no roadblocks in the mountains.

Reluctantly, I told myself that, maybe, I was being irresponsible in not giving this possibility more credence.

"How long would it take to investigate the huts in the mountains?"

"Three days. Two nights away."

I thought. "Can you ski, Fräulein Stempel?"

She didn't reply in words but gave me a look that was enough. A look which told me that, as an Austrian, she had been skiing for very nearly as long as she could walk.

"Sorry." I smiled sheepishly. "Do you know your way about up there? Would you be my guide?"

I can remember the look she gave me then as if this all happened yesterday. No actress could ever simulate it—it said a hundred and one different things at the same time. There was surprise in it, that I should be so forward as to suggest such a thing. There was pity, I think, since I was so obviously desperate to catch my man and so lacking in ideas as to where he was. There was hostility, that I should not have more tact in raising the subject. And there was an affronted air to it, that I should presume she had nothing else to do with her time except help me. But she was excited, too, there was a sparkle in her eyes, and—yes—more, perhaps. She was tough but she was a sport. And maybe life had been just a little bit boring recently.

"Perhaps," she said, teasing. "But can *you* ski?"

"A bit. Nowhere near as well as you, I expect."

She liked the flattery, I could tell. A glow spread across her face. Yes, I thought, life *has* been on the dull side lately. I offer adventure.

I played up to it. "I don't think it will be dangerous—I wouldn't suggest it if I did. But it could be exciting if we do find him. It will be in all the papers. And we are old friends, you and I, compared with the guides I would find in the village."

She liked that—the "old friends" quip, I mean. And she made up her mind: I was all right. She gave me a wide smile and said, "When would you like to start, General?"

"Tomorrow, as soon as you are free. But I need skis and ski clothes."

"You can rent them in town. No problem." A thought struck her. "Why don't you stay here tonight? It's a big house and the hotels in Berchtesgaden are expensive. You may have Rudolf's room."

That was how it was settled. She never actually said, "Yes, I'll come." Just invited me to stay the night.

The idea of sleeping in von Zell's bed struck me as a bit bizarre, though I didn't know why, and could think of no objection. I asked, "Will your father agree to having me here?"

She got down from her stool and put another log on the fire. "Oh yes. Since Rudi left, we have led a quiet life, and father likes company. He's bathing now, and will be down soon. We'll have a drink then."

I got down from my stool, too, and sat near her in front of the fire. "Your Austrian accent is still strong. You have not lived in Berchtesgaden long?"

She thought back. "Nearly five years now. After Mama died, Father was restless. He is a sausage-maker and you know how the Germans are about sausage. Rudi loved papa's sausages."

There was movement above and the man in question appeared. Tall, but stooped, about sixty or a little more, he swung down the stairs, a coil of energy in his every step. He was thin but had huge hands and eyebrows, which, I remember, didn't go across his face but sloped diagonally out and down, giving a permanent lugubrious cast to his expression.

His hand, though huge, was very gentle when we were introduced, but his eye didn't meet mine. Instead, he fixed on a point slightly to one side and below, my own gaze. For a moment I put this down to chronic shyness, what the psychiatrists, these days, call "gaze avoidance." But then I noticed his daughter smiling and looking at the same spot and I realized I had a packet of American pipe tobacco in my breast pocket.

Immediately, I took it from my tunic and offered some to the old man. To my dismay, and his daughter's amusement, he turned and slowly took down from the wall over the hearth an enormous alpine pipe which he proceeded to fill. His daughter explained my presence while he was doing this and outlined our plan to explore the mountains. Without waiting for her to ask his permission, he, too, extended an invitation for me to spend the night there. No doubt he had his eye on more tobacco.

The girl, who now insisted I call her Allie, showed me to my room. It was comfortable, not large but with a radio, a double bed and a window looking out to the Hagen Gebirge. I imagined von Zell spending quiet nights in this room, listening to music on the radio, while his wife also listened, over the mountains in Austria. I bathed, changed my shirt and went back downstairs, taking a pair of nylons with me, for Allie.

Herr Stempel offered me a beer and we chatted in a relaxed, unforced way while Allie clattered around in the kitchen. We sat down, twenty minutes later, to a dinner that consisted of three kinds of sausage, cabbage, potatoes in their skins, beer that had been left outside to chill, black bread and, afterward, Swiss cheese.

As we ate the sausages, accompanied by a local mustard, Allie did most of the talking. She had been engaged to an Austrian boy who was named Walter, also, when Hitler had invaded their country in 1938. The boy, for he was little more than that, had eventually been conscripted to fight on the Russian front where he had been killed seven months later. She still grieved in her own way, she said, but she was practical and now the war was over she intended to move to a big city, Munich, Vienna or Frankfurt maybe. She would take her father with her and get work in the fashion business. The clothes industry would boom, now that the war had ended, and her Walter had been a tailor. She felt it was right.

Allie's father relit his pipe when she had finished her story—there was still plenty left in it to smoke. He then disappeared for a moment, presumably to some secret prewar horde, for he returned with a bottle of Armagnac. Jealously, he poured me a finger of the pale foxy-colored liquid. It wasn't much but it was generous of him all the same; people like the Stempels had little enough in the way of luxuries at that time.

We sat by the hearth and I told them about my war, stretching the Armagnac, lingering over each sip as it slithered down my throat. I explained how I had not become a naturalized American until 1941 and so could not enlist until then. How I had been married for nearly a year when I left for my military training. How my wife and I had never learned to know each other in those first months. I didn't say it had been simply a sexual attraction; one didn't talk as freely in those days as now. I described London, which had been my first posting, and how the normality of life in 1942 had surprised me.

"For instance, I remember one night, I was walking home late, after studying intelligence reports at the embassy. I had a leather overcoat, in those days, a long one, double-breasted, that I had bought in Italy years earlier. As I walked down South Audley Street, I passed a group of three or four girls, obviously prostitutes who had just finished working. They admired my coat as I went by and we stopped to talk. I had assumed they were on their way home, but no, they said they were just off to their club and would I like to come. They were attractive girls and I was a soldier and intrigued by the idea of a club. Along I went.

"The club was amazing. It was in a basement just off Portman Square and it was beautifully decorated, with a small band, reasonable food, which was wonderful by wartime standards, and lots of drink. All the staff were men, and, I later learned, retired policemen. To be a member you had to be a prostitute; the club had been founded by a group of wealthy clients and given to the girls as a 'thank you.' Not even those men were allowed in except as guests of the members. Only the members could sign for things, as in any club, and it became a treat for the girls to repay some of their more favored clients. It was a masterstroke for it gave the girls, and their customers, a dignity they might otherwise not have possessed.

"War does that, I think. It makes people conscious of their dignity, I mean. After D Day, I followed the main invasion force forty-eight hours later. By then I was attached to the outfit I'm in now—the art recovery unit. Our job was partly to recover looted art but, during the invasion itself, also to advise artillery officers on what not to bomb, if it could be avoided. The basic decision was always made on military grounds, of course, but if there *was* a particularly noteworthy building at risk from our shells, it was my job to draw it to the attention of the local commander. As you may imagine, some commanders were easier to deal with than others.

"However, the particular episode I am thinking of took place in Mondoubleau, a small town near Orléans, in northern France. The unit I was with, a British company of grenadiers, was temporarily billeted there for two nights, regrouping ready for the race south, around Paris. I spent the nights foisted on a family of farmers. The sons were away—fighting in the resistance—and no one knew if they were dead or alive. The grandfather of the house, the only man of the family, was on his last legs, dying from one of those mysterious liver complaints that you hear about

only in France. The old man had hung on for months apparently, knowing that the invasion must come. Now that it had happened and was
coming—quite literally—through his house, he was, if not ready to go, at
least reconciled to his death and pleased that he had lived so long. The
family were Huguenots so there was no question of the last rights, but
the old man was determined all the same to go with dignity and not a
little style.

"For months he had prepared for his last moment on earth. He was
determined that it would not be just an exit but a proper farewell. So,
whenever he felt his condition deteriorate, he would sink back and call
the family, or whoever was at hand, including me, around him. Then,
when a quorum was gathered, he would speak his final words. Or what
were intended to be his closing lines. And the touching thing was that he
had a whole anthology of last good-byes, a litany of final words, all
worked out inside his head.

"The trouble was that he never did actually die. It was, in its macabre
way, hilarious. One time he might whisper, 'Well, friends, it looks like
the ship has slipped its moorings,' or 'Time to turn the page,' or 'My
own D Day has come.' And he would lie back, with his eyes closed.

"The family would wait by the bed. But he would continue breathing.
By the time I stayed there it had reached the point where some members
of the family hoped he *would* die after one of these little speeches, since
it would have given him so much satisfaction. Instead, after a while, the
old man would pretend to be asleep and the family would creep out,
embarrassed. Then, a few hours later, they would go through it all again.
'Close the book, the story is ended,' or 'The last leaf has fallen, winter is
here.' Soon I had to move on, to Blois and Bourges, with the grenadiers,
but the old man was still at it. Trying hard to go with some dignity but,
for all that, still alive."

In what seemed like no time, it was ten o'clock. Not late but it felt as
though it was. Allie and her father had listened to me attentively
enough, but they were both fading. The Armagnac was finished and we
went to bed.

I awoke to find the sun in my room and the smack of freshly brewing
coffee in my nostrils—it was barely 7:00 but Allie must already be about.
Wrong: it was her father who was cooking breakfast, hot bread and fried
sausage. She followed me down, dressed in a mustard-yellow ski overall
and together we stepped outside to try the raw morning air. The house

was in shadow but the scalloped white shoulders of the Hagen Gebirge were already soused in sunshine. It was going to be a spectacular day.

"Father says you may borrow his skis and sticks," said Allie, her breath forming little clouds in front of her face. "So all you need to get from the town is a suit, some gloves and boots. We have a knapsack for you and some snowglasses."

During breakfast I put a call through to Maurice and left word that I would not be able to phone again for a couple of days. I tried to do the same with Sammy but there was no reply from the office in Salzburg— too early. It took me half an hour in the town to find the right equipment but I also had to inform the military commander of the area that I was going out of uniform. Back at the house, I finally got through to Hartt, who listened to my change of plan without a word, then calmly informed me that my shares had dropped another five cents the previous day on account of a rumor that the president of the company was being recruited by President Truman to help organize the administration of postwar Germany. My "grand" was now worth $941.28. I was amazed that one man could have such effect but Sammy was beyond that, trying to find out what substance there was to the rumor before deciding whether to sell or not.

I had to ask, of course. "And paper?"

He sighed. "Up four—points, not dollars. But that still takes your friend to a thousand and twenty-two."

I was glad I had already been in touch with Maurice's office that day. He could sweat in ignorance for a while.

"How long will you be on this mountain jaunt?" Sammy asked.

"Two nights."

"There'll be no phones up where you are going, presumably?"

"Correct, Sammy."

"Well, this thing will have cleared by then—so call me as soon as you can. You'll have to trust me to do what I think is right."

"I know." I *did* trust him, although my thousand dollars was now worth nine hundred and forty-one, give or take the change. "How's Hobel?"

"Caught up with something else, so you are not at the center of his thoughts for the moment. But don't worry, he'll plague you soon enough. Now remember, call me as soon as you can."

We set off. Earlier that morning I had bought chocolate and more tobacco from the American officer's mess in Berchtesgaden and I left some for Allie's father. He waved to us as we turned toward the mountains at the end of the street. He didn't seem to mind his daughter going off with a total stranger. A track rose steadily for a mile or more and we followed this until another path turned off, leading to a ski lift. At that time of year it was quiet and there was no queue; the package tour was a thing of the future. The cable car, cold and primitive compared with what you get today, rose silently and the valley and Berchtesgaden began to stretch out below us, green and, in the distance, a fuzzy blue. After about six or seven minutes we reached the snow line and it grew very quiet. The cold closed around us, too, an intimate chill that drove us in on ourselves as we concentrated on keeping warm, blowing on our fingers, rubbing our ears, wriggling our toes. We were rising steeply now, past short, upright firs and the occasional small deer. Ski marks appeared in what seemed to me impossible locations. Silver-black burns slithered by, scratch marks in the snow, narrow and too fast to freeze.

No matter how much we rubbed, wriggled or blew, by the time the cable car suddenly slowed, rounded a corner and arrived at a squat, red-gray shed, ugly as only human indifference can make something, we were solid blocks of cold. Beyond the shed we could see meadows of smooth deep powder, white but becoming buttery in the high sunshine. And, save for the trees, deliciously empty.

We fixed our skis and inspected the map Allie had brought with her. We began to thaw. We double-checked that we had all the essentials we needed: coffee, chocolate, sleeping bags, tins of food, biscuits. Then we snapped on our glasses, I gave her a mock salute and we were off, down a slope and following the line of many ski tracks that had gone before but were now frozen over.

In no time we were out of sight and earshot of the ski lift and a bright, shiny silence folded around us. Our breath floated out before us when we stopped to rest, though before long we were both glowing with sweat. Allie knew the mountains very well and led me with unerring speed. She knew which downward slopes could be used to pick up momentum, so we could coast up as many inclines as possible, and she appeared to know all the safe shortcuts through the trees. The deer were more plentiful up here and they seemed somehow in less of a hurry to escape. It was a glorious day and we were enjoying ourselves.

I noticed that the ski marks grew scarcer as we went deeper into the mountains but that they never disappeared entirely. There was activity of some sort up here. Occasionally, we glimpsed villages far below, in the green valleys, still in shadow. Sometimes faraway rivers glinted in the sun. Before long I felt my skin beginning to itch in response to the sunshine.

After an hour, perhaps more, we stopped for chocolate. I was fairly exhausted by now, having used muscles in a way I was unaccustomed to. "But," said Allie mischievously, "we are not even halfway to the first hut. Shall we go more slowly?"

The next hour, naturally, became a race. I didn't do too badly since, to my relief, I found that I had gained my second wind. I was also learning how to relax on the downward runs so as to conserve energy for the hills. And on this sector we had to negotiate our way across, rather than down, a very steep precipice and that required a different kind of strength where Allie had to rely on me. By the time the first hut came into view, shortly before one o'clock, I was feeling very fit, my face roasting in the sunshine, and it was as much as Allie could do to keep in front of me. Indeed, my only complaint was that I was ravenously hungry.

The hut was empty, but warm; someone had slept there the night before. There was fresh water outside, in a large canister, so we lit a fire and brewed coffee in no time. We ate biscuits, cheese, some fish paste Allie had brought and two apples I didn't know she had. And we lay flat out on long benches to rest our aching bones.

"What is our best strategy?" I asked. I had been doing some thinking. "Does it actually make sense to visit all the huts, or should we just stay in one place for a couple of days? If he *is* up here and he moves around, aren't we more likely to catch him that way?"

Allie shook her head. "The huts are strung out in a straight line, more or less. If we visit all the huts our paths must cross. If we wait in just one hut, it may take days before we see him. We can go back a different way, and take the train to Berchtesgaden."

We had a second coffee, then filled the canister again with melted snow, collected kindling from nearby, so it would dry for the next visitor, and moved on. Thankfully, the sun was on our backs that afternoon; I don't think my face could have taken any more of its rays.

I had not discussed it with Allie, but although I had changed out of uniform, I was armed still. I had a pistol and it occurred to me that von Zell, if we came across him, would almost certainly have a gun, too, conceivably a rifle. As the English would say, it might get very tricky. I resolved to approach the other huts with more care.

No sooner had all this passed through my mind than I noticed that Allie, who was about fifty meters ahead of me, had stopped. About a mile away a figure was coming toward us. It was impossible, at that stage, to say whether it was a man or a woman, though surely, I thought, no woman would be up here by herself. A moment later and this query was answered: another figure appeared. I drew up alongside Allie and, without making any sudden moves, took off my right-hand glove and reached into my knapsack for the pistol. I hid it in my jacket pocket but not before Allie had seen it. She started to say something but I silenced her quickly, saying, "What did you expect? More chocolate?"

The figures approached, closer together now. One was all in white, with red skis, the other in blue. When they were within earshot, I waved at them. They had not intended to stop but now they veered toward us.

I was tense. What was I going to say? A horrible thought struck me: would I recognize von Zell if it were indeed him? Who on earth could he have with him?

The two skiers slid to a halt about fifteen meters away and slightly below us. The smaller of the two immediately removed his snowglasses and I was relieved and disappointed at the same time. It was a boy of no more than eighteen. "Good afternoon," he said, in German.

Feeling overdramatic, and foolish, I nevertheless pulled out my gun. "I am sorry," I said loudly. (We had been taught to talk loudly and slowly while pointing a gun at someone.) "I am a U.S. military officer and I am searching for a fugitive Nazi commander who is believed to be hiding out in these mountains." I turned to the taller man. "Sir, please take off your snowglasses."

He refused. At least, for one horrible, agonizing, minute that's what I thought had happened. I found myself wondering with dismay what I would do should the man make a dash for it. Would I shoot? No. I had spent the war in intelligence of one sort or another and had not fired a gun in anger once. I tried to remember von Zell's description. Was this man in front of me too tall, too lean? Was he dark enough?

Then, with an exaggerated slowness, to show his distaste for my "request," the man lowered his glasses, and I pocketed my pistol. He was almost certainly German, probably an aristocrat, possibly an ex-Nazi, for he had a dueling scar ripped down his right cheek. But he also had a black eye patch over his right eye where the duel, no doubt, had left him blind. And I did remember that von Zell's scar was on the *left* cheek.

"Thank you. I'm sorry to have detained you," I said, in as matter-of-fact tone as I could muster. "Please be on your way."

They turned down the slope and were gone. The one-eyed aristocrat had not spoken a word.

Allie moved on without a word too. The sight of the gun had shocked her; until then our time together had been fun. But now I had brought the war back into her life, a war which had made life hard for so many years and killed her fiancé. I wouldn't apologize for this "tidying up" that I was doing, but I knew how she felt. We saw a lot of it in our work. I let her ski on ahead for a while, so she could be alone.

Around four, as the strength was beginning to go out of the sun, we stopped for more chocolate by a waterfall where we could also take a drink. We took off our skis and sat on some rocks where we could see across to the Hochkönig, the peak that overlooked Arthurhaus. Allie washed her face and hands in the waterfall, which was much too cold for me. I didn't notice, but she must then have cupped her hands under the waterfall and crept up behind me. Before I grasped what was happening, she had tipped the raw-cold liquid down my neck.

God, it was shocking. I exploded to my feet and Allie collapsed in laughter. It was more than just a joke, though. In part, she was paying me back for how horrid she thought I had been earlier on, when I had pulled out my gun. And in part the episode was, in its way, the beginning of physical contact between us. As I stood there, glaring at her, glacial rivulets chasing down my back, I was conscious that she had wanted to bring me up here, on the mountains, to be alone with me, away from her father. What had happened between Allie and von Zell up here? I wondered. We stepped into our skis and set off on the final sector of the day.

During that last hour the light began to go, and I, who had become perhaps overconfident after a day's skiing, stumbled once or twice. So I was grateful when, around five, we topped a ridge and there, below us, was the second hut. It was somewhat larger than the one we had eaten lunch in, with a woodshed at the back and a large porch in front which, earlier in the day, would have been bathed in sunshine. I motioned to Allie to remain where she was and again rummaged for the pistol in my knapsack.

There were no lights on in the hut, but then we had been chatting away as we approached and sound travels long distances over mountain snow. If there had been anyone there who wanted to avoid company, he would have heard us coming and would have had a chance to hide. I slid down the last slope and took off my skis some way from the front door. Quietly, carefully, I approached the hut from the side, and then went around to the back. There were no windows at the rear of the chalet, since it backed on to the mountain, but there was a red door that opened into a covered walkway connecting to the woodshed.

Gingerly, I tried the door. It squeaked open. Inside, it was very dark and I had to allow time for my eyes to adjust. I wasn't certain if, as I waited, I heard movement elsewhere or not. Houses have all sorts of sounds that they make by themselves.

The bathrooms, I found, were at the rear of the building and I examined them first, one for men and another for women. Nothing. Next to the bathrooms was a large kitchen, also empty, and this gave on to the large living room, with chairs and a fireplace. That, too, was deserted. The staircase to the bedrooms led directly out of the living room, exactly as in Allie's own house. I felt melodramatic again, climbing the stairs with my gun at the ready; this sort of thing had never happened to me while the war was in full swing. There were four bedrooms, each with enough beds to sleep four people. All were neat and tidy, ready as they should have been, for travelers such as we. But they, too, were empty.

In fact, it looked like the whole place was empty, and so, not for the first time that day, I felt both relieved and disappointed. Quickly, I went downstairs and outside to call Allie.

The light was failing rapidly now, and it was clouding over, so while she was negotiating the final slope and taking off her skis, I fished out a couple of hurricane lamps which I had noticed in the kitchen and went to meet her on the porch.

"Welcome," I said, making a mock bow and holding open the door. "No Nazis tonight. We have the hut all to ourselves. If I light a fire, will you cook?"

Allie cocked her head to one side, as if considering whether the deal was a fair exchange. Then, with a smile, she leaned forward and gave me the briefest of kisses on my cheek. Her lips were as warm as those rivulets of water had been cold.

The hut had a clever, if primitive, system whereby the fire in the living room backed on to the kitchen, giving off heat in both directions *and* warming a water tank above, which I had to fill if we wanted a bath. It did not prove easy to light the fire, but a previous traveler had observed the mountain code well and there was plenty of kindling. Allie had brought pasta—vermicelli because it was light and lacked bulk—plus tomato puree and some sausage which she could cut up and mix with the puree for sauce. We also had fruit, chocolate and coffee. Sadly, no wine.

We both worked hard. It had been a tiring day and we knew that as soon as we stopped our bones would refuse to move again.

After some coaxing, the logs caught and soon the chill began to leave the room. The water tank, too, began to warm up. Allie went upstairs to change and I lay on one of the sofas, relaxing. There were books and magazines on the rack near the hearth, unbelievably out of date, but not necessarily less interesting for all that. I could hear Allie upstairs, moving around, readying the beds, and I dozed off.

The next thing I knew she was standing over me, with her hair pinned up and dressed in nothing but a towel.

"Wake up. I need help with the water." She handed me a magazine that I had dropped as I had fallen asleep.

I ran her bath, filling the room with steam. She disappeared into it and I could hear her splashing and making contented noises. While she let the water swirl around her bones I began to slice the sausage. I soaked the puree in a little salted water and put it in a saucepan with the sausage. I laid the table and put the apples and the chocolate in a wicker bowl at the center. By the time Allie emerged from the tub, her hair shampooed and her skin rubbed raw, everything was ready to go. She was, I think, pleased that I had not been completely idle and hugged my arm. "As soon as you are out of the bath, we will be ready to eat," and she stroked the back of my hand with her finger.

Then it was my turn to sink into the tub. The water could have been hotter and, since Allie had already used it, cleaner. But at least it smelled of her and, before long, what was left of the heat began to penetrate to my marrow and muscles. I was looking forward to the evening, though it had been an unproductive day. Would tomorrow be as fruitless, I wondered? Had Maurice's man in the Wachau already located von Zell?

Back in the living room, I found that the fire had been primed by Allie and was now billowing with flame, giving off light as well as heat. Its shadows, moving now rhythmically, now fitfully about the room, and the mingled smells of pasta, puree and sausage, all laid over the musty timber flavor of the hut itself, I can recall now as keenly as if it had all happened last week. The smells are what I remember best, but the shadows, too, are vivid, a warm red blanket all around.

We sat and, to begin with, ate in silence, both surprised, I think, at how ravenous we were. The pasta dwindled until there was none left and we wiped the plates dry. When I broke the silence it was to say, "Let's rest before we have the fruit and chocolate. Otherwise, all these good things will be over too soon." And I refilled our pale blue coffee cups.

Allie needed no persuading. She set her napkin down and leaned back in her chair. In the firelight her skin was a warm ivory, the shadows from the fire swooping across it like fingers of wind on a field of barley. I got to my feet and put more logs on the fire, then stood with my back to the flames. Stabs of soreness here and there in my muscles warned me that tomorrow's skiing might not be straightforward.

Allie got up to move away from the heat of the fire; the side of her face nearest the hearth had a reddish flush to it, which she massaged. One of the hurricane lamps was nearby on a table and, taking it with her, she walked to the door and out into the night. No sooner had she disappeared, however, than she called back, "Oh, Walter, *please* come and look. It has started snowing!"

I followed her outside. She had hung the lamp from a hook on one of the beams that supported the porch so that it threw light for twenty or thirty meters, enough to spotlight thousands of thick tussocks of snow settling.

"This could slow us down tomorrow, if it goes on for long."

"Walter!" Her voice rustled with exasperation, disappointment and reproach. "How can you be so unromantic: It's bewitching." And she stepped forward, from under the porch and into the blizzard. For a few moments she stood there, with her arms outstretched and her face turned up, being snowed on. In no time her hair, her eyebrows, her arms were encrusted.

Then she turned and came back in. Mounting the steps to the porch, she stopped in front of me and put her wet, flake-covered arms around my shoulders. In the light of the hurricane I could see the snow melting on her lashes and the lobes of her ears. Drops from spent flakes were caught in the down of her cheeks and glistened in the yellow light. Her forehead, her chin, her neck were all soaking.

I kissed her. Her lips—wet from melted snow—were cold, cold as the mountain. I put my arms around her. When she had reached up to embrace me, her shirt had pulled out of her trousers and my hand brushed the skin of her waist.

She kissed me back, her mouth slightly open, promising. "In the mountains," she whispered, "people get up with the sun." She kissed me again. Her lips were drier now, and warming. "So they go to bed early too."

Behind Allie I could see the snow getting thicker, the flakes falling faster. Despite what she said, about me being unromantic, I couldn't help but worry that the search would be spoiled the next day by the snow. I didn't want to spend any longer in the mountains than I needed to. Still, there was nothing to be gained that night from worrying.

"I have a suggestion."

"Mmnnmm?"

"It's already nine o'clock—quite late really, for up here. Why don't we eat our fruit and chocolate in bed?"

She dropped her arms to my waist and squeezed. "You'd better make sure the fire is safe. I'll look after the apples and things."

I took down the hurricane, inspecting the snow for the last time, and made sure that none of the logs could roll out of the hearth or do any damage. I then followed Allie upstairs, carrying the hurricane with me. I was amused to find, when I got there, that she had made up only one bed. When she had puttered around up here, earlier in the evening, she must have already been certain that we would sleep together. I'm not sure why but the knowledge gave me a pleasurable smack of anticipation.

"You must get into bed first," she whimpered, as I set down the lamp, "and warm it up for me. I hate cold beds. I'll sit here and drink my coffee."

I did as I was told. Undressed, and watched by Allie in an open, appraising way, I dived under the quilt cover, kicking and thrashing with my legs to warm the linen as quickly as possible. She laughed.

Once the chill had been taken off, I lay still and gave her a mock salute. I reached for my pipe and began to fill it with tobacco.

Now it was Allie's turn. The first thing she did was to blow out the hurricane—very unfair, I thought. As my eyes became adjusted to the glow, I could see that the room was bathed not so much in light proper but a soft red wash that had somehow percolated upstairs from the remains of the log fire below. I could see Allie getting undressed in silhouette, in shadow. Dark and still darker shades of red. It was not unlike looking through those infrared night-scopes that the Army was to invent just after the war.

There are three things I remember about Allie on that red night, three things besides the fact that she had let down her long hair and that her skin, in the fire glow, seemed to be more a liquid, a cream or a lacquer of some kind, rather than skin itself, so shifting were its shadows. One thing I remember noticing were her breasts. It was not so much that they were large, though they were certainly not small. It was more that, at twenty-six (or whatever age she really was), her breasts seemed *full*, as if they were ripe and just waiting to feed a child. The thought crossed my mind, with a sudden painful jab, that Allie would be one of those European women whose bodies seem to give up after they have had children, to expand and settle. To age before their time. The second thing I noticed was that Allie slipped into bed alongside me not entirely naked. She still had on a pair of silk, lace panties, so feminine but so old-fashioned that they can only have been her mother's. In the glow from the embers they looked almost black.

As her skin touched the sheets Allie let out an involuntary sob. "Walter! It's *freezing.*" And she pressed herself against me for warmth.

I reached across her to the table at the side of the bed and set down my pipe. As I brought back my hand she caught it in hers and pressed it to her cheek.

"Your hand is warm, though." And slowly she guided my fingers across her shoulder, up over the swollen circumference of her breasts, down into the recess of her waist, over her hip to the silk on her thigh. And she shivered.

The third thing I remember that red night was the soap Allie smelled of. It wasn't expensive, and was a little too sweet for today's taste, probably. But I can recall it as vividly as ever. It had the tang of gentian, the spring flower of the mountains.

5

THE next day was uneventful, until evening. The blizzard had blown out during the night, without doing too much damage to our plans, and the sun was back, as if it had never been away. Allie was right, we awoke with the sun. We made love a second time—slower now, shier, perhaps because we could see each other's faces. Allie's skin was different in the morning, too, pale in comparison to how it had been the night before, and showing all its blemishes—scars, birthmarks, vaccinations. It was another reason, I think, why she was shy. I didn't mind, far from it: I have always found shy women far more erotic. And I think she was flattered as it ended: although I had lived in America for six years by then, I still broke into German.

We visited two huts in the morning and saw no one. The first hut was cold but the second had been slept in the previous night; the embers were warm. I also noticed in that hut a fresh newspaper lying by the kindling. It was dated only a few days before and it was a local paper, from Worms, in Germany.

"Von Zell's mother lives in Worms," I told Allie. "That's where he came from originally."

The only other thing that needs mentioning occurred around 3:30 in the afternoon. Just then the sun had disappeared behind a raft of cloud and, for a while, it grew rather cold. I thought it odd how, in the mountains, the noise level changed, or appeared to change, with the weather. When the sun was out, and you could see birds, black against the sky, you were unconscious of the deep silence around you. Yet, once the cloud had covered the sun and there was nothing to look up for, your skis immediately seemed to slither over the snow with a more deliberate, a louder swish and this only emphasized the cold, white quiet at 1,000 meters.

We were immersed in this white-gray light when Allie, who was about a hundred meters in front of me, suddenly pulled up. "What is it?" I said, coming alongside some moments later.

She did not reply and I followed her gaze, across and down the slope, toward some large black boulders drenched in water as the snow on them had melted earlier in the day. Just beyond was a blotchy, black-red stain on the snow. Blood.

I took out my pistol and went over. Allie followed, although I asked her not to. Close up, the blood was redder-looking; it had not been there very long.

"It's not human," I said. "Look!" I pointed to some hoof marks and then to some scratches on the bark of nearby trees. "There was probably a deer trap here. Then someone came along and shot the poor thing." I had stepped out of my skis and stooped down to examine the snow around the blood. I looked up at Allie. "Whether or not it's von Zell, it looks as though we have found someone who is living up here. Whoever it is must be in hiding—and that could make him dangerous. Keep very close from now on." Stepping back into my skis, I said, as forcefully as I could, "Tell me when we get close to the next hut; then we'll go even more carefully." I didn't say so to Allie, but I was anxious that we reach the hut in full daylight. If we were to arrive at dusk or in the dark our reception might be, as Maurice would say, "sticky." I skied on now as fast as I could push myself, even though some of my muscles had other ideas.

For three quarters of an hour I even managed to keep up with Allie. She was surprised, I think, at the reserves of strength I could draw upon when I really needed to. And, in fact, I was slightly ahead of her at the point when she suddenly called out. We were in a kind of dip, a saucer-shaped hollow with some young trees growing safely out of the wind.

"The hut is about a kilometer away." There was probably no need for Allie to whisper but she did so in any case. "We go over that ridge, out of this hollow here, then across another ridge, higher still; then we descend through many trees, and there's the hut."

"Very well," I said. "I've been thinking. We are safest as a couple. We shall pretend we are on our honeymoon and don't know each other at all well yet. We shall say that we live in Vienna now but that your father has a house in Berchtesgaden, which is where we started out from, as is true. If von Zell *is* there, act as if you are mildly surprised, but introduce me. Say we met about six months ago, after he moved out. That you are moving to Vienna after our honeymoon and will look for a job. I will pretend to have a new job at the university, teaching English. I've been to Vienna a couple of times so I can say something sensible." Another thought occurred to me. "We should approach the hut talking. We are just married, happily married, and chattering away. A couple of innocents enjoying the mountains, not sneaking up on anyone. Okay?"

"If we are married, why haven't I got a wedding ring?"

"You have your mother's—she is dead now and your father decided to give it to you only on the day before our wedding. It's in Berchtesgaden, at a jeweler's, having the size changed. It'll be there when we get down again."

The last kilometer was downhill mostly and, all the way, Allie and I talked gaily. I told Allie about my family—telling her the truth except that I moved them from Heidelberg to Linz. I told her about my brother, how we had never been close, about my mother, how she hated being separated from her sons during the war and how she was now trapped in East Germany, in Leipzig, and how I was trying to get her out. Allie played her part well, asking questions—did I have photographs? was my mother pretty?—exactly the way a newlywed might.

The hut came into view and immediately I noticed that there was smoke rising from the chimney. We would not be alone tonight. We skied right up to the front of the building and shouted. While we were taking off our skis, still talking, the door opened and a man came out.

"Good evening," I said, smiling in what I hoped was an easy, friendly way. "We just made it before the light goes."

The man was tall, with vivid gray hair, lank and bushy. He was thin but looked strong, sinewy, with a long chin and a mouth wide as the Mississippi. He didn't smile.

He didn't say anything at that point, either, so I collected the skis and spoke again to Allie. "I'll put these away, darling. You go and get warm."

Allie—bless her—was superb. She stood in front of the man, with her hand held out. "Alessandra Stempel—oh, sorry, I mean Wolff. We've only been married a few days. This is our honeymoon."

The man had no choice but to take her hand and now he *had* to say something. "Reimer," he said, nodding to me. "Eric Reimer." He stood aside and followed Allie back into the hut.

I packed the skis away at the end of the hut where there was a shed especially for the purpose. I couldn't help but notice that the shed was full—Herr Reimer was not alone. I judged it best to leave my gun in the knapsack. I would try to keep that near me, just in case, but I didn't foresee any real danger, not just yet. I took the bag off my back and went along the porch and into the hut.

I shook hands with Reimer and inspected the room. As Allie had predicted, it was bigger than the previous night's and I calculated that at least six, and perhaps eight, bedrooms opened off the gallery upstairs.

"Are you here alone, Herr Reimer?" I asked.

"No." He paused. "There are others."

"Yes." I nodded, stepping forward to stand by the fire. "I noticed the skis in the shed just now." If I was just a little bit sharp, that could do no harm. "Where is everybody?"

"Collecting wood, two of them. One is in the kitchen, another upstairs, resting."

"There are five of you?"

"Yes."

"How long have you been up here in the mountains?"

"Nearly two weeks. We are going home soon."

"You are German?" I said. "Your accent is not Austrian, I think."

He hesitated again and I realized with a start that I had been acting quite naturally like the interrogator I was. "Sorry," I said. "I wasn't meaning to be inquisitive. I'm from Vienna and we are naturally nosy. Come on, Allie," I called across the room, changing course into safer waters. "Let's find a room and relax a bit. We can fix supper later."

"The end one is free," said Reimer, pointing. "It is larger than the others. Why not take that?"

"Thank you," I said, beaming. "We will."

As we mounted the stairs and walked along the gallery, I noticed that all the rooms had their doors closed. Did that mean anything? I wondered. Were the doors hiding anything? My suspicions were interrupted, however, by a friendly shout from Reimer. "Water is warming. There will be baths in half an hour."

"Thank you again," I shouted down, following Allie through the only open doorway into the end room. I closed it firmly behind me and went instinctively to the window, looking out.

"That's funny," I murmured, mostly to myself.

"What is?" said Allie, lying on the bed, a high, wooden thing. She stretched her limbs.

"Two men walking toward the hut. They must have been gone at least twenty minutes . . . after all, we've been here that long. They must be the two men who Reimer says had gone to fetch kindling. Yet they are carrying no wood."

"Darling," said Allie, imitating the word and the intonation I had used before. "There's half an hour before bath time . . ." I looked across. She was unbuttoning her shirt.

Afterward, with her kind of mind, Allie returned without preamble to the conversation we had been having before. "What was that about the two men outside?"

I had developed a sudden craving for a pipe, so I filled that first. "It just struck me as odd that the two men should have been gone for so long and to have returned empty-handed. It's almost as if . . . they had left the hut to avoid us."

"Why would they do that?" She tried my pipe, imitating the way I held it.

"I don't know but it worries me because, if that's what they did do, then they knew we were coming. Which means they have a lookout. And why would they need *that?*"

I don't think Allie really took in what I was saying just then, for suddenly she was racked by a spasm of coughing brought on by the pipe, which she didn't know how to handle. I laughed and took it from her. "Come on, let's have our bath."

When she had subsided we went downstairs. There was no one about, but I noticed that the fire had been built up with more logs and that the table was laid for seven.

Back in our room after the bath, while Allie spent time combing and recombing her hair, I stretched out on the bed and took from my knapsack the Worms newspaper I had found earlier in the day. On closer inspection I could see now that it was not a daily but one of those local weeklies in which the news consists entirely of parochial events—a new road being planned, repairs to the church, damaged in the war, local sports news, a big wedding in the offing. The fact that the paper was in these mountains in the first place meant that *someone* had close links with Worms. But that's all it told me until I noticed that, near the back, in the classified advertisement section, a small notice had been ringed in pencil.

It was a curious ad. Most of those around it were straightforward: legal notices, a big section for secondhand clothes, this being just after the war, bicycles for sale, sewing machines, moneylenders. But the one that had been ringed said, as I recall:

"MOTHER. Missing you as always. Looking forward
to Sunday, at the usual place. No flowers. R."

It made no obvious sense but it was the fact that it began with "Mother" and was signed "R" that drew my attention. Some newspapers, of course, make a feature of this kind of coded message—that's what it seemed to be. But not a local paper. It must have been unusual, very unusual, in that context. Could it really be Rudolf von Zell keeping in touch with his mother? Or was it a coincidence? Worms was a big place, the war had forced many, many people to move around; perhaps it should come as no surprise that someone from the Worms area was here in the mountains. And the message could be code for all sorts of things. "Mother" itself might not mean what it said, or "Sunday," or "flowers."

I didn't believe in coincidences. With luck the editor of the paper would remember who had placed such an unusual ad. I folded that page of the paper and tucked it into my knapsack. At the very least it was another lead if everything else came to nothing.

Allie finished combing her hair and put on the trousers and shirt she had brought for the evenings. They were both a dark, cobalt color and, though they had seen better days, managed exactly to release the dash of blue locked somewhere in her eyes. I was already dressed by then, with my pipe relit. We went down.

Everyone else was now assembled and the men fell silent as we appeared, then stood up. They were drinking beer and there was a jug of it on the table. So far as I could tell, von Zell was not among them.

Reimer came forward and made the introductions. "Good evening. May I welcome you more formally now. Mr. and Mrs. Wolff, I would like you to meet Gunther Kerschner." Kerschner was a small, round, florid man with a high forehead, aged fifty to fifty-five. He shook hands and bowed slightly, saying he was from Innsbruck and a builder. Next came George Lammers, an engineer from Augsburg. He was in his mid-forties, I would have said, a blond man who had once been handsome but was now running to fat and, probably, hitting the bottle. He had a fine nose, deep-set blue eyes with a rather misty glaze to them which, for me, suggested that he was hardly the most intelligent of the group. The third man was called Joseph Muhlman. He had a rather English appearance, for his most telling characteristic was his posture, which was erect, aristocratic, self-possessed, arrogant even. Above all, elegant. He had lank brown hair, fine strands of which fell down across his forehead. His voice was a soft drawl with vowels as long as his hands, which had never, I was sure, done any manual work in their life. He was described as a farmer from the Tyrol. In that case, I thought, a gentleman farmer. Age forty-eight, slightly more maybe. And, finally, Oskar Handler, a ruddy-faced man with masses of hair—on his cheeks, the backs of his hands, in his ears even. He was in his fifties and had a vineyard on the Mosel, he said. In contrast to Muhlman, his hands were gnarled, coarse and criss-crossed with runnels of ingrained grime.

Introductions over, Reimer offered us beer. It was piercingly cold, making the glasses almost too frozen to hold. As on the previous day, when we had stopped the two skiers on the mountain, I was relieved but also disappointed that von Zell was not one of the five men standing around us. Even so, there was something odd—sinister almost—about them. I couldn't place it yet, but it would come. Meanwhile, Allie was holding the fort.

She was explaining to the other four about our "wedding," telling them we were on our "honeymoon." The men were listening rather stiffly.

"But, my dear," said Muhlman tartly, "you have no wedding ring."

I caught my breath, but Allie took it in her stride.

"Oh, but I *do*. I have my mother's, bless her. It's being made smaller, at Laurin's in Berchtesgaden." She flashed Muhlman a firework of a smile. "In time for our return tomorrow."

"That's a short honeymoon," said Handler. "When I was married my wife and I had two weeks in Italy."

"You're lucky," said Allie easily. "But Walter has to get back to Vienna. He's an architect and you can imagine how much rebuilding there is to do."

I marveled at this invention of Allie's. She had obviously forgotten what we agreed, but I had to admit that her improvisation was just as good as my idea, if not better. I was qualified in architecture, even if it was medieval architecture. And it was most certainly true about the rebuilding in Vienna.

Reimer had disappeared into the kitchen and Handler was playing host. He refilled my glass. "What kind of architecture do you specialize in, Herr Doktor?" he said, holding the jug of beer.

Now it was my turn to be convincing. "Renovation. I rescue old buildings—churches, monasteries, taverns. Anything that has been corroded by age or damaged by bombs. I'm an historical architect, if you like." That seemed to satisfy Handler, but he asked another question, almost as aggressively.

"You don't have an Austrain accent, Dr. Wolff. Where are you from?"

So Reimer had told them of our earlier conversation, as I thought he might. But I had seen this question coming and had my answer ready.

"I am Viennese, born and bred. But as a boy I had a governess from Heidelberg and later on I studied there. I picked up a lot of their intonations and rhythms. What you can hear is what the English call a 'mongrel' mixture of suburban Vienna and my governess's German."

This made them all smile and the atmosphere eased a little. Handler helped everyone to beer, but now Kerschner took up the interrogation.

"What did you do in the war, Herr Doktor?"

I noticed Allie's smile take on a fixed, unfocused quality. She had described me as an architect and she was worried inside that she might have landed me in a spot, without a ready answer. But I had seen this coming too.

"Much the same. I worked for the Ministry of Buildings and Public Works. I surveyed bridges to see how strong they were; I designed air-raid shelters; I made surveys of what we should do if certain monuments were to be bombed—how we would have repaired them, and with what, after the war."

"What about before the war? Were you never attached to any fighting forces?"

I had realized during this exchange what it was about the group that was odd, which made them sinister and, possibly, dangerous. It was their social mix. Handler was a coarse man, the more so when set beside the cool, elegant, aristocratic Muhlman. But Handler was just as much at ease with the aristocrat as he was with all the others. Everybody treated everybody else as an equal. That could mean only one thing, so far as I was concerned.

"I suffered from depression as a boy," I said. Everyone in the room was now listening to me, so I raised my voice slightly. "As a result I was turned down by the Army." My heart giddy inside my ribs, I added,

"After Germany annexed Austria, my brother joined the Nazis, but my medical record was still against me."

"And where is your brother now?"

"In an internment camp, in the British zone, I think. Near Hanover."

"He is well?"

"Yes, I believe so. My mother hears from time to time."

Reimer reappeared and announced dinner. Muhlman took command again and invited Allie to sit on his right, me on his left. The beer jug had been refilled and the company was beginning to relax.

"I'll bet you can't guess what we are having to eat." Muhlman looked from Allie to me with a rather liverish luster in his eyes. Allie confessed that no, she didn't know what to expect. I knew exactly what we were getting but pretended I didn't. No point in letting on how clever I was. I never knew when I might want them to underestimate me.

"Venison?" said Allie when it was announced and brought in from the kitchen with a flourish. "But . . ." And I watched her face as she realized we were to eat the beast whose blood we had inspected earlier in the day, spread out on the snow. She stifled her revulsion. ". . . but how wonderful. How clever. And *such* a change from the pasta we had last night."

The meat was of course a little young to be really good but it had been overcooked to take away the stringiness. The mood of the evening was loosening all the time but I still judged that, to keep us out of the danger we might have to face, some gesture on my part was called for. I waited until we were all midway through our meat and another round of beer had disappeared. Then, as he was the most aggressive man present, I addressed Handler.

"I hear they have a socialist government in England now. Serves them right."

Handler looked at me hard, still chewing. Trying to work out what I was playing at. Allie stared at me, too, horrified at what I was doing. I smiled mischievously.

"Why do you say that, Dr. Wolff?" It was Muhlman who replied first, setting down his fork and drinking some beer.

I finished what I was chewing. "England, like other countries, responds to strong government. The British Labour Party cannot provide that—it is too divided against itself and Churchill is too strong an opposition. Hitler's only mistake was to expand too fast. He should have consolidated, not opened up two fronts. Then he would have beaten England. He would have been invincible."

There was silence around the table. "I hope you don't mind me putting these views," I added after a pause. "In Vienna it is fashionable now to disparage Hitler but, as an historian, even though I am only an historian of buildings, I like to think I can be more objective, more scholarly, than most. Hitler will be judged more kindly in the future than he is now."

Muhlman turned in his seat to look at me. Then he glanced around the table. Then back at me.

"Reimer!" he barked. "Fill Dr. Wolff's glass." He waited while Reimer did as he was told. Then: "Dr. Wolff, you appear to be a clever man. The question is—are you also an honest one?"

A thin smile on his face, he looked from me to Allie, and then to Handler. "Oskar!"

Handler rose from the table. He made straight for a jacket hanging against the wall by the main door and, I was horrified to see, took from it a pistol. He turned and stood near the door, facing us. The message was unmistakable.

"Now," said Muhlman, "how did you guess?"

"Guess what?" said Allie, mystified. I put my finger to my lips to quieten her. The less she said now the better.

"I didn't guess," I said, with what I hoped was a cocky smirk on my face. "I worked it out. We saw the deer trap this afternoon. That meant someone was up here for long enough to be able to trap food. Then, although we arrived late, there was only one person here—Reimer, who turns out to be the waiter, and is probably head cook and bottle washer as well. Two of you were supposed to be off collecting kindling but I saw you return empty-handed. So what did that mean? That two people had deliberately disappeared to avoid being seen by us, at least to begin with. And how could they have been warned about our arrival in advance unless you have a lookout? And why should you need a lookout? Why do you all keep your doors firmly shut? You have something to hide.

"Then I look at the five of you. Very different people, whether the stories you told us, about who you are and what you do, are true or not. It seems to me that, except for Herr Reimer here, or whatever his real name is, you are, all of you, German officers. There is no other way that you, Dr. Muhlman, and Dr. Handler here, could regard each other, and *behave* toward each other, as equals, as you so clearly do. Socially, you are poles apart but you must have spent years thrown together in the mess hall. Probably, you have been under fire together, in danger side by side. May have saved each other's lives, for all I know. But enough, clearly, to make you absolute equals, men who enjoy mutual respect.

"In short, you are all Nazis—I will not call you ex-Nazis as others probably do, for my sympathies are with you. You are fugitives, exiles, on the run. Whatever. That explains why you have to be so careful when anyone approaches. You have been safe up here these past winter months but from now on the weather will improve, more and more people will come up here as the world settles down again. Earlier on, I tried to hint that I had worked out your secret. Maybe I can help. You can't stay here forever, or indeed for much longer. As I say, my sympathies are with you, all the more so as my condition prevented me from fighting during the war."

The others were silent, quite still, as I said all this. They scarcely breathed. This was the stage of maximum danger for Allie and me.

Muhlman smiled vaguely—it might have been friendly, it might have been menacing. After some time, he addressed Kerschner. "What do you think, Gunther? Is he telling the truth?"

Kerschner nodded. "I see no reason to disbelieve him. We *do* have a lookout."

I relaxed. But not for long.

"I don't believe a word." It was Lammers. "He could be anyone. He may even have been sent up here to look for us. He doesn't have a Viennese accent and the girl could be his cover. She doesn't have a wedding ring, after all."

"But she has already explained about her ring." Kerschner was speaking again. "And if they were going to concoct a story like that, would they be so stupid as to turn up without a ring? That's what real honeymooners do, not undercover agents. Don't be so paranoid."

"Hhmmmmnn," said Muhlman, who seemed to be in the skeptical camp. He addressed Allie. "Where did you send the ring?"

"Laurin's." Allie said nothing more. It was a perfect answer, utterly convincing in its brevity.

"I have a thought." Kerschner said, again facing me. "On the evenings we have fresh meat, we try to make it a bit of a party. We end our dinner with a few songs. We sing German songs, Prussian songs, Bavarian songs, Austrian songs. We sing Nazi songs they used to hum in the Vienna coffeehouses." He turned to Muhlman. "If he is who he says he is, he'll be able to join in."

It was a vile idea but crafty. I saw a smirk of wicked satisfaction worm its way up Muhlman's cheek.

No one exactly felt like singing, given the general mood at the table, but Kerschner, since it was his idea, eventually found his voice. He began with a German song, with words by Goethe, about a river sailor of the Rhine. By the third verse others were joining in, but I sat still and silent. The song finished. There was a short pause before, this time, Lammers started up. This was a Nazi song, of the most venomous kind, equating Jews with rodents. Everyone looked at me but I didn't move. Allie— bless her—must have been terrified but, by some superhuman effort, she managed to look thoroughly calm, as if she knew I was just biding my time.

The second song ended. One or two of the men took nervous gulps of their beer, though Muhlman was not among them. He kept his gaze fixed on me but it was not easy to tell what he was thinking. He wiped his lips with the back of his hand, then it was his turn to sing.

His was a vicious lyric, too, all about the glorious blond youth of Bavaria and how it had to remain pure and uncontaminated with hebraic sewer mongers and malcontents. Or some such ponderous rubbish which I have long since forgotten. As the second verse began, and even Allie's smile was beginning to grow a little worn at the edges, I joined in. Tentatively at first, but that was because my voice was—has always been —so awful. But there was no problem with the words—I knew *those* only too well. Each verse of this song had to be delivered faster and louder and, as it progressed, the others joined in. Expressions around the table opened up, as they ignored the painful sounds that issued from my throat; they had ears only for the fact that my knowledge of the words was almost faultless. Allie looked at me, her expression much the same.

The song finished and Muhlman held up his hand. "Before we sing again, let's have some of that French brandy you have tucked away, Reimer. To celebrate."

While it was being brought out and the glasses readied, he turned back to me, beaming. "I thought . . . we thought . . ." He waved his hand across his face. "You know what we thought."

I nodded and spoke quietly. I did feel quite winded. "I didn't know

the first song. I knew the words to the second but . . . it was—is—a
favorite of my brother's. For a moment there, you brought him back."

It was a hammy lie. But they had all been drinking, were separated
from their own families and so were inclined to sentimentality. There
were morose nods from all around the table.

Then the brandy arrived and the group started drinking what the
English call "chasers"—cognac "chased down" with beer. The singing
went on for another hour and I joined in as lustily as I could. Or at least I
seemed to. In fact, I kept a firm eye on the time and, at the earliest
moment I felt it safe to do so, I said, during a convenient lull, "Gentlemen, we *are* on our honeymoon. Will you excuse us?" I held up my ring
finger. "I have a wedding ring—see?"

The singing, not to mention the chasers, ensured that my announce-
ment was greeted with loud cheers and applause. Allie did her best to
play the part of the blushing bride and kissed each man good night in
turn. She slipped her arm in mine and kissed my shoulder. They all stood
and we went upstairs.

Inside the room, I fell onto the bed. Now that I was no longer "on
show," so to speak, the shaking started. My hands, my jaw, the backs of
my knees especially, and all sorts of organs inside me, shivered and trembled, wavered as if with a life of their own. I could hear my heart
thumping in my ears, going much too fast. Sweat streamed from my
scalp and fell in cold trickles to my neck. Muscles trembled where I
didn't know I had muscles.

Allie was in much the same state and neither of us spoke for ages. I
had promised her adventure—but not a close shave with the wrong end
of Handler's pistol.

I closed my eyes. The faces of Muhlman and Lammers swam before
me in the dark, singing, drinking, leering.

But for me the fear—no, the terror—of the evening was not as bad as
the humiliation. Those horrible, disgusting, ridiculous songs! I felt sick—
my throat gagged and I had to sit up, choking and retching. It broke the
silence between us.

"How did you know the words?" Allie whispered. "I was terrified."

"That's why it was so humiliating." I pulled Allie toward me and put
my arms around her, clinging for nourishment. "You see, my brother
really *is* a Nazi. Or was. I despised him. I despised all Nazis. But because
of him, because we were in competition all our lives as boys, because I

wanted to understand him better, I got to know all about the Party—their arguments, their beliefs, their theories, their slang words—and, yes, their songs. Then, as an interrogator trying to recover looted art, I came across many people who denied that they were, or had been, Nazis. I sometimes found it quite effective to play some of those songs softly in the background. Germans are a sentimental race and it had an insidious effect on some prisoners—the songs, often so certain in their sentiments that Germany was right and bound to win the war, rubbed it in that Germany was losing. After they lost, it worked equally well. Those songs even made some people cry. I couldn't join in straightaway tonight; I had to wait for the words to come back to me. What a humiliation."

"But, under the circumstances—"

"I know," I said quickly. "But it was still hard."

Allie said nothing more, but kissed me. She understood that there was something corrosive inside me that night, a malignant mood that meant I was not yet ready for lovemaking. She closed my eyes and massaged my temples. She took off my shoes and my socks. She turned me over onto my stomach. She massaged my feet. She unclipped her hair and let it hang down over her face, holding her head so that the hair fell across the undersides of my feet. Slowly she pressed her fingers, through the hair, against my soles. The texture was smooth, cool, yet slightly grainy too. New, unexpected and quite unlike a normal oily massage. Unhurriedly, still swishing her hair back and forth across my feet, I felt her take off her shirt and brassiere. Now, in the most unexpected move of all, she held her breasts to the soles of my feet. She moved them from side to side, then pressed hard.

All my adult life I had been an anti-Nazi. That's why I had eventually arrived in America, and become a professor of art history there. My two great teachers, Erwin Panofsky and Bernard Berenson, were both Jewish. Panofsky had sent me to Berenson, in Italy, when the political situation had become too uncomfortable for him in Hamburg. I had been glad to get away, relieved to have an excuse to leave a Germany I no longer cared for. But even in Italy I had been too obviously an anti-Fascist and had been escorted to the railroad station and put on a train for Genoa, where I caught the boat for America. By then it was 1938. I did not return to Europe for a number of years. In America I had been content at first to ignore Europe and get on with my work as a professor. But when your brother is a Nazi you can't ignore evil forever. By the time my naturalization papers came through it was Christmas 1941, Pearl Harbor had been bombed and I enlisted. The Allied invasion of northern France, in 1944, and the advance northward through Italy had given me greater satisfaction than anything else in my life up to that point, my marriage included. To have been part of it was for me, an ex-German, a privilege. To have missed it would have been unthinkable. So, although it was necessary, that night in the mountains, to pretend that I was actually enjoying those offensive songs, I still felt deeply humiliated.

Allie's massage was relaxing. In other circumstances it would also have been highly erotic—but not that night, not in the mood I was in. Allie sensed it and, before long, I felt her come around to the side of the bed and fumble with my shirt. She was undressing me. Then she got into bed, put her arms around me just above the waist and pressed her body against my back. In that way, like two spoons side by side in a drawer, we fell asleep.

Sleep releases all but the heaviest of my moods, so we were both cheerful enough the next day when we awoke. We got dressed and went downstairs. Everyone else was already up and any doubts that Muhlman or the others might once have felt now seemed to be a thing of the past. There were one or two honeymoon-type jokes and Reimer produced coffee and a little cheese with some bread.

But if the others were relaxed, I was not. My snooping was not yet done.

I had noticed, on our way downstairs, that once again all the bedrooms were closed. There was something they had to hide, even from Nazi sympathizers. Could it be linked in any way to that Worms newspaper with the unusual ad? I was as certain as I could be that it was this group who had left it behind in the other hut. It might be a link between one of them and von Zell. But how could I broach the subject before we left without appearing to pry? I nibbled my cheese slowly.

I thought back to the paper itself and all those classified ads. There was something there I could use, I thought. It might rock the boat and make them suspicious again, after we had gained their confidence, but, on reflection, I thought it worth a try. In any case, I had to make up my mind quickly—we were coming to the end of our breakfast and it might seem curious if we didn't move off soon. Trying to appear casual, I spoke with my mouth full of cheese.

"Before we leave," I mumbled. "I wonder if any of you gentlemen,

Herr Doktor Lammers, perhaps, or Herr Handler, here, can give me some information. About Worms."

Muhlman was superb. That I remember. Everyone else—Lammers, Kerschner, Handler, even Reimer, who was just bringing more coffee into the room—stopped what they were doing. They just stopped. Lammers was spooning sugar into his coffee and, as his hand stopped, the sugar spilled on to the table. Kerschner, about to take a bite of cheese, stopped and looked up. I don't remember what Handler was doing, but I know he stopped whatever it was. Only Muhlman carried on smoothly as before. He had balanced a lump of cheese on his bread and, when I dropped my bombshell, propelled it neatly into his mouth.

He smiled at me as he chewed. Whether the menace had reappeared in the grin I couldn't say. As he finished he wiped his lips with the back of his hand—there was no such thing as a paper napkin in the mountains in those days. "I don't follow you, Dr. Wolff. Why on earth should George or Oskar or indeed any of us know anything about Worms?" He turned his head and, in the most relaxed manner, smiled at them. "Well? George? Oskar?"

They both shook their heads.

Movement had returned to the table as Muhlman had spoken. Lammers was scooping up the sugar he had spilled, Kerschner was chewing his cheese. Handler was busy again with this or that. Muhlman looked back at me, a definite glint of something other than casual friendship in his smile. He didn't say anything but he didn't need to. It was again my turn to explain.

I smiled back. "You must know what Worms is famous for, Dr. Muhlman. Wood. Teak especially. Teak floors from Worms are known all over Germany, Alsace, Switzerland—even Vienna." This is what I had remembered from the newspaper. There had been a big section of ads for timber yards, job ads mainly, as these businesses got going again after the war. And what I said was true up to a point: Worms floors *were* widely known for being very good. "I am renovating old buildings and the floors in many of them have been very badly damaged, burned from the bombing. Even though the war is over, in Vienna good wood is still hard to come by. Herr Lammers is from Augsberg, you said, and Dr. Handler is from the Mosel—neither is very far from Worms. I thought you might know someone in a timber yard, arrange an introduction perhaps . . ." I trailed off and refilled my coffee cup from the jug

Reimer had now placed on the table. "In business, it's who you know—
not what."

I couldn't tell if Muhlman, or the others, were taken in by my expla-
nation, which may have been overelaborate. However, Allie, bless her,
once more, came to my rescue. She linked her arm in mine and kissed
my shoulder. "Walter!" she hissed loudly. "We are on a honeymoon.
Switch off, *please*. You can be an architect tomorrow, but not today."

She was masterly, her intervention coming at just the right moment
psychologically. Muhlman may not have been entirely convinced by
what I had said, and he knew, of course, that I had seen the reaction that
the mention of Worms had produced in the others. So *he* knew that *I*
knew that Worms was, in some mysterious way, special. Which was
probably grounds for detaining us. On the other hand, he may have
judged that to do anything to Allie or me would inflict more harm than
good in calling attention to his group here in the mountains. If I was
more than I seemed, then my nonappearance after a day or so would be
just as alarming and inconvenient to him and his group as if I went back
to wherever I had come from and sent out a larger patrol. If I really was
what I seemed, an architect from Vienna, there was no harm in letting
me go.

If Muhlman's group *was* connected with von Zell, then they were also
connected with the conduit of leading Nazi war criminals to South
America. Which meant they would almost certainly have intended to
move on soon anyway. A group like that was too important to stay in any
one place for very long. The safest course for Muhlman now, as far as his
treatment of me was concerned, was to make sure that I left soon, and
really did leave so that I was not in a position to follow them; and then
they would evacuate the hut and disappear into an even more remote
region of the mountains.

So my question about Worms wouldn't kill me, but it did mean that
Muhlman and his gang would stay free for a little bit longer than they
might have done if I had played things differently. I would alert the
military authorities in Berchtesgaden, of course, but it would be largely
pointless by then.

I turned to Allie, rubbing my fingers through her hair. "Sorry," I said.
"You're right. Would you like to stay here this morning and get some
sun?"

Out of the corner of my eye I noticed a jab of agitation flicker through

Muhlman, exactly as I had hoped it would. If my reasoning about him was correct, and he half-suspected me, he would now want to get rid of me—us—as soon as possible. If I pretended we were going to stay, he would be the more ready to see us leave. I wasn't going to find out why Worms meant so much to them, nor did it look as though I was going to have a chance to poke about their rooms. But it couldn't be helped. I had gone as far as I could.

Fortunately, Allie was playing her part, though unscripted, to perfection.

"No, Walter, we can't stay. You are forgetting—we have to pick up the ring."

Muhlman relaxed and we got to our feet. The others did so, too, and followed us outside into the sun—I had not noticed until then that it was another very beautiful day. I went to retrieve our skis from the shed and Allie said her good-byes. Then I shook hands with the men. Muhlman, on guard to the last, could not let me go without one final dig. "Sorry we couldn't help you with Worms, Doktor Wolff. But good luck with the renovations. If you run short of ideas, have a look at Hitler's plans for Linz. They are too good to be wasted."

I smiled weakly but said nothing and stepped into my skis. He had had the last word and it was probably safer that way.

And that, for the time being, was that. We saw no one else in the mountains and, in the afternoon, descended first on skis and then by cable car to Königsee, a pretty village with trees and a bandstand at the northern end of a lake. We strolled into the town around three o'clock and had just a short wait before a red and yellow train took us back to Berchtesgaden. It was getting dark, past five, as we walked up the dead-end road to Allie's father's house.

During the train ride Allie had sat next to me, close by, her arm in mine, watching the lake go by.

Judging the moment just right, I asked her about von Zell. "What sort of man was he?"

"Quiet. Strong. With two parts to him. One part was the efficient Nazi. His briefcase and his room were always incredibly tidy, and he always finished all his outstanding work before going to sleep." Allie shifted on the seat. "But when you could persuade him to talk about his wife and his son, he was quite different."

She squeezed my arm and rested her head on my shoulder. "He had a wonderful skin; that I *do* remember."

I looked down at her. The lake slipped by outside.

"Only once," she said softly, in reply to my glance. "Only once. He regretted it, I think." She squeezed my arm again. "He had invited me out to lunch—father was away—one Saturday. We ate fish and ice cream and red wine. I told him that I didn't realize he had French habits—red wine with almost everything. But he said he didn't know France very well. He had been there on his honeymoon, to the Loire. He laughed. The first days of the honeymoon had been spoiled by an electrical storm which had brought on the mosquitoes. Both he and Mrs. von Zell had erupted and been covered with scores of bites. At night they couldn't make love and they couldn't sleep: it was very warm, and in any case they were itching and scratching so much. So they had talked. In fact their talking got them thrown out of their hotel since they couldn't stop laughing at their spotty appearance and kept waking up everyone else. Rudolf loved looking back. After two or three days of putting cool cream on each other's skin, and yet not being able to make love, they were I think all the more ready when the rashes died down."

Allie looked up at me. "Telling me that story obviously had an effect on Rudolf. And remember, we had drunk quite a lot of wine. We went back to the house and—just the once. It was lovely, but he wasn't really unfaithful. He was, I think, thinking of her. I hope you weren't thinking of anyone, Walter."

I smiled and shook my head. Then she had slept with her head on my shoulder. Or at least she had pretended to sleep. We had both felt sad, I think, that our adventure was nearly over, and any more words would have been out of place. As the train had rocked and clanged into the station at Berchtesgaden and we got to our feet, she had given my arm one last hug and had kissed my shoulder. We never touched again.

"I won't come in, Allie," I said softly as we reached the house. "I must get to Salzburg tonight." She nodded.

"But may I ask a favor?"

"Ask it."

"Those books of sheet music, the ones von Zell left. May I take them?"

"Of course," she whispered. "You start your lovely car. I'll fetch them."

I did as I was told. She reappeared with half a dozen wafer-thin book-lets. Printed during wartime, the paper was pathetic and off-white, as if it had been made from scorched trees. She handed them to me with a melancholy smile. "It was an adventure, Walter. A real honeymoon. I shan't forget it."

"No. Nor shall I."

"Will—would you ever come back?"

"No."

But I held out my fist, cupped upward. In it was the gold ring I always wore on the little finger of my left hand. "This belonged to my father; my mother gave it to him. You could have the size changed. I'm told that Laurin's here in Berchtesgaden does a good job."

She frowned. At first I think she thought the gift too personal. But, when I kept my arm outstretched, she suddenly beamed and accepted it. She took it with her, back into the house, without once turning around.

PART TWO
THE
LETTERS

CHAPTER THREE

1

I had lied to Allie when I said I had to get back to Salzburg that night.
I *had* to do no such thing. I was very largely my own master, and, up to a
point, no one really cared where I was. I had said that because I felt a
need to get away from her; the episode was over—it was time to move
on. However, after I had been to the office of the military government in
Berchtesgaden, to report Muhlman and his cronies, the response was so
depressing that, coming so soon after my good-bye to Allie, I suddenly
became rather morose and was filled with an urge to return straightaway
to the Goldener Hirsch, as if it were home.

The military governor in Berchtesgaden, a cocky young colonel from
the Midwest, had listened to my story but said he could not help. He
had very few people on his staff who could ski, he said, and nowhere near
fifteen, which would be the minimum number needed to chase five
fugitives who were armed. On top of that, he imagined that the Germans, being skilled skiers and familiar with the mountains, would easily
outpace greenhorn Americans, so we wouldn't get near them anyway.
Furthermore, this being Hitler's retreat, he said that the population of
Berchtesgaden could not be relied upon to provide help—there were
secret Nazi sympathizers everywhere. I explained about the conduit and
I showed him Eisenhower's orders but it did no good. The colonel didn't
have the men. He agreed with me that Muhlman would have moved on

by the time any patrol he sent out reached the mountains and that there were all sorts of remote places where they could hide away forever. What he said made sense but it didn't help.

It was a clean, clear night for the drive back to Salzburg and, as usual, the roads were as jammed with traffic as the sky was cluttered with stars.

To my depression could be added confusion. I now had not one but two theories about von Zell, both of which were plausible but, for the moment, hardly more than that. I had no real evidence to support either. Tomorrow Hobel would demand to know what progress I had made, what I had to show him. I had been away five nights. I had, I thought, gone a lot further in my reasoning than any of my predecessors but, when it came down to it, I still hadn't produced von Zell. Worse, it now looked as though, if he *was* hiding in the mountains, I would never be able to get at him. Or, if we were to send a patrol after Muhlman and the others, in the hope of them leading us to von Zell, that patrol would have to be specially drafted for the purpose. I had no idea whether Hobel would sanction that, whether he had the power to do so. Even if he did, and the patrol was sent out, if it then drew a blank, as was quite likely given how many mountains there were, it would be such a spectacular failure on my part that it would more than wipe out any acclaim I had achieved with the Holy Roman Crown Jewels. There would be no medals. I just had to hope against hope that when I called him the next morning Maurice would have some good news for me.

The yellow and green light over the main door of the Goldener Hirsch was a welcome sight when I reached it around ten that night. More, the staff acted like family, remembering my name, all smiles, solicitous of my welfare while I had been away. The restaurant was closing but they held it open for me, provided I had my bath afterward, and I treated myself to a whole bottle of wine with the roast chicken; I had been away five nights, hadn't eaten properly on any of them, and had almost forgotten what it was like to be tipsy.

After dinner I bathed, in clean, unlimited hot water, then crept in between fresh, cool, clean linen sheets. I didn't think much about Allie. I hadn't met Konstanze then and until that time I had always been able to put affairs behind me with little trouble—I suppose because I had never really fallen for anyone, rather, the reverse was true. But I did dream about Allie. We were back on the mountain and Muhlman was being far nastier than he had been in real life. He was wearing his Nazi uniform, my brother was there, also in uniform, telling all the others who I really was. Allie was stripped to her underwear (her mother's) and tied to a tree that appeared to be growing inside the hut. One of her legs was in the deer trap and bleeding. A psychiatrist would no doubt make much of the fear, family jealousy and eroticism mixed into my dream, but I couldn't have told him where the dream went for it didn't go anywhere. Maurice called in the middle of it.

I had dropped off so suddenly, so painlessly, so easily that, when I heard the phone, I thought it was still evening. In fact, it was 9:30 the next day.

"Yes," I said, wide awake as soon as I realized who it was. "Any news?"

"I am afraid, dear boy, that so far we have drawn a blank."

"Damn. Tell me."

"Simply no sign of your man, either as von Zell or as von Haltern."

"Have they checked *all* the vineyards?"

"Of course not, not yet. But they did find the most obvious ones, three vineyards near Zöbing, were those Benedictine monks you mentioned—the ones expelled from Kremsmünster—had been housed. The monks had gone back to their monasteries but there was no doubt they were the right vineyards. I've had a second man there since yesterday morning and they were allowed to search everywhere and to look at all the books. No one at the vineyards or in the surrounding villages has heard of your man."

"But there are still plenty of other vineyards to try?" I realized I sounded desperate.

"Yes, Walter, but . . ."

"But what? But *what*, Maurice?"

"We'll keep searching, Walter, of course. But you should know that, at two of the vineyards, the owners did know von Zell. They remembered that he had visited them before the war, for an article he was writing. Now, don't you think that if he was going to stay anywhere, Walter, it would be with those people? People he knew well enough for them to remember him eight years later?"

Maurice was right, damn him. I knew it, but the more I thought of my meeting with Hobel later that morning, the more desperate I became.

"Keep looking, Maurice, please. Another day—no, two days. If you haven't found him by tomorrow night you can call your people off, and many thanks. Okay?"

I put the phone down before I realized that our stock market "race" had not even been mentioned. I was in such a state it felt as though the chicken I had eaten the night before was still alive inside my stomach, fluttering its wings and trying to get away. My dream had been bad enough, leaving me with a vague, unpleasant sensation; but the news from Maurice was worse, much worse. My theories about von Zell were fine, as theories. But if they didn't check out, they were so much hot air, empty reasoning, as Hobel would be the first to tell me. I thought I had been so clever with my hunch about the vineyards of Austria, and it would have been such a *coup* if it had worked out. But it now began to seem that I had flattered myself into believing a silly theory, just because it was clever. Hobel would see that too. As for my other theory, about von Zell's hideaway in the mountains, well, I had no way of knowing what he would think of *that*. I decided to take my time over breakfast and, since I could see that it was another beautiful day, walk to the office.

I stopped on the Market Bridge; the sun was strong and the green waters of the Salzach were swollen with melted snow. There were two nuns shopping for vegetables on the Rudolfskai. I stood and watched as they felt everything carefully, badgered the greengrocer into fetching his freshest merchandise from the back of the store, then counted out their money very carefully. I was no further forward in working out how to catch von Zell, still dreading the I-told-you-so reception I knew I would get from Hobel. I envied the nuns their simple, straightforward, certain life.

I was like a little boy who, having been to the dentist, delays his return to school for as long as possible. I looked in every shop window that morning and found something of interest in everything that was happening on the street—scenery being unloaded from a truck and carried into the theater, a choir progressing in purple cassocks from one church to another, a consignment of new bicycles on display outside a garage. Finally, I could put off my arrival no longer.

I smile when I think back now—for Hobel wasn't in the office that day and I still wonder if the whole investigation would have taken a different course if he had been, if he had heard what I had to say, laughed in my face, then fired me from the case, as he might have been able to do. But the major had gone to Munich, three or four hours away, and had left word that, should I show up, or call, he wanted to speak to me. I was not to leave Salzburg again before he had seen me and I was to study carefully the file from him which I would also find on my desk. He was getting impatient for results.

Nonetheless, he *was* out of the way, temporarily, so despite his heavy-handed message I relaxed and was soon caught up in the details of office life. It appeared that a dance had been organized for the following Saturday and this was the single most important topic of conversation for most of the men in the building, Sammy not excluded. Army trucks were being sent out into the surrounding countryside to bring girls into Salzburg for the big occasion. A band was coming from Munich; in fact, that was one of the reasons Hobel had gone there, to choose the musicians and settle various other details.

There was a pile of messages waiting for me on my desk, a letter in my wife's handwriting, another in my mother's and a cream-colored folder, presumably Hobel's file. They could wait. "Well, Sammy," I said, as cheerfully as I could. "What news from the bulls and the bears of Wall Street?"

He was working at his typewriter and didn't look up. "I sold." He didn't so much say it as sing it, his voice rising a note or two.

"Oh yes?" But I meant "Oh, *no!*"

"Yeah. But don't worry. I bought some other stuff."

I sat down on top of my desk, directly across from him. "Very smart. But all this activity on my behalf must mean I've lost, right? It's going to be that sort of day, I can feel it. Give me the gory details, Sammy, so I can swear and get to confession before lunch."

He finished a sentence on his typewriter, then finally looked up. "The rumor was true. The guy from Consolidated Automobiles was recruited by Truman and is coming to Germany."

"And?"

"And so the shares dropped some more—"

"How much? No—hold on. Let me get more comfortable." I slumped into my chair, threw back my head and closed my eyes. Then I opened one and squinted at Sammy.

He looked at his watch, pushing his eyeglasses back up his nose with the other hand. "This time yesterday, your original thousand dollars was worth"—he looked in his book—"eight hundred and seventy-two, plus forty-six cents. Each share dropped thirty-one points."

"Confession, here I come. . . . Shit!"

"Remember," said Sammy calmly, "that for every dollar you have lost, I have lost five."

"Shit!" I said again, more softly. "So what did you do, Sammy? What did you do with the money?"

"Insurance. I bought into insurance."

"Why?"

"Simple. In wars insurance companies have a hard time, especially this last war with its blitz bombing. Nothing, and no one, is safe. You can't insure your house, or your furniture or your life, so it's hardly Christmas and birthday time all at once for insurance companies. Not that I feel sorry for them. But now that the war's over, it will be different. Life insurance, house insurance, health insurance, even jewelry insurance will all start up again."

He waved a sheet of paper as he put it fresh into his typewriter. "I bought you seven hundred shares of Atlantic Insurance, at one twenty-five a share. Grand total—eight hundred and seventy-five dollars. And that means you owe me two dollars fifty-four cents."

As I paid him the money, I took a deep breath. "And I suppose Confederate Paper went up yet again?"

He reached across and took the notes and change before answering. " 'fraid so. Steady rise—good share that, I reckon. Up six since you last asked. Your friend Ghent is now worth . . . one o three four."

That meant Maurice was $159 ahead of me in no time. He would be unbearably cocky and the helmet was surely already his. A thought struck me. "Did *you* buy into Confederate Paper, Sammy?"

He looked up, shoving his eyeglasses back yet again. "No. I put my spare cash into automobiles, with you."

"That's *some* consolation."

Sammy grinned. "You need nerve in this game, Walter. You'll get your money back, later or sooner."

"I don't like the way you said that."

But he was already busy again with his paperwork.

I turned wearily to the mail and the messages on my desk, thinking again of those nuns I had seen on the Rudolfskai. Were they really as content as they looked? Or did they, too, have their problems? Did a convent harbor all manner of jealousies and rivalries? Did each job—choirmistress, say, or librarian—carry with it responsibilities that gave the nuns sleepless nights? The nuns I had seen had both been attractive women and the thought occurred to me that they might enjoy the dance being planned for the following Saturday. The image of Major Hobel, his watery eyes bulging with lust, dancing with a nun cheered me as I picked up the papers.

I put the letter from my wife, and the one from my mother, in my pocket. I would look at those when I was alone. Gingerly, I opened the folder that Hobel had left. It contained a single sheet, a newspaper clipping—in German—and no sooner had I read the headline than I groaned aloud. No wonder Hobel had passed it on to me. No wonder he wanted to talk. No wonder I was not allowed to leave Salzburg beforehand.

The clipping described how, two days before—the day Allie and I had found the deer blood in the snow and sung those sickening songs with Muhlman and his troupe—a motor cruiser had been intercepted by the Swiss police on lake Geneva near midnight. It was found to contain three small-time ex-Nazis and, according to the police, had probably set out from Cully, in Switzerland, bound for Meillerie, in France. Neither the Germans nor the Swiss helmsman would talk. The newspaper speculated that this was a crossing point, from Switzerland to France, for the notorious secret conduit set up to help ex-Nazis escape. It suggested that, since the figures apprehended were relatively minor, this might have been the first time this route was used, that the three men were, in a sense, guinea pigs. All that was bad enough, but what had particularly drawn Hobel's attention, and incensed him, was the last paragraph, which went something like this: "Police have traced the boat to the yard of M. Gilbert Lenoir, which is situated farther along the shore, at Château de Chillon. M. Lenoir says he sold the boat to a 'tall, swarthy man, French-speaking, perhaps an Algerian,' about two months ago. He said that there was nothing suspicious about the transaction, the man did not seem in a hurry to buy and came back several times to argue over the price. 'The only thing that was remotely unusual or strange,' said M. Lenoir, 'was that the man paid in gold. He had several small bars of it in a briefcase. The last time that happened to me was in 1940.' " The boat had cost the equivalent of $1,200, a lot of money in 1946.

Hobel, of course, had ringed the word "gold" several times with his pen. His eyes, I thought spitefully, must certainly have fallen from their sockets as he had done so.

But, I had to admit, it stepped up the pressure on us, on me. This story, small enough in itself, would nonetheless wing its way around the news service wires across the world. With the Nuremberg trials still in full flood, with Kaltenbrunner on the stand at that very moment, Nazis and ex-Nazis were news. Almost certainly, Wren and General Eisenhower himself would see the item, or have it drawn to their attention. Questions would be asked about the progress I was making—whether I was in fact *making* any progress. I would be left to continue for a while but somewhere, in the recesses of Wren's mind perhaps, or in one of those offices near Eisenhower's, where smart staff officers from good families had enjoyed safe wars, a contingency plan would be drawn up. In case I should fail.

I took out my pipe and sucked it for comfort, as I sometimes did, even though there was no tobacco in it. So far it was not proving to be a good day. I closed the folder and picked up the next thing, a telegram from Henry de Jaeger in Hamburg. More bad news, I supposed, and I was right.

He had been unable to get hold of me while I was in the mountains so had wired the results of his investigations direct to Salzburg. He had contacted the von Halterns, as discussed, he said, and had spent two or three hours with the family at their farm in Tegernsee, just outside Hamburg. Von Zell was not there, he wrote. He was also convinced, he said, that no one was hiding out at the von Halterns. The Baroness claimed she had not seen von Zell since her own son, Eric, had been killed and "Rudi," as she called him familiarly, had come to the funeral. De Jaeger was convinced by her story but had searched the farm in any case and asked shopkeepers and policemen in the surrounding village. All told the same story: the Baroness, having lost her husband just before the war, then her son-in-law, and finally her son *in* the war, had been devastated by these events. She now went nowhere and saw no one. It was rare for her to go shopping, even in the village; most of the time the local traders made deliveries. De Jaeger added that the farmhouse itself was not large and that the various outbuildings had been searched simultaneously by the four men he had taken with him. So he felt pretty sure that von Zell was not at Tegernsee. I could just imagine him saying "Sure as shee-it."

What really made it seem as though the Baroness was telling the truth was her confession to de Jaeger that her son's documents—army ID documents, passport, driver's license—*had* survived the bombing in Koblenz but that she could not find them now. "So make of that what you will," de Jaeger had concluded. "Good hunting."

That sign-off phrase "Good hunting" made me think of deer and my feast of venison in the mountains. And that reminded me of how little progress I was making. Both the Wachau and Hamburg leads had proven to be blind alleys that day and my third lead, Muhlman and the mountains, looked too difficult to follow up. Terrific! And, on top of it all, I was $125 poorer. It was only a little over a week since I had found the Holy Roman jewels and been the envy of all my colleagues. But it felt like a lifetime.

I suddenly noticed on my desk a large bundle of papers that looked like letters but which obviously didn't belong to me. They were wrapped untidily with a dark blue ribbon.

"What are these?" I asked, looking across at Sammy. Still concentrating on his typing, he didn't hear me at first. "Sammy! Do you know what these are?"

He didn't look up and he didn't stop typing. "They came for you. A couple of days ago."

"They came for me? Do you know what they are? Who sent them?"

He came to the end of his sentence before speaking. Then he looked up, pushing back his eyeglasses, which had fallen forward, over the bridge of his nose.

"Well, they weren't addressed to you personally. They were just sent to this office by Lieutenant Bloch, the last person to interrogate Mrs. von Zell. He was the man who threatened to deport her to the Russian zone."

"Yes, I remember."

"As soon as he had seen Mrs. von Zell, and she had failed to be intimidated by his threat to send her to Berlin, Bloch was recalled to the U.S. His wife was taken ill. In his scramble to leave he took a lot of documents with him that he should have left behind." Sammy motioned to the bundle on my desk. "I had a letter from him two days ago—I helped him with some shares too." Sammy smiled. "Those papers were included in the parcel. He finally got around to sorting his things out."

"Yes, but what are they?"

"Letters mostly, I think. Bloch confiscated lots of things from the von Zells—he wasn't exactly our best example of American tact, but he never read them; he never had time. No one has read them. I thought they might contain something useful, some reference to a location where von Zell might hide out. But I'm guessing; I don't know what's in the bundle. It might be a waste of time. Then again, it might prove very useful."

I looked at the bundle without undoing it or touching it. When I think back now, and remember that I came close to not untying that ribbon, I have to smile to myself.

That bundle changed everything. It changed my life.

The papers or documents, whatever they were, looked old and there seemed to be scores, if not hundreds, of them. That was daunting. In my interrogation work I had learned one thing at least: that important clues could turn up in the most unlikely places—like that ad, for instance, which I had found in the newspaper in the alpine hut where Allie and I spent the night. Which meant that I had learned to concentrate on even the most unprepossessing documentation. But that didn't make the job of reading such things any more interesting or less daunting. On the contrary, I had also learned to dread the fact that, on the way to an important clue, one usually found oneself reading the dullest, most obscure or banal rubbish. So those documents on my desk were, at that point, just another chore for me and I wasn't exactly overjoyed with Sammy or Lieutenant Bloch for their part in returning them. What's more, it looked as though a good number of them were handwritten, which would make reading them even more difficult. I weighed, as I had done on similar occasions before, whether I could get away with not reading them. On balance I decided I could not. If Sammy was right, and some of them were letters, they might indeed tell me something about von Zell's habits, something that might be a clue. I brushed my hand through my hair and stood up.

Sammy had gone back to his work and I walked through into the little cubicle that adjoined our office, the small room with the window. I looked out onto the city. Salzburg really was pretty, its roofs all different colors—black, green, yellow and reddish clay. And, from where I was standing, I realized I could see the brand-new powdery-blue spring gentian on the Gaisberg.

In my bones I had no real hope that Maurice's men would come up with anything, but, even so, I had to wait for him to get back to me. I also had to wait for Hobel to come back before I could tell him what I had done and discuss the possibility, however unlikely, of sending a patrol into the mountains. Hamburg was a dead end and I had no more ideas where, if he wasn't in the Wachau, von Zell might be. There was nothing for me to do that day but wait.

Looking out over the glorious Salzburg roofs, blotched with gold from the sun, I turned and went back to my desk to examine the bundle of papers with the blue ribbon.

Hartt was right about one thing—they *were* letters. Quite how useful they were was at first not easy to say. As I had feared, they were mostly handwritten and that made them difficult to decipher. I leafed through them, picking some out, leaving others on the desk. Some had been unfolded, others were tucked into their envelopes and still others were scrunched up, the pages stuck together with coffee or wine or something of that sort. The earliest ones were written on rather good paper in fountain-pen ink, rich and deep in color; later ones were scrawled in pencil on thin, discolored wartime sheets.

There were perhaps two hundred letters in the bundle, in no order or sequence that I could discern. It was when I noticed that there were only three hands doing the writing, three signatures at the end of the letters, that I began to take more than a casual interest in them. One signature was Mrs. von Zell's—her letters were clearly signed "Konstanze," in an upright, round hand. Funny how, the world over, women seem to write in one style and men in another. One hand was her husband's and those were signed either "Rudolf," "Rudi" or just "R." But the third hand belonged to someone who signed himself "Bruno."

Glancing briefly at a couple of the letters signed by Bruno, I kicked myself. Until then I had spent a great deal of energy in trying to find out if Rudolf von Zell had a mistress, in the hope that, if he did, she might lead us to him. For some reason, chauvinism, I suppose one would call it, it had simply never occurred to me that Mrs. von Zell might have a lover. Yet that is what Bruno seemed to be, if the few letters of his that I read that day were any guide.

I considered the letters in front of me. There were an awful lot of them. But, I decided, if Mrs. von Zell *did* have a lover, if she *was* at the center of a triangle, then who knew what sorts of jealousies might have been unleashed, jealousies that I might be able to use, emotions that might induce Konstanze's lover to betray his rival? I decided that the letters might just repay the effort it would take to read them.

Easier said than done. The letters had been confiscated by Lieutenant Bloch against Mrs. von Zell's wishes and certainly without her consent. So, as I say, they were not arranged in any sensible order and my first task was to shuffle them into chronological sequence. There were so many that the task took me most of the day. Quite a few bore only the day of the month and the month itself and I had to guess the year by matching the paper and the ink to surrounding letters.

The ordering of the letters was helpful in showing me two things: first, Mrs. von Zell was not deceiving her husband, at least not with Bruno. All the letters to and from him predated the letters to and from Rudolf. Second, *both* sides of the correspondence were there. That intrigued me, the more so as it was immediately obvious that the letters were all love letters of the most intimate kind. I could understand Mrs. von Zell keeping the letters she had received, but it also seemed that she had been given back the letters she *herself* had written. That was unusual, to say the least.

It was almost midnight as I finished putting the letters in order. Hartt had gone, leaving me with the news that Atlantic Insurance had dropped a point—I was now down to $868, and that Confederate Paper Mills was up two cents, making Maurice $168 dollars ahead of me at $1,036. The office was quiet around me, though still blazing with light. Hobel, apparently detained in Munich, had not appeared.

In sorting the letters I lost my hope that they might provide me with a jealous lover. But, I have to say, I glimpsed enough of their contents to want to know more than I did. They were *extremely* intimate, and although Bruno did not appear to be in touch with Mrs. von Zell at that time, the mid-1940s, it occurred to me that the letters were personal enough and detailed enough to contain information which I might find invaluable if ever I decided to interrogate her.

I shuffled the most recent letters into place at the bottom of the pile. The cathedral bell had clanged midnight about ten minutes before. I wrapped the dark blue ribbon back around the bundle, which was far more neatly stacked now. I paused to consider whether I did, in fact, have the right to read the letters. There was probably nothing in the Geneva convention about it; and historians of the Second World War would probably not regard the reading of enemy correspondence as a major war crime. Nonetheless, a woman's love letters were scarcely to be regarded as enemy intelligence.

I walked back through the town. It was another clear, cold, very quiet night. I cannot say that I pondered very deeply over Mrs. von Zell's correspondence. Curiosity, which is after all a quality you are supposed to have in abundance as an interrogator, would easily get the better of me.

Across the Market Bridge, I turned left rather than right toward my hotel. I was not at all sleepy and had been told of a brasserie, tucked away behind the cathedral, which kept late hours and served hot, if primitive, food and good beer. Then I would go back to the hotel and, if I still felt as wide awake as I did now, start reading the letters properly.

In later years I would look back upon the need to read the letters with mixed feelings. They were engrossing pieces of paper: enchanting, sad, funny, by turns passionate, moving, occasionally erotic, always intimate and never, never dull. But they took me where I had no right to go—and that, later, caused all the problems.

At the brasserie I was given Middle-European stodge—sausage, cabbage and potatoes—spicy and served very quickly. Two beers and I was back at the Goldener Hirsch before one o'clock. I was still wide awake so I undid my tie, slipped off my shoes and lay across my bed with the bundle.

2

THE first letters were the easiest to read, being written on the best quality paper and in fountain-pen ink. We don't remember today what an effort people used to make when using a fountain pen; handwriting could be quite beautiful then. The letters started in 1933, in the late summer. These early ones had been read and reread so many times that the paper was almost worn through at the folds. Bruno had been just as conscientious a letter writer as Konstanze; each would write once a week, waiting for the other's to arrive, then reply the next day.

To begin with, I read the correspondence with a pencil and notebook handy, so that I might jot down anything that struck me as relevant or interesting and which, if I did interrogate Mrs. von Zell, I might need. But, as that first night wore on, I was very soon caught up in Konstanze's story. It was, without a doubt, her story, rather than Bruno's or her husband's, that held my interest, and my note-taking fell by the wayside.

I can remember the chain of events perfectly, even after all this time. But, of course, in the letters it emerged only gradually, eliptically, and not in the more straightforward way that I am now going to describe. In the early letters Konstanze and Bruno each assumed that the other would understand all their references to the past or the world around them, naturally, and, of course, they met between letters and wrote things down against the background of their conversations. This meant that I had to read quite a way into the correspondence before I understood fully what was going on. When I did, though, it only made Konstanze's situation and character all the more intriguing.

This is Konstanze's story, for it is now that I begin to think of her as Konstanze and not as Mrs. von Zell. It started when she was eighteen and met Bruno, who was two, no, nearly three years older. She had a sister, Rosamunde, and came from quite an exotic background; her father was an actor from Munich who was well known in Bavaria in his day, and her mother, an Austrian, was a musician who played piano and organ. I learned that the most important effect Konstanze's parents had on her was that she and her sister had grown up in an emotional household that was used to drama. No one, so I gathered from what she told Bruno, had been afraid to show their feelings. Her father played all the great tragedies on the stage—by Goethe, Schiller and Shakespeare, who was his favorite, to name a few. The father came across in the letters as somewhat lacking in a sense of humor but Konstanze seemed genuinely fond of him and more than once referred to him as a King Lear figure. She pictured him as a kind but misguided old man, too often taken advantage of by her elder sister.

Her mother seemed to have been a somewhat more distant parent, not austere exactly but disciplined, perhaps as a result of being a musician and having to practice so rigorously. She was a good pianist, apparently, and played in a small but highly regarded orchestra, which meant that she had to travel—and therefore be away from home—a great deal. On Sundays she played the organ in one of Munich's main churches.

After her husband, her main loves, so it would seem from the letters, were Schubert, Mozart and the massive organ works of Bruckner, all of them, interestingly enough, Austrian, rather than German, composers. Konstanze and her sister were never neglected exactly and TB, which they both contracted, was not uncommon; but they definitely came second in the household, after art.

To begin with, as you would expect, both sisters had rebelled against their parents, but Konstanze had been won around by the time she was twelve and started to learn the piano. Her sister went the other way, and eventually became a scientist. More significant perhaps, being raised in the family atmosphere that she was, Konstanze regarded all human relationships as passionate and inevitably tragic. I imagine that her father probably agreed with her, while her mother was too busy to disagree. Schubert, Mozart and Bruckner all had tragic aspects to their lives. Lear and Faust were her father's favorite dramas and his quotations and misquotations, like Mephistopheles' "Blood is a juice of quality most rare," peppered Konstanze's letters.

Reading between the lines and, at this point, paying more heed to Bruno's asides than to Konstanze's, it seemed to me that she grew up into a melancholic young woman. Melancholic was a word still in use then, despite the existence of Dr. Freud, not far away in Vienna. So, in 1933, when Konstanze met Bruno in the—for her—highly charged surroundings of a concert, he immediately fell for her modesty, her reticence, her inner sadness or, as he put it, her desolate sense of doom, from which he was determined to rescue her.

He was in uniform that night, the handsome gray-green of a Luftwaffe pilot, sharing a box with three others, all the same—laughing, dashing figures with the world, and not just the theater stalls, at their feet. It was a typically south German, or Austrian, concert, maudlin or moving depending on your point of view: a series of sad songs, all by Schubert, written in the last two years of his life and describing the pain and sorrow that he couldn't shake off. In fact, precisely the kind of melancholic evening so suited to Konstanze's character. In the first intermission Bruno and the other pilots in his box had been introduced to her by mutual friends. In the crush they had been jostled to one side and he had a chance to whisper, "The next songs are much too sad for someone as beautiful as you. May I console you afterward with some champagne?"

Melodramatic perhaps, but an unusual approach nonetheless. Bruno, whoever he was, knew something about Schubert, and he was also sensitive enough to spot the melancholy in Konstanze. She agreed.

They had spent the second intermission talking. He had been a pilot for two years now and was, he told her with an eager pride, highly regarded. She laughed at his immodesty, but also liked his confidence in himself, so different from her own. She found that, besides music and aircraft, he was mad about automobiles, trains, yachts, motorcycles, the faster the better. They had to part for the last songs, but arranged to meet again the following day. In the darkened hall the music swelled to the finale of *"Rastlöse Liebe,"* based on Goethe's poem expressing the mysterious melancholy which always mingles with the joy when one heart is spontaneously attracted to another. It could not have been better suited to her mood and she closed her eyes and tried to imagine Bruno's face.

It was a short flirtation because it soon blossomed into something more; that was Konstanze's way. They would meet twice a week in Munich. There was much for her to show him in the city, since he was from Berlin and therefore a relative stranger. She was happy being his guide and took him to the museums, where he admired the works of Dürer, Cranach and the other German masters. There was the library, the bridges across the river, with their medieval carvings, the churches—the Dreifaltigkeitskirche, with its frescoes by Asam, the church of St. John Nepomuk, built so that the congregation sits in shadow while the rest of the church is lit radiantly from above—and any number of music shops where they could inspect beautifully carved woodwind instruments and violins. There were restaurants with their terraces still open in the late summer where they would talk for hours over a single glass of white wine. As a pilot, Bruno would permit himself no more alcohol than this.

When the two had exhausted the city they bicycled into the country, a real pleasure in those days. Cars were few, almost nonexistent and certainly rarer than horses. Country roads were clean, refreshing places, as strange as that may seem these days. Cycling was a joy because bicycles were so quiet, and the wildlife in the hedgerows often could not hear you coming. Hedges in the 1930s were cluttered with life: different varieties of birds, rabbits, field mice, hedgehogs, squirrels, occasionally a fox. Far busier than the roads.

It had been a happy time for both of them, too happy for letter-writing—I had to piece much of this information together later. In the

face of so much unadulterated pleasure—sunshine, countryside, affection
—Konstanze had even begun to lose her melancholic bent. Bruno knew
far more about wildlife than she did, surprising for someone who came
from Berlin, and he was a patient teacher. What he knew about the
habits of bees, foxes or elms amazed and seduced her.

Three weeks passed without any shadow. September turned into October. The bees became less populous on their jaunts into the country,
and the leaves of the elms began to change color.

Then one day they sat by the river Isar, south of Munich, watching
the white lock gates open to let a motor cruiser downstream. There was a
bite in the air that had been absent before; they would not be able to sit
out like this for much longer.

Bruno was trying to guess how fast the motor cruiser could go with all
throttles open. Konstanze, for a while, was silent, pondering a question
that had been on her mind for some time.

The cruiser passed them, the chug of its engines so deep, so powerful
that they could feel its vibrations on the riverbank. Together they
watched it disappear.

"Bruno."

"Yes?"

"Why don't you make love to me?"

He lay back in the long green grass.

"Why, Bruno? Why not?" It was a question, not a complaint. "I
would like you to, very much."

At length he said, "I thought you might have guessed." He sat up,
biting his lip. "I only ever see you during the week, never at weekends. I
have never invited you to the base. In the circumstances it wouldn't be
fair."

"What circumstances, Bruno? Say."

He looked downstream. The river was quite smooth again now, the
wake of the motor cruiser washed entirely away. "I'm married."

She had half-guessed, of course. Her question gave her away. A strict
Catholic woman doesn't ask a man into bed, as she had just done, without knowing the answer in advance. But, when she heard his reply, she
was still shocked. At first she had felt sick, then the bite in the air got to
her and she shivered. The sediment of TB in her lungs made her cough.
Bruno had taken off his tunic and put it around her shoulders; but she
hadn't thanked him and didn't even look at him. She couldn't. Despite

her inexperience, however, her instincts told her that any sudden gesture —like breaking off the affair there and then—would be rash, that she would soon regret it. In the long run that might have been better, cleaner certainly and less tragic.

That day they had made their way home on their bicycles as best they could, not speaking and ignoring the countryside all around them. That night she had written to him that she could never see him again, that it was wrong for the two of them to deceive his wife. I must say that my heart really went out to Konstanze at this point; for what this letter showed, above all, was not her anger at his deception, or her pity for his wife, or any kind of self pity on her part, but a simple *bewilderment* that people could behave so badly, so selfishly. As the days went by she was bewildered, too, by her own feelings. As a Catholic she was in no doubt that what she was involved in was wrong. At the same time, as she lived through the next few days without seeing him, without contact of any sort save her letters to him, with any *prospect* of seeing him, so she reacted as a woman in love for the first time: she was desolate, rudderless, adrift. She had written later—much later, when she was strong enough to admit it—that she never knew what it was like to cry until that week. The uncontrollable nature of the crying, I think, frightened her.

She might have weathered it, though I doubt it, and as it was she didn't see Bruno for a full week. But then two things happened. In the first place, they met by accident. She had gone to see the doctor, since she was feeling so ill, and Bruno had been in the town with his fellow pilots. He had left them and insisted on seeing her home. It was enough to renew her grief; she grew yet more bewildered at the strength of feeling within her and the kind of peace she felt when Bruno was around.

There was also, I think, a second something that had an effect on Konstanze, something that made her even more attractive in my eyes. With her family upbringing, the father and mother she had, Konstanze was very familiar with tragedy. In a sense she had been prepared for it all her life and, in the affair with Bruno, had been rewarded with her very own. His unattainability was, for her, almost a natural state of affairs, no more than she had come to expect. It was invariably what happened to lovers in Shakespeare or Goethe.

And so, after their accidental meeting, they went on seeing each other. She fell into the new relationship a bit like her father assumed a new role onstage. She never demanded to see Bruno, never made scenes, was content to have him when he could get away. She was still living with her parents, but she never told them or her sister. They knew she was seeing someone but did not question why she never brought him home.

These were terrible, wonderful weeks for Konstanze. The weather improved so that the countryside was available to them as never before. Bruno, trying harder now because he sensed she might call a halt at any minute, was at his most enchanting, giving her little lectures about badger life, or what goes on inside a tree. In those days the rivers and streams of Europe were much cleaner than now, and Bruno would collect fresh river water and take it home for Konstanze to wash her hair in. When they were together they kept busy, moving around or concertgoing: both knew that it was dangerous to slow down, that that would, paradoxically, hasten a breach.

When she was with Bruno, Konstanze thought about nothing but that day. She made sure she always had a surprise for him: one time it might be a pair of gloves she had found; on another occasion it was a medieval map of the area on which she had marked all the places they had visited by bicycle.

When she wasn't with him, Konstanze was very different. The day after a jaunt, she would be ready to end it again. The affair was wrong; she was strong enough to make it on her own and, in any case, she wanted children some day. That could never happen with Bruno.

She would go to confession. I was never very sure whether Konstanze's confessor was good for her or not. By today's standards, he would no doubt be regarded as terrific, since he listened to Konstanze's story and was not very censorious. He had obviously decided that here was a young, attractive woman who had got herself into a terrible predicament and that to punish her for it only added to her difficulties. Which was fine as far as it went, except that the confessor's approach simply meant that she was allowed to unburden herself every time she sat in the confessional. And that was undoubtedly therapeutic. The priest, I believe, helped the affair continue.

And so Konstanze's emotions seesawed horribly, or wonderfully, depending on the direction they were going in. One day she ate voraciously, the next nothing at all as she worried over her appearance and whether Bruno preferred her in this skirt or that—tighter—dress.

Somehow the first few traumatic days turned into weeks, then months. On the days she didn't see Bruno she felt, she had written, that there was a hand around her heart, squeezing it so that it slowed down and hurt. She hated the way her feelings were beyond her control. She imagined bumping into him as she had done that day after the doctor's and often walked miles out of her way in case that should happen; it never did. But on the days before she was to see Bruno, she developed a routine, getting ready to make herself extra pretty for him, planning their trips and so forth. Then, on the mornings of the days on which they did meet, a wonderful calm settled on her—or, rather, it arose from within her, the hand was released from around her heart and she knew, she wrote, that such a wonderful feeling could not be wrong, whatever the Catholic church might say.

Up to a point the new arrangement worked. Konstanze was not a woman to plot or scheme. In no sense did she try to ensnare Bruno. Their love affair simply suited her personality as if it had been made for her. Konstanze asked only two things. First, that she be allowed to write to him at his base. It was a way of being with him. Since Bruno's wife lived off base, and he visited her on weekends, he agreed to this. Thus the letter-writing began.

Konstanze's second condition was that Bruno make love to her. At first he was reluctant, for he was not entirely without honor, either toward his wife or Konstanze. *And,* in those days contraception was an unreliable, as well as an ugly, business. But inevitably, of course, it happened.

It was not until this point in the letters that Konstanze's Catholicism began to matter. As a fellow Catholic, I found her behavior and attitude extraordinary. Later, I began to understand.

I came to realize that, as a Catholic, she regarded Bruno as her chosen love. She had no ambitions outside of this relationship and so, believed that she should give herself to him totally. She could never marry him, barring the death of his wife, but in a sense she was willing to be a wife to him. She convinced herself that he didn't love his wife, that she— Konstanze—was really the person he had been intended for. She knew she couldn't have all of him, but she couldn't live without him, either, so she settled willingly, if not entirely happily, for what she could have. In a way it was perfect that the relationship suffered a flaw; the melancholy twist to her nature actually meant that she *enjoyed* her unhappiness.

She moved out of her parents' house and found an apartment in Munich. That was a great success, and for a while, being out of the family hothouse, her melancholic streak disappeared. Though she clearly still had enormous guilt feelings about Bruno and could not stop being a Catholic overnight, yet she was able to screen them from him when they were together. She even became flirtatious—well, as flirtatious as someone with her constitution could be.

They discovered a number of boat rides on the Isar and other rivers and would take their bicycles on board, sail downstream for an hour or so, then cycle back. Gradually—I could sense it—she began to relax. She loved picnics and was never happier than when she and Bruno had stumbled upon a new spot.

Their favorite location was on a small river, the Amper, above a watermill. Centuries before, the ox-bows of this river had been straightened by diligent monks in order to hasten the water race and, by speeding up the mill, make it more efficient. So that made the river unusual: it was flowing water and had the mini-ecology of a stream, but at that spot it was as straight as a canal. This had made it ideal for a family of kingfishers. Their vivid blue bodies hurtled along the stream just above the water line and under the tunnel of overhanging trees, dead straight like fighter planes. Bruno, I read, loved that. He climbed the willows on the banks so he could get an early warning before the blue flashes whizzed by.

One day they made love by the river and Konstanze teased Bruno wonderfully. I found myself grinning as I read the letter. At quite the wrong moment she had told him that a kingfisher had just zoomed past. The look on his face, at what he had missed, made her helpless with laughter.

When he realized it had been a joke, he playfully pretended to throw Konstanze into the river. Equally playfully, she resisted. When, however, a kingfisher really had hurtled by, Bruno had looked up and stopped what he was doing. The couple became unbalanced and, screaming and laughing, they had *both* toppled into the stream.

And so, after a fashion, they were happy. They had a routine, but she was more in love with him than he was with her; since he was married, that was probably for the best.

This balance didn't last. She had been right in her instincts: Bruno did love her and his feelings deepened and strengthened.

For his birthday she had planned a special treat, including lunch at their favorite restaurant in Munich. It took a bit of arranging but, in the end, she managed it. It poured with rain that day so it was just as well she had decided not to have a picnic, which had been her other thought.

They met at the restaurant and, as usual, Bruno was late. After he had taken off his soaking raincoat, and ordered his one glass of wine, and she had kissed him happy birthday, he had glanced at the menu.

"Good God!" he exclaimed.

"Bruno, what is it?" She appeared very calm.

"Have you seen what's on the menu?"

"What do you mean?"

For reply he beckoned to the waiter. "George, what on earth is this?"

The waiter hurried over. "What's that, Herr Bruno?" The couple were well known in the restaurant by now.

"Kingfisher's eggs, that's what. You can't eat them, can you?"

"Oh, but yes. They are delicious. We don't often get them; they are quite rare. But when we do, they always go very quickly. Would you like some?"

"No, I would *not,*" said Bruno firmly, disgusted. Then, as an afterthought: "Where do you get them from? The market?"

"No, no. They are local, from the river Amp . . ."

"Where?" Bruno exploded.

". . . the river Amper. The eggs are quite expensive and the monks can use the money."

"Damn mon—" Bruno was in the middle of speaking when Konstanze and the waiter could hold out no longer. Both of them collapsed into laughter.

"Chump," said Konstanze, lifting a package onto the table. "You'd believe anything. I hope you like this: happy birthday, darling."

Bruno, who had been bewildered for a moment, before he realized he was having his leg pulled, now marvelled at Konstanze. As a pilot in the Luftwaffe, he was used to being treated as little short of a god, by women especially. That Konstanze thought of him as all too mortal he liked. In fact he more than liked it.

By the time Konstanze had moved out of her parents' house it was already 1934. As the year turned into 1935, and Bruno was promoted, it became clear that he was falling more and more heavily for Konstanze. His letters became longer, more intimate. Hers for a time became responses to his whereas before it had been the other way around. He began to talk of having children. I gained the impression that Bruno had become a little frightened at the strength of his feeling for Konstanze and often tried out new thoughts, new ideas, on paper rather than bring them up in conversation. Whether it was the lovemaking, which Konstanze described in vivid and moving detail later, or whether Bruno's marriage was deteriorating for different reasons, eventually, he introduced into one of his letters the dreaded word. Divorce.

In one sense, of course, there was nothing either of them wanted more than for this to happen. But Bruno, now quite miserable, insufficiently appreciated Konstanze's Catholicism, which forced her to forbid divorce despite the love she felt for him. Also, her sense of the tragic was still with her after all this time. She would not let Bruno leave his wife. She had achieved a kind of tragic happiness. I imagined that she thought of herself as an amalgam of Lear's Cordelia and Faust's Margareta.

At this point I noticed—with a start—the first chalky streaks of daylight slithering into the room; the cathedral bells would soon be sounding six o'clock, but I was still wide awake, engrossed in my reading.

The more Konstanze's insistence on her tragic stance grew, the more bewildered Bruno became. He wanted to tell his wife about their affair; Konstanze forbade it. He wanted her to come to a dance at the base with him, but she had been to confession again and the priest had told her plainly that what she was doing was a sin. She could certainly *not* appear in public at a dance. He wanted a photograph of her to carry in his wallet; she said it was "too dangerous."

His letters became more frequent than once a week, and his writing, once so precise and level on the page, became unwieldy and difficult to read. He declared his love for Konstanze repeatedly in the letters of these weeks, so much so that it became monotonous and his were the only pages of the entire correspondence that I began to skip over. Then he began to discuss his wife, not her faults, as one might have expected under the circumstances, but her strengths and the reasons he had fallen in love with her and married her in the first place. Konstanze didn't recognize the warning signs. I'm not sure that I would have either, but, when his revelation came, it was not quite the surprise to me that it obviously had been for her.

His wife had guessed there was another woman. The two women had never met and never did meet, but Bruno could not have gone on loving Konstanze for very much longer without any wife in the world guessing that something was wrong. They were lucky to have had the time they did.

With the benefit of hindsight, I saw that Bruno's untidy scrawl was the first outward sign of what was going on inside his head. The second sign may have come when he started singing his wife's praises to Konstanze. He may have felt that he would lose both of them, when his wife found out about his affair, and threatened to leave him. His letters made it clear that his wife wanted to divorce him; that she was trying hard to find out through his friends who Konstanze was, so that she could cite her in the petition.

Konstanze, of course, was devastated all over again, only more so this time. Over the previous weeks she had learned to relax with Bruno, to hold the awful truth of his adultery—and her complicity—in suspension. It had never gone away entirely but it had become manageable. Now, like a huge black weight, her sin engulfed her. She could not see other women in the street as other than wives who might be wronged by someone such as she. She could look no other woman in the face, nor yet herself in the mirror. She broke down three times in confession, the third time so badly that the priest was moved to come round to her side of the confessional and comfort her. One day she had to travel out of Munich in connection with her job, and the bus went near the spot on the Isar where Bruno had first told her he was married. Again, the deep sobs were unstoppable, to the bewildered concern of the other passengers on the bus.

After this short trip, and the anguish and public discomfort it had caused her, Konstanze had returned to Munich with her mind made up. Bruno should do all he could to save his marriage. She still loved him and would remain faithful to him, but she would not marry him, even if he was divorced, because she could not recognize that divorce; her church forbade it. She advised him to devote all his attentions to his wife for a while.

Konstanze's strength, or stubbornness, must have been thoroughly perplexing to Bruno. She refused to see that his wife might never take him back and he could not believe that Konstanze would wait for him while he tried to make a new start with his wife. In his eyes he was losing both of them.

Briefly—very briefly—his letters became viciously angry. He accused Konstanze of being a masochist and a sadist, of reveling in the mess they had all created. Konstanze, I have to say, did not entirely disagree. In reply to Bruno's short, angry period, she wrote him a considerate, loving letter, in which she set out many of her own feelings on meeting him. It was from this letter that I was able to reconstruct much of their earlier relationship.

In it she admitted tacitly that there might be something of the masochist in her, that she thought she had always been destined for just such a tragic relationship as theirs had become. I cannot remember the exact words, of course, but she had concluded along these lines:

> So you see, Bruno darling, you have arrived at the emotional state I have been in since we met; one in which you fiercely love the person you cannot have completely. At last we are, in a strange way, equal. We can be together but we can never be married. We may never have children.

It was the worst letter she ever wrote. At least the worst one that I read. Konstanze was a Catholic, brought up to her own brand of interesting but futile melancholia. She could not betray her religion. Bruno was a Protestant who wanted to make a fresh start. He now loved Konstanze wholeheartedly, but for him the natural culmination of that love was, ironically, the same as the Catholic Church's: he wanted children.

After she had written the letter, Konstanze had gone away. She had met friends through her job who lived in Bernkastel. She closed up the flat and left no forwarding address. Bruno called there, and at her office; he even paid a visit to her parents' house, but no one knew where she was.

She was gone two weeks, and it was while she was away that Bruno was killed.

At the end of April, Bruno and two friends who had been with him in the box at the concert when he had first met Konstanze, had finally been awarded their "wings" and had graduated to full-pilot status within their unit. They thus joined a military elite who were the pride and joy of mothers up and down Germany, the envy of almost every schoolboy and the heroes of many young women.

The official ceremony for the graduation was a parade at which the "wings" badge was awarded, followed by a cocktail party given by the unit's commanding officer. Bruno never mentioned it in his letters, but it occurred to me that he would have attended the party, the peak of his flying career to date, without either his wife or Konstanze. Despite the fact that they were little short of gods, Bruno was probably the only young pilot at the ceremony without a woman.

However, besides the official graduation ceremony, there was an unofficial one, quite different from the commander's cocktail party. It was, in fact, a highly dangerous affair but, because the Luftwaffe was such an elite organization, and carried with it such an enviable reputation, a blind eye was turned. It was also a ceremony that was not without its poignancy as far as Bruno was concerned.

To the south of Munich, near where Konstanze and he had bicycled on their early rides, where they had watched the motor cruiser slip through those white lock gates, there were three bridges across the river Isar. Two were railway bridges, high iron cobwebs, red with rust in places. The third was a road bridge, a small but elegant suspension bridge with wires spraying out from each support like an enormous coxcomb. At some point in the days that followed the official ceremony— for obvious reasons the exact time was kept secret—new pilots from the Luftwaffe's Munich squadron were expected to take off and fly their planes under the two railway bridges and, most dangerous of all, through the suspension bridge, above the roadway and between the two sets of wires.

Each time the stunt was tried there was a hullabaloo, from the local bishops, the newspapers, and the sensible citizens, but nothing was ever done. Indeed, as I was to learn from later letters, there had only been two accidents in the seven years the Luftwaffe squadron had been stationed in Munich.

Bruno and his colleagues had made their attempt in the late afternoon of the first Wednesday in May. As sometimes happens in Europe in May or June, there was a heat wave and that may have been part of the trouble, for the air was very unstable. Another problem may have been the sun, which was setting at the time the three pilots embarked on their victory flight. Where the three bridges cross the river, the waters of the Isar flow east to west—into the setting sun—for a few miles before turning south.

The valley and the river are wide, for the most part, and so, in good conditions, for a pilot who keeps his nerve, the bridges present no real problem. But on a hot May evening, with an inexperienced, possibly emotional, pilot it is another matter.

As the youngest of the three pilots, Bruno went last. They approached the first of the bridges shortly after six o'clock. There was hardly anyone to watch as they swooped under the railway line, the twin exhausts of their early Messerschmidts rattling the metal webbing in a prolonged echo. But a passenger train was just crossing the second bridge as the three aircraft approached. The train was bound for Basle and the passengers in the dining car were just beginning to enjoy a predinner drink when, all at the same time, they noticed with horrified fascination the three black shapes shooting toward them a few feet below. In no time, however, the aircraft had come and gone, out the other side, leaving nothing but curdled air reeling like thunder under the bridge.

Then it was on to the third and final bridge.

It may have been that Bruno was flying too close to the aircraft in front of him. Perhaps he was slicing through air that had already been clotted by his colleagues in front. We will never know, but, in any event, the starboard wing of Bruno's plane clipped the outermost wire on the third—the suspension—bridge.

The wire had carved Bruno's wing in a neat way, slicing about two feet off. This meant that the forward thrust of the aircraft had scarcely been checked at all and that the bridge, save for that solitary wire, was left intact and the people on it safe. The attitude of the plane, however, had changed drastically; it wheeled and rolled downward, to its right.

Had Bruno plunged straight into the river, less of a disaster might have occurred. As it was, the Messerschmidt curled around and, almost deliberately it seemed, aimed itself, still moving at 150 knots, into a riverside gas station—the kind reserved for the refueling of barges.

The explosion occurred on impact. Bruno must have been killed instantly for his body was never found. The fire defied control for more than a day with the gas station and the Messerschmidt roasted out of recognition.

The letters did not reveal how or when Konstanze found out about Bruno's death, whether she was told privately by a friend from the base or whether she read about it in the newspaper; nor did the letters say whether she cried.

She did not go to the memorial service held in his honor—his wife would have been there. But she was sent the hymn sheet, from which she learned that his favorite had been sung, the one based on the last psalm, about praising God with music.

If Konstanze had suffered an emotional battering while Bruno was alive, it was nothing as compared with her grief now. Naturally, she blamed herself. If she had not gone away, if he had just had his mind on flying, not on her, if she hadn't been so stubborn, forcing him back to his wife; if she hadn't been so quick in leaving Munich. The tragedy—even though it fulfilled the expectations for herself that she had always held—overwhelmed her.

Her grief was crushing. It might have been even worse than that except that she discovered for herself the one prop, the one psychological device that kept her going.

Her letters to Bruno continued for a whole year after his death. Once a week, on Sunday, she sat down to write to him. She never posted the letters but she did keep them. She must have been very lonely.

His death alone may have prompted this behavior on her part but, it seemed to me, it was as likely that the return of all Konstanze's letters to Bruno, a day or so after the crash, by a fellow officer from his base, might have caused her to continue the correspondence. Presumably the letters were returned to avoid embarrassment for Bruno's widow, who had taken his other things.

It was now that Konstanze began to go over her initial meetings with Bruno, and, with this new insight, I was able to construct a full picture of their relationship and its development. She talked to him as though he were still alive. She was conversational, as intimate as ever—even, on occasion, erotic, as when she reminisced about some aspect of their lovemaking.

In these letters I found out things that at the time seemed inconsequential but later on became all-important. Things like her favorite color, her birthday, her favorite cigarettes, her shoe size, the fact that she adored asphodel—the yellow variety, not the white—mosaics, omelets and nougat. I discovered that she was a romantic about dates. She invariably remembered birthdays and anniversaries and would often know, on any particular day, what she had been doing on that date a year, two years, five years before. I found out that she was meticulous and proud about her clothes. Her parents had never been really interested in her appearance and so she had not been given many good dresses. She, for her part, was fanatical about looking clean and well-turned-out. She kept everything she had in excellent repair. She was a sentimental hoarder of things too. She kept photographs, theater programs, pressed flowers, empty perfume bottles, railway tickets. Finally, I learned that she had a secret fancy, a fetish almost, for pens. She loved new pens and could browse in stationery shops for whole afternoons without getting bored.

This was all in passing. Her letters to Bruno were far more discursive. There was, after all, no hurry now. She told him about the new things in her life that year: she was promoted in her music publishing company and in her new capacity as the editor responsible for opera she had met the famous composer Richard Strauss. His opera *The Woman Without a Shadow* was new to her and it had a profound effect, given her own situation. The opera tells of a woman who, in order to have a child, is instructed by the devil to steal another woman's shadow. This she refuses to do since it would spark tragedy for the second woman's husband. I could see why Konstanze was affected by the opera—the parallels with her own situation were all too close.

For nearly a year Konstanze kept Bruno alive, describing the concerts she had heard, the music she was publishing. She became an expert on the Luftwaffe and wrote to him of all the new details and developments she could find from the newspapers and the radio. She followed his unit, which had moved from Munich to Hamburg, and she gave him news of that. Her letters of this time were quite long, four or five pages, and must have taken an hour or more to compose. Konstanze can have done very little else on Sunday nights for nearly a year.

In fact, I had begun to wonder whether, at this stage, she could properly be called well. Everyone should grieve, but a year writing to someone who is no longer alive? She had started subscribing to aircraft magazines and described to Bruno all the refinements that were taking place.

The more the year wore on, I noticed, the more Konstanze looked back.

"Yesterday, I cycled south along the river Amper. It was a gray day, and the clouds were dirty, like the exhausts you get from trucks. There were swans on the river, very proud and lofty but they, too, were grayer than usual. The only color came from a tribe of house martins, blue-black as ink, with dashes of lemon and very, very busy. Being near the

Amper reminded me that it will be two years next Wednesday since we, or rather you, discovered that inn called The Watermill—by the bridge where they had such delicious radishes and cheese. I remember we got very merry and that you fell off your bicycle into a ditch. Very undignified for such an elite pilot! The swans I met yesterday would not have approved."

To my untutored way of thinking, her condition seemed to be deteriorating.

What saved her, I think, was that she met Rudolf. The first thing I noticed was a gap in the letters, almost ten months. After the first encounter there came a point when she stopped writing to Bruno.

When she met Rudolf there was no question that Konstanze was still in love with Bruno, or with his memory. Once again, from the later letters I was able to deduce that she didn't grow to love Rudolf for some time. He was very different from the young pilot, about whom Konstanze never told him. In no way could he be described as the kind of elitist god that Bruno, as a Luftwaffe pilot, had been. Rudolf was five or six years older than Konstanze, already a major in the Army, a professional. He was the quiet type, authoritative, serious, but not without a dry wit. He did not actively seek the company of women, as Bruno had done, and so could not be considered a ladies' man in any way.

They met through friends. Konstanze had been invited back for the weekend to Bernkastel. Rudolf had also been a guest for the weekend and the couple had, inadvertently and unexpectedly, been a great success. This was all because their host's idea of fun was to have endless games. Before dinner on the Saturday, the man had organized a wine tasting of German wines. Rudolf, who, as I already knew, was a self-taught expert on wine, romped home the clear winner. After dinner the quiz game was devoted to music. The host played tunes on his piano and the others had to guess the composer. Here, of course, Konstanze had an advantage. The host played ten tunes and Konstanze correctly identified eight of them. No one got near her, though Rudolf came second with four. The host was delighted at the success of his games and everyone applauded Konstanze.

Her prize—more a forfeit really—was to play the piano for everyone. She chose Strauss's Piano Sonata in B and it was after the applause had died down that Rudolf went up to her. They chatted. Rudolf complimented her, saying that she knew far more about music than he did about wine. She countered, saying that he knew more about music than she did about wine. He laughed, and she always remembered that. She had never made Bruno laugh and it was a new, and pleasant, sensation for her. Relaxed, and emboldened by her success, she said how much she would like to know more about wine, that it had always fascinated her but that she had never mastered its mysteries.

"There are no mysteries," Rudolf had said. "Only hard work . . . and"—he added with a jot of mischief in his eyes—"lots of practice."

Now it was her turn to smile.

Just then the butler brought them a late-night glass of champagne and, still smiling, they toasted one another.

"Do you really want to learn about wine?" asked Rudolf as they finished sipping. "Or was that just polite conversation, Munich-style?"

She registered the fact that he knew she came from Munich. Interesting. "But of course," she said. "I feel . . . well, I feel that it's a whole area of pleasure that is passing me by. As rich as music and, probably, as varied. But I know music and I miss not knowing about wine."

"May I teach you?"

Careful. She thought of Bruno. There would be so much to tell him in this week's letter. And, she acknowledged with a shiver, so much to leave out.

Something like that must have gone through her mind, for she had answered, "Well—yes . . . if you really want to."

"Good," he said, finishing his champagne. "Meet me on the bridge, tomorrow, at eleven." He drifted away then, being polite and careful not to monopolize any one of the party for too long. She had gone to bed feeling more buoyed up than she had for some time and, in the morning, changed her habit and wrote to Bruno. She had later confessed that, by writing that letter early in the day, what she wrote would be less deceitful. That's how bad her condition was at the time.

When she stepped onto the bridge a few minutes after eleven, Rudolf was already there. They shook hands formally.

"It is such a golden day," she said. "Why are you in that stuffy uniform?"

"I have been to Mass," he said apologetically. "There wasn't time to change afterward."

He was a Catholic too. Konstanze was composed. "I went early," she said. Then, in case she sounded a little too holy: "I couldn't sleep. Too much champagne."

He looked surprised, but pleased of course, that she was a Catholic also. "Let's walk by the river. That leads to Braunes, it's as good a place as any to start."

I shifted on the bed. Noises in the street told me that the working day was starting and my stomach told me that breakfast was not too far off.

Rudolf had led the way down the steps at the end of the bridge. It seemed to Konstanze as if all the wildlife in the valley had rolled down the slopes and collected at the bottom along the river. Yellow hammers and jays wheeled and dipped, moorhens—little black tugs—shunted about on the river, and sedge, in wet, clotted swags, glinted beneath the surface of the water. Looking up, it seemed as though the whole valley was swept with a green-gold wash as the sun glazed the vines.

They walked for perhaps a mile until they were well away from the town. Rudolf talked when the absence of wildlife gave him the chance. He was affectionate about their host and about his village and, I was most interested to read, said that he admired very much the local wines of Bernkastel. In a perfect world, he had sighed, he would be a wine man, not a soldier.

Why *was* he a soldier then? Konstanze had asked.

He shrugged. "My father, my grandfather. The usual reason. It runs in the family, I'm afraid, like twins or red hair. And about as useful."

She laughed again. "And where are you stationed?"

He looked at her. "Didn't you know? Munich."

It was silly but Konstanze blushed. Not only was the man single and a Catholic but he lived in the same city as she did. She blushed because she was pleased when he told her that and pleasure was for her at that time something of a novelty, and so something to feel guilty about.

He stopped on the path near a stile. "I don't know why we never met before, Konstanze . . . but I hope that from now on we shall meet often."

It was the first time anyone had said anything like that to her for a very long time. The blushes started again. She searched for a few words.

"I . . . I don't know much about . . . uniforms, army uniforms. Are you a captain, or a lieutenant . . . a general?" She trailed off.

"Major. But, now that you know my secret, forget it. Rudolf was good enough for two emperors and it's good enough for me." He led the way across the stile into the vineyard and turned back to help Konstanze. "This way."

That morning the couple visited three vineyards. Besides Braunes, they went to Schlossberg and to Doktor, so named because a Prince Bishop of Trier once believed that he was cured of an illness by the wine. In later years Konstanze would say that this wine, her first tasting of it, marked the beginning of her own recovery from the death of Bruno. Certainly, from what I could make out, the letter she wrote that weekend was one of the last she ever devoted to him.

I had read all night. The early morning noises of Salzburg rose from the street and the curtains fought a losing battle with the sun; light washed the room. Now was as good a place as any to stop, although, to judge from the piles in front of me, I was not yet halfway through the collection. I had long ago kicked off my shoes; now I shed the rest of my uniform and crept between the sheets. I called down to the front desk and left word that I was not to be disturbed. From my watch I could see that it was 6:45 A.M., but in no time I was fast asleep.

3

I awoke at two that afternoon. I shaved and hurried downstairs for a late lunch and then took a brisk walk along the riverbank for exercise. If anything, the weather was improving. It was sunny, with only the lightest of breezes, barely strong enough to carry off the river the slight and not unpleasant nip of sodden weed and mud.

I bought a paper and caught up on other events. At Nuremberg, Kaltenbrunner was still on the stand. There was no news about insurance or paper prices on the stock exchange but I did read that U.S. railroads were doing well, so was Cunard, so was cotton. I read that the West Vlahfontein gold mine, in South Africa, was to reopen, operations having been suspended in June 1940, and that, consequently, gold would not be quite so rare. Sickeningly, I read that Chrysler was doing well too.

I stuffed the newspaper into a wastebin and went back to the letters. I thought I could see a line of interrogation developing and I was anxious to discover what was in the remainder.

As I entered the Goldener Hirsch the receptionist waved a piece of paper at me but I motioned for him to put it back in my pigeonhole. It would be from Hobel and I now wanted to avoid him until I had finished the letters. Then at least I would be able to tell him my plans for interrogating Mrs. von Zell. I would simply pretend that I hadn't received his note, which, in a sense, would be true. A white lie.

The high afternoon sun slanted into my room, drenching in light six bottles of beer which I had placed on the table in anticipation of another long session. I opened one, sat back in my chair and picked up the next batch of letters.

Major von Zell drove Konstanze back to Munich in his official car after the weekend. He had bought some wine for her at the vineyards they had visited and she invited him to dinner to help her drink it, and to teach her more about wines in general. She promised to play the piano for him.

They met several times more and began to make discoveries about each other. Like the fact that they were both more religious than they had let on when they had been talking about Mass on Bernkastel Bridge. They would enjoy—really savor—going to the church of St. John Nepomuk in Munich on Sundays. The music was of a high standard, which is why Konstanze went, and she was able to teach Rudolf about the organ, which, until that point, had been one of his least favorite instruments.

They also found that they both had a weakness for apples, not always plentiful in those days, and that they both disliked pets, especially dogs.

Rudolf's passion, besides wine, was rivers. Not what went on around them, but what happened in them. He was knowledgeable about the botany and biology of rivers and he was also a keen explorer. Over the next weeks and months, I read, he took Konstanze farther and farther afield. They started, ironically enough, with the Isar, visiting among other places the lock with the white gates where Bruno had first confessed to Konstanze that he was married, which, of course, she never mentioned to Rudolf. What would have been the point? They explored the Inn River and the deep valley between the Patscherkofel and the Hafelekar Spitze, the Würm, the Rissbach and, eventually, the Danube itself. I read very closely the letters that described their voyage down the Danube, for this journey took them through Linz and right by the famous monastery of Melk, with its twin towers overshadowing the river. It took them on into Wachau, to the region where Maurice's men were still searching on my behalf. But, to begin with, Konstanze's letters revealed nothing specific that might be of help.

As I have said, it was some time before Konstanze came to love Rudolf. But in some ways he was, from the start, better for her than Bruno had been. For example, since he was in no sense an heroic or tragic figure, that side of her nature had to take a backseat. Rudolf was down-to-earth, not what you would call an outrageously romantic figure, but then neither was he undemonstrative. He would send her little gifts—yellow flowers of some kind, which he knew were her favorites—and he, too, would remember dates, like the anniversary of their first meeting, or the first time they had heard a Bruckner organ concert. He knew those things, however silly, were important to her. He quickly developed his own nickname for her—Stanzl—and that, being young and tomboyish in its associations, forced Konstanze still further from her melancholic self-image and brought her back safely from the edge she had been near when she had first met him.

She bought plenty of new clothes, which she could afford because of her promotion, became reasonably knowledgeable about wines, and together they took out a subscription to the Munich Opera and became a familiar couple there. Her parents were never mentioned. Rudolf, so it seemed to me, had by his manner rescued her from her melancholy nature.

Sex alone posed a problem. They were both a long way from being teenagers, but at the same time they were each devout Catholics. Curiously, I believe that music had a great deal to do with the fact that Konstanze and Rudi, which was now her nickname for him, never slept together before they were married. Their love of music took them to the cathedral every Sunday, and on many other occasions also, and that helped to keep alive their faith, to force them into confession and to keep their consciences to the fore. In turn, that may have made them get married sooner than otherwise.

Though Rudolf was not the romantic figure Bruno had been, he was

determined to be imaginative about his courtship of Konstanze. For
instance, he proposed to her while they were sailing down the Danube,
at Passau, where the waters flowed from Germany, his country, into
Austria, the land of her ancestors. Konstanze, I was not surprised to read,
did not accept him straightaway. Rudolf, so I gathered, was not disappointed. He had expected to be turned down and when she gave no
answer either way he was, if anything, optimistic rather than the reverse.
Two weeks later it was Haydn's birthday and they went to Mass to hear a
special concert. She whispered her acceptance as they received the sacra-
ments.

They did not rush into marriage immediately. Rudolf had met Konstanze's parents once or twice I discovered and I suspect they found him
rather dull—but she had never met his mother. Rudi was from Worms,
as I already knew. And it was because Worms was on the Rhine and so
close to the Mosel that he had developed his interest in both rivers and
wine.

Rudolf's mother had been relieved that her son had found a Catholic
girl and delighted that she was as serious as Konstanze. For some reason
Mrs. von Zell regarded music as a serious profession.

Konstanze, for her part, naturally compared Mrs. von Zell with her
own parents. This was a new experience for her since she had never met
Bruno's family. She found her future mother-in-law on the old-fashioned
side but also a stabilizing influence in Rudolf's life that she had never
had with her own parents. The first time the two women met, Rudolf's
mother talked about his boyhood in an affectionate way, showing almost
total recall. Obviously, he came first with his mother in a way that
Konstanze and her sister had never done with their parents. I read that
on their first visit to Worms, Rudolf and Konstanze had gone for a walk
with Mrs. von Zell across the family farmland. The older woman had
pointed out the fence where her husband, Rudolf's father, had been
killed, thrown in a hunting accident. She gestured to the copse where, as
a boy, Rudolf used to hide when he ran away from home. It was apparently a regular practice and the family always knew where to find him.
The idea of the quiet, efficient, down-to-earth Rudolf being out of control enough to run away delighted Konstanze.

On this walk Konstanze had been fortunate to find, in the copse, an
entire family of yellow hammers and was able to win Mrs. von Zell by
her knowledge of the creatures' habits and behavior. So effective had she

been that, on her second visit to Worms, Mrs. von Zell had given Konstanze a neck brooch, yellowish diamonds set in an ivory carving of a bird, which had been her grandmother's. It was the first gift of any real value that Konstanze had received and she swelled with pleasure inside. Thereafter she wore the brooch whenever she could.

Rudolf's second original move was the wedding itself. He persuaded the owner of the castle where they had first met, the host from Bernkastel who loved games, to let them be married there. He was a Catholic also and there was a private chapel in the castle.

It was exactly the sort of gesture which Konstanze relished. They were married, typically, on Schubert's birthday, in front of about forty people, including Konstanze's parents, of course, and Eric von Haltern. Konstanze wore a long cream dress with the diamond and ivory brooch at her throat. She carried—naturally—a small bunch of yellow asphodel.

She confessed later, when she *was* in love with Rudi, that she had not been so on the day they were married. Fond—yes. Learning to love him —yes. But at the time she did not feel for Rudolf what she had felt for Bruno. Among the hymns sung during the ceremony was Bruno's favorite, which had been played at his memorial service, the one based on Psalm 150, about music and the praise of God. She didn't tell Rudi why she had chosen it.

The honeymoon was, inevitably perhaps, spent exploring a river new to both of them: the Loire. Starting at Orléans, they visited Blois, Tours, Saumur and Angers and introduced themselves to the wines of Anjou and Jasnieres, Muscadet and Quincy, Sancerre and Reuilly. After ten days they returned via Paris, where Konstanze was able to hear Artur Rubinstein in concert.

Back in Munich, they moved into a fairly large house in the Grünwald district; it had a garden and was near the river. To begin with, Konstanze kept her job at the music publishers and to their rapidly expanding circle of friends they were a colorful couple. They turned one of the rooms in their house into a music room and lined it with wine bottles. Their parties were always a great success.

Remember that I had to piece together this phase in Konstanze and Rudolf's relationship from letters written somewhat later since, as they were man and wife living together, there was not much need for correspondence. I worked out from these later letters that it was about this time, just after their marriage in 1937, that Rudolf was promoted from major to colonel. This was good news—up to a point. It meant recognition for Rudolf, for although he was older than Konstanze, he was still relatively young in army terms. It meant more pay, and it was from this time, I think, that the couple began to think about having a family. But the higher you went in the German Army in those days, the harder it became to escape contact with the Nazis. The letters were not clear about when exactly he joined the Party but it must have been around the time he was promoted to colonel. Otherwise, I doubt very much if more promotion would have come his way.

I also noticed from the same batch of retrospective letters, mostly written by Konstanze after Rudolf had been posted to Berlin, of which more later, that it was about this time that the couple took a second trip down the Danube, accompanied on this occasion by Eric von Haltern. I cannot remember exactly but it must have been later in 1937. This was not the time when they researched their wine article but it was this trip, and their visits to vineyards, which gave them the idea to write it later.

I was about to open another bottle of beer when I saw, in Konstanze's handwriting, the names of three specific vineyards they had visited: Traeger, Kleiber and Salz. At last!

I opened the beer and looked at my watch. It was already eight o'clock. I had burned my boats with Hobel. Since I had not been back to him, he would think that I had left Salzburg, against his orders. It was too late to do anything tonight, but tomorrow I would try to calm him down. My plans for the interrogation of Mrs. von Zell were coming along and I should finish the letters sometime during the coming night.

But first I had to call Maurice.

The woman on the hotel switchboard said that Major Hobel had tried to reach me three times during the afternoon but that since I had been so strict with my embargo, they had not disturbed me. I thanked her and said I would buy her a drink for her courtesy.

It took about twenty minutes to get through to Vienna at that time of night but Maurice was still at the office.

"No wenching tonight, Maurice?"

He howled into the phone. "Jeeesus, you have a cheek, Wolff. I cancel a bloody date, what we in Vienna call an assignation, so that I can be here in the office when my man calls from the Wachau, just in case we have found your goddamn runaway Nazi. And what do I get for my trouble? Hassle. If Hermann *is* pregnant, I hope he lays his pups in *your* shirts."

I smiled into the phone. When Maurice was truly angry, he went deadly silent. "So you haven't heard from your man yet?"

"Too bloody right, I haven't. He should have called two hours ago."

"Is that good news?"

"Might be. Might mean his car wouldn't start. Might mean *he's* got an assignation. How long did it take for you to get through?"

"Twenty minutes."

"If he's calling from a small town, or a village, it might take him hours to get through. The phones here are as unreliable as an Italian tank. Sorry we've nothing more concrete. What news from Wall Street, dear boy? Am I a millionaire yet?"

I ignored him. "I'm sorry to upset your love life, Maurice, but it *is* important. Now listen, I have some more information, more specific details." I told him about Konstanze's letter. "So if, when your man calls, he *hasn't* found von Zell, ask him if he's tried those three vineyards —Traeger, Kleiber and Salz. If he has checked them out already, and drawn a blank, then call him off and thanks for your help. But if any of those three have not been checked, could you ask him to do so? Please?"

Maurice hesitated. That was unlike him. He must be under some pressure of his own, something he wasn't telling me about. Perhaps that was the real reason he was working so late.

"Maurice . . ." I stammered. "If it puts you in a difficult situ—"

"Dear boy, don't jabber. Where are you?" I told him. "Don't leave. I'll get back to you tonight, I promise. Have dinner in the hotel, if you must eat. We have to get this thing tidied up."

I was grateful to Maurice. I recognized the signs; he *was* under pressure of his own and was deliberately not telling me. He was a good friend. I gave him the latest on our race.

"A thousand and thirty-six, Maurice, that's what you're worth."

"Is that all? I thought Hartt was a genius?"

"Don't moan, Maurice. You might have had *my* shares which have slipped to under nine hundred. Eight hundred and sixty-eight. So you're doing relatively well."

"Mmmnnn. Looks like the helmet's mine, dear boy. Sorry about that too."

As I ate dinner, I wondered whether it was a good sign that his man had not yet reported back. If he *had* found von Zell then, besides a medal, for wrecking the underground conduit, I reckoned I could go home soon. Coming on top of the Crown Jewels affair, I would be a hero. Maybe there would be a book of my reminiscences, or a movie even. I had been told several times that I bore a passing likeness to Gregory Peck; maybe he would like to play me. I chuckled, still recovering from my night with the letters.

If Konstanze's condition had been deteriorating before she met Rudolf, my own condition was also deteriorating. By the time I had finished dinner, and no doubt because I had an entire bottle of wine inside me, I talked to myself as if the whole thing was sewn up. What an ass I was.

The phone was ringing as I reached my room.

"Dear boy, did you enjoy your dinner?"

"Maurice! What news?"

"Bad—and good. My man just came through. The reason he was so late was because he thought he had found your man. Someone answering von Zell's description, dark-haired with a dueling scar, worked in a vineyard at Kottes until last week."

"Yes—go on!"

"Well, it's difficult to know exactly what we have. He answers your description but his name was Aubing, Franz-Josef Aubing."

I didn't know what to think. The man's name spoiled my theory but. . . . "What was his job at the vineyard?"

"Accountant."

"Why did he leave?"

"A woman, so he said. He was getting married to a girl in Zurich and was going to live there."

It might be true, and it might not be.

"Which vineyard was that, Maurice?"

"Let me see." There was a pause as Maurice searched his notes. "Mmmmm . . . Mildorfer. Not one of your top three, I am afraid."

"What about those three names, Maurice? Has your man checked them out?"

"Two of them, he has. Hold on. . . ." He looked back at his notes. "Yes, he's been to Salz and to Kleiber but not to Traeger. Never heard of it. Do you know where it is?"

"Sorry, just that it's near the Danube and in the Wachau region." I was thinking fast. "Maurice, you've been terrific; I owe you a big favor.

But could you *please* have your man find the Traeger vineyard and check it out? I would kick myself if it turned out that's where von Zell was hiding and we had overlooked it. Leave this Aubing character to me. I believe I know the man to find him. Another day, Maurice, please. Give me your men for another day—to find Traeger?" I was pleading.

"Dear boy, don't get in such a state. The war's over, you know. Of course you may have them. I just hope they can find this Traeger place in one day."

"Bless you, Maurice," I said. "I owe you two favors. And I tell you what—"

"What?" he butted in.

"When Hermann delivers, *you* can choose the names of the pups. Is that fair?"

"Thank you *very* much. I can tell you now that Walter will not be one of them. Now good night. One may keep a lady waiting but not a cognac."

I looked at my watch: 10:45 and too late to make the second call to Vienna that I had planned. It would have to wait until the next day. There were still some beers left on the table from the afternoon, so I opened one of them, lay on the bed and kicked off my shoes. I picked up the next batch of letters.

4

I read a few letters but nothing very significant happened for a while. I did learn that Konstanze's favorite character in the Bible was Paul and her favorite story the one about his conversion. Again, I believe she found parallels with her own situation; in a way she was being converted also, from not loving Rudolf to loving him. And I found out that she had a sweet tooth for chocolate as well as nougat. These things meant little to me at the time; it was only later that I was able to make crucial use of facts like these.

The next thing of real importance to be reported in the letters occurred in early 1938, when Konstanze found that she was pregnant. The child was very welcome, not least among their friends, who, I gathered, found a great deal of amusement in the couple's behavior during Konstanze's confinement. Instead of spending the usual amount of time that ordinary parents devote to the names they will give to their son or daughter, the von Zells expended their energy trying to decide what instrument he or she should play. Konstanze favored the oboe, whose creamy murmur probably satisfied some final vestige of the melancholic hidden inside her. Rudi preferred the cello, which, he said forthrightly in his letters, offered greater satisfaction, being a sensual instrument to play, using most of the body, with a broad range and producing the most "composed" of tones. That was the word he had used and, later, I was to pick it out as the word which best described his wife. Composed, Rudolf said in one of his lyrical sections, meant the best possible combination of independence and understanding for others. And that was why I applied it to Konstanze. But I am running ahead.

Before Konstanze could give birth, their happy period of anticipation was roughly disturbed. Rudolf was promoted again, to full colonel. This meant a large pay raise but, more important, it also followed that he was admitted to an inner circle of men with great influence. It was 1938 and the world was preparing for war.

He had to leave Munich, and his pregnant wife, for Berlin. Someone on Martin Bormann's staff, an old friend of Rudolf's from Worms, had recommended him. It meant an exciting life for Rudolf: power, prestige, fame even, if Germany were to win the coming war. But it also meant of course that he had to embrace the aims and ideals, if you can call them that, of the Nazi Party.

Again, I had to reconstruct all this from later letters. This part was particularly difficult since Konstanze and Rudolf never discussed politics in their letters so I never had any real idea what sort of Nazi Rudolf was. I never knew whether he was an enthusiastic brute, someone who ran with the crowd, or a reluctant convert, though, I suppose, as a colonel, he couldn't have been *that*.

In the later letters Konstanze was also to describe their rending farewell at Munich's *hauptbahnhof*. They had gifts for each other. She had bought him a new biography of Schubert; he had saved and secretly bought her a bracelet, tiny diamonds set in an ivory band, to go with the brooch his mother had given her. By this time, too, they had begun their practice of listening to concerts together on the radio and they promised each other they would continue to do so, each Thursday and Sunday, as a way of being together, even though Munich was nearly a thousand kilometers from Berlin.

And so Rudolf left. Three weeks later Germany annexed Austria.

With Konstanze separated from Rudi, pregnant, and the political situation constantly deteriorating, it was no surprise to find that the letters started up again.

Konstanze's letters were not so long now, compared with those she had written to Bruno, and they were less self-indulgent. Her sense of the tragic was absent. In one way, however, the letters were just as unreal— they had a pact never to mention the war. It was prompted by Konstanze but Rudolf didn't need much persuading; it was something they both wanted. Whatever it meant, they agreed to keep the war and Nazism out of their private life.

Konstanze wrote every week and so did Rudolf. I was surprised to find that his were handwritten, not dictated or typed. And I watched with interest as his style developed: stilted at first and not at all intimate; but, with Konstanze's example, this undemonstrative German soldier blossomed to become in time more oblique, more lyrical.

In one letter that I remember vividly Rudolf described the parts of his wife's body that he missed the most. This is of course precisely the sort of letter that I should never have read. But I did.

Stanzl, dearest . . . [He always started his letters differently, that was another original touch which I liked and admired.]

It is 2:00 A.M. and I am having to snatch a few moments to write while I can. We are all busy, bobbing in and out of our offices just like those moorhens we watched on our first walk in Bernkastel. Anyone would think there was a war on.

But busyness is all on the outside—what is going on inside my head is what counts. And my head cannot stop thinking about your body, swelling now with a little soul inside, someone who will grow up in a greater Germany, or else in an unthinkable wasteland.

I picture you lying in bed, perhaps uncomfortable now, not knowing which way to hold yourself. And I miss you. You won't know this yet, for I do not think I have ever told you, but since our first trip on the Danube, I have had my favorite places on your body. Just as when we were on our honeymoon, and you preferred Blois to Saumur, Sancerre to Quincy (or was it the other way around?), so there are parts of you that I prefer. Not that I loathe the others, of course, simply that some are what we would label here "For my eyes only."

One you have not even glimpsed, save perhaps in a mirror, is the deep, shapely runnel at the base of your back, the most sunken spinal column I have ever seen, deeper than I thought a spine ever *could* be, until I saw yours. It is more beautiful than anything I could find on the nudes in the Alta Pinakothek, which, as you know, are all I have to compare you with, not being a widely experienced man.

Second, I miss your ankles—yes, don't laugh. Women underrate ankles, I think. A woman who is glamorous, who has the kind of cheekbones you see on models, who has a good figure and the right sort of posture, is spoiled totally if her ankles are too thick or too thin. And the worst of it is—there is nothing to be done about it. A brassiere can help her figure; makeup can improve her skin and totally transform her eyes; the right shoes may—just—alter her overall proportions. But the ankles are there for all to see and cannot be changed.

Third, I miss that horrible scar at the top of your thigh. Only a delightful tomboy who climbed trees to steal fruit, or got herself chased by a farmer because she had frightened his geese and then fell over a wire fence, could get a scar like that. Perhaps you have never noticed, but sometimes, when we make love, or rather before we make love, I touch your scar in the dark. When I do that I feel very tender toward you but sad, in a way, that I didn't know you then, when, almost certainly, you were even lovelier than you are now. If we could have been lovers then, how much less time we would have wasted.

I must go, but one last thing. You know what I think of A.H., but one thing I do agree with him about is the Bruckner center at Linz. In case I haven't told you, Hitler wants to build a Bruckner hall on the Danube because B was an organist near Linz for ages and wrote most of his symphonies there. Rather like Bayreuth and Wagner. It's a marvelous idea and it reminds me that there is a performance of B's Mass, in E, being broadcast on Sunday. I shall listen here in Berlin. I now have a radio in my office. If you were to listen, I should feel very close to you.

My love to you and a small prayer for the soul we and God are creating inside you. R.

Rudolf, it appeared, managed to get away from Berlin every six weeks or so for a long weekend, when he would spend the time with Konstanze in Munich. Despite the war the couple were very happy. Each was now fulfilled by the other, complete and unambitious for anything, or anyone, else. As Konstanze became more knowledgeable about wine, the language of the wine snobs provided them with much amusement. For instance, when Rudolf was unusually pompous in one of his letters, or just plain wrong about something, she would refer to him as her little Goldtröpchen, a wine which, she wrote, was a bit like a Zurich banker, "safe but dull." If she was coquettish, or a shade too persnickety in her letters, Rudolf would tell her to be more careful or she would go the way of Brunellesco, an Italian concoction which should not be touched for fifty years.

And Rudi took up the piano. Which meant that, from then on, they started to occasionally enclose music with their letters and he would report progress on what he could play.

The baby arrived. It was a boy and there were no serious complications or worrying delay. In the weeks that followed, both Konstanze and Rudolf appeared extravagantly, prodigiously happy, and for ages talk of the baby, its personality and its progress, took up nearly all of the ink in their correspondence. Rudolf went home immediately after the birth on special leave and accompanied by a magnum of champagne from Bormann himself. Konstanze was already back on her feet by the time he arrived so they left the infant with Rudolf's mother, who was in Munich to visit her grandchild, and motored to the Isar to open the champagne there.

I skipped across most of this domestic chatter, except for one point that did claim my attention.

I had almost forgotten the existence of Bruno by this point, but, when it came to the christening of their son, he was given the names Dieter Anton Bruno von Zell. Dieter had been Rudolf's father's name, Anton was for Bruckner, and Bruno was for—Bruno.

I didn't know whether to feel touched by this or vaguely disturbed. I had assumed that by now Konstanze had put the pilot behind her, but here she was naming her child after him. Rudolf, as far as I could make out, never knew the real reason why she named their boy Bruno and I concluded that Konstanze always kept the existence and the fate of the pilot a secret from her husband.

On the other hand, it was about this time that Konstanze told Rudolf that she had finally come to love him. It must have been some time in 1940 or thereabouts. The phony war, as it was called in Europe, when war had been declared but hostilities had not started in earnest, was over and the battle of Britain was just beginning. It was a very hectic time for Rudolf and, I noticed from the dates on the letters, he was not writing as regularly as he had been. Perhaps that was the first time Konstanze realized how much she depended on Rudolf emotionally, how much she *liked* him, how supportive of her he was.

All sorts of things were probably going on inside her head. It occurred to me that the war may have reawakened in her some of her old tragic self-consciousness—her letters did get a shade indulgent, if not yet melancholic. Later, it also crossed my mind that naming her son after Bruno might have been the act that finally laid his memory to rest. Knowing Konstanze as I now felt I did, I thought that she might have harbored some need to pay a final tribute to him and giving his name to her son was that tribute. Bruno would live on, she had restored him to life after having had a hand in his death. And, once it was done, she could forget him and get on with the business of learning to love Rudolf.

Later, in 1941, they visited the Rhône, then in Vichy France. In 1942 they went to Prague and traveled down the Elbe; also in that year they took in the Garonne and the *canal du midi.* Finally, in 1943 they visited Arezzo and followed the Arno to Florence and Pisa.

With prodigious calmness, they kept up their letters, their concert-listening, their music-swapping. I found myself, not for the first time, envying them. True, in 1943, Konstanze complained that she was seeing less and less of Rudolf, but that was the only shadow.

And that changed, or appeared to, late in the same year when Rudolf was transferred to Berchtesgaden. This was where Hitler's own retreat was located, where he would sometimes spend his weekends, so the transfer did not mean that Rudolf was in any way demoted. Quite the contrary. I got the impression he had been sent because he was a man to be trusted outside Berlin, away from the entourage around the Führer.

Rudolf was put in charge of the arrangements for the Führermuseum, which Hitler planned for Linz. As part of this, he also had to help arrange the administration of the salt mine at Alt Aussee in Austria, where all the so-called liberated art, from museums in France and Italy, and from the great Jewish collections of Paris, Vienna or Siena, was to be hidden until after the war.

It was about this time that the couple found a house at Mondsee, on the edge of an enchanting small lake just outside of Salzburg in Austria. Konstanze had given up her job when Dieter was born and was delighted with the move to the country both for the boy's sake; and her own. Also, she would be near Rudolf. I wasn't so sure that he had bought the house simply for the convenience of his wife and child. I suspected that early in the game von Zell had begun to think that the war might go against Germany and that, afterward, living in Austria would be better than living in Germany. But nothing was ever said in the letters.

Whatever the reason, things continued to go well for Rudolf and Konstanze after the move. He was able to get home every weekend and they would walk in the mountains and explore the Salzach River, not the least of whose attractions were the waterfalls at Krimml, which Konstanze once described as "crowded with light."

At this time, when they were seeing a lot of each other, relatively speaking, Konstanze took up cooking more seriously and took advantage also of the space they had in Mondsee to make a kitchen garden. They resurrected their Munich concept of music room cum wine cellar. Another advantage of Mondsee, so I learned, was the village church, which had an impressive organ, and the family became a familiar sight on Sundays.

The love between them by now seemed to be fairly equal. Konstanze had at last "caught up." Her letters to Rudi were very affectionate and sentimental. She would remind him of any anniversary to do with Dieter —when he had cut his first tooth, for instance, or taken his first steps. She even remembered Bormann's birthday for Rudolf.

They had, with enviable skill, transferred their happiness from Munich to Mondsee, and so it was ironic that no sooner had they settled into their new life than the Allies invaded France, soon to be followed by the push north, from Africa into Italy. The final squeeze had begun.

The letter-writing continued, less frequently perhaps, but if so not by much. Shorter letters, but no less loving. In fact, the turning of the tide in military terms had mixed consequences for the von Zells. It meant that they saw less of each other, since Rudi was so busy, but they could look forward also to a time when the war would be over, when Rudolf could leave the Army and they could be completely on their own again.

By now, I judged, the tables had been turned and Konstanze was, if anything, more in love with Rudi than he was with her. To prove it, the less they saw of each other, the more she took care to make her letters intimate, to show him how much she missed him. Dieter had developed a touch of TB and a slight problem with his eyes but nonetheless had expressed a wish to learn the piano! And so, Konstanze wrote, there would soon be *three* pianists in the family. Not even Schubert wrote pieces for *six* hands.

Also, Konstanze's letters took on a definite erotic flavor. In no way pornographic but merely more explicit in her tender expressions of longing. This may have been triggered by the increasingly bleak news about the conduct of the war, meaning that the sense of impermanence at last got to her. I don't know. I'm not sure either whether I should have read those erotic letters of hers. But I did.

One nickname she sometimes used for Rudi was "Musketeer," which she thought had a proud romantic ring to it. I can remember at least one letter of this period which began like that.

Dear Mad Musketeer,

Dieter is asleep, more snow has fallen and everything is quiet. I listened to the concert tonight as, I hope, did you. Bruckner was never lovelier. Now I am alone, with just one light on in the whole house, so I may see to write to you. The light throws a yellow beam through the window onto the smooth snow, white and untouched, like the skin on my belly.

I wonder why we have never made love in the snow. I laugh as I write this. I am sure it would be *very* uncomfortable. But wouldn't it be lovely to be outside in the fresh air, surrounded by it, *and* warm? Do you remember the evening by the Elbe two years ago? There was no snow but it was very cold and our breath was like stabs of steam. The war will end soon and there will be snow every year. We have time.

Do you know how I miss you, my darling? My prayers, tonight and every night, are for you and our dear son.

I kiss you and put out the light. K.

By Christmas 1944 the letters finally started to show signs of change. Rudolf's got shorter and more irregular. Eventually he said he was returning her letters because, if there *was* a collapse, he didn't know what would happen or how safe he would be.

And that explained how Konstanze came to be in possession of the whole three-way correspondence.

When the collapse did come and Rudolf disappeared, the letters stopped entirely for a while. Then something interesting happened. Just as she had done with Bruno, Konstanze took to writing letters but did not post them. What did that mean? I asked myself. Could it be that Rudolf was, after all, dead? Surely there would have been acknowledgment of the fact somewhere in the letters. No, he wasn't dead.

I examined these letters carefully. And, on inspection, I could see that they were not at all like her last letters had been to Bruno—they were more chatty, less tragic. She wrote about music, their son, about wine and their kitchen garden, and developments at the church in the village, where she was now deputy organist. As I read these letters I began to realize what was going on. No place names, other than those in the immediate vicinity of Mondsee, were ever mentioned. There was no reference to the future; everything was in the past tense. But, in fact, the letters of this period were written almost as a diary, as a record, a reminder of what took place. She continued to record Dieter's progress, with his handwriting, his awareness of wildlife, the friends he had made. The fact that his TB got better but never disappeared entirely. Konstanze even included photographs to go with the chronology. And she included details of who had been born in the village, who had been married, whose funerals she had played at. She enclosed little snippets from the newspaper—where the fishing was particularly good on the lake, which stretches of the Salzach looked like they were becoming polluted, which of the locals was in favor of the new road planned to link Mondsee and Salzburg and which ones were against it. The politics of the local chamber of commerce.

These letters became a record, a means by which Rudolf could catch up on life in Mondsee *when he came home.* Konstanze might think, if anyone took the trouble to read her letters, as I was now doing, that she had written to a dead man before, as her way of grieving, and that she was now doing so again. I was not convinced. She might not know exactly where her husband was, might have to contact him through an intermediary, but she had access, of that I had not the slightest doubt.

The fact that she might be able to reach Rudolf only with difficulty suggested to me two things. First, that one of my hunches about him must be right—he was masquerading as someone else so that *he* had to contact her. Or he was hiding out in the mountains, part of the covey of exiles I had seen with Allie. Second, it began to look as though he was in charge of this conduit which ferried ex-Nazis to safety. He was an able administrator, a man who had access to the top echelons of the Nazi Party; he knew everyone. He had his hands on the funds; and, if he was not in some way involved in the running of the pipeline, surely he would have taken advantage of it himself by now, gone to South America and sent for his wife and child.

In 1946 it was not yet all that obvious that many ex-Nazis, or Nazi sympathizers, would retain their positions and their influence in postwar Germany. Rudolf possibly knew his Germany better than most and may have realized that, in running the conduit and helping some powerful people to safety, he, in his turn, would be looked after. It had occurred to me that this is why he had bought the house in Mondsee. Perhaps Bormann or Hitler himself had seen the end coming, put von Zell in charge of building up the pipeline and then authorized the confiscation of the gold coins.

I picked up the last letter, the last only in the sense that it had been written shortly before Lieutenant Bloch interrogated Konstanze and confiscated her papers. So there was no suggestion of this last letter being a final episode in a story I had been intrigued by and enchanted with, a tale which had spanned more than ten years and taken me thirty solid hours to read. There was no feeling of climax or conclusion. The letter simply went on for a couple of pages, then trailed off, as a run-of-the-mill letter does.

Dieter had started to learn English at school because Konstanze agreed with the local headmaster that English was the language of the future. The Salzburg festival, abandoned in 1944, was to be revived that year, though the new Strauss opera, *Die Liebe der Danae*, which had been in rehearsal when the cancellation had been announced, was not to be brought back. Having once been Strauss' editor, she was disappointed. There were no elaborate endearments in this last letter, save for a brief "I miss you" at the very end. Presumably, Konstanze felt that was how it should be if Rudolf was supposed to be dead. But this one did have a P.S.

Dieter has at last mastered the bicycle. Better still, I have managed to wangle one which fits him from Herr Polten, that small, roly-poly man who helps the butcher. We have already ridden around the lake almost as far as Plomberg. What a pity we cannot make the ride together, the three of us. The road goes right by that spot on the lake where the good fish may be found. K.

I looked at the postscript again. Something—I couldn't think what—was scraping at the back of my brain. I lay on the bed, chewing my lip. It would soon be light. The trees lining the river, a hundred meters away, were alive with the rustle and chatter of birds. The last sentence of the postscript was half familiar. No, that wasn't quite true. Then it came to me.

After she had first started writing to Rudolf, while Bruno's memory was still far from dead, he had used the word "never" in one of his letters when, strictly speaking, he had not meant it. Something like "It will never work," meaning, "I'm not in favor of it."

Konstanze had scolded him. " 'Never' is an awful word if you don't mean it. When I was a child, no more than six, I did something to annoy my father; in anger, he said he never wanted to see me again. Then, the next day, before I awoke, he left on tour for two weeks. I didn't understand where he was. I was too young to know what a tour was, and, in any case, two weeks is an eternity to a six-year-old. For all that time I thought I was never going to see him again. I was desolate. He, of course, had forgotten what he had said, but I never did and I never have. Since then I have tried never to say the word except when I mean it."

I pulled the letter containing this exchange from earlier in the correspondence and I recalled Konstanze's letters to Bruno. She had used "never" when she wrote that they could never be married, never have children—when she had meant it. Throughout her last letters to him, when he was dead, she had used it quite a lot too. I now checked back to be doubly certain. Yes, I was right.

In her letters to Rudolf she hardly ever used the word. She never exaggerated the meaning and used the word only when the sense justified it; at all other times she used a simple negative. So when she wrote "What a pity we cannot make the ride together . . ." she emphatically did *not* mean "What a pity we can *never* make the ride together. . . ." That word gave her away. Rudolf wasn't dead. He was alive. She was in touch with him, if not regularly then occasionally, and looked forward to a time when they could be together again.

I folded the letter and replaced it on the pile. I put the various packets together and carefully tied the blue ribbon around them. I slipped the bundle into my briefcase. Then I lay back on the bed and switched off the lamp. It was 5:30 A.M. and the light showing through the curtains was beginning to sweep away the shadows. I was tired and not a little sad that I had come to the end of the story. Bruno I wasn't sure about. But I liked the Rudolf of the letters. As for Konstanze, I think I already felt more than liking. I couldn't wait to meet her.

I fell asleep without taking off the rest of my uniform.

CHAPTER FOUR

1

I slept through lunch and reached the office only at three that same afternoon. On my desk top there was yet another envelope in my wife's handwriting, which reminded me that I had still not opened her earlier letter or the one from my mother. I put the new one in my tunic pocket, promising myself that I would open it later.

I was also surprised to find a hand-scribbled note saying that a Lieutenant Ghent had phoned from Vienna.

"Dear boy," he said, when I got through. "I called at noon and they said you were asleep and not to be disturbed. What on earth are you doing in bed at such an hour? Anything I should be jealous about?"

"You've got an easily aroused imagination, Maurice. Well, my friend, do we have anything?"

"Sorry, Walter, but we found Traeger easily and my man went down there first thing this morning. The place is closed up; it went out of business two years ago when the owners got permission to rezone the land. They promptly sold it and someone's building on it now. Forty houses and a hospital. The main house is still there but closed, waiting for someone who wants to live in a large house surrounded by forty smaller ones."

I groaned. My "cleverness" had really backfired this time. My theory about the vineyard had been wrong from the start and I should have known it. I had insisted on the search when all the evidence showed that I was reading too much into too little.

"Are you there, dear boy?" Maurice asked, after I had been silent for too long. "Show signs of life, will you?"

"Yes, I'm here," I sighed. "But for how much longer, I don't know. I haven't got much to show for all my effort. The C.O. here will not be pleased."

"The future could be worse," said Maurice, trying to sound cheerful. "Hermann might still lay her pups in your shirts."

"You are about as comical as Mussolini, Maurice. And deserve the same fate. I know I owe you a favor but perhaps you'll think I've repaid you already with that introduction to Sammy Hartt." And I told him about the state of his shares and how far ahead of me he was.

"What can I say, dear boy? Splendid, absolutely splendid. No more than I deserve, of course, but keep your chin up. You're not going to make a very good American after you return to California, are you? Don't be so pessimistic. Where are we now? . . . April 3. Nearly two months to the finishing wire. Anything can happen, Walter. Anything."

"Yes," I joked. "You could recover those Italian old masters you're looking for. That would put the lid on it for me."

There was complete silence at the other end of the line.

"Maurice?" No reply.

"Maurice! You haven't found them, have you? Tell me!"

His voice rustled as he breathed in. "I wasn't going to tell you. Not yet anyway. I know how you're feeling and it's not good."

Too right. "But you've found them? Yes?"

" 'fraid so. Fourteen old masters, property of the Kunsthistorisches Museum in Vienna, recovered yesterday by yours truly. Two Bellinis, a Vermeer, two Rubens, a Veronese and assorted others."

"Fantastic! Congratulations!" I said, genuinely pleased for him. "Where did you find them?"

"Don't ask. Very grisly. They had been buried and disguised as a new grave. Fortunately, we had a tip-off and the small cemetery had just three burials during the entire war. So we had to exume only two bodies, but that was bad enough."

I shuddered. "A colorful story for your memoirs, Maurice. But seriously, very well done. I really am dropping behind."

"Well, it's about time you Americans came second at something."

He told me it would take him a day or two to clean up in Vienna, then he would head back to the flat in Offenbach but would keep in touch. I took the opportunity to introduce him to Sammy, who had come into the office during my conversation with Maurice. There was no point in my being an intermediary between the two of them. Maurice might want to sell his shares and buy others while I was away. It turned out that Sammy had a brother at Cambridge, in the same college as Maurice, and they talked for ages.

I was, therefore, a shade irritated when Sammy finally came off the phone and said, "Hobel wants to see you. Sorry, I should have told you earlier but I forgot."

I shoveled a weary hand through my hair, but instead of hurrying into Hobel's office I picked up the phone again. I wasn't *quite* ready to talk to the major, not yet.

"Yeeees?" said the voice that I recognized. Suspicious, doubting, uncertain.

"You don't remember me, do you? It's Walter Wolff. We sat next to each other at dinner, in the mess at Salzburg. You were there to arrest a man but having a rough time yourself. I'm an architect, too, of sorts."

"Of course, of course." He relaxed once he recognized my voice. "How are you, Walter? It's good to hear from you."

We exchanged pleasantries for a while. His case was coming along well and he expected to go back to Florence for the trial in about a month's time. Then I brought the conversation around to business. "Saul, I need your help, your professional skills."

"Oh yes?"

He was already familiar with the bones of the von Zell story, since I had filled him in when we sat together at dinner. I brought him up to date as quickly as I could, concentrating on the investigations by Maurice's men. "So you see, Saul, I could be in better shape. However, I do have this one lead, this character named Franz-Josef Aubing, who did work in one of the vineyards but left to get married in Zurich. He answered the description of von Zell."

"And you want me to trace him for you?"

"Could you, Saul? I would be so grateful if you could help. But have I given you enough to go on—a name, a description and a destination? It's all I have."

He thought. "The short answer, Walter, is that I don't know. It ought to be easy enough to check the forthcoming marriages in Zurich. But if he was lying, and if he's your man he *will* have been lying, it will be ten, a hundred times more difficult. Maybe impossible."

To stress the urgency of my predicament I told Saul about the recent discovery of the pipeline for ex-Nazis across lake Geneva and von Zell's alleged role in that. "And I'm worried, too, that his secretary, this Breker woman, might just have enough savvy to try to contact him, to alert him about me."

Saul listened attentively. "Hhmmmnnn. All right. You've convinced me that he needs our attention. I'll do what I can, I promise. It may take a few days, of course, so let me know where I can find you."

I gave him my numbers at the office and at the hotel. "The minute you get anything positive, Saul, let me know, will you? I've got a commanding officer breathing down my neck. I'm sure you are familiar with the type."

But he stifled my whining succinctly. "That's what commanding officers are *for*, my friend." And he hung up.

I looked at my watch. It was almost five o'clock. I could put if off no longer.

I got up, made a face at Sammy and headed along the corridor toward Hobel's office. Lucy, his secretary, gave out a whelp of predatory recognition as I stepped through the doorway.

"We've been trying to get you for *days*," she said, obviously delighted that she hadn't been able to find me. "Where *have* you been?"

"Reading," I said, and savored the puzzled look on her face.

"You're to go straight in," she said triumphantly, almost solicitously— the kind of concern that the guards in a prison reserve for the really important convicts.

Hobel was engrossed in the inevitable paperwork. As I entered he couldn't help but flinch with anger. He steadied himself and finished what he was doing before he looked up again. It was as quiet as a hangman's cell. You could have heard the noose drop.

I remained standing until Hobel finished what was in front of him and waved me to a seat. He sat back, almost entirely still save for his lower jaw, the teeth of which picked away at the inside of his cheek. His eyes were as gummy as lard.

The silence lengthened dangerously. It was colorless, but it had a texture like that of boiled rice, fluffy, gray, warm and damp, clinging.

Hobel's breath came in grunts, few and far between; he was wrestling to control himself. The attempt showed in little patches of sweat on his forehead, which caught the light. I was apprehensive, but not really nervous now that the confrontation had finally arrived.

At last he said one word:

"Speak."

If he had not been in such a volcanic mood, it would have been comical. Looking back, it *was* comical, but not at the time.

I spoke. I gave him a slanted version of events, calculated to calm him, an optimistic interpretation of what had gone before. I concluded with the information that Saul Wolfert, an expert in finding people, had joined me on the case, and I told Hobel that I had read the entire correspondence of Konstanze von Zell and now felt I could do a better job of interrogating her than the others had.

"That's why I have been closeted in my hotel room, sir. The letters took me days to read; there were more than two hundred of them. But they were full of vital information."

"What sort of vital information?"

It would have sounded silly to say something like: her favorite color; her birthday; the fact that she likes Bruckner and yellow flowers; but that's what I meant. "Difficult to say at this stage, sir. All sorts of personal details. But I know what kind of person she is now. I think I know how to build up a relationship with her. I feel fairly certain I can trick her into revealing that she does know where her husband is. I am convinced she does know, by the way. Once she admits that, the rest will be easy." Put like that, I almost convinced myself that I was making progress.

But not Hobel. He shook his head. It was time he had his say. "You were foisted on me; I suppose you know that, Wolff. It was Wren's idea. He was the one who convinced Eisenhower that you were the man for this job, not me. Oh, I know you recovered those Crown Jewels, but you were lucky, really, weren't you? You were tipped off."

I was surprised. That was the official version, that we had been tipped off by an anonymous informer, but it wasn't true. It was just a line to protect the city official whom I had "broken" during interrogation. It was part of the deal, part of the exchange I had to arrange in order to extract his confession. I had assumed that Hobel knew that. If he didn't, he wasn't as much in touch as he thought.

"It's disappointing, Wolff, isn't it? After how many days—nine?—you are not really any further along. By your own admission you've scared off those renegade Nazis, if that's what they really were. So we stand no chance of finding them, let alone von Zell, if I were mad enough to agree to your idea of a search of the mountains. Whoever heard of searching mountains? It's crazy."

He held up three fingers and folded one down. "So, there goes theory number one. Second, you've got a suspect, who may be von Zell but isn't using his real name or the one alias that would make chasing him plausible, who may or may not be in Zurich." He curled down the second finger. "And you have read a pile of letters which, you say, gives you an inside edge interrogating this woman." He waggled his third finger, so that it trembled. "You will forgive me, I hope, if I do not regard that as a real theory. I don't need to remind you that three people have interrogated Mrs. von Zell already. And failed." He curled the third, quivering finger over. That left a fist, clenched and bald, staring at me across the desk. The sentiment was unmistakable.

That wasn't how I saw the results of my efforts over the previous few days, not at all. Still, unlikable as Hobel was, he had a case. I knew a great deal about the von Zells, more than anyone else and probably more than I would ever need to know. But I was still a "million miles," from the gold coins.

"I don't agree, sir," I said vigorously, deciding that what was needed was a bit of bluster. "I've explained why I think Mrs. von Zell knows where her husband is and I think my reasoning is sound. I don't imagine for a minute that I can just amble over to Mondsee and expect her to tell me what we want to know. But if I can have a few weeks"—Hobel twisted again, as if in pain—"if I can have a week or two," I repeated in a stronger, more self-assured tone, "then I believe I can force her, or trick her, or persuade her, to at least acknowledge that she knows where her husband is, that she has access to him, however indirect. I know enough to be able to convince her, I think, that we know that she knows. Once she understands that she will realize that we are not going away."

Hobel looked interested at this line of reasoning, so I pressed it.

"All the other interrogators have been in too much of a hurry. This is a case that has to be built up slowly but insistently. If I turn up for a few days in a row, she will realize, or come to realize, that I won't go away until she cooperates. It won't work overnight—she's too strong. Too many of us have failed already. But it *will* work, eventually. I know Eisenhower must be impatient for results. But my way may be the only way that will work. Remember, Bloch's form of torture failed miserably. I need a week, maybe two, possibly three. To make a nuisance of myself."

Those bulging greasy eyes fixed on me. Hobel was calculating just how rude he could be. His hidden teeth chewed away at his inner cheek, gyrating rhythmically, side to side. He opted for the frontal attack.

"I don't like you, Wolff. I don't like you as an individual and I don't like the type of person you represent. Fucking European intellectual. If my own career didn't depend on this fucking case, I would be reveling in your failure. As it is, I'm stuck with you. You haven't fucked up enough yet for me to fire you. You're still Eisenhower's baby. But you saw that newspaper clipping I sent you, the one about the three renegades captured on the lake near Geneva. Anything else like that, Wolff, and you're finished. I will fire you before Eisenhower, or Wren, ditches me. There's no way you are going to survive this if I don't. Is that fucking clear?"

Yes, I thought, it fucking well is. But I said nothing. I just stood up. I'd bought time and, under the circumstances, that was as much as I could hope for. I saluted and left the room without speaking. In the outer office the secretary looked up eagerly to see just how bruised I was. I grinned, blew her a kiss and laughed wickedly as her face fell.

Sammy looked up as I slumped into my seat. I held up one hand with my fingers crossed. "I'm still on the case. Just."

"The omens are better," he said in the grave manner he reserved for good news. "Atlantic Insurance failed to fall this morning—the tide has been stemmed."

"Oh yes?" I mumbled. The aggression I felt toward Hobel had left me sapped of energy. "Terrific. But I haven't actually *made* anything yet—right?"

"Can't have everything," Sammy said. "Be grateful the slide has stopped."

"I suppose Confederate Paper went up again."

"But only a cent," he announced cheerfully as he left me with my head in my hands.

I had been with Hobel nearly a half-hour and it was almost six o'clock. The office was winding down. Saturday's dance was still the main topic of conversation, for Hobel had hired a band that did imitations of Glen

Miller and managed to seduce a company of women infantry who were stationed not too far away to attend. For the time being, therefore, he could do no wrong in the eyes of most of the men.

Sammy returned and began packing up. He suggested a drink in the mess, but I told him to go on ahead, that I would follow in a few moments. I still had one more piece of tricky navigation that day—my wife's letters.

Alone in the office, I slit them open with a Swiss army knife I had picked up years ago. All thought of a drink went out of mind—for they were unnerving. In the first letter Nancy wrote that she had fallen in love with a sailboat manufacturer; and in the second that she had found a lawyer—here was his name and address—and he would be handling her end of the divorce. Just like that. No preamble, no buildup, no discussion. No second chance. I didn't expect the relationship to get a second chance and perhaps I didn't mind the divorce anyway. But, a failure is a failure, and combined with the rest of the news that day, I suddenly felt very lonely. Looking back, I wonder if those curt, unaffectionate, businesslike letters from my wife had anything to do with what happened later. They were in such marked contrast to the letters Konstanze had written and received.

PART THREE
KONSTANZE

CHAPTER FIVE

1

THE next day I met Konstanze for the first time. It was April 4. The morning was even warmer and brighter than on the preceding days and I sat on the hotel terrace taking my time over breakfast. Across the roofs of the old town, the Gaisberg rose impressively, poking into the sun, which had not yet cleared its rim. The day promised to be glorious.

Afterward I put down the top of the BMW and decided there would be no need even for a neck scarf. It was not a long drive to Mondsee. The road chased a broad valley, curving steadily to the left, following the river Fuschl. In those days it was more a lane for farm vehicles, narrow, winding, slow and flat—perfect for bicycles, I thought, remembering the letters. Horses and mechanical tractors existed in about equal numbers at that time, each as slow as the other, and I had to pick my way around both several times before I glimpsed the lake.

It was a pretty village, when I came to it. The first thing you saw was an area of formally planted trees on the lakeshore, making it look more French or Swiss than Austrian. There was a long, crude canoe—a hollowed-out tree trunk—on show near the water's edge. An historical monument, I suppose. A white wood and glass conservatory of some sort stood on a point, drawing the eye. Numerous small jetties ran around the northern curve of the lake, trodden by the slapping feet of hundreds of mallards, moorhens and other ducks.

From the shore area an avenue, or boulevard, led into the village itself, the houses beginning where the trees ended. Almost immediately the street widened into an irregularly shaped market place, with a cafe and shops. All the houses lining the market had shutters and were painted in bright, primary colors. The church was set back, basking in a relatively new coat of sand- and cream-colored paint. It was much larger than I had expected.

I stopped the car outside the church and went inside. Since Mrs. von Zell was deputy organist, I knew someone h ·e would be able to direct me to her house. The church was ornate but remarkably light considering the amount of black stucco that adorned it. As an art historian I was very familiar with white stucco work but had forgotten how dramatic black moldings can be, especially when lined and highlighted with gold. It was like being inside a big box of chocolates.

I entered the church under a gallery and as I walked into the nave the huge organ became visible above and behind me, an impressive engine of black pipes. I stopped to admire it as the sunlight threw high beams across the tubes, stippling the far wall with broken shadows and colored patches from the stained-glass windows.

A woman was cleaning the steps that led to the high altar and she was only too happy for an excuse to break from her sweeping. To get to the von Zells' house, I was told, I had to go back the way I had come, along the boulevard which led back to the lake. I was to turn left at the end, away from Salzburg and follow the shore road, which led south along the east side of the lake. The house was easily recognizable, the woman said, because it had a swing outside, for Dieter, dangling from a tree. It was no more than a kilometer away.

The shore road was pretty and narrow, with sudden, open glimpses of the lake. Many of the homes, to the left of the road, away from the water, were set back a bit on a slope, with the mountain behind them. These had better views, and most of them had small summer houses, or huts, on the right-hand side of the road, on the lake. These were for swimming and boating, tea parties and fishing hideaways. The von Zell house was no different, though slightly larger than most. The summer house, like the main building, was wooden, not painted but skinned with a thick, clear varnish, so that it gleamed in the sun.

I didn't stop outside the house but drove on for a couple of hundred yards to where there were some trees between the road and the lake. I parked the car, switched off the engine and sat for a moment or two. I fished out my pipe and found a patch of grass among the trees quite close to the water's edge. I had to be very relaxed when I met Mrs. von Zell. Not only did I need to give the impression that I was totally in command of myself, which, since my wife's letters, was something less than the truth, but I also had to make it seem that I had all the time in the world. That my interrogation of her was quite unlike the ones which had gone before. I was here, and here I would stay until I got what I had come for. I needed to pretend that I had that kind of personality, the kind that is undisturbed and undisturbable.

For now I needed to wind down, to let the sensations of the day before wash out of me. I leaned back against a tree and lit my pipe. I could smell the lake from where I was and listen to the irregular smack of the waves as they beat against the beach. Twenty yards out two trout slapped the surface as they sucked in flies. There was a light, warm breeze and the smell of cut grass, or cut something, in among it, over and above the tang of the lake. Behind me the road was empty.

I waited until I had finished my pipe. I wasn't looking forward to what I was about to start. Here, in what was quite possibly the most soothing spot I had ever found, I had to—well, I had to drag on the war in my own particular way. I was tidying up the war and, in the process, harshly interfering in the life of a woman who, under different circumstances, I felt sure I would like. It was, in a way, crazy.

I knocked my pipe out on a tree, got to my feet and, leaving the car where it was, walked back along the shore to the von Zell house.

There was a wooden balcony running the length of the house on the upper floor and a few steps, also wooden, leading up to the main door. The garden was large, with a low, unpainted fence around its perimeter. Three trees threw hundreds of tiny shadows onto the grass. The child's swing, red and peeling, hung forgotten in the almost still air.

As I unclipped the latch on the gate I could see a piano in one of the rooms to the side of the house, as well as wine bottles in racks. This would be the wine and music room I had read so much about in the letters and which the von Zells had brought with them when they moved from Munich.

My boots scraped so loudly on the wooden landing that I didn't need to knock on the door. I had been heard and footsteps inside the house moved toward me. To my surprise, a small, leathery woman with dark hair opened the door; she must have been a housekeeper. She had never been mentioned in the letters.

She scrutinized my uniform as if she had never seen an American soldier before and scowled.

"Is Mrs. von Zell at home? Please."

She shook her head, jerkily, from side to side, like a rook or raven looking for worms. "No."

"Has she gone far?"

"No." She paused, determined to be no more helpful than she needed to be. "She's in the village."

"When do you expect her back?"

"Very soon."

"Then I will wait, if I may."

She said nothing but simply turned around and walked back into the house, leaving the door open. I closed it behind me as she led the way into a sort of study cum sewing room. There was a rocking chair, covered with curtains, bedcovers and other bits of cloth, and a small, upright, very uncomfortable-looking wooden chair by a fireplace. I was invited to sit on that.

"Mrs. von Zell does not allow smoking in here," said the old woman and went out.

I looked around the room. There were a few photographs—Bloch had not taken them all—including a large one of Rudolf with Dieter and another print of the picture I had seen in the library at the Schloss Haltern in Koblenz: Rudolf and Eric together. There were also a number of maps on the walls, of rivers: the Mosel, the Loire, the Elbe and the Danube. This last I examined carefully, especially its path through the Wachau region. No one else knew about Rudolf's passion for wine, or his interest in the vineyards of Austria, so there might be some sort of cryptic mark on the map. It would mean nothing to the casual eye. *There was:* a small circle, drawn in smudged pencil, around a town called Krumau. It was at the foot of a small lake, no more than a swelling in the river Kamp, about eighty kilometers from Vienna, and right on the edge of the wine-growing region.

I sat on the chair to think. God, it was uncomfortable. I don't think my spine had ever been so upright. What did that circle mean? That I had been unlucky but right all along, that von Zell *was* hiding out in the wine region? How could I find out without arousing suspicion? At least I now had a location for Saul Wolfert to concentrate his search. I wouldn't tell Hobel about this latest find. Instead, I would quietly ask Wolfert to check it out. If and when we got something positive, I would tell the major.

I heard noises outside. A child speaking and a woman laughing. I also noticed for the first time that the room I was in had a door which opened directly on to the side of the house. It was through this door that I could make out the approaching voices. I did what I could to compose myself.

I realize that I have not properly explained my feelings on that day when I first found myself in Mondsee. I was nervous because I had never interviewed a woman who had access to vital information. I was not, in theory, affected by her sex. Women, I believed, could be guilty of the same crimes as men, but I had never had to face a woman in quite these circumstances. I was, therefore, apprehensive. Also, having read the correspondence, I did feel somewhat guilty. I knew that I had no choice, but my actions were still quite reprehensible. I was not proud of what I had done. What made it worse was the knowledge that I would be unable to resist using the information I had, should the need arise. So, in a way, I resented Mrs. von Zell, Hobel, the war, for putting me into such a bind. I wished that my two hunches about Rudolf von Zell had come to something. By this stage, what with Major Hobel's hostility, my professional pride had been dented and I was smarting for results. If, therefore, I could crack Mrs. von Zell, making use of knowledge I had gained from the correspondence, then I could satisfy some of the boiling motives inside me and further justify my indiscretion and assuage my guilt as well.

Underneath these more specific feelings ran two deeper, general ones. I had left Germany as an anti-Nazi and had joined the U.S. Army enthusiastically, as soon as it would have me. In 1946, therefore, as far as the Nazis were concerned, I suppose I was a bit of a zealot, and so were a lot of people. I say that here because, since then, I think tempers have cooled. Finally, there were the general feelings I had about human nature and I wanted to see whether they applied to Mrs. von Zell. She had been a tragic, melancholic young woman and appeared to have changed into a mature, composed mother. Was that change real? I suppose I held the view that people do not change fundamentally, that with Konstanze the earlier woman lay not far underneath.

From the distance of time I can also admit to myself that as I heard her footstep outside the door there was another emotion inside me. Until that moment I had never met her though, in a way, I felt I knew her quite well. I had never been in a situation where I knew so much about a person, possessed so many intimate details before I met them. I had never known so much about someone who didn't want me to know those kinds of details. My reading of the correspondence was supposed to give me an advantage over her and so, in a sense, it did. Yet what I knew about Konstanze I liked and it gave her an advantage over me. Before we met she didn't even know I existed; yet I was already half in love with her.

The door banged open and, as I have said, the sunlight splashed in. Within the room swirls of dust rose lazily in the straw-colored beams.

She was taller than I imagined, more erect, yet her features were softer than they appeared in her photographs. Under the oatmeal-colored cloak she wore, her figure was that of a woman, not a girl.

Her distaste for me was quick to appear. She saw absolutely nothing to smile about when her son crashed into her legs, spilling the groceries.

As calmly as I could, I wiped the spittle from where it landed on the collar of my uniform. She and I remained frozen and I do not know how long we would have both stood like that had not the housekeeper, hearing the commotion, stepped into the room from the kitchen and, without a word, taken the eggs from Mrs. von Zell and led the boy away.

Left alone, I wanted to do something which would ease the tension but also stress, right from the start, that I had power and *time*. Slowly, deliberately, I began to fill my pipe. I knew that she didn't allow smoking in the room. She knew that the housekeeper would have told me that. Still, I took out the tobacco pouch and scooped bundles of leaves into the bowl.

She stood there, not moving except for her heavy breathing. Behind her the door was still open, the sunlight streaming in. I remember thinking that she must have washed her hair that morning for it was slightly unruly and gave her a ragged, flickering halo of gold where the sun caught the edges.

It sounds perverse to say, but I was encouraged by the fact that she had spat at me. It had never happened to me before, but I had heard of it happening to other interrogators. And, strange as it may seem, it was not always the disaster it at first appeared to be. The ideal with any new interrogation is to get the person to react, to communicate with you. The person who just sits there impassively is the worst, the cleverest. Because they give you nothing. So, in spitting at me, an extreme act in any language, at least Konstanze was reacting. And two important things follow from this. One, the person who does the spitting feels guilty, in however small a way. Two, things can only improve. Konstanze and I had started off in the worst possible way, but now that we had touched bottom, we could only go up.

I made no attempt to shake hands—no point in risking a rebuff. Softly, in a voice designed to sound relaxed and patient, I repeated myself. "I suppose you know why I am here."

This time she did reply, but in a much harsher tone than I had hoped for. "Yes," she hissed, hardly moving her jaws and in no way relaxing her frame. "You want my husband."

I let a silence hang between us for a few moments. "No."

She moved her head, surprised. I had given this exchange some thought.

"I have not the slightest interest in your husband. Or his whereabouts." Again there was a silence between us, as I pretended to be the patient, unflappable type. I smiled and moved about the room, in another attempt to defrost the atmosphere. "My job is to recover some gold coins."

I was now standing next to a radio—in those days they were much larger than now—wooden and elaborately carved, as this one was. It occurred to me that it was probably on this set that she listened to the concerts while Rudolf did the same, miles away, wherever he was. There was a photograph of the two of them with Dieter on the top of the radio. I moved my body so that her view of the photograph was blocked.

"I do not know where my husband is. I cannot help you find the coins. I told that to the other men who came." Her voice was soft, yet deep, a tall person's voice. The sound was drawn all the way up from her chest— like an actor's, I thought to myself, remembering her father. It was a tutored voice in which the consonants rang out as clearly as the vowels. Funny that neither Bruno nor Rudolf had commented on her voice, for it was beautiful.

This was what Maurice, with his British taste for understatement, would have called the "tricky" moment. It always was, in any interrogation. The first exchange was over, each side's position stated. It was

unavoidable, but now I had to move things a stage further. Experience
had taught me that it helped at this point to talk about other things.
One had to be careful. The object was to get the other person to talk, so
the subject matter could not be too threatening. It couldn't be too
obviously a complete change, either. That was unrealistic and just as
intimidating. The most I could hope for at this early stage was that she
should be intrigued by me and have *some* respect for me. It was, in its
way, like a seduction.

I sat down. It was impolite, but it conveyed my intention to stay
better than any words could. She looked at me with ill-concealed hatred.

I had not yet lit my pipe, so I took out some cigarettes. Mrs. von Zell
might not allow smoking in this room but I knew from the letters that
she liked Virginia tobacco, the milder the better, and that is what I had
brought with me. I also knew that in Austria, in fact throughout Europe,
good cigarettes were in short supply.

I offered her one. She didn't move. But then she didn't tell me not to
smoke, so it occurred to me that she was more tempted than she let on. I
left the pack on a table, open, and started to light my pipe. The blue
smoke filled the room.

I knew that I would have to talk and that everything would depend on
how successful my little speech was. Patiently, or at least with the sem-
blance of patience, I made sure my pipe was properly on the go before I
spoke again.

"I know a little bit about you, Mrs. von Zell, from our files. Not
much, you understand, but a bit. And nowhere does it say how beautiful
you are. If I had been the author of one of those reports, I would have
put it in the first sentence. But I suppose"—I tried to make it a joke—
"you would have been visited by many more interrogators, and they
would not have sent me. This is my first time in Austria, so I am grateful
to you." I sucked contentedly on my pipe. The sweet smell floated about
the room, like the smoke. Sunshine continued to pour in from the open
door, behind where she stood.

There was method in what I was saying. She might have no relationship with me, no feeling beyond a general loathing for my uniform, but I
was saying I was human, a person, and that I was not indifferent. She
was a beautiful woman and I was grateful to her for bringing me to a
beautiful country.

"I am German by birth, from Heidelberg. That explains my German.

I emigrated from Hamburg to Italy in 1936. Then to America in 1938. Since 1940 I have been a professor of art history in California. So, for me, Austria has always been the country of baroque churches and lovely, lonely monasteries—Melk, Wilhering, St. Florian or Klosterneuburg. I haven't seen anything yet, but I shall. It feels good to be back.

"I write to my mother—she is in Leipzig, separated from the rest of the family, and I am trying to bring her west—and I say that I am in Austria. 'Tell me about the churches, Walter,' she writes, for she is very religious, but so far I have not been able to report anything."

I was establishing that I was a German, too, a European. It might do some good. Inside my uniform there was an individual, someone with a Christian name, a life outside the Army. I, too, was separated from loved ones and my mother, if not I, was a devout Catholic, like Konstanze.

"Soon, though, I will get a chance to see the monasteries and I shall write to my mother. The world is returning to normal. Most of our work recovering art treasures is complete. You are lucky—oh, I know you are separated from your husband, but you have a child, this home. I have been away now for four years. I have a new set of friends, people I would never have met except for the war. But I have no wife, no children. The war destroyed my marriage, though perhaps it was too fragile to last, war or no war. I had to leave for Europe before we had been married a year. I would no longer feel at home in my house, I am sure. I have not written an academic paper or given a lecture for so long that I am no doubt rusty. I can get cigarettes, the Army feeds me, but I can't get the books I enjoy.

"Some of the new friends I have made, I have already lost, of course. That's a curious thing about the war that I hadn't expected. All the activity is interesting, not least for the fact that it introduces you to many new people. You are always moving around, making new friends— there are more people to care about during a war than there ever are in peacetime. Then a lot of them go off and die. Disappearing acts, as someone said. That's the cruelest thing about war—not that it kills people, but that, because of the pressures, the unusual hours, the life-style, it produces a hothouse in which you make friends rapidly, in which people develop themselves in extraordinary ways that wouldn't happen in peacetime, so that their deaths matter even more."

I wasn't talking about winners and losers, about Nazis and Allies. I was aligning myself with Konstanze, saying that we were all victims in war, whichever side we were on. That although I was here to interrogate her, maybe I had more problems than she did. She was still standing stiffly, but she was listening.

"The other thing that amazes me is how everyday life goes on. People continue, not just to work, but to have a good time. When I arrived in London in 1942, it was my birthday"—I was cheating shamelessly, making use of what I had found out in the letters—"January 27, the same as Mozart's. Some friends had arranged a party for me at a club in Soho. I was tired from the flight—sixteen hours via Gander and Shannon—but I was determined to have a good time. Imagine my frustration, then, when for some unaccountable reason I was held up at immigration. At first it didn't bother me that one official took his time scrutinizing my papers; there was a war on, after all. But he called in his superior. The two of them huddled, inspecting my documents, conferring. I didn't like that. Then, to my utter astonishment, they called in the superior's superior. All three of them examined the papers. I was *itching* to get on. My party was about to start and I was still eight miles from the center of London. However, from the way they all pointed their fingers there seemed to be something wrong with one particular detail in my documents. I had no idea what it could be and the people in line behind me were getting very impatient. Finally, after what seemed a terrible delay, all three officials came over to where I was standing. As you may imagine, I was by now a little angry, though my anger was mixed with nervousness. What was wrong?

"I was totally unprepared for what happened next. As one man, they burst out singing 'Happy birthday, dear Walter, happy birthday to you. . . .' They'd spotted my date of birth on my papers. Was I relieved!"

I was by no means certain that Mrs. von Zell found my story as amusing as I meant her to. She had yet to move. I hurried on.

"After the invasion I noticed that life went on normally in France and I expect it was true also of Germany. In fact, I was surprised to be told here that the Salzburg festival has been canceled. I was looking forward to that. I understand that Strauss's new opera *Die Liebe der Danae* was in rehearsal in 1944, before the festival was abandoned, and I had rather hoped it might be revived."

Now, I was cheating very badly. Insofar as I knew anything about music, I hated Strauss, yet here I was pretending to like him. More subtly, by referring to the festival, which was held in the summer, I was implying that I would be around that long, that I was not going away.

Still she said nothing.

"I see you have a music room here, Mrs. von Zell. I envy you. I don't play, though I did start to learn the oboe when I was a boy. My brother, however, is a really good pianist—Chopin, Schubert, Haydn—he can play beautifully. It's strange, but music is the only thing he and I have in common. In all other things we are so different. He is three years younger than I and, where I am tall, he is short. I am dark, he is fair. At school I was always interested in art and architecture, the countryside and literature. He was keen on science, math, sports. I was interested in travel, in other countries. He was a German and Germany was his love. I was interested in history but the present and the future were everything to him. Sometimes I think that's what brothers—families—are for. If I'd been an only child I could have been interested in anything I chose, and, as a result, my personality might have been so vague I would never have chosen a career and just drifted. But with us being so different—and of course we became determined to be different from each other—we came to represent each other's opposite. When I left Heidelberg I went to study with the great Erwin Panofsky in Hamburg. He was one of the most famous art historians of his time and, for me, it was a great honor. But of course he was Jewish. We could see what was beginning to happen, though never in our wildest dreams did we imagine what would come to pass.

"In '36, however, Panofsky thought it was too risky for him to go on teaching. I was disturbed but still very young. I asked him what I should do. He asked me if I wanted to stay in Germany and I told him I didn't care. Within a fortnight he had arranged for me to study with Bernard Berenson in Italy.

"That is how I came to leave Germany. In 1938 things got so bad in Italy that I left for the United States.

"But I was talking about brothers, and whether we become what we are because other people in our families are something else. Who can say? But I do know that after I left Germany to study in Italy, my brother, already a scientist, embraced the present at home by joining the Nazis.

"We have fought this war on opposite sides. Think what that means for my—our—mother. Maybe one son would shoot the other, either wittingly or unwittingly. As it happens, my work has always been in intelligence and I have not fired my gun except on the practice range, but Mother could not know that. For six years I have heard nothing from my brother. And, since my mother lives in the eastern sector of Germany now, I have heard only infrequently and inadequately from her. As I mentioned, I am trying to bring her west but I don't know if I will succeed.

"But, and this may sound strange after what I've said, I miss my brother. It's true. I would love to have *a* brother again. With friends, even with husbands and wives, a certain equality must be established, otherwise the relationship can't last. That equality is by no means easy to achieve and often it is impossible. But with a brother, or a sister for that matter, equality is imposed. My mother never had a favorite, and even though Martin and I are very different, to her we are equals. I would love to see him again."

I stood up. She remained where she was, but her eyes followed my movements as I walked across the room and stood by the open door looking out. "Why am I telling you this?" I turned and relit my pipe, which had gone out as I talked. "Music, that was it. I don't really have a favorite composer but I like Bruckner a lot. Mother's favorite is Schubert. Martin, being a modern, went for Strauss. Very German, he said. What about you, Mrs. von Zell, are you a Strauss fan?"

It was the gamble I had to take at some point. I had talked at length about myself, deliberately, to show that I was a German, that I shared with her the problems of separation, that I had a family life, with its riches and its problems. But I had also tried to make my conversation as interesting as possible. I gambled that, since Rudolf had stopped writing to her, Konstanze had been starved of proper companionship, tucked away as she was with just her son and the housekeeper. In the later letters, the ones she had not posted, only local matters or family affairs were discussed; the old housekeeper could hardly be an emotional or an intellectual equal. I had lied about my brother's favorite composer; he preferred Beethoven but that wasn't the point. Konstanze had contact with Strauss; Strauss had been involved at one time with the Nazis. For me to have talked only about music in the abstract would have been too bland. Introducing Strauss brought things back to the present, to the very room we were in. I had established, or tried to establish, a link between myself and Konstanze. What I hoped would be the beginning of a relationship.

She didn't answer. Maybe Strauss was too direct, too close to her. Too close to the Nazi issue. I tried again.

"You have a piano here, Mrs. von Zell. A music room. I take it you play. Who are *your* favorite composers?"

She appeared to consider this. I could see her thinking to herself, What kind of interrogation *is* this? All he wants is what the others wanted, to know Rudolf's whereabouts. Yet, at the same time, he's different from the others; none of them took this line.

She examined my question from every angle and decided she was giving nothing away if she answered. That was a mistake. After all, that's why I had asked the question in the first place; because it wasn't threatening and carried no risk.

"Schubert, like your mother; Strauss, like your brother; Bruckner, like you; Mozart, like everybody."

"Why?" I said it softly but quickly to keep her talking.

She shrugged. "It would take too long." She was telling me to keep away, that I had no right to probe. It was her business. "Let's just say they made the nights of the war bearable."

"But why Bruckner?" I wasn't put off so easily. "I've never met anyone before who said that Bruckner was a favorite composer." Maybe she would notice my use of the word "never" and wonder whether I used it lightly or took it as seriously as she.

"Bruckner was a silly old man, always falling for girls young enough to be his granddaughter, but his organ music is magnificent. Only a man who has never been loved by a woman could write music that is so beautiful and yet so angry, so loud and yet so lonely. I play the organ at the church in the village. I know just how different Bruckner's music is from anyone else's."

Splendid. I was, I thought, doing rather well. This was quite an exchange, considering it was our first encounter and after such a difficult beginning. Perhaps she was feeling guilty for having spat on me.

"I suppose that if Hitler *had* built a Bruckner center in Linz, as he planned, it is one thing the whole world would have thanked him for."

Did the look in her eyes take on a more cutting glint? She nodded, but noncommittally. She wasn't going to approve or disapprove of anything

Hitler had done, or not done, not in front of a stranger in an American uniform.

I moved across to the fireplace and reached for the cigarettes I had left on the table. I offered the pack to her again. She refused, but for the first time her gaze left my face and followed my hand as it replaced the cigarettes. I let my hand rest on the pack for a moment, then picked it up again. I held it out once more, this time taking a step forward so that I was now physically closer to her than before. I remember noticing that her ears were pierced.

"These are very mild," I said. "Pure Virginia. I hope you like mild cigarettes. Please have one."

She hesitated, uncertain that such an act of collaboration was not treason. Then, with a quick gesture, she took one from the pack. She insisted on lighting it for herself but this meant she had to move forward, to take the matches from my hand. The door, which she had been holding open, clanged shut behind her, plunging the room into what, by comparison with the sunshine that had gone before, seemed like soupy gloom. The movement, the change in light, and the scraping noise of the match on the box eased the tension between us. Not that she was friendly yet. She was still hostile, but in a different way. It was as if her policy of silence, or utter noncooperation, had been superseded by a determination on her part not to be outwitted in whatever game it was that I was playing. At last I had an opponent.

All of this meant that I was ahead. I had made an impact of sorts on her. It didn't matter what it was. What mattered was that I had proved myself to be more than a hated figure in a uniform. It was as much as I could reasonably hope for a first meeting. Time to quit. I had noticed, as she lit her cigarette, that some extremely appetizing smells were sliding under the door from the direction of the kitchen. No doubt a few of those big brown eggs were going into an omelet of some sort. I recalled that in the letters omelets had emerged as one of Konstanze's favorite things. Nothing, just then, could have given me greater pleasure than a fresh omelet eaten in the company of such a beautiful woman. But I wasn't going to be asked and, in any case, now was the right time to leave. If I left of my own accord, it would be easier to come back again.

I pocketed my pipe and picked up my hat. "I must go. There are other people I have to see and, from what I can tell"—I tapped the side of my nose with a finger—"your lunch is ready. Can't keep a growing boy waiting."

Maybe she smiled, maybe she didn't.

I held out my hand stiffly and she took it. I left by the side door, before she could speak again. I didn't stop or turn around to see if she was watching me go. I would be back and she knew it. She had mixed feelings about me, of course. But, as I walked back to my car along the lakeshore, I felt better than I had in days. And it wasn't just the sunshine. I had quite deliberately left the cigarettes on the table where she had watched me pick up my cap. She had made no attempt to give them back.

2

I didn't go back the next day. All the other interrogators had dashed in, spent three or four hours with Mrs. von Zell, failed, then dashed off again. For my approach to work I had to be as different from them as Rudolf was from Bruno. I also had to give the impression that I was in no special hurry, that time was on my side and not her ally as it had been against all the others. I wanted to make it appear that I had other things on my mind—that, to me, there were more important things in life than military affairs.

Fortunately the good weather held. In fact, it continued to improve as if the military authorities in the area had decreed that April was to be officially a part of summer. I spent the intervening day exploring the surrounding countryside: I had plans. And I spent a while on the phone talking to Saul Wolfert. As yet he had no news for me but I told him about the pencil mark around the village of Krumau on that swelling in the river Kamp. He agreed to search in the village once he had checked out the forthcoming marriages in Zurich. He was enjoying Vienna, finding it just as enticing as Maurice had—girls, coffeehouses, the architecture. I was envious. Just then I seemed to envy a lot of people.

Two days after my first visit to Mondsee I again followed the winding road along the Fuschl Valley. I took care this time to arrive later in the morning so that the sun was well clear of the mountains and the air already hot. Again I parked in the trees at the edge of the lake. Three figures, in a low black boat, fished for saibling.

I walked back along the empty road, aware that the heat of the day was already melting stretches of tar on its surface. It smelled fusty, not unlike coal.

This time I didn't knock at the door but instead I sat down unannounced beneath one of the trees in the garden. I put down the parcel I had brought with me and started to light my pipe. I reclined, listening to the sounds around me: a tractor, like a huge and insistent dentist's drill boring into the mountainside; the creak of the tree above me; a lawn mower somewhere rasping through the grass; birds, cleverly finding the silences in between everything else. Seven or eight minutes passed before I heard a door click open.

There was a pause. I looked around.

"I didn't recognize you without your uniform. What are you doing there in my garden? I told you, I do not know where my husband is."

I held up my package. "I have something for you. I didn't know whether you were in, and since I'm in no hurry, I thought I'd enjoy the sun and the smells until you came out. America doesn't smell like Europe. America doesn't really smell. That's one of the things I miss."

She sniffed.

I held up the package again. "Music. Schubert, Chopin, Mozart's Adagio in B." They were the booklets I had been given by Allie, the ones Rudolf had left in Berchtesgaden. But Konstanze didn't know that, yet.

She looked at me, trying to work out my motives for bringing the package and her own true reaction. As before, she was pulled between an entirely natural distrust of me and an equally natural curiosity about the music. And we were both aware that she had accepted those cigarettes the last time. Until now she hadn't realized it, but she was already compromised.

Before she could say anything, I spoke again. "There is a price, however."

She kept her expression as impenetrable as she could, moving her head just a fraction. But I could see her thinking, Surely he doesn't imagine I will tell him where my husband is just for some sheets of music?

"Two eggs," I said, and enjoyed the surprised look that, for an instant, passed across her face. "You may have the music in exchange for two of those fresh eggs you were carrying the other day. Beaten into an omelet, of course."

I couldn't be certain she would have any eggs left, but I had gambled that, since they were such a luxury, she would probably husband them for as long as they remained fresh.

A silence passed between us as she tried to size up what was happening. By not coming in uniform that day, I was trying to make it easier for Konstanze to accept me. I was wearing the one suit I carried with me, a rather dreary gray one flecked in white, like the stones they spill between railway lines. It was double-breasted and with it I wore a mustard-yellow tie, luckily her favorite color.

She was wearing a smock, very similar to the one my mother used to wear before the war, only Konstanze's was light brown whereas my mother's was faded blue. But otherwise it had the same halter neckline, the same untidy A shape, the same pockets in front where Konstanze now hid her hands. The smock only partially hid her figure, and I found it unexpectedly arousing. She noticed this, I believe, and curiously it played its part in her decision to allow me in that day to sample her omelet. She may have felt that since I was obviously drawn to her sexually, whereas she was merely intrigued by me, she could easily retain control of the situation. She stepped back and, taking one hand from her smock, pushed open the door for me to enter.

"Come in then. There are a few eggs left."

Behind my back, where I had kept the hand not holding the package of music, I uncrossed my fingers. That old trick, in use since childhood, had worked again.

Although I don't think she realized it, Mrs. von Zell had just made another mistake, just lowered an important psychological barrier: she had invited me inside. That is the real reason I had stayed in the garden that day and not knocked for admission; that is why I was out of uniform. Now I was a guest of sorts, not an enemy.

She showed me into the kitchen, a large, bright room. There was a cooking range with a large chimney on one side, a long wooden table in the center and, on the wall opposite the range, a large picture window with a view of the lake and mountains in the south.

"Where is your son?"

"Dieter is in the village, with Martha, our housekeeper."

She pulled out a chair at the end of the table. I sat down. She placed two of the biggest eggs in front of me. The shells were coated with a dusty stipple—browns and whites the color of bread, pepper, oatmeal and whiskey.

"Won't you have some?"

"No." She was firm. "I shall wait for Dieter. We always eat lunch together."

I was going too fast; I told myself to slow down.

"What would you like with the eggs?"

"Whatever is produced locally, or nothing. Some pepper, maybe."

"Sausage? Bread?"

"Perfect."

She stood in front of the range, so erect she was almost leaning back. I watched as she cracked the eggs into the pan with one hand. The shells snapped like crisp straw in a hot sun. Below the hem of her smock her legs swerved down to the narrow ankles Rudolf had praised so well.

"I like your smock," I said. "It suits you."

She acknowledged my compliment with a nod. I knew from the letters how meticulous she was about her clothes. Every time I met her, after that, I never failed to praise her dress sense.

The eggs slithered into the pan. The smells that began to come off the range I had anticipated, but what was unexpected was the comforting effect which the spitting of the eggs produced. It was a homey cooking sizzle that I had forgotten and it made me suddenly nostalgic. I told her.

She was suspicious. She could not believe, I suppose, that an interrogation could take this form. Nor could she understand when I made a fuss as she laid the table. She found it extraordinary, and perhaps a little false, which it was not, that I took such pleasure in knives with real bone handles, or napkins made out of flowered material. Without asking, almost without thinking, she poured me half a glass of red wine to have with the omelet. It was light, young, red as a damson and from a bottle that was already open. I realized with a jerk how much I missed a culture where wine was taken for granted.

"When shall you return home, Lieutenant?"

A normal question at last! That was a good sign. If we could have an ordinary, plain, *dull* conversation, I was truly making progress. Yet maybe that question was more than it seemed. Konstanze von Zell, I reminded myself, was not to be underestimated.

I lied. "Not for ages yet. The American Government has made the university promise to keep my job open indefinitely, another year at least. But I don't know where home is anymore." I expanded upon what I had already told her about my wife and her new companion. I explained that I was not looking forward to my return.

She was back by the range, standing in front of the frying pan. She had thrown in a piece of bread, which was smoking. She didn't look at me as she said, "You are a good-looking man. You will have no problems."

"Looks aren't everything. Some of the most happily married couples I know started off by not being in love with each other because one was perhaps much better-looking than the other. Their feelings grew."

I had bent my words deliberately to suit Konstanze's situation in the early days with Rudolf. She looked across and gave me a smile of agreement. It was thin, brief, but a smile nonetheless. The first.

She served the eggs and sausage with the fried bread, which was rusty-looking and sodden with cooking fat. She sat down at the other end of the table, not so much to be away from me as to catch the sun, fingering in through the window. She made no attempt at conversation; she distrusted me too much for that. Yet I had the feeling she wanted to talk. She sat with her elbows on the table, her arms wrapped around her shoulders. She looked out through the window, to a point far away. Again I was aroused; she looked starved of more than companionship—a healthy, *full* body, unused in months.

In between mouthfuls—which were so hot, yellow and fresh that it was like swallowing the sunshine outside—I took a small book from my pocket. "I came across this yesterday, in Linz. I'm hoping to get a chance to use it." It was called *The Baroque Churches of Central Europe* by an English schoolmaster.

She stopped looking out of the window, stopped being concerned with that point, some way off, and reached across for the book. She glanced at the spine and leafed through it.

"You play the organ at the church in Mondsee, Mrs. von Zell. Have you visited many other churches?"

"No. I am only the deputy organist here, so I play perhaps once a week, practice twice." She put the book down, not really a bookish person. "But I go to church every day. I have not been anywhere else."

Who, I wondered, did she pray for when she went to church?

"The Mondsee church is in the book. I checked. It says the church has a wonderful altar as well as a fine organ."

"Yes, they both *are* rather lovely. The stained glass is worth seeing too."

She had again been gazing out the window, lost in her own private world, as remote as the mountains she could see but wasn't looking at. Absently, she cut me another slice of bread, more a wedge really, from the outer crust of a round, flat loaf. I used it to wipe what was left of the eggs from my plate. I finished my wine.

"That was delicious. The best fresh eggs I've had since breakfast."

She looked sharply at me, but I was smiling, and she relaxed. She shoved the book back along the table with another small smile. Her second.

I sat back. Any smoker will know that, after such a treat, only a cigarette, or in my case a pipe, can complete the enjoyment. I squirmed in my pocket and put the pipe on the table. Then, along with my tobacco, I brought out another pack of Mrs. von Zell's favorite cigarettes. She hesitated, but not for long, and this time allowed me to light it for her. I cannot say that, in smoking together after the eggs, any kind of intimacy was beginning to grow between us. That wasn't true. She was still stiff, still distrustful of me, still distant. But, compared with how they had been, things *were* easier. The tension was going, whatever she might do to maintain it. I felt more confident of what I was about to say, which, I am ashamed to recall, I had rehearsed in some detail.

"You know, five years ago today, I was married." I smiled sadly. "It was one of the few days in history that it has rained in California. We had invited fifty people to the reception, in a garden. They all had to fit into one tiny room. It was awful—it was because of the crush that my new wife and I had our first argument. Then two years ago today, in 1944, I remember that I was in Cambridge, making a survey of beautiful buildings in northern France and Holland. We didn't know where the invasion was coming, or when, so we had been told to prepare a list of buildings to be spared the shells and bombs, if possible, a list to be handed out to colonels at the last minute. It would be an interesting historical document now, that list. It stretched from the tip of Britanny nearly into Denmark. Last year at this time I was in the Loire, trying to locate some tapestries that had disappeared from Chenonceaux. Funny how you remember certain dates. Have you ever been to the Loire, Mrs. von Zell?"

"No."

Why was she lying? Was it because I had intruded again into her private life? Or was it perhaps because she had gone to the Loire with Rudolf to sample wines and wine was dangerous territory? Tantalizing.

"My memories of Europe before the war—my family's part of Germany at any rate—were of endless days of sunshine. But that time in Cambridge and last year in the Loire were just like my wedding day—wet, wet, wet. Thank God the weather is different now."

Smile number three. "This weather is more typical than you think. Everyone imagines Austria under fathoms of snow, but spring and summer here are much more interesting. The countryside is so mountainous, and the altitude varies so much, we have far more flowers, and birds, than flatter places. Fewer trees, maybe, but trees are much duller than flowers, don't you agree? If you do look at the churches, Lieutenant—or should I say Professor?—don't ignore the flowers."

Privately, I thought botany was beyond me. You don't get to thirty and not know what a narcissus looks like, or an elm, without having a "block" of some sort. But I made agreeable noises about the flowers and brought the conversation back to more useful things, more in line with the plan that was beginning to form inside my head.

"You know, I am amazed that more churches have not been bombed out of existence. The town of Donauwörth, for instance, was very largely destroyed, but Heiligkreuz, its most imposing church, survived. Innsbruck was badly hit, but otherwise churches there are intact. It probably has something to do with the many pilgrimage churches in these parts, which were usually built in the countryside, unlike in Italy, where the churches are all at the center of busy towns."

But I had lost her attention. There were voices on the path—her son and the housekeeper had returned. She rose and I got up too. It was, in any case, time to leave. I had more or less achieved what I had set out to do that second day—to bring her the music, persuade her to invite me in, to raise the question of dates, showing her slyly how similar we were in some respects. To show her that I was first and foremost a professor, interested in art and architecture, not an intimidating soldier.

This time she shook hands less stiffly and smiled again. Four.

3

THE next day was Saturday, the day of the dance. I set off early to explore the countryside around Salzburg. I visited the waterfalls at Krimml, the ones Konstanze had described in her letters as "crowded with light." The weather was brilliant and I saw what she meant. I went to the glacier at Dachstein and I followed the Salzach River in my car, noting its features, the countryside and the villages it flowed through. I didn't get back to the hotel until nearly seven o'clock, leaving me not much time to change. One couldn't arrive late at the dance; it would be like a cattle market—men would choose an available woman and then stick to her all night. Army dances abroad were like that.

Ulrich, the Oliver Hardy look-alike concierge at the hotel, gave me two messages when I arrived back.

The first was in Sammy's writing; he must have dropped it off earlier in the day. It read, "Bad news and even worse news I am afraid. The bad news is that at close of business last night Confederate Paper was up twelve cents on the day, following an agreement between the U.S. and several European countries, concerning the supply of certain basics, paper included. That takes your friend Ghent's stake to $1,062 by my calculation. The worse news, I'm afraid, is that while people don't appear yet to have picked up the habit of insuring things—Atlantic Insurance hasn't moved either way—Metropolitan Motors are on the way up again—don't groan but they rose yesterday by all of fifty cents. Hope this doesn't spoil the dance for you. S.H."

I sighed.

Sammy must have come into the office that day and brought the second message with him, for it was a wire from Maurice, now back home in Offenbach, and it had been sent to my headquarters.

"Hermann doing well after her confinement," he had written. "But your Panama hat has seen better days. Two pups only are left; number three—a girl—has disappeared, possibly eaten by something or other.

The survivors move about, squeak, eat shirts and do all sorts of unspeakable things which I shall clean up before you return. They appear to be boys so suggest Dwight and Winston unless you prefer Monty and Patton. Hurry home. M."

Before going up to my room I scribbled a reply on the bottom and asked Ulrich to send it. I had written, "They appear to be doing too much damage to be Dwight or Winston. How about Spitfire and Messerschmidt? Shares now $1,062–$868 in your favor. Are you sure helmet will fit your big head? W."

The dance that night was a riot—I mean it literally. It would be talked about for weeks to come. The band was terrific but that only made people all the more crazy to dance and that, in turn, made things worse. An entire busload of women failed to arrive. The bus broke down and, in those days, breakdowns could be very final affairs. Which meant that women were in far shorter supply than liquor. Inevitably men without girls fell out with men who had girls. Men who had girls left them to get drinks from the bar and returned to find the girls they claimed as theirs being pawed by other men, very often men from a different state, a different ethnic group or a different army unit. In other words there was no shortage of reasons for disagreement. Sooner or later a brawl was inevitable. We were lucky in a way that it didn't happen until ten o'clock had come and gone.

One of the topics mulled over in the messes for weeks to come was whether there had been more damage inflicted on the dance hall itself or on the people in it. There was certainly a lot of blood, and a lot of light bulbs seemed to be broken. By general consent the band had the best of the deal, being paid in full yet having to play for only half the evening.

I managed to steer clear of the fighting just as what few women were there managed to steer clear of me. I did have two dances with a tall, sad-eyed Austrian girl who spoke no English and so found the fact that I was fluent in German not unattractive. But someone stole her while I was getting her a drink and before we had so much as exchanged names. I was in bed by eleven.

I went back to Mondsee on Monday. That way, I figured, it would convey the impression that what I was doing was a job. I had taken the weekend off to do more interesting things; now it was back to work. I was still around, and would stay until I got what I had come for.

I did not, however, go to the house this time. I went to the church.

The main door, large, worn and wooden, with two arches, was locked and I let myself in by a side entrance through a curtain. It was cool inside the church, but already sunny. On the far side of the nave was a huge stone font, carved, with a bronze plate on the top. I sat beyond this so I could not easily be seen.

I noticed that there was a high ornate pulpit halfway down the nave—perfect for hectoring anti-Protestant sermons. There was a small private chapel on the far side, with white flowers, lilies. The main altar, in black and gilded stucco and deep green marble, was closed off behind an elaborate wrought-iron gate, which was also black. Green, smooth steps rose to this gate from a wood-dark choir, earthy in its simplicity. Beyond the altar two slender stained-glass windows showed the life of the Virgin in all its primitive ecstasy. None of the individual features of the church was magnificent but the overall effect was—and that, for me, was the essence of baroque. The whole was greater, much greater, than the sum of its parts. I opened the book I had brought with me and settled down to wait.

Konstanze didn't appear until nearly two hours later, right at the end of the morning. She came in, walked quickly down the aisle and, without once looking back at her beloved organ and thus seeing me, sat in one of the front pews, crossed herself, knelt to pray. I had guessed that she would come. In the first place she had told me that she went to the church nearly every day. Second, today was exactly a year since she had gone with her husband and Dieter to the waterfalls at Krimml, when they had used the name von Haltern. It was the kind of thing I thought she would remember. She had come to pray for Rudolf.

Quietly, while she was absorbed in prayer, I moved to the back of the nave and sat where she could not fail to see me as she left. I had to wait, however, for the priest came by and, when she saw him, she got up and stood talking to him in the main aisle. From what I could hear they were discussing next Sunday's services, at which she was to play. Slowly they began to come toward me, down the aisle, still talking.

Because of the gloom, she didn't recognize me right away, but then she stopped and looked again. The uniform was unmistakable. The priest, who was doing most of the talking, stopped also. He looked at Mrs. von Zell, then at me, then back to her.

Her hostility was quite frank this time. She clearly felt that I had followed her into the church and was, in a way, eavesdropping on her prayers. It was too much.

It may have been clever of me to anticipate that she would come to the church today, but it was a mistake to surprise her as I had done. She was so angry that all the progress I had made before the weekend looked like it was ruined unless I could do something, say something, to calm her.

"I'm sorry if I startled you," I said and held up my book. "I've been looking at churches in the last few days. I started with Salzburg and Innsbruck, but I thought it was time to try some of the smaller towns. This seemed as good a place as any to start." I pointed across the nave. "I was sitting over there, by the font, when you came in. I didn't want to disturb you, so I waited back here."

"Waited? What for?" She was aggressive, but maybe there was a touch of curiosity in there too.

The priest, who until then had been standing nearby, mute and embarrassed, now muttered something and moved away. She turned to him, smiling. As she turned back to me, I led the way out of the church. Only when we were outside, in the bright sun, did I realize how cool it had been in there. We stood in front of the creamy building, squinting up at the twin towers, with their black clock faces and relief statues of the Virgin. To the right of the main facade a small fountain dripped disconsolately.

"Well, Lieutenant? What is it you were waiting for? I thought you said you were just looking at churches?" I had lost the advantage of the previous meeting. She was frankly suspicious and hostile.

"Yes," I said. "But looking at the few churches I have seen has given me an idea." I took her elbow and gently moved her down the slope in front of the church and toward the main market square. As we went I took care to compliment her on her dress, which that day was white with yellow zigzags. Ahead of us the sun glinted on the iron balustrade in front of the Café Braun, the main gathering place in Mondsee, not counting the church.

"I have my car here," I said. "Let me give you a ride back to your house. We can talk as we go."

I had parked the BMW in a side street, not far away but out of sight so that she would not see it on her way into the church. The top was down and, when I opened the passenger door for her, she got in gracefully.

Nowadays, so long after the war, a drive in an open car in the sunshine along the edge of a lake is pleasant but hardly special. In 1946 it was quite different. For most of us, and for Mrs. von Zell certainly, it was a new and intoxicating experience. It didn't take very long to get back to her house, and that may have been why the ride was so successful; it gave her the briefest of tastes of the pleasures of the BMW.

The lake, as I had come to expect, was black and glittering. The mountains beyond were beautiful. I knew Mrs. von Zell was enjoying herself, because she didn't confront me again about what it was I was waiting to say to her in the church. She just enjoyed the mixed sensations of the car's noises, the smell of the exhaust and the shimmering haze that the sun produced on the black, melting road. In fact, the ride that day, in perfect weather, could well have been the reason why the rest of this story turned out the way it did.

I drove past Mrs. von Zell's house to the spot amid the trees where I had parked on my first visits. The engine died and the sounds of the lake took over. There were a few more fishing boats out today. The water was warming up all the time and the saibling were becoming more and more active. As we sat we could hear them feeding, soft but deep-sounding, comfortable swishes, as they took the flies and sank from the surface.

In front of us the road stretched in a straight line for almost a kilometer, unusually straight considering it ran along the lakeshore. There were two figures at the far end walking toward us. What looked like a child and an adult.

"It's Dieter," said Konstanze. "With Martha." And, oddly, I got the impression she was disappointed, as though her son's return with the housekeeper would curtail her enjoyment of the open car. She was running her hand along the edge of the door, the top edge, almost caressing it as if it were alive, like a pet or a child. There was a sudden commotion on the lake—one of the silhouettes had caught a fish. His black rod was warped in a perfect parabola. We looked on as the trout was hauled in, glistening purple and brown, slapping helplessly.

Dieter, I noticed, kept stopping by the roadside, picking things.

"He's a strange and wonderful child," said Mrs. von Zell when I remarked on this. "He has decided that, since everyone else takes so much interest in flowers, he will be interested in leaves. He makes up his own words for their shapes and their different shades of green. He says leaves are nature's underdogs. Can you imagine that?"

I saw my chance. "Do you think it matters, having a son, with your husband away such a lot?"

She surprised me by the frankness of her answer. "Yes," she said plainly. "Dieter has not seen his father at all since the war ended. But he had seen him only infrequently before that. I'm sure it has made a difference. It may not show for years. But it's there."

Martha and the child were barely a hundred yards away now, still picking leaves. I knew that their arrival would break the spell that had been accidentally woven by the weather, the fish and the open car.

"I envy you, Dieter," I said. "In America, because I am a well-paid professor and have no children, I am everybody's favorite godfather. All my friends ask me when a Christening is coming up. I have *seven* godchildren—Katie is my favorite, then there is William, Simon, Christina, Pietr, Sally, and another whose name I can't even remember, there are so many. I am flattered, of course, and it means that when I do go back to America, a bachelor again, there are always plenty of invitations to spend Christmas, Easter or Thanksgiving. But it gets expensive, with gifts at Christmas, and hardly a month without someone's birthday."

I laughed. "I complain, but I miss them, you know. Every month I write them a letter—I send the same one to everybody." I looked at Konstanze and smiled again. "You can't imagine how hard it is to get six sheets of carbon paper into an army typewriter."

She was holding back her head, letting a sudden gust of wind tug at her hair. Her eyes were closed and she was smiling, either at my story or at her own recollections of some of Dieter's foibles in the past, things he had done or said that made her laugh.

The spell was working on her too. I would not get a better opportunity for what I planned. I glanced down the road to see how far away Dieter and Martha were. They were part of my plan too. I had a speech to make to Konstanze, a speech I wanted her to think about before replying, before saying no, as she would do if she had the chance to answer right away. If I could time my speech so that it ended just as Dieter arrived, then the spell might be broken at just the right time.

"Mrs. von Zell, you give me an idea. I hope that by now I have persuaded you I am not like the other men sent to find your husband's whereabouts. I am not going to threaten you with deportation to the

Russian zone, or anything like that. I am who I say I am and I do want to explore the architecture of this country. Therefore my idea is this. Come and explore the countryside with me for a few days. We can walk in the hills, explore the lakes, collect the flowers, see the rivers, visit churches. I have the perfect car for it—there is room for Dieter and the weather is on our side. You can keep me company and I can do the same for you. You have been separated for a year, you say, from your husband, so you must be a *little* bored at being confined to your house and to Mondsee. You must have some curiosity about the rest of this lovely country. I am tired of being married to the Army, of spending my life with other men or alone. I miss children. I have my army wages, saved up for months because there is so little I want to spend them on. I need a holiday.

"I lied to you before. I gave you the impression I have all the time in the world for this case. I don't. If I don't get the information in a few weeks, I'll be pulled off the case. The deal is this. Spend the days with me, in the countryside, looking at churches, picnicking, enjoying ourselves. Then, at the end of ten days, if you feel like helping me with the gold coins, all well and good. If not, I'll go away. I promise never to raise the subject of the coins until the very end. But even then, no pressure. If you don't want to tell me, I'll just go away.

"Think of it, if you like, as a game. It lasts ten days and there is a winner and a loser. If you think you can hold out, what have you got to lose? You will enjoy the fields, my car, the churches—and keep your secret."

Martha and Dieter had started walking toward us again but had still not seen the car, parked in among the trees. Dieter's mother had stopped stroking the door. Instead she used the other hand to fiddle with the gear shift.

"I could teach you to drive," I murmured.

She leaned forward and touched the dials closest to her on the dashboard, the fuel gauge, the rev counter, the battery charger, one by one, like a blind person feeling a lover's face. She spoke softly, without looking at me.

"A game? It is like making a pact with the devil. You promise me . . . pleasure, relief, learning for a few days . . . but at what risk? I may regret it for the rest of my life. The hardships of the war lasted six long years. You offer respite for less than two weeks. You are not brutal, Lieutenant, that I accept. But maybe your plan is cruel."

"Mummy!" Dieter had seen us at last. He left Martha and galloped toward the car, wrenching open the passenger door and scrambling onto his mother's lap.

"Can we go for a ride? Please, Mummy, say yes! I've never been in a car like this before, all open. And Daddy always had that horrid driver, Kleiber. *Please.*"

He looked at me, expecting me to start the car. I looked across to his mother.

"Just along the lake then, as far as Sterneck. Then back home."

We left poor Martha to walk back to the house alone and drove south along the shore to the next village. Dieter hung his head out of the side of the car so that he could feel the slipstream swish through his hair. He yelled loudly at all the children he knew as we passed, showing off. At Sterneck I pulled into the main square, turned the car and stopped by the café.

"Shall we have a pastry?" I asked generally.

Dieter's smile said "Yes, please" but his mother was equally clear. "No. Please start the engine. We must go back." I was being too familiar again.

Dieter's disappointment vanished as soon as we were on the move again. "Can you go faster?" he said, but we were already doing seventy kilometers an hour and that was quite enough on a lakeshore road in those days.

When I pulled up outside the latch gate at their house, there was no sign of Martha. Mrs. von Zell opened the passenger door and said to her son, "Say 'Thank you' to the lieutenant. Then run in and find Martha. Tell her I have some fish for lunch."

The boy squirmed around on his mother's lap and held out his hand in that extremely old-fashioned manner some young children have. "Thank you, sir," he said. "Can we go farther next time? And faster?"

I nodded noncommittally, looking over his head at his mother.

He got down and skipped into the house. I waited. The car engine was still running. I noticed Martha sneak a look from one of the windows. Her glance was dark and disapproving.

"There is one condition," said Mrs. von Zell after a short while. She was still not looking at me. "We must drive away from here to villages where they do not know me. Not Salzburg, not Mondsee, not Sterneck. Not anywhere on this lake or in the Fuschl Valley. You understand? It would look—unusual." She stopped and at last turned her head toward me. "Those are my terms."

"I understand."

"Then I accept the risk. It will be good for Dieter to get out and about. You may call for us tomorrow. At ten-thirty."

CHAPTER SIX

1

AND so the game I had planned began. The next ten days are the ones which, looking back, I most regret. I behaved brilliantly at times, and I behaved badly. Enough to say, perhaps, that my shame has stayed with me throughout the years since the war, growing more secret maybe, as each April passes and, once more, I think back. But it does not diminish. It is unfashionable now to admit to regrets, so let me say, plainly, that I am the exception. I regret what I did in those ten days: I regretted it as soon as I had done it and I have regretted it ever since. Some time ago I broke my ankle. It healed so that it is again as strong as ever; however, the bone has thickened fractionally and this small deformity serves to remind me of the injury every morning when I put on my socks. My shame is like that: emotionally I am deformed and a day never goes by without my remembering, with a shiver, what I did during those ten wonderful, terrible days.

We met the next day as arranged. I had polished the BMW for the adventure and Dieter was delighted, pulling faces in the bright chrome of the headlamps. Konstanze had dressed him in a thick jumper (no one said sweater in those days), bright green with red birds knitted into it. I admired it. She had on a cloak of some autumn color, russet or mahogany, maybe, under a cheerful butter-cup-colored hat and shiny brown boots. We were all, I think, looking forward to the day, all that is except Martha, who stared suspiciously from the balcony and waved back peremptorily as we shot off.

Having Dieter with me, I remember noticing that day how much the waxy undersides of the leaves on the trees shimmered in the sunshine. It was hotter than ever. Each time we slowed for a bend or a turn, or because we were held up by farm traffic, we could feel the sun beat on our necks. The exposed leather of the car seats began to smell with the heat.

I had studied our army maps overnight and had brought the local one with me. We could escape Mondsee by the back roads to meet Konstanze's condition. It meant taking the least direct route a couple of times but the day was so glorious no one minded that. None of us spoke for a while, each of us adjusting to what the other's company felt like. There was plenty to see.

Eventually I could no longer avoid the more important roads and we found ourselves in a line of traffic, army trucks mainly.

"I thought we'd start with Krimml," I said above the noise. "I'm told the waterfall there is wonderful and I thought it would be more fun for Dieter than spending the whole day in dreary churches."

"It's *ever* so high," Dieter piped up. "We went last year, with Daddy. It takes the water six and a half seconds to fall from top to bottom. Someone timed it."

"The church *is* interesting, though," I added, again falling back on what I knew from the letters. "It has some fine mosaics showing the lives of the saints, which is unusual for a baroque church."

"What's a mosaic?" said Dieter.

His mother answered, sounding a little bit like Sammy Hartt, except that she wasn't trying to flatter anyone or ingratiate herself. She was genuinely interested in the subject and quite knowledgeable. It had been a good ploy of mine to raise the topic; Konstanze relaxed as she spoke to her son.

It took just over an hour to arrive at Krimml, not bad considering we didn't go through Salzburg. Dieter was a definite speed fanatic, urging me to go faster whenever we could. At Krimml, Konstanze insisted on going to the church first. "Dieter will be tired later, so I'd like him to have a quick look now." She led the way inside, marching purposefully and pulling the boy with her.

The church was an all-white building on the outside with the now familiar twin towers. Once inside Konstanze made no immediate attempt to view the decorations or the pictures, but walked down the main aisle halfway, stopped, lowered herself on to one knee and crossed herself. Then she slid into a pew to pray. Dieter, beside her, copied her movements. He'd been in similar situations before, in Mondsee.

This posed a problem for me. What did *I* do? I was not a religious man. I *was* eager to ingratiate myself with Konstanze, to make her like me, but religion is one of those things people have difficulty lying about —even me. So I hesitated. I knew she might think less of me if I didn't say a short prayer, but I had my own conscience to think about. A malleable commodity, I know, but there was still a little of it left. In the end I sat a row or two behind the other two, looked about the church and waited.

As she raised her head and slid back onto her seat, I rose and walked forward, down the main aisle, looking up at the dark, carved pulpit. She might assume that, behind her, I had been praying also. She followed me, our boots clacking in unison on the white marble floor. I pointed out the carvings on the pulpit, which were scenes from Paul's conversion (her favorite story as I knew, but was not supposed to know). She was pleased, as I had intended her to be; the day was going well. As we circled around the nave, looking up at the pulpit, the pictures, the ceiling and down at the mosaics, I found that I returned with ease to my old lecturing style. My gestures and mannerisms came back from my subconscious where they had been buried. Students had told me that I had a way of hesitating, of biting my bottom lip, when I wished to indicate that I had reached a point about which even I, as a professor, was uncertain. I had forgotten this, but it came back now, as strong as the tide.

Mrs. von Zell was no ordinary student, and it was she more than I who set the tone and the flavor of our relationship that morning. She listened to me civilly enough for a while but then let me know that she saw me for what I was—an educated but godless professor who saw only stones, carved wood and paintings where she saw—well, the glories of worship, love, pity, the search for companionship, for meaning.

"Don't whisper, Professor," she boomed at one point. "There's nothing shameful here. If you don't believe in God, there's no one to overhear you. If you do, He can hear you anyway." It was a reprimand to emphasize that she could tell I did not spend my time in churches as a worshiper, and that whispering was my way of keeping my distance. But she made it a joke nonetheless and we both managed to smile.

We took some postcards of the church, which, as a sentimental hoarder of things, I knew Konstanze would appreciate. We sat in the churchyard writing. I had a brand-new pen which Dieter admired, the latest issue from the Army, with an eraser on the end. Konstanze, with her passion for pens, liked it, too, I could tell. But she didn't say much.

We left the church and explored the tow ; the waterfalls were to be saved until after lunch. Krimml was a small place, built on a steep slope just below the tree line, so it was pleasantly leafy. There seemed to be nothing but patisseries, but eventually we found a restaurant proper with a terrace that overlooked a skating rink. I ordered wine, an Austrian Welsch-Riesling, and we chose to eat fresh trout from the local river. While we waited for our food Dieter ran off to take a closer look at the skaters.

I got out some cigarettes, more of the type Konstanze preferred, and as we sat in the sun, smoking. I thought what a good-looking couple we must make. Under normal circumstances I would have enjoyed my time with Konstanze, even though her child and her religion would have made her a difficult prize. But that day in Krimml I was in a hurry. I had ten days to get somewhere with her, ten days to develop our relationship to the point where she would help me. I had to move fast, to create a cocoon around us in order to distort her perspective. And to do that I had only one weapon, the personal information and the inside track the letters gave me. They had already helped me enormously, providing me with details about her love of music, her concern with dates and all the other things I had used to gain her attention and sympathy, and they had been invaluable in speeding me to the point where I was now sitting in this restaurant with her in the sun. Sooner or later it would become obvious to her that I had access to her most intimate thoughts. What then? Should I try to stage-manage things so that she gradually realized what had happened? Or would it be better if I suddenly revealed all? It might ruin everything but, on the other hand, it might advance our intimacy rapidly. What kind of man *was* I to be thinking in such manipulative terms anyway? My instincts were to keep quiet and use the letters as much to my advantage as possible. Slowly, slyly, I would plot my course, at least for the time being. Konstanze was very clever, very cunning, and would realize soon enough where I had found my information and what I was up to. She might even know where those booklets of music had come from.

The waiter brought the wine and she looked at me and said, "That's a coincidence, that was one of Rudi's favorite wines. I didn't recognize the name when you ordered it but I know the label. He always preferred the Austrian Riesling to the German. He said they were softer, more feminine wines. The actual word he used was 'shyer.' "

Fortunately I was squinting into the sun as she said all this, so I could smother my reaction. She was speaking of a wine I had selected quite by accident. I looked at the label, as she was doing, and my heart changed gears. The wine came from Krumau, the town that was circled in pencil on the map in her sewing room.

"Was your husband an expert on wines, Mrs. von Zell?"

She savored the Riesling before replying. "An expert amateur, I think you would have called him. That's what he called himself. But"—she looked around, searching for Dieter—"we agreed not to mention him. It was my fault this time, I know, but you mustn't encourage me."

Dieter came running up, hot and excited from the skating rink, as our food arrived. Mother and child had an easy relationship. She did not talk down to him but neither did she stand for any nonsense. Dieter was well-mannered and polite. He was, at the moment, mad to go skating and his mother agreed he could, but insisted he eat his lunch calmly first. I said I would pay for the rent of the skates as my gift for the day. Dieter looked delighted but Konstanze was thoughtful.

But I still had to move things along, using my inside knowledge. I waited until we had finished the fish and Dieter had dashed off again to the rink. "I'm a terrible skater," I said, looking after him. "How about you?"

She shook her head from side to side, smiling. "Awful."

"In fact, I'm not athletic in any real sense," I went on. "I always left those activities to my brother. I can't run very fast, or swim well or water ski at all. The only physical exercise that I ever get in America is bicycling."

Music had started up at the skating rink, a raucous, repetitive organ piece—hardly church music. She put her fingers in her ears, smiling at me. She was relaxing.

"You know, if you had not laid down your rule—that we get away from Mondsee—we could have gone bicycling around the lake today. It would have been marvelous in this weather, and good for us to get some exercise."

She shook her head, wildly, as if she were trying to shake the skaters' music out of her brain. "No. Dieter would soon have tired; and we would not have seen many churches that way, would we? No cathedrals or abbeys?"

This was the game which, time and again, we would play in the days to come. I would invent a conversation, starting with something I had remembered from the letters. *My* side of the exchanges were designed to show how similar we were, to give her yet more reason for liking me, so that at the end of our time she would want to help me find the coins. *Her* responses were invariably wary. It was some time before she realized I had read all her letters in close detail. Usually, as on that first day when we discussed bicycling, the conversations were left unresolved; they just trailed off and each of us would read into them what we could.

We lingered over the coffee, feeling the sun radiate off the tablecloth between us, warming our faces. Dieter eventually came back from the rink, his shins aching from the exercise. Konstanze rubbed them briskly but wasted no more attention than that on him. We were ready to explore the waterfalls.

To some people the falls of Krimml are more impressive than either Niagara or Victoria. I had been to neither but the setting of Krimml, overlooking the beautiful Inn Valley, must take some beating. The water, boiling and giddy with millions of bubbles, launches itself down a three hundred-foot twist of rainbow to a waxy green pool below.

Standing by the pool at the bottom, deafened by the roar, we watched the same bubbles, now silently simmering. Here the waterfall created its own climate, cold and damp, the rocks behind us permanently wet from the spray that escaped the pool. Behind the falls itself a natural cave had been formed in the stone at the insistence of the water. Dieter, being too small, could not see over the concrete balustrade designed to protect people just like him. I signaled silently to Konstanze to ask if I might lift him up so that he could see the cave. She nodded her consent.

He was heavier than I expected. He looked lean but, as I held him, I could feel that he was in fact quite chubby. Many children in Europe, this close to the war, were still suffering its nutritional effects—under-nourishment, vitamin deficiencies and so on. Not everyone of course, but these things were not uncommon. As I held Dieter aloft, and his young imagination searched the cave for demons and serpents and vipers, I wondered if his chubbiness should be a clue for me. His green and red sweater was nearly new and of fine quality. For the first time I wondered if those gold coins were helping to keep Mrs. von Zell and Dieter in reasonable comfort. Shaken, I thought: Perhaps that's why she can get eggs—she pays in gold.

Dieter signaled he had had enough and I put him down. Back at the car, I suggested we take the quiet road back, the one which stuck close to the river Inn; then we could find somewhere pretty to have tea. Dieter enthusiastically agreed but his mother insisted that we head straight home.

"He's exhausted; he won't enjoy the tea and we won't enjoy having him lolling about all over us."

So that was that—but she was right. We had not gone ten minutes that afternoon before the swaying of the car and the sweet air had sent Dieter fast asleep on the backseat. At Mondsee I was able to lift him up, carry him in and hand him over to Martha without so much as a murmur.

2

THE next day I had to disappoint Dieter, who, I know, was looking forward to a second jaunt. I had to disappoint myself, come to that. When I had arrived back at the hotel after the Krimml expedition, I found a note addressed to me from Hobel. "Please come to the office tomorrow. And keep lunch free."

It turned out that a party of American and British journalists were in town and Hobel wanted me to brief them over lunch on the workings of the art recovery unit. They were like most journalists, a suspicious bunch, aggressively unashamed of their ignorance in both military and artistic matters, certain in themselves that, however philistine they were, their readers were even more so. I am sure they thought me a strange bird, if I do say so myself, with my old-fashioned pipe and a command of several languages. I am afraid that I was unable to hide my contempt for them and lunch was not a success.

That afternoon I had a long conversation on the phone with Saul Wolfert. He was making progress. It had been fairly easy to check the forthcoming marriages in Zurich, the Swiss being a methodical and puritanical nation, and his inquiries had convinced him that Aubing, or von Zell, or whoever he was, was not going to be married in Zurich. So he had a suspect who lied, who had a reason to lie, and that interested him much more. He had already dispatched two men to Krumau with orders to be discreet and not do anything that might frighten von Zell away. If they did find him they were to watch him for a while. We needed the coins back, or what was left of them, but we also wanted to destroy the underground conduit if we could. I told Saul about the Welsch-Riesling from Krumau that had been von Zell's favorite. That encouraged him still further.

I reported all this to Hobel, or rather to his secretary, since he was out somewhere. She listened and said she would pass on the message, but I could tell she was disappointed I had not already been fired.

"I didn't see you at the dance on Saturday," I said politely.

She sniffed. "Dance? It was a riot. The men here are rude and contemptible."

"Then they have a great deal in common with the women."

It was unfair of me to stoop to petty exchanges, but I was in a bad mood all day that day. I felt that I was wasting time in not being able to get to Mondsee. I spent what was left of the day at Mozart's house in Salzburg, which I had not yet seen, then had dinner alone in the hotel.

As I ate I considered my moods during the day. I had hated having lunch with those journalists but, as the wine began to relax me, I had to admit that it had been an entirely reasonable request of Hobel's to have me brief them. There was no imminent development in the von Zell case and I was the ranking officer in the area, with the experience and the knowledge. Why then was I so moody?

I sipped my after-dinner coffee. The letters I had read were supposed to have given me an advantage over Mrs. von Zell. Yet, sitting there in the hotel, I wasn't sure. I didn't *feel* as though I had the upper hand. Not by a long shot. For the first time it crossed my mind that I might lose the game.

The following day was a Thursday and was marred by the ice-cream incident.

It had started well enough. Dieter was waiting on the swing in the garden when I pulled up outside the house. All the doors and windows of the building were wide-open as the unseasonably warm weather continued. After just a few days of sunshine we were all behaving as if we were used to such a glorious climate, could rely on it and assumed it would continue forever. I sounded the horn to call Dieter's mother from the house and then got out of the car brandishing two long, French-style *baguette* loaves.

My plan that day was for us to follow the Salzach River, a device to remind her of the romantic times she had spent on or near rivers, years before with Bruno and her husband. South of Salzburg the river slips through succulent countryside, rich meadows of barley studded with knots of birch. We could picnic at a spot I had in mind, a place I had reconnoitered over the weekend, and in the afternoon there were churches to visit at Kuchl and Golling. Besides the bread, I was equipped with all sorts of treats including a bottle of Welsch-Riesling, which I was trying to keep cool under my seat.

When Konstanze appeared it seemed as if she, too, had thought of having a picnic. She was dressed in a pair of dark green trousers, with a yellow shirt under a white sweater. As she walked across the lawn to where I was gently beating Dieter's head with one of the *baguettes,* I noticed that she had washed her hair again that morning; it was silky and fluffy and had been pinned back with two bright yellow combs. Her face was blotched from washing—a clean but imperfect look. Her well-kept beauty was to please herself, not me.

"Eggs," I cried. "That's what we need—hard-boiled eggs. I have bread"—and I tapped Dieter's head again with the loaf—"cheese, salami, wine and an army map of the Salzach, showing churches and picnic spots." As she came close I could smell the soap she had scrubbed her face with and I felt an unwinding inside me. "You look good enough to eat too," I said before I could stop myself. Several expressions competed for her features—a shy, embarrassed smile, suspicion and anger at my tactlessness in front of the boy. But embarrassment won the day and more blotches marked her cheeks. She covered by stooping down and shooing Dieter back into the house to fetch his jacket, just in case.

"Give me five minutes to boil the eggs," she murmured to me, straightening up. "I have some honey, too, if you like that."

I waved expansively, as if the sunshine were an endless gift. "We have all day." Was honey expensive? I wondered. Where did she get it? How did she pay for it? How did she pay for *anything?*

It was barely noon as I nosed the BMW into the green Salzach Valley and turned south, upstream. The Salzach is not one of Europe's grandest rivers but it is one of the most beautiful. Its valley is narrow, its course straight and fast, its waters clear, except where the cold rocks punch the flow into white rapids. At that time cars were a real luxury and, between villages, we more or less had the road to ourselves. Before long I spotted the wooden bridge that led across the river. A narrow lane wound behind some trees, emerging as no more than a track between the water and a strip of meadow beyond. I stopped the car and the engine died.

One advantage of this spot, as I had found on my previous visit, was that the current slowed here, allowing sedges and cress of various kinds to take hold, attracting in turn all kinds of wildlife. Dieter was the first out, naturally, seemingly anxious to frighten off any birds or fish that we might have seen.

His mother clacked her tongue on the roof of her mouth. "Now I see what his schoolmasters mean when they say he's 'volcanic.' No wonder they moved him out of the main dormitory."

I didn't know until then that the boy went away to school. It must be recent because it wasn't mentioned in any of the letters. How could she afford *that?* I wondered.

We took out the food and set it down on the bank. From the basket she had brought for the eggs and honey she took a yellow gingham cloth and spread it over the grass.

While the lunch was being laid out I searched the trunk of the car. I soon found what I needed—a long length of string. I gave it a yank and tore it in two. One length I tied around the neck of the wine bottle, which I was then able to suspend in the river to cool it. The other length of string I took back to the car, where I picked up a slice of salami I had cut before setting out for Mondsee. With a series of knots I managed to tie a couple of pieces of this to one end of the string.

"Fish won't eat that, will they?" asked Dieter, skipping over to where I was kneeling. "Those lumps are much too big."

I winked and said, "Come with me." I took him to a point about fifty meters away, where the bank jutted out into the river and the water slowed still further. I stood on the point and, taking firm hold of one end of the string, threw the sausages as far as I could into the river, upstream. "Now we wait," I whispered. "It shouldn't take more than a few minutes."

But it did. It took longer than Dieter had the patience for. He had noticed some ducks downstream and just had to dash off and scare them. Mrs. von Zell was much less fretful; she was sitting contentedly, arranging the lunch. She had managed to light my portable army stove and was warming the water with which we would make coffee.

Suddenly, though, not more than a minute or two later, her calm was disturbed by the "volcano"—Dieter—who hurtled back. The ducks had turned out to be cygnets and their mother, a Hindenburg of a swan only much more ferocious, had appeared from nowhere and cawed menacingly at the boy the minute he had ventured too close.

While I was laughing at the story Dieter was telling his mother, with an air of perplexed indignation, as if the swan had disturbed *his* natural habitat, I felt a tug on the string. I said nothing but, very gently, pulled it in. You couldn't rush these things. I knew from the weight that I had quite a catch and, sure enough, as I pulled the string free of the river, I could see there were two of them—a good start. When they were safely on the bank I called out, "Dieter, Mrs. von Zell, come and see. I've caught something!"

Dieter barreled right over, nearly treading on them as he skidded to a halt. Mrs. von Zell stopped what she was doing and joined us.

"See," I said. "We can have a hot lunch after all." Crawling about on the bank at my feet were two wet, crackly, parchment-colored crayfish. "Pieces of old chicken are the best bait for these," I said, reloading my string. "But sausage works almost as well."

Dieter was delighted; crayfish were exactly the kinds of creepy-crawly things he liked. He asked if he might be allowed to hold the line from now on.

I noticed his mother looking doubtfully at our luncheon guests.

"Don't worry," I reassured her. "They are delicious when they are this fresh. The water in this river is quite clean, so there is no danger of disease. Just pop them in the boiling water with a little salt. With that fresh crusty bread I brought, we'll have a real feast."

She was not convinced and just stood there, looking at them, not moving. I had to carry them over to the stove myself and place them in the water. I added salt and said, "I thought you enjoyed rivers. You must have fished before. Have you never caught crayfish?"

She shook her head. She was about to say something when Dieter erupted again. "I've got one! I've got one!"

I stood up. "Pull it in slowly," I shouted. "Or you may lose it." We both hurried over to the point, where Dieter, with total concentration, was pulling in the string very slowly indeed. We got there just in time to see him yank the string clear of the water. A single, dripping crayfish, larger and darker than the two we had already landed, was feeding greedily off the sausage.

Dieter swelled with pride.

"Well done!" I said. "Now we all have some lunch."

We returned to the picnic site, Dieter triumphantly carrying his trophy, which he dropped with relish into the boiling water.

I retrieved the wine from the river, opened it and presented a glass to Mrs. von Zell. The acrid bite of the cooking crayfish began to flavor the air about us. I sampled the wine myself and lay back on the gingham cloth. Dieter was standing, inspecting his crayfish as it cooked in the water.

"How long do they take to cook?" He was transfixed by what was happening in the pot.

"A few more minutes. Until I finish this glass of wine."

"What will they taste like?"

"Have you never had shellfish?"

"Have I, Mummy?"

"Never." And that, I knew, meant never.

I rolled over and looked at Konstanze. "What would you say shellfish are like? How would you describe the taste?"

She was cutting the *baguettes* into small pieces. She stopped, looked at the boy, then at me. "Warm, salty, rubber bands."

I laughed as Dieter pulled a face.

I got to my knees. "I think they should be done now, if there are any takers, after that." I put on one of my army gloves and pulled the pot from the stove, tipping the hot water into the river. "Now the shells are very hot," I said, gingerly lifting the crayfish out of the pot and sliding them onto the plates. "Let them cool for a while; then we spread a little butter over them, a little more salt, maybe. Then . . . *ecrevisse pique-nique.*" I turned to Mrs. von Zell. "Shall I peel Dieter's for him?"

She smiled and nodded and I began, the boy standing over me to watch. I spread butter on the pale gray meat, added salt and handed the plate to Dieter. Although he took it, he said, "You first."

"Not as tough as you look, eh," I said, laughing, and started to peel my own. I garnished it and, without a second thought, munched away in front of them. I shook my head in admiration, the butter slithering between my lips. "Delicious." Neither Dieter nor his mother moved. I appealed to them. "It *has* to be. The poor creature was swimming around alive less than fifteen minutes ago. This is a treat you rarely get, I promise you. Come on—eat up."

Dieter at last nibbled on his. Tentative at first, but as soon as he found it was not like a medicine he admitted that he liked it and chewed with increasing gusto. "We get rubber bands at school," he said, joining the joke. "And boiled seaweed, and cardboard. This is much nicer."

Mrs. von Zell picked at hers. She took off the tail and ate some of that, but she didn't even attempt to touch the claws. I passed her the cheese and salami; no point in forcing the crayfish on her. The crusty bread, golden as autumn, was delicious with butter.

Dieter did most of the talking. He was on holiday from school just now, he said breathlessly when I questioned him, and had only a few more days before he must go back. He didn't mind, though. It was unusual, but for a boy of his years he seemed to enjoy school, mathematics and music especially, and, of course, games. They had soccer every Tuesday afternoon; he played and loved it.

"Bet you can't guess what instrument I play," he said, fidgeting over and standing right above me. "Go on, guess."

He was so earnest, just then, so certain that I would never in a thousand years be able to guess his instrument, that I couldn't resist it.

"Let's see," I said. "How about . . . how about . . . the cello." I felt slightly guilty at the sudden flash of disappointment that he showed.

His eyes widened. "Gosh! That's clever. How did you know?" He looked at his mother. "How did he know?"

"Just a lucky guess," I said, making light of it and offering him some salami. I had the army map in front of me. "Now," I said loudly, in a way designed to change the mood. "Why don't we explore the river. According to this there should be another bridge farther downstream, where we can cross. And there should be some waterfalls beyond that. What do you say?"

Dieter was delighted to be on the move again and pulled his mother up from the grass. We left the picnic things as they were. We had seen no one during lunch, so it seemed quite safe.

Left to himself, the boy would have run on ahead and I would have been able to talk to Konstanze. But she was wary; it was a river, after all, and quite deep in places. Dieter could swim, she said, but since he was so young, not strongly. She made him stick close.

On that walk, I remember, she did most of the talking. Maybe she wanted to prevent me leading the conversation into areas she didn't wish to go. She knew a great deal about the plant life you find on riverbanks and she talked interestingly and clearly, keeping Dieter's attention as well as mine. She never talked down to the boy and treated him just as she treated me. If either of us said something silly, she told us so. If either of us asked a question, the answer to which we could have worked out ourselves, she was short with us. Dieter might be only seven but he was already treated as an equal. I found myself thinking that, whatever happened, when I returned to America I would want to have a family.

We reached the bridge, crossed to the other bank and followed the river as far as the waterfall. It wasn't really a waterfall as much as a stretch of rapids, and below these, we were fascinated to see, stood a solitary fisherman, up to his shins in the water, a whiskey-colored cane rod in his hands. He was wearing a floppy green hat with a wide brim to protect his eyes from the glare of the sun, and as we stood watching he cast and recast with an easy but powerful grace. The white-green line curled lazily behind him, not unlike the long tentacles of a crayfish; then, smoothly, he flicked it forward again so that it reached out across the river, farther and farther, quite level, before it finally gave up and sank as if exhausted onto the water all at once, the artificial fly dipping and skidding just like a real insect.

As we watched, the three of us standing close, I caught occasional, elusive snatches of Mrs. von Zell's smell—mainly the smack of clean clothes hung out to dry in the warm, fresh air. I was standing behind her and found myself staring at the collar of her yellow shirt; it looked quite new. It went against the grain, but once more I found myself wondering whether the gold coins had paid for it.

The fisherman caught nothing—much to Dieter's sorrow—and after a while we turned back. On this return trek Konstanze noticed, across the river on the opposite bank, a very rare species of plant. I forget what it was but I do remember that she got quite excited. So much so that, when we crossed the bridge again, we had to turn back and examine the spot in more detail. We found it without any difficulty and once again she gave us both a mini-lecture. As she spoke I was amused to note the similarity between mother and child. When she was preoccupied she held her face in exactly the same way as Dieter: her mouth slightly open, her eyes fixed on a point somewhere beyond us, the slightest of puzzled frowns on her forehead. What she said was as clear as the waters of the Salzach. She would make a fine university lecturer in botany or biology, I thought as we listened.

After the lecture, on the way back to the car, we passed the spot where Dieter had his encounter with the swans. They had disappeared but I now noticed something that would make a perfect memento for the day—a dislodged white swan's feather. I gave it to Dieter to keep safe for his mother until they got home.

As we neared the picnic spot Dieter was allowed at last to skip on ahead while Konstanze spotted another plant that she didn't recognize and stopped to examine it. She stooped, snapped off a couple of shoots, straightened up and fixed me with those sharp eyes.

"You are right, Lieutenant. I *am* interested in rivers. But how did you know?"

She didn't miss a thing, Mrs. von Zell. I had deliberately planted that but she hadn't responded at the time and I thought she hadn't noticed. Remember, I told myself—do not underestimate this woman.

"It was in the file on you," I lied. "The report I read back at the base."

She had walked on a step. Now she wheeled and faced me again. "And how did you know that Dieter plays the cello?"

"That was a lucky guess. Really. It's my own favorite instrument. Why are you asking all these questions?"

Now it was her turn not to reply. At least for a while. We walked on in thoughtful silence until the car came into view and Dieter saw us and waved. He had tied a piece of uneaten sausage to the string and was fishing again for crayfish. Mrs. von Zell stopped out of earshot of the boy and looked at me. "It is not only swans who will turn nasty to protect their families, Lieutenant. Remember that."

We packed the picnic things away in silence. I didn't quite know what to make of her reference to the swans. Did it mean that she had realized I had read the letters? I had introduced those references partly because it was the only way I knew to accelerate our intimacy and partly because I wanted to see how she would react once she knew I had read the letters. Of course I was cheating in the game. I was not supposed to make any direct reference to her husband or the coins. But in constantly raising material from the letters I was keeping up the pressure, as I had to do. Maybe she had not fully realized yet what I was up to. At this stage she might have found it difficult to believe that anyone could be so dedicated, so intrusive, as to have read the entire correspondence so closely. If so, she would be disillusioned.

We dragged Dieter away from his crayfish and drove on down the river. The two churches we visited that afternoon were smaller than the one we had seen at Krimml but in some ways they were better examples of stucco work. That afternoon we established a routine. Konstanze and Dieter would pray in each church when we arrived while I examined the outside of the building. Then I would show them quickly around. Dieter would disappear, to play outside, while his mother and I went around again, this time more slowly. I remember that afternoon we saw some fine examples of Beduzzi frescoes and statues by Peter Widerin.

And I must say Konstanze began to teach me something about art. Not factual things. But her reactions to paintings, and especially to sculpture, were quite different than mine. In the first place, she responded more to sculpture than to painting. Whereas I had always found paintings more expressive, more subtle, she seemed to find the three dimensions of sculpture more real. For me, someone like Peter Widerin was a series of dates, with a known *oeuvre* which fitted into the development of sculpture in Europe. Konstanze saw none of that. She saw a religious man who had no knowledge of evolution, no scientific doubt, a man for whom the ordinary emotions of the flesh were as nothing when compared with his feelings for God. She used sculpture, as she used paintings, to try to understand what the emotional life of mankind was like before the corrosive influences of modern times. That seemed to be her aim—to recover that emotional texture. That was what her religion meant to her. She couldn't understand why I didn't long for the same thing. In time I came to understand what she meant.

It was on the drive back that day that the ice-cream incident occurred.

At Vigaun, a town about an hour south of Salzburg, I stopped when I noticed a café that had just put out its tables for the summer season. Dieter had announced that he was thirsty, and so was I. We had tea, lemonade for Dieter, and ice cream. I had to spend my wages on *something* and the ice cream was my gift for the day, I said.

I read out the flavors from the menu. "Vanilla, of course. Strawberry, chocolate, mint—"

"Daddy used to buy me Italian ice cream. He said it was the best," the boy chirped up eagerly.

"Dieter!" his mother shouted sharply, glaring at me. "I told you, father has gone away and until he comes back again, you are never, *never* to mention him." She was extraordinarily angry. She stood up. There would be no ice cream today.

Dieter, naturally, could not see that he had done anything wrong. He retreated into a sulk, with the odd tear or two. And there was the added injustice that he now wouldn't get any ice cream. I paid the bill, leaving a large tip to compensate the waitress for the sudden loss of business, and we got back into the car.

The boy's silence soon turned to sleep and, as before, he curled up in the backseat and was no bother. When she was quite sure he wouldn't hear, his mother turned to me.

"We have an agreement, Lieutenant. We are to enjoy these few days —you in your way, I in mine. And the strongest person wins. You seem to know a lot about me, far more than I expected. . . . There's nothing I can do about that, I suppose. But don't pick on the boy. You must play fair or it's all off."

But he said nothing wrong, I thought to myself. The tenses he had used were all past tenses. If Dieter was a weak link, it could mean only one thing. He still saw his father from time to time. . . .

I should have found this deduction encouraging. Part of me did. But for some reason my main reaction was disappointment. It was as if part of me, paradoxically, did not want Mrs. von Zell to be in touch with Rudolf. I should have recognized the signs. As we drove back along the Mondsee lakeshore, with the afternoon sun to our left, glittering on the small waves like a million gold coins, I found myself thinking for the first time that I was torn, torn between pushing the "case" as fast as I dared and drawing out these pleasant days with Mrs. von Zell for as long as I could. Certainly for as long as the good weather lasted.

Nothing more was said until we arrived back at the house. But she hadn't finished with me, not yet. As we slowed and I applied the hand brake, Dieter awoke. "Where are we going tomorrow?"

"Sadly, nowhere. There are other things I must do. But don't worry, I'll come the day after. I thought we'd explore the Löser."

"What's that?"

"A mountain," said his mother.

"You can see fourteen lakes from there," I added. "Or so I've read."

"I'll look it up in the atlas," he said, "so I know all of them." And he disappeared into the house, running, to tell Martha about the crayfish he had caught.

Mrs. von Zell stood by the car. "He enjoyed it. Thank you."

"So did I." A pause. "And you?"

She nodded. "Except for the rubber bands. And the ice cream."

"Maybe we should steer clear of rivers," I said, crossing my fingers and hoping that I wasn't going too far.

She ignored the remark. Or appeared to until, as she turned, she said, "I would invite you inside, for a glass of wine. But I have a letter to write."

3

THAT night Hartt and I were attending a concert in the cathedral at Salzburg—the profits to help repair the bomb-damaged roof—and as I dressed I pondered Mrs. von Zell's throwaway remark: "I have a letter to write." Letter. It could have been a coincidence, but the word leapt at me. *She was playing me at my own game.* Earlier in the day I had sought to confuse her by mentioning things, intimate things, I had read in her letters, then pretending they were coincidences. Now she was returning the favor. She might really have had a letter to write, it might indeed have been a coincidence. On the other hand, she needn't have mentioned it. She could have made some other excuse for not inviting me in. She needn't have said anything at all. Was she telling me that she had realized I had read the letters? On balance, I decided, she was probably uncertain. And she was paying me back for that uncertainty. Mention of a letter told me that she was onto me; it was a tease, a deliberate ploy to confuse me in return. Who was she writing to? Rudolf? She was telling me, in the most deliciously tantalizing manner, that she had my measure. That she could play any game I played, and just as well.

Dammit, she was clever. And the worst thing about her cleverness was that it was so attractive. The cleverer she was, the harder it made my job. But I found I liked it. My situation was becoming paradoxical. She had pictured the game, from her point of view, as a pact with the devil. But if I was the devil, I wasn't a very good one. That night I got the first inkling that it was I who was being ensnared, not she.

I half expected her to be at the cathedral that night. Besides Mozart the program included Schubert and Bruckner, her favorites, but although the cathedral was full, nearly a thousand people in all, and although I looked hard for her during the intermission (feeling a bit like Bruno, all those years ago), I didn't find her. It would have been difficult, I suppose, for her to have returned to Mondsee after the concert, which didn't end until 9:30. There were hardly any buses in the area in those days and, of course, she had no car.

The next morning my uncertainty had disappeared. Konstanze was nothing if not suspicious, those suspicions sharpened on earlier interrogators. She would wake this morning, just as I had done, with her mind made up. She would *know* that I had read the letters. Next time we met the rules would be different.

As I ate breakfast I wondered whether I should regret giving myself away so quickly. So far I had been able to use the knowledge I had gained from the letters to good advantage. I had, I thought, persuaded her to like me and to respect me. I had been able to pretend that I was more like her than I really was. Otherwise, being the woman she was, she would probably have never agreed to our deal. I had needed the advantage which the letters gave me. Now I no longer had it. On top of that, she might wake up this morning, or any morning, so appalled by my intrusion into her privacy that she would never agree to see me again.

By the time the breakfast things were cleared away I had thought myself into a panic. I had gone as far as I ever would. I had made a fatal blunder the day before in trying to be too clever over Dieter's cello. What I wanted to do was see for myself by driving straight out to

Mondsee. But I had saved today to do more reconnoitering. If Konstanze would not see me again, that was it. The end. But if she would, I had to stage-manage our future expeditions just as I had managed the Krimml trip and the picnic by the Salzach. So today I wanted to explore the countryside east of Salzburg.

My chore was pleasant enough, though nowhere near as much fun as if I'd had company. And I could not stop thinking about her remark: "I have a letter to write. . . . I have a letter to write." It kept going around and around in my head. I would not have been surprised, on my return that afternoon, if there had been a letter or note from her calling off all future meetings, canceling the rest of the game. But, save for my room key, my pigeonhole at the Goldener Hirsch was mercifully clear. I was ridiculously pleased.

As I drove along the Fuschl Valley the next day I prayed that Konstanze would not cancel out. It was Saturday and the weather mocked me; the sun was as cheerful as ever and, along the lakeshore, the barks of the birches gleamed as if some giant hand had silver-polished them moments before I passed by.

She had my measure, all right. Far from giving me a cool reception, Mrs. von Zell was waiting in the garden, with Dieter, and was wearing not only a creamy-lemon dress of the finest silk but a simple gold necklace and, in her hair, a lemon ribbon. She looked fantastic and, I guessed, she knew it. As I arrived she stopped pushing Dieter on the swing and picked up an envelope that had been lying on the grass.

Dieter dashed across to the fence first. "May I ride in the front today? Please!"

"If your mother agrees."

"Good morning!" she said brightly, coming to stand behind her son and placing her hands affectionately on his shoulders. They looked so healthy, the pair of them, that it was hard to believe they had once had TB.

"Good morning," I replied, surprised at the warmth of her welcome. "Dieter would like to ride in the front today. What do you say?" Was she going to back out? I kept my fingers crossed.

"Yes, of course." She smiled radiantly. "So long as he is careful. And so are you."

Since Dieter had already clambered into his privileged position in the front seat, I got out and held forward mine so that his mother could slip into the back. As we drove off she tapped me on the shoulder and said, "Could we go via the main square in Mondsee, please? I have a letter to post."

I said nothing, but that was a very odd request. In Mondsee it was market day, the square choked with vegetables, flowers, even cows. At the post office I turned and offered to take the letter for her but Mrs. von Zell insisted on getting out and mailing it personally. It was already stamped, so all she had to do was pop it into the mailbox. It took her seconds, then she was back in the car and we headed east, into the mountains.

After the crayfish, and the swan incident, Dieter treated me as a firm friend; I knew what he liked and I knew at least one of his weaknesses. The business about the ice cream seemed to have been forgotten. As we drove he spoke about school, about the other boys who, on the whole, he liked and the masters whom he didn't. And he spoke about cars—he was as mad about them as Bruno had been. One of the masters at school had a Bugatti; some of the other boys had been in it, but not Dieter. His rides in the BMW were clearly intended to make up for that deficiency and, when he went back to school, he would have such stories to tell. He made it clear that if I would let him sit at the wheel once or twice I would be an even firmer friend.

Although I readily promised Dieter that, at some point, he could "drive" the car, I had only half an ear for his chatter. My mind was on his mother. It was silly but what disturbed me was the friendly reception I had received, the way she was dressed and the fuss she had made about posting the letter. Yet again I found myself admiring her cleverness, especially over the letter. It *might* have been an innocuous note. On the other hand, the packet she posted was just bulky enough, and the right shape, for it to have contained the sheets of music, Rudolf's, which I had given to her. And the fact that she insisted on mailing it herself at the mailbox, when it would have been much easier for me to have dropped it in, meant that she was deliberately teasing me, leading me to wonder whether she was in touch with her husband and sending back to him the music which he had unfortunately left behind in his hurry to leave Berchtesgaden. She had mailed the packet herself so as not to show me the address on it. If that was the case, then I was being made a fool of, and God help me if Hobel or Eisenhower, for that matter, should ever find out. I had the power to intercept mail, but she knew that I would not risk it. She might only be testing me and, if she was, and I did intercept that packet, the interrogation was all over. I would have lost. Christ, she was clever. It also occurred to me, as I headed the car off the main Salzburg-Linz road into the valley that led to the Löser, that if she was again corresponding with her husband, she was saying to me that at any time she wanted she could regain the privacy that I had, in effect, stolen from her by reading the letters.

She had the better of me. My dilemma was of my own making.

Then there was her dress that day. That was a different kind of tease. Until now she had dressed tastefully but modestly. Her clothes were well chosen for her coloring and figure but almost all, save for the yellow shirt, prewar. The creamy-lemon dress, however, was not only frankly sexy, it was also very obviously brand new. It was as if she could read my mind with uncanny accuracy; she knew what my suspicions were, and what I felt about her. And proceeded to tease me about it.

How soon, and how often, in a relationship does the balance change? Until very recently I had felt myself well in control of this interrogation. It had been going slowly, as I had known it would, but it had been going according to plan.

Now things were different. The balance was changing, may already have changed. I was, in some unaccountable way, losing control. I could feel it, but I could not stop it. That was a terrible thing from a strictly military point of view. On the other hand I *liked* what was happening.

All my life I had been attractive to women and attracted by many types of women. A few had meant more to me than the others, but, invariably, I was more loved than loving. One effect of this was that I usually saw affairs as competitions, with winners and losers, where to be in love was more a handicap, a hindrance, than the object of the whole business. It meant that I tired of my companions easily, but then relationships were by nature difficult. It had never seemed a problem. Mrs. von Zell was different. On paper she should have been easier than most: I had lots of inside information about her, she was lonely, she had been on the losing side in the war. I had a car, money. She should have capitulated. Yet here she was, controlling me in all sorts of ways, large and small, telling me that, whatever our relationship was or might become, it would be equal. *She* had to be treated as an equal, with care, or not at all. I might have inside information about her but that was simply an accident of history; it had not been earned.

You can see how she had set me thinking. What I had not anticipated —because, I suppose, I had simply not thought about it—was how enticing I found Konstanze's reaction. I had not imagined that the game between us would be an easy one, but that I would win I had never doubted, until recently.

The approach to the Löser is very steep toward the end, where the road rises above the tree line. The grass survives to quite a height, however, so in spring the slopes are green, sprinkled in places with yellow crocuses and the glacier blue of the gentian. Dieter had turned around in his seat so that he could see the view that began to stretch out behind us. He hadn't stopped talking the entire trip. He was particularly interested in buffalo and questioned me closely about how common they were in America and what they tasted like. I told him that, sadly, I had never seen any, nor had I come across buffalo steak in California restaurants.

A few minutes after we had left the trees behind us, the road curled through a small gully, widened into a turning circle and stopped. From here we would have to walk.

"Are you going to be warm enough?" I said to Mrs. von Zell as we got out, thinking of her history of TB. "That dress looks pretty thin to me."

She stretched after so long in the car, and for a moment the smooth outline of her breasts could be seen, pummeled by the silk. But it appeared to have been done entirely unself-consciously so that I was unable to be sure whether she was being deliberately provocative or not.

"No," she replied. "Silk is quite warm, thank you. Especially after we have started to walk."

"Come *on!*" yelled Dieter impatiently, already fifty meters along the path. "I can see three lakes even from here."

I made to follow the boy but his mother put a restraining hand on my arm. "Professor . . . Professor Wolff—you know, I prefer that to lieutenant—military ranks are so out of date now, don't you think? Professor is much more civilized . . . much nicer. Don't you think that first names might be easier, friendlier? It would certainly be more natural for me. The war *is* over." She paused, looking at me with a smile but also, I thought, with a trace of nervousness in her face, as if, for once, she wasn't too sure of my reaction. "My name is Konstanze, as I am sure you know."

There it was again: ". . . as I'm sure you know." The breeze was sweet up here. It stroked our faces, lifted up our hair, then, unhurried, moved on. I knew that Mrs. von Zell—Konstanze—was trying to be friendly but, at the same time, she could not help chiding me for having delved so deeply. She wouldn't admit it openly; but neither would she let it go.

When she touched me with her hand I felt the opposite of an electric shock sear through me. A bolt of relaxation imploded across my shoulders and down my spine. Now she took her hand away and with it went my sense of well-being.

"My first name is Walter," I said. "I should be happy for you to call me that."

She nodded and walked on. The wind pressed her hair flat to the back of her head, emphasizing the rich varieties of autumn blond that made up her coloring: whiskey, corn, crocus. I fell into step on the path behind her.

We walked for perhaps ten minutes, rising steadily all the while. Dieter had again run on well ahead, far out of sight. Konstanze walked strongly, used to mountain paths, but at one point she stopped to pick at some loose pebbles that had become lodged in her shoes. As she did, she looked up at me.

"Tell me about your wife, Walter. Why didn't it work?"

Her tone was so warm, so friendly, so *confidential* that I had no problem responding. Or, rather, I had no problem wanting to respond. Another part of me, however, grew alarmed at her questions. Now it felt as if *I* was being seduced, interrogated. It occurred to me that I knew a great deal about the von Zells; she now wanted to know about the Wolffs, and why not?

It was also true that I was relieved to talk about myself. She had, at that point, beaten me to the extent that I actually felt eager to redress some of the balance between us if I could.

I suppose that day on the Löser, when Konstanze and I moved on to first-name terms, was the first moment that I regretted reading the letters. The war perhaps justified what I had done. But, on the mountain with Konstanze in that lovely dress, the war seemed a long way away.

"My wife is as American as apple pie—that's what they say over there. She is blond, like you, tall. Her name is Nancy. Her family were Dutch originally but they were early immigrants so that even Nancy's great-grandparents were born in America. We met at a sailing club—I am a Sunday sailor and Nancy likes to drink. She is a scientist—well, a psychologist anyway. I thought at first that science and the arts could mix. We had a wonderful six-month romance. We honeymooned on the Mississippi, taking a boat from St. Louis to New Orleans.

"I remember two things from our honeymoon—aside from the things everyone remembers. First, we had a family in the cabin next to us who had two children—twins, a boy and a girl. The young children, Dorothy and Dashiell, could speak English very well if they needed to, but they had their own form of the language. Many twins do that, I understand, and only they can decipher this private language.

"When we got back to California there was a letter waiting for Nancy. It was an incredible coincidence, for the letter was from a woman in New York who said she was Nancy's twin. Nancy had never known she was a twin but this other woman—Brooke—had known since she was sixteen. She had never done anything about it but suddenly, God knows why, she had decided to look for her sister. She had employed someone trained in tracing people and had been looking for Nancy for almost a year. She said she wanted to meet her twin and that she had some information about their parents."

The path was growing steeper, the view improving all the time. The Wolfgangsee stretched out far below us, black and glittering. Konstanze put her hand on my shoulder as she negotiated some boulders poking into the path. Far ahead and above, we could hear Dieter, yelling then waiting, listening to his echo.

"What happened then? Go on."

"Brooke said she was taking up a new job in Los Angeles and asked Nancy to meet her there. I was against it. I thought it might be disturbing for Nancy and that Brooke might prove such a disappointment she would be depressed. Brooke might want money. But Nancy had been fascinated by the twin children on the boat, with their secret language and intimacy, and there was nothing I could do to stop the meeting. Brooke was coming out by train so they did not plan to meet for about three weeks. During that time Nancy and I set up housekeeping in Berkeley. We had a lovely house; no garden or pool but a big balcony with a view of the Bay. It was all I wanted and I was very happy. But things had already started to change for Nancy. She began to say that she had always felt 'incomplete' but had never known how to put it into words. Now she knew she was a twin and that seemed to her to explain everything.

"Off she went to LA at the appointed time and from that day it was all over between us."

"What do you mean?"

"It's simple really; Nancy and Brooke became obsessed with each other."

Konstanze stopped and turned around.

"I looked into it," I said. "I asked psychologists and doctors who specialize in these kinds of matters. Apparently it is not uncommon for twins who have been separated, then reunited, to become obsessed with each other for a while. They are inseparable, talk constantly, and compare notes, as it were. This period is very distressing for their families but it passes, and everyone settles down again. Unfortunately, for me, I went into the Army and had to leave California at this time. Nancy hardly had time to adjust to married life, and so, after I came to Europe, she moved out of the house and went to LA to live with Brooke."

"Live with?" said Konstanze, noticing where I was fudging things.

"It's quite natural for two sisters to decide to share expenses and keep one another company during a husband's prolonged absence."

"Go on. You are still in touch, of course?"

"Yes. But not long letters. I began by telling her what London was like, then my impressions of France. Brooke had a job as a casting director at Galaxy Studios and Nancy worked there for a while. So she told me some Hollywood stories. She sent me photographs—but always with Brooke. Would you like to see?"

We had reached a fairly flat part of the path, as good a place as any to rest. I took out a folded photograph showing two women on a beach.

"That's the Pacific behind them," I said as I handed the photograph to her.

She stared at it for a while. "What does it feel like, seeing your wife's double?"

I took back the picture. "Eerie. You ask yourself questions like . . . does she whisper in the same way? Does she slam the door like Nancy? What presents does she like? Does she insist on putting the cream in her cup before the coffee, just like Nancy?"

"What presents *does* Nancy like?"

I laughed, crossing my fingers behind me. "Nancy loves pens. Every new pen she saw she had to have. It was almost a fetishism. And earrings, she adored earrings, the long dangling types especially. The more gipsy-like the better."

"But you are getting divorced?" Sharp, snappy questions now. A frank interrogation.

"Oh yes. At her request, but I had been half expecting it, I must say. We just didn't have time to develop a solid relationship. She met a sailboat manufacturer at a Hollywood party. He was an adviser on one of Galaxy Studio's films. She says he's there for her when she needs him. Unlike me. Apparently he believes the United States should never have become mixed up in this war." Konstanze, who had been admiring the view, looked sharply at me. I went on. "Many people in America want to become isolationists. I find it very depressing. Nancy and her new man are starting up a business together. He will make the boats and she will sell them."

We moved off again as she spoke. "And are you sad? That it's over, I mean."

"Difficult to answer. Sometimes, of course, when I think about our courtship, our honeymoon on the Mississippi. She was truly a lovely woman. I remember what she was like before Brooke's letter turned up. Nancy changed. Had I not come away to the war, maybe we would have found one another again. Who can tell? Our marriage was a mistake."

Just then we reached the top of the Löser, to find Dieter crying. His mother was with him in no time, our discussions forgotten for the time being. But it wasn't serious. Dieter had dropped his binoculars and cracked them. Konstanze wiped the boy's eyes while I examined the glasses. They were beyond repair. One lens had been shattered completely and the chamber cracked along its entire length. It would be cheaper to get new ones, except that such things were not easy to come by in Europe at that time.

"I can't see fourteen lakes," Dieter coughed, emerging from the folds of his mother's handkerchief. It was the only time I saw evidence of *his* TB. "Only twelve."

I counted them. He was right. I looked around. "Ah! But maybe you're not supposed to be able to see all fourteen at once. Only that you can see fourteen from the top of the Löser." I pointed south. "There's a grassy ledge over there. Maybe there are a couple of lakes in that direction which we can't see from here."

We moved over and, sure enough, two small black lakes, like patches of oil on a garage floor, became visible far below.

"But that's cheating!" complained Dieter, unimpressed and still hurting from his clumsiness with the binoculars.

"Don't grumble, Dieter," said his mother firmly. "Professor Wolff has gone to a lot of trouble to bring you up here and the view is marvelous. Not many boys have had the chance to see this, binoculars or no binoculars."

Dieter was silent but moved closer to his mother and held her hand. Not being a parent, it always amazed me how independent children could be at one minute and how childlike the next.

"Is that a restaurant down there?" Konstanze asked.

Indeed it was. About four hundred feet below us, in what looked like a hanging valley, was a brand-new, raw concrete building with rather too many windows and a terrace. It looked beckoning; in the thin mountain air we could hear the waiters chatting as they laid the tables for lunch. Konstanze and Dieter led the way, still holding hands, and I followed, carrying the broken binoculars.

Because it was very early in the season, the restaurant was almost empty. But that didn't prevent it from being very good. I forget what we ate, but I do remember asking for an omelet. Eggs in restaurants were nonexistent just then and the waiter smiled sympathetically at my request—he, too, wanted eggs, but he shook his head, an omelet was out of the question. Of course, I just wanted to make Konstanze feel special about the omelet she had cooked for me, to show her that I had not taken it for granted. I was being manipulative, then settled willingly for whatever they had.

We sat outside in the sunshine while Dieter counted the lakes from the table. He could see five. He counted them again in the hope of finding more, but five there were. The concrete walls of the terrace were a perfect sun-trap and in front of us the hanging valley stretched out for perhaps three hundred yards and then just stopped, giving way to an enormous deep valley, hazy and blue far below us. Sounds carried long distances on such a clear day and the mixed noises of cars, cowbells, the excited shouts of children and the very far-off trundle of trains reached us in steady progression as they rose from the valleys to the blue heavens.

Konstanze's questions seemed to be over, and for the first time in her company I began to feel quiet inside. The climb and the fresh air had made us all hungry. The food wiped away Dieter's disappointment and he soon rushed off again out of sight. Around us the lakes began to change color as the sun moved.

"I could stay here forever," I said, leaning back in my chair and closing my eyes.

"Is it more beautiful than America, Walter? Than the Mississippi?"

"At this moment, yes. With you."

I wasn't sure whether I had meant to say that. The phrase "with you" had just formed in my mouth of its own accord. I felt embarrassed but not wildly so. I was glad I had my eyes closed anyway—I would not have said it otherwise, but that meant I couldn't see her reaction.

For a while there was silence between us. A waiter came to take our empty plates and glasses. I opened my eyes and, without looking at Konstanze, asked him to bring me a brandy. I asked her if she wanted one.

"No, thank you, Walter. But I'll taste some of yours."

Her willingness to share my glass, to put her mouth where mine had been, seemed to be a kind of promise. Unless, of course, it was all calculation on her part. What was I thinking? The day was too perfect and I tried to put the thought from my mind.

She was as good as her word. When the cognac came she took the glass and swirled the liquid around in a way that showed she had done it before. When she threw her head back to sip the drink, I was able to study the rhythmic contractions of the muscles in her throat as she swallowed. My God, she was beautiful.

The first to arrive, we were the last to leave the restaurant. The plan that day was to visit Gosau and Steeg and see the churches there on our way back. We returned to the car by a different route and, when we arrived, Dieter was curled up asleep in the backseat.

Something changed between Konstanze and me that day. Some invisible line was crossed. The business about the letter, which she had insisted on mailing herself, had started it. Her new dress, her decision to move on to first-name terms, the incident with the brandy all contributed, but it was also Dieter's total acceptance of me. Everything else about us might look calculated, might *be* calculated, but not that. It was as if, in spite of ourselves, we had grown closer.

Konstanze felt the same, I am sure, for as we descended the mountain road she began to talk about herself, something she had never done before. She spoke about her parents and her childhood. She said she felt her early life had been boring, that she had been a spectator until she grew up. It had left her with the feeling, she said, that childhood was safe but dull. She found children difficult to be with, she said, including her own son. Children had a false sense of time, when even tomorrow or next week seemed an age away. That gave them a false sense of drama. Whenever she read a biography, she said, she would skip the early pages until the person in question was at least into adolescence. It was because of Dieter that she had first agreed to come out with me. Since the war had ended she had been bored. That was, of course, when Rudolf disappeared. She loved Dieter, but she couldn't say yet whether she liked him —he was too young. Of her own childhood she could remember only incidents when she had tried to behave as an adult. Once she had stolen a couple of dozen of her father's favorite cigarettes (the brand I had left on her table the first day we met) and given one each to all of the children in her gang. The children had met one afternoon for an illicit, communal smoking spree. Fortunately, an observant neighbor spotted the smoke that was beginning to billow from the basement and alerted the fire department. The children were discovered—it was anyone's guess as to who was more surprised, they or the fire department—and Konstanze identified as the ringleader. As a consequence her father had given her a sound spanking. On another occasion, when she was nearing adolescence, a friend and she had sneaked into an "adult-only" horror movie in Munich. The escapade was designed for retelling to other girl-friends since it was a mark of great daring, conferring much prestige on a thirteen-year-old, to have slipped past the cinema cashier, who was supposed to prevent anyone under sixteen from entering the cinema. Unfortunately for Konstanze and her friend, it was one thing to make up like a sixteen-year-old but quite another to behave like one. They had been exposed and forced to leave when the movie had reached the really horrifying scenes and both girls had started to cry.

She laughed now, retelling this story. In general, she said, her school days had not been hugely successful or happy. Her French had always been bad but she was at the top of her class in music. That was how she had come to take up music publishing in Munich; her headmistress had introduced her to the firm.

Apparently she was quite a good publisher. She had seen the potential of the guitar in modern music as an instrument which, though not as versatile as the piano, was as self-sufficient and much, much cheaper. So, as well as publishing music for piano and voice, she developed her ideas for the guitar long before records, TV and, in some cases, radio became the household items of the future. The publishers had been very pleased with her.

Suddenly the conversation changed direction and switched back to Dieter. His arrival, she said, had caused some anxious moments. Not the birth—that itself had gone well enough—but he had had a squint and needed an operation. It was successful, but it might not have been and they had all been very worried.

It was the choppiness and changed direction in her conversation that suddenly made me realize what was happening, what she was doing. Until then I had been sitting back happily, as we swished downhill into the valley, listening to what she had to say and congratulating myself on at last getting through her reserve. I now realized that everything she was telling me was distinguished by the fact that *it had not been referred to in the letters*. She was gently but insistently rubbing in the fact that she was aware of what I knew about her but also, in telling me some new stories, what I *didn't* know. Unlike me, she *hadn't* switched off; she was still working. If I needed a reason to respect her more, here it was.

The churches that day were disappointing. They must have been, for I remember nothing of them. I was too preoccupied with Konstanze. The balance had shifted firmly into her favor now—I was sure it had. I was lost, torn between the feeling that I was getting somewhere with her, softening her up, so to speak, and the feeling that I was drowning. She could just as easily have been playing with me, tormenting me. I had never been as uncertain of a woman as I was of Konstanze. It was a new sensation for me, half painful, half exquisite and wholly addictive.

4

THE next excursion, on Monday, to the glacier at Dachstein, was to be Dieter's last. The following day he would return to his school at

Stockerau, near Vienna. On Monday, therefore, I arrived late at Mond-see. I had shopping to do and, I had to stop off at the office to see whether there was any news from Saul Wolfert. There was. He had called the previous day. When I got him on the phone his voice had a subdued excitement in it.

"We haven't seen your man yet, but something's going on in Krumau and we don't think it's wine-making."

My stomach tightened and I realized I didn't *want* Saul to find von Zell. Not just yet anyway.

"Oh yes?" I said into the phone. "Why is that?"

"You don't sound very thrilled," said Saul, not missing a thing. "Don't forget we're going to all this trouble just for you. You do still think he's here, don't you? You haven't changed your mind?"

"Don't be silly," I said. "I'm just preoccupied, that's all. What have your men found?"

"Well, don't forget, they're undercover, posing as tourists. They can't ask too many direct questions or spend too long in one place. So nothing is certain yet." He paused for effect. "But it begins to look as though one of the vineyards is far busier at night than during the day."

"What do you mean?"

"Just that. My men have been watching the vineyards one by one. Naturally they took a particular interest in anything disused. And, taking a stroll around Krumau one night after dinner, they spotted a truck drawn up outside a warehouse that was boarded up during the day. Several men got out of the truck."

"What time of night was this?"

"Ten forty-five."

"Could mean anything."

"Of course it could. But it could be interesting. The truck was not there last night but they will try to watch tonight. It could be that your man, von Zell, has a cover job in one of the vineyards that leaves him free to organize this conduit, hiding ex-Nazis in the warehouse, where he equips them with money, documents and all the rest."

"We shouldn't read too much into one late-night truck."

Saul sounded exasperated. "God, you're a skeptic, Walter. I thought you'd be pleased."

"I'm sorry, Saul. It's just that Hobel here doesn't like theories. He wants results. I've had so many theories on this case, I'm a bit frightened of another. But press on, of course. If that vineyard should turn out to be the start of the conduit, it will be a feather in all our caps. Yours most of all. So I'm sorry—good luck. Call me tomorrow if you've made any progress."

Sammy came into the room just then.

"You look relaxed."

"That's not how I feel, Sammy. I've been thinking."

"Want to pull out?"

"No, not yet. But I think we should sell Atlantic Insurance and buy something else. Maybe even get back into Metropolitan Motors."

He sat down. "You shouldn't chop and change too much, you know. Otherwise you keep missing the boat."

"Perhaps. But Maurice is two hundred and four dollars ahead of me. I've got to *try* and catch him."

Sammy put his feet up, just as I was doing, and rocked back in his chair. "What's your first priority, Walter? To make a little money or to catch your pal?"

"Does it matter? Don't they add up to the same thing in this case?"

"Not necessarily. Some stock grows steadily, so you go on getting modestly richer as you grow older. Other stocks, as you have found to your cost, fall. But there are some that are much riskier than anything else but which, if the idea behind them turns out to be the right one, take off like a shot."

"Yes. Go on. I'm listening."

"I've got my eye on such a stock right now. I haven't put any of my own money into it yet, but I just might. It could work . . . it *could* work spectacularly. On the other hand . . ." He drew his hand across his throat, making a clicking sound.

"What's the stock?" I said.

"You'll laugh."

"Maybe I will. But what is it?"

He hesitated. "Gramophones."

"Why? What's wrong with the radio?"

"Simple." Things always were for Sammy. "People are tired of war; it's time for leisure. The radio is fine but gramophone records give you the music you want when you want it. The quality will go on improving and the machines will get cheaper and cheaper. Best of all, the war stimulated the synthetics industry. We'll have better and better forms of plastic from which to make records."

"What company do you suggest?"

"RMC, the Recorded Music Company, out of New York."

"Do they make the records or the machines to play them on?"

"Records, for the moment."

"You mean you've heard something?"

"I mean it's a risk, but maybe it's not a bad risk. Remember what I said. It's speculative."

I thought it over, but not for long. I had to get out to Mondsee. I fished in my wallet and took out some money. "Here you are, Sammy. This has to be the last company I try. Atlantic Insurance is worth eight hundred and sixty eight dollars . . . here's another seven dollars. Do as you did before and buy me eight hundred and seventy five dollars worth of RMC. Or as close to that as you can get. And let's pray this works."

We grinned at one another. He was a good man.

When I arrived at Mondsee that day Konstanze and Dieter were waiting on the other side of the road, in the summerhouse. I turned the car before parking so that it was facing the way we needed to go to get to Dachstein, then I let myself in through the wooden gate. The heat that had accumulated over the previous days was reflected off the lake, now very still, and from the walls of the summerhouse, waxy and shiny.

I had brought with me a brown paper parcel. Fancy wrapping paper was a thing of the future. I handed it to Dieter. "For your return to school. And happy birthday on Friday."

He took the packet, delighted. "Gosh!" he said. "You know my birthday. You know everything." He tore at the paper. Inside was a box wrapped in tape, which his mother helped him to open. Inside the box was some white tissue paper, which Dieter sent tumbling to the floor in his hurry, and a new pair of binoculars, very similar to the ones he had cracked on the Löser. He grabbed them and scanned the lake, searching out some fisherman in the hazy distance. "They're good," he said in a mature tone. "Very good."

"They were made in America."

Dieter examined the maker's mark critically. It had not occurred to him that such good equipment could be other than German. At first, I think, he was disappointed—not being German, to Dieter, meant that the binoculars were not the best. So I added, quite correctly, "They are what we use in the Army." That made all the difference. Now he had something to show off at school; no other boy could boast a piece of genuine U.S. Army equipment so soon after the war. He turned to me and gravely shook my hand, his way of saying thank you in a man-to-man fashion.

Konstanze, I noticed, had turned her back on this scene. She had been delighted with the gift but, obviously, shocked when I had revealed that I knew Dieter's birthday. I realized why. Not only did this confirm that I had read her letters, but also that I had been through them again, perhaps recently, perhaps as recently as the night before in order to check Dieter's birthday.

I had been deliberately obvious in my approach that day. It was the only way for me to gain the upper hand, to bring everything out into the open.

And for a time it seemed to work. During the drive to Dachstein, Konstanze was moody and she let Dieter do most of the talking. Since it was his last day I had promised to let him sit at the wheel and now the boy kept up a number of technical inquiries about cars which, at the least, filled in the time.

Dachstein was one of our most distant destinations and, as on previous occasions, the plan was to take in a couple of churches after visiting the glacier. This we reached shortly after noon. Dachstein is fairly spectacular, as glaciers go. The observation point is, or it was then, a little way above the ice and from there you can see not only the two-kilometer-long silver tongue slithering out of the mountains but also the end of the ice, thick as a New York skyscraper is high. I had no idea how noisy glaciers are; the dripping and the cracking could be heard from where we were, a hundred meters away. A notice on the railing of the observation point drew the visitor's attention to the fact that the glacier was 3.6 million years old and grew at the rate of forty-three centimeters a year. Just to emphasize how slow that was, forty-three centimeters was marked on the railing by two deep cuts in the wood.

For a brief moment I borrowed the glasses from Dieter. There was something on the far side of the valley which I wanted to show him. I found it.

I pointed, handing back the binoculars. "A frozen waterfall," I said.

"Scan along the edge of the glacier till you come to the waterfall, then track up the cascade of ice. When you come to it, you'll recognize it."

"Recognize what?" said Dieter, looking up at me.

"Wait and see."

He fiddled with the glasses to get them focused. Slowly he moved up the glacier, stopping at the foot of the waterfall, inspecting the peculiar shapes of the ice at this point of collision and the strange ways the light was trapped and reflected. Then he began to follow the line of the waterfall back up the way it had come, millions of years ago, before it had been frozen.

"The shapes get better and better," he said. "Wait till I tell the boys at school. Is that what you mean? Long white needles." A thought struck him. "Surgeons should use stalactites as operating needles. They wouldn't need to sterilize them and they could throw them away after."

I said nothing.

His glasses continued to slant upward toward the top of the waterfall. I was just beginning to think that he had missed it when, to my satisfaction, he let out a scream, a half-swallowed shout, both excited and repelled.

"Ahhhrrgh! Is . . . is . . . he dead?"

"Is who dead?" Konstanze flashed me a look of anger as she snatched the glasses from Dieter and searched the waterfall herself.

The boy was horrified but enthralled too. All children are morbid and he was no different from anyone else. The grin on his face may have been macabre but it was a grin all the same. He couldn't wait to have the binoculars back from his mother.

"It happened in 1938," I said. "Eight years ago. His name is Albert Fest and he used to be well known in Austrian climbing circles." I had been told the story at the dance in Salzburg by another lieutenant, from a different unit, who had also had his woman of the evening stolen from him. "Besides being a climber he was a gambler and, one day for a bet, he was challenged that he could not climb the waterfall. It's a sheer drop, of course, but on the other hand the ice is as hard as iron; a fit, experienced climber should have no difficulty hammering in those metal pitons they use. The chief problem is the cold, but there again an experienced climber could foresee that and plan accordingly. As you can see, Fest nearly made it; in fact he got higher than where he is now before he slipped. Unfortunately for him the waterfall had been hit by debris from an avalanche a couple of weeks before and some of those slender icicles you were talking about had been snapped in two, turning them into jagged daggers sticking up in the air. He slipped onto one of those and it pierced his lung."

"How do they know?" said Dieter. His mother had given him back his glasses now. "I can't see that clearly from here."

"There is a closer spot, above the glacier. Fortunately, Fest died instantly. But as it's so cold up there, his body just froze and will not decompose."

Dieter's eyes widened in wonder. "You mean he will stay there like that . . . forever?" What a story for the other boys at school.

I nodded and Konstanze gave me another black look.

"What happened to the bet?" Dieter asked carefully. "How could the loser pay?"

"Good question. Apparently the man who won felt so guilty at being the cause of Fest's death—however accidentally—that he behaved as if he had lost and donated the money to a charity which helps the families of climbers who have been killed in the mountains."

"What a cheerful story," said Konstanze, speaking at last. "Don't you think we have had enough of ice and glaciers, Dieter?"

"Yes. All right," he said, taking a last glimpse through his glasses at the body. Then a fresh thought struck him. "Can I have my driving lesson now, please? You did promise."

This was much more to his mother's liking. His legs were much too short to reach the clutch or the accelerator pedal but I let him sit on my lap and steer the car as we drove back down the mountain. I found a track which turned off the road and led around a tiny lake; there he could steer legally and make all the mistakes he wanted.

Seeing her son so absorbed helped to relax Konstanze that day but even so she remained on edge much more than on any of our other excursions. It was the effect, I suppose, of my having harped on about the letters. It became more obvious when we finally managed to prize Dieter away from the wheel and we visited the churches at Schladming and Radstadt. They were small but exceptionally elaborate, making up in prettiness for what they lacked in grandeur. By now Dieter would do anything to avoid the dark interiors of the churches and he dashed off to play in the cemeteries. Konstanze, for her part, introduced a new ploy that day. On entering each church, she simply knelt in prayer for what seemed, to me, an eternity. I wandered about for minutes on end all by myself looking at stained glass and inspecting the stucco, and trying to work out what was going on inside her head.

Was she really praying, or just avoiding me? Was she praying for Rudolf? In any event, she was showing me that she was capable of having a private life into which I could not pry. At Radstadt, the second church we visited that afternoon, she kept me waiting for twenty-five minutes. Who could pray for that long? And about what?

I wrote a postcard to my mother and one to Konstanze. I drew pictures of the frescoes and the mosaics on the back of Konstanze's, so she would remember what she had seen, but even then she kept her distance.

As we drove back along the Enns Valley, with Dieter once more curled up asleep on the backseat, his binoculars wrapped around his neck, I reflected that what should have been a very successful day had backfired in some ways. I had thought myself so clever to have remembered, dimly, from the letters, that Dieter had been born about this time of the year. And I had been really pleased with myself, the night before, when I had found the letter which confirmed the date. A lot of good it had done me. It was as if the intimacies of the previous day—the move to first names, sharing the brandy—had never happened.

At home Dieter woke and thanked me again for the binoculars and his driving lesson. He promised to write me a proper thank-you note from school. He ran off across the lawn to show his new acquisition to Martha.

"Tomorrow?" I said diffidently, trying to show Konstanze that I was aware of her mood. She was bending down to pick up Dieter's jacket, which he had left lying on the backseat.

She shook her head. "We have to visit the doctor—to check Dieter's TB. Then I must take him to the railway station at eleven. He has a heavy trunk."

"I could help."

"No. The train is always late. And I hate long good-byes. We are always very sad. Let us be alone."

5

I sat at my desk the next morning watching the clock. I had looked at the map and knew that, to get to Vienna by rail, Konstanze and Dieter and Martha would have to travel to Frankenmarkt to catch the train. I knew that it would take them about an hour to get there and that the train was supposed to leave at eleven. I was therefore able to follow their movements inside my head.

I can admit my feelings now better than I could then. I missed Konstanze. Having to be by myself, even for a day, in Salzburg seemed an endless ordeal. Worse, Konstanze had left me with words which suggested she was not overanxious to see me again. I had blundered that day. I should not have looked up Dieter's birthday; we had been set back yet again. I should never have read those letters. For the first time I saw what I had done from a different perspective. I would have hated it if anyone had read *my* correspondence. It was like been burgled psychologically, like having your past stolen. Now that I had become something rather more than Konstanze's interrogator, I could see that. And I was, for the first time, truly sorry. So I was eager to see her once more and try to set things on an even keel.

That day I performed all sorts of time-wasting chores to fill up the hours as best I could. I walked to the office. I read the paper thoroughly. I answered my mail, writing to my wife, giving her the name of a mutual friend in San Francisco who, I told her, would be my lawyer and handle our divorce.

I called Maurice, just for a chat. He was cheerful, friendly as ever, but his news upset me. He was going home. He had heard from Wren, he said, who had told him that the art recovery unit was winding down and that in view of his success with the old masters stolen from Vienna, Ghent could be one of the first to leave, having done his bit.

"When are you going, Maurice?" I asked, feeling suddenly bereft.

"Two, three weeks, dear boy. Got to bring all my reports up to date first. Then it's back to Cambridge in time for the summer term. That's the best of all. Punting on the river, summer tea parties, the rowing races, the May balls. All that will be getting going again. Time to put away wartime things, eh?"

It was not what I wanted to hear. "What about Hermann, Maurice? And Spitfire and Messerschmidt?"

He chortled. "For a start, they've become Spit and Mess. Very apt names, Walter, I congratulate you. Everything they touch is disarranged and covered in slobber. We are all good friends except that, since they were born here, they treat this place as home. It's as if they just evacuated to the trees for the duration of the war and are now back in their real habitat. You'll never wear your cap again, Walter. I'm afraid it now looks like what it has become—a squirrels' nest. But I'm sure they're very grateful. Hermann licks them all the time, her way of cleaning them, I guess. But it does tend to make everything wet."

"I wonder if I'll see you again, Maurice, before you go? I'm stuck down here."

"How's it going? No news of—von what's-his-name yet?"

"It's the most difficult case I've had, dear boy," I quipped, imitating his accent. "I'm probably going to have to crack the wife, who's very tough and very beautiful."

"Well, I'll definitely be here for two weeks," said Maurice. "If you are not back by then you'll just have to come visit me in Cambridge. You could do worse."

We hung up. Our "race" had not even been mentioned. I felt very envious of him. He had not a care. He had never been married, had had a good war, finishing it with a great coup, and he was going back to a peace which for him was just as exciting and satisfying as the war had been. "Time to put away wartime things." Those words had stung.

A corporal came in and said that Hobel wanted to see me. Thankfully, the old man's secretary wasn't at her desk as I went through. There was enough bad news around that day; I didn't need her. Hobel was his usual watery self.

"I talked with Eisenhower's office," he snarled, without greeting or preamble of any kind. "The art recovery unit is winding up soon. You've got another week. Then I can play this case the way it suits me. Either bring me the information a week from now or get lost."

I didn't even sit down. He wasn't interested in the progress I was, or wasn't, making. He just wanted to be rid of me and he had finally managed it. So he could shove it. I wouldn't tell him anything. At least I now had a week entirely to myself. I turned, but as I did so he spoke again.

"You know why you've got only a week?"

I stared at him.

"Two nights ago a U.S. Army staff car was hijacked in Southern France. No one was injured but the car disappeared. The same night, in Augsberg, a consignment of officers' uniforms disappeared, stolen from a quartermaster's warehouse." Hobel permitted himself a sneer. "The guard responsible has been interrogated by real interrogators and has already confessed. He was paid off to turn a blind eye. The people who paid him were German or, at least, spoke German. They paid cash. Gold."

I wanted to hit him.

"Who would need U.S. Army officers' uniforms? Who would need a staff car? It would be a swift way of traveling, eh? There are hundreds of staff cars, all over Europe. The underground would have to change only the license plate. We know they are already able to get access to ID documents. They can buy their way into anything, with all the gold they have. These people are getting away, Wolff. And you are doing fuck all to stop them. Well, not for much longer."

It may have been that interview with Hobel that caused me to think the way I did that day. Or it may have been my conversation with Saul Wolfert, who had telephoned while I was out of the office and whose call I returned at once.

"It's slow, Walter, when your men are having to work undercover, but there is some progress to report. This man Aubing hasn't showed yet, but it appears that the warehouse I told you about is busy most nights and continues to look abandoned during the day. *Something* is going on there. A truckload of something is delivered every night. More exciting, though, my men have discovered that an inn backs onto the warehouse and they think that people go in via that. People walk in and out of the inn perfectly naturally all the time, as though they are going for a drink; but they slip through into the warehouse. My men have followed people into the inn, only to find they are not there."

"What do you want to do?"

"That partly depends on you. I don't want to let this situation in

Krumau go on for too long. It might come to an end naturally, my men might be spotted—all sorts of things might go wrong. So I want to raid the place as soon as I can, one night after there has been an influx of people and after a truckload of whatever it is has just arrived. But how are you getting on? What would suit you? You've probably heard about these uniforms that are missing. It occurs to me they might turn up in Krumau."

I was thinking fast, but not in directions I was supposed to. "Can you hold off for a week?"

Saul hesitated. "That's on the long side, Walter. Longer than I had anticipated."

"If you can't, Saul, you can't. But if you can, it might help me."

"You're playing a deep game, Wolff. I won't ask you what it is, because I know you won't tell me, so I'll try to hold off for as long as you ask. I owe you something. But let's talk daily. I may have to go ahead if anything changes. Okay?"

"Thank you, Saul. Yes, let's talk every day. Thanks again."

I left the office that day around lunchtime and strolled back to the Goldener Hirsch, where I picked up my car. I had one or two places to reconnoiter and, in any case, being behind the wheel was relaxing.

As I drove, first south to Bischofshofen, then east to Liezen, then north to Steyr and Enns, and finally west, back to Salzburg, I turned a new thought over in my mind. It had occurred to me while I was listening to Maurice talk about going home. It had grown while Hobel had harangued me and it had matured after Saul Wolfert had agreed to lay off raiding the warehouse in Krumau for a week.

I had a week left with Konstanze, at most. After that—what? I was inclined to think that she would be able to resist me quite well. I passed meadows of young barley that would soon take on the color of Konstanze's hair. Would Konstanze still be here when the barley was ripe? I knew I would not. When I thought of the weeks ahead I could not help but feel disappointed. A new sensation for me, to be sure.

The road curved between the white peaks of the Hochwildstelle and the Hoher Dachstein, a geological stand-off that had been going on for millions of years. The enormity of these two mountains suddenly emphasized the puny dimensions of the BMW, and me inside it, but that in turn only directed my attention to the huge well of feelings I was harboring. There were these giant cold mountains to my right and left, totally inert, and here was I, in the middle, minuscule by comparison, but seething with emotion.

When I have a problem making up my mind there are two stages to the decision. First, there is the stage when your intuition decides but your conscious brain has yet to find the courage of your body's convictions. Then that conviction seeps upward, like an invisible hormone, and enters your brain. There is nothing sudden about this. It is a subtle process of osmosis in which your brain changes without your being aware of it.

As I wound my way between the Austrian alps that afternoon, my mind was made up for me by my body. I didn't know it until later.

6

THE garden outside Konstanze's house seemed curiously empty when I arrived the next day. The swing had been taken down, all the balls and other toys removed, the balcony tidied. In fact, all signs of childhood had been eradicated as if, it seemed, Dieter was never coming back.

I remarked on this when Konstanze answered the door.

"Oh—no! That's just Martha. She worships Dieter and always lets him have his way. Then when he goes back to school she collects up his things and looks after them until next time. She's like a mother hen."

"Did she like the binoculars?" I stepped aside to let Konstanze into the sunshine. She didn't *seem* unwilling for me to be there.

"Yes. Except for the fact that they were American-made, but Dieter set her right about that." She smiled to herself as she said this and I began to wonder what she had planned for me this time. Usually, whenever I had made a move forward, she responded. What would she do today, after my gaff about her son's birthday?

For the time being she just stood in the garden, letting the sun shine on her face.

"I thought we might venture farther afield today," I said, trying to sound bright, breezy, innocuous. "Now that we have no Dieter to go with us and get tired, we could look at some of the large monasteries as well as the churches."

"Martha wants to go with us."

"What?" I was flummoxed. "Is she really interested in religious architecture and art?"

"She thinks we need a chaperone."

"You're kidding!"

"It's true. She says Dieter was a chaperone of sorts. Now there's no one. So she must come."

Martha I could do without. But what I said was, "What do you think?"

"That depends," she said, the glimmer of a mocking smirk about her lips, "on what your designs are."

"I don't *have* any designs," I said quickly—perhaps too quickly. I looked straight at her. "We have a pact. I played fair and did as you asked with Dieter." I paused. "I don't think it would be fair to take Martha."

She chuckled. "Don't worry. I wouldn't dream of it. But it was worth pretending, just to see the look of horror on your silly face. To know that you *can* be human."

Before I met Konstanze I had liked to pride myself on the fact that, as with all good interrogators, I could blow hot and cold whenever I wished, to soften up the opposition. I had planned something of the kind for her at first and to begin with I had achieved it. Now, however, I had the distinct impression that she was returning the compliment. On our last outing I had blundered, and she had been chilly. Now, instead of being just as cold, as she was entitled to be, she was—for no reason that I could see—being wonderfully warm. I was the one being confused.

Rather than think more, I sought refuge in action. "Let's sneak off," I whispered. "Before Martha has a chance to invite herself."

Together, like a pair of teenage elopers, we slipped quietly across the grass and into the car. Unfortunately, the BMW did not start at first and I had to try again, making an awful din. The noise brought Martha to the window of the music room, where she was cleaning. She shouted something we couldn't hear, but her expression said it all. The engine barked into life and we sped off.

The BMW purred along smoothly as we headed for the Enns Valley, which I had reconnoitered the day before. The escape from Martha had tickled Konstanze just as much as it had me and put us in a relaxed, familiar frame of mind.

Over the next few days Martha became increasingly forbidding and angry. Each morning she would come to the balcony of the house and watch in fierce silence as we left without her. If it was designed to deter me and to make Konstanze feel guilty, it didn't succeed. If anything, it had the opposite effect. She simply made Konstanze and me feel like disobedient children and forced us closer together. Unintentionally, Martha was an ally.

In the days after Dieter went back to school, his mother and I moved farther and farther afield, as I had hoped. We visited monasteries that were more arresting architecturally and more interesting historically than the small churches we had already seen.

We went to Melk, which was built by the Benedictines in 1111. Positioned dramatically on top of a rock two hundred feet above an arm of the Danube, it can claim to be one of the more beautiful sites in Europe. Inside, the church is a mass of gold and reddish ocher, with little wall space that is not decorated.

Wilhering, I explained when we visited it the next day, was just thirty-five years younger than Melk, founded in 1146. The entire abbey, except for the porch, had been burned down in 1733 and rebuilt with a glorious reddish cornice running around the entire church.

Konstanze listened attentively to my occasional art history lectures, and she seemed impressed by my scholarship. She was a good listener and a quick learner. But even in this she insisted on equality. She was, for instance, familiar with many of the lesser-known saints represented in the stuccowork and with whom I was completely unfamiliar. People like St. Notburga, who was the patron saint of hired hands. According to legend, as Konstanze told me, this saint had refused to reap corn on a Sunday and, when forced to do so, her scythe had jumped miraculously from her hand and suspended itself in midair, just out of reach. Another was St. Dorothy, who, on the way to her execution for converting heathens, was asked mockingly to send down flowers and fruit when she got to the heavenly garden; after her death a child miraculously appeared with a basket of fruit and roses. And St. Genevieve, St. Ursula, St. Marcella . . . I was not unaware that all Konstanze's saints were female.

I was impressed by her knowledge and her devotion. More than once she was visibly moved when I described the circumstances surrounding the building of the churches or abbeys we visited. At some a vision had been seen there, or a miracle performed, or a martyr killed. Her ability to identify with religious suffering was remarkable. It was old-fashioned but it also had a link with that melancholic streak she had grown up with. Perhaps, I thought to myself, that streak helped Konstanze become so devout.

It was now that she began to take confession. This disturbed me even more than her prayers. What was she confessing? The little lapses in her life? Her thoughts? What thoughts? Perhaps—I imagined—she was confessing to her relationship with me. But if so, what relationship? We hadn't so much as touched. I found myself wondering whether, in her own mind, she had betrayed Rudolf yet and whether that was what she was discussing with the priest.

I wasn't the first authority figure in history to want to know what was going on inside the confessional, and that provoked another thought. If she could confess her sins and be absolved, didn't that give her an advantage in our game? She was aware that a safety valve was available to her through confession that was not available to me.

Sitting in those monasteries and abbeys, I would be deliciously content one minute, happy that I was with the most interesting and complex woman I had ever met, and tormented by doubts the next, painfully aware of the fact that, three weeks after I had started this "interrogation," I could not be certain that I was any further along.

It was while I was sitting in the nave at Sonntagberg, a magnificent church on the top of a hill, where you can see for fifteen kilometers in every direction, and which has a striking fresco above the altar, a masterpiece by Daniel Gran in gray, green and gold, that I first began to concede to the feeling that had formed in my unconscious the day I drove in that large circle from Salzburg. At last I could see that there was an alternative to my plan for worming information out of Konstanze. I believe that in the stillness of the church, the late sun washing the plasterwork beneath the dome, I actually whispered my thoughts aloud. *I could let the interrogation fail.* I remember repeating the sentence to myself, amazed that the church walls around me didn't tremble and fall down. Konstanze had finished praying and had disappeared into the confessional. The more I thought about my change of plan, the better I liked it and the easier it seemed to bring it off. Three other interrogators had failed before me, so it would not look suspicious. Hobel was a fool and there was no way that he would succeed where I had failed. It meant that a handful of Nazis—Bormann, maybe, Eichmann perhaps, Mengele —would scramble to safety in South America. But, I found myself thinking, the war was over; it was time to put away wartime things, as Maurice had said. And did all that matter anyway, if I could persuade Konstanze to come back to America with me?

Then I would check myself. These were ridiculous, even dangerous, thoughts. Probably treasonable. I had my job to do; I had been an anti-Nazi all my adult life. And, for all I knew, the feelings I had developed for Konstanze were part of *her* counterplot, her plan to resist me. She had made me fall for her so that I would have the ideas I was now having, so that I would think along precisely these lines.

As these subversive notions raced in and out of my mind, Konstanze had still not appeared from behind the confessional curtain. Sometimes I could hear the murmur of her voice, or the brief, gruff tones of the priest as he replied. But never could I decipher what was being said.

I got up and went outside to try to catch whatever breeze there was and clear my mind.

In this uncertain and unsatisfactory way we visited monasteries at Garsten and Christkindl, Krems and Schlierbach, Traisen and St. Pölten.

The more monasteries we visited, the more expert Konstanze became at recognizing the style of Prandtauer, a fresco by Altomonte or a painting by Troger. Being Konstanze, she was not content to be the passive recipient of the knowledge I gave her. She had to twist it to her own use. Troger she called "the Dragon" because she spotted his aptitude for painting this mythical animal; Altomonte she called "Adolf," since he seemed unusually keen to paint people with mustaches—very rare in religious art where the male figures are either clean shaven or bearded. These were not idle nicknames, as I had to admit. Konstanze was making points about both painters that I had overlooked.

Nonetheless, it was also true that I was giving Konstanze something— knowledge which fitted well with her religious devotion, something that added to her understanding of religion and that could not fail to produce a growing intimacy between us. I was pleased. The letters, or rather the fact that I had read them, began to bother me more and more. It had been wrong. I wanted to make amends.

For a couple of days, as I recall, the pattern of our expeditions changed. Sight-seeing and lunch played less of a part. We concentrated on the churches and the monasteries, sometimes visiting three or four a day. In its turn this produced a change in us. Whatever the reason for our initial "pact," by this point the relationship had taken on a vigor of its own. It had its own humor, its own rhythms, most important, its own satisfactions. We were now growing more at ease with one another. Sometimes, if I inadvertently revealed something gained from the letters, as when I drew her attention to a nougat factory in Wels, knowing that nougat was her favorite, she would sink back into silence for a while. But these periods got shorter and shorter.

For two days we concentrated on religion and on architecture. For my part, I was so anxious to preserve the tone of things that I stopped going into the office. I had nothing to say to Hobel, Sammy's news seemed unimportant. I called Saul each night, as arranged, and managed to delay his raid on the warehouse in Krumau. I said my end of the investigation was "too delicate." And so it was, though not in the sense he thought I meant.

Although it may have been a treasonable notion to consider deliberately failing in my duty, it was one which would not go away. I had no idea whether Konstanze's feelings would ever be such that she would leave Austria, leave Rudolf and return to California with me, but the day we visited Christkindl gave me hope.

Christkindl is not a monastery but a pilgrimage church, near Steyr, completed by Prandtauer and known for its altar, which shows God, a dove and a child, and for its globe-shaped tabernacle. Konstanze had been in confession and, as we stepped out of the church into the afternoon sun, she said, "Would *I* like America, Walter? Would Dieter?"

Her question came out of the blue, or out of the gloom of the church porch, and so it may have sounded more significant than she meant it to. Certainly, in my mood, I took it as significant.

"Dieter would love it," I answered quickly. "That bit is easily settled. It's a boy's country. There's plenty of space—more space than anyone knows what to do with. Sports and games galore, a very different wildlife —coyotes, raccoons, cardinals, different kinds of owls, buffalo. Seventeen-year-olds have their own cars. He would love it."

She smiled, agreeing.

"As for you, I don't know. It's not a truly religious country. There are a lot of religious groups, and many kinds of bossy interfering puritans, even among the Catholics, but the Church has no sense of history; and it is, of course, the century of science. So on both counts there is no real humility. However, the land itself is beautiful. San Francisco Bay is probably the most beautiful large bay in the world. My house overlooks it. Some mornings a mist rolls in from the ocean, like a huge layer of cotton batting. Occasionally the Golden Gate Bridge pokes up through the wool. It is an eerie but wonderful sight, and typically American. They have interfered with natural beauty and improved it! You would love the climate in California; it's like April in Austria throughout the year. No snow, lots of fresh fruit and flowers, lots of crayfish.

"Both of you would love the Rockies—raw, red, hard and bony, not at all like the mountains here. No pretty flowers or soft green grass, but deliciously cold rivers, clear and shining with trout. The clothes are ugly —you wouldn't like that—and so are a surprisingly large number of the people. But, away from New York, their manners are open and welcoming. It's not just a different country or continent. It's a different mood.

"In the office we have a man who is a genius at speculating on the stock market. At least I hope he is because some of the money he is using is mine. But he says, for instance, that now that the war is over America is *the* place to live. Europe will get going again but it will never be as prosperous as the United States. In twenty years, he predicts, everyone will own a car and a television set. And who knows what else?"

I knew it would take more than one conversation to convince Konstanze to come to America, but I had made a start. Mention of cars gave me the idea to repeat my invitation to teach her to drive. That might lead somewhere too.

She was nervous at first, but I kept her on the quiet lanes until she had mastered the foot pedals and was sure that her perception of speed and stopping distances was safe. As in other things, she was a fast learner, and the more practice she had, the more she enjoyed driving and the more she wanted to do. I was content to be the passenger for a while, as this allowed me the chance to examine the map and I was able to locate some of the more out-of-the-way churches and monasteries.

Indirectly, this arrangement led to one incident we had while Konstanze was at the wheel that caused us much merriment. We had been to Garsten, a Benedictine abbey church with some of the finest stuccowork anywhere. Garsten is on a narrow tongue of land between the river Steyr and the river Enns, so that there is no shortage of water in the area:

lakes, marshes, small rivers and streams which occasionally, but especially in spring, flood the roads. We had come to one of these spring fords and Konstanze had stopped the car just where the water began. She was, she said, nervous. Owing to the layout of the river, which ran alongside the road for a while before crossing it diagonally, the actual area of metal under water was quite extensive. I told her to drive slowly through the stream to avoid doing any damage to the engine and as a way of ensuring that water did not splash into the carburetor or distributor.

That was *my* mistake, for Konstanze drove so slowly that, right in the middle of the water, she stalled. Though she was at first mortified at what she had done, she was soon helpless with laughter after I, complaining, had removed my shoes and socks, rolled up my trousers and then stepped into the water to push the car clear. What man can keep his dignity under such circumstances? In fact, she was so amused that I was tempted to believe that she had stalled the damn thing on purpose. I was very uncomfortable in the cold water but that only made her laugh the more, and eventually I joined in.

I took the opportunity of the driving lesson to give Konstanze the BMW badge off the car as a memento of her driving lessons that day. It wasn't my car and, therefore, strictly speaking, the badge wasn't mine to give. But I gave it to her all the same and she accepted.

Farther up the river Steyr is Schlierbach, a small Cistercian abbey church surrounded by an eighteenth-century courtyard built of multicolored brick, with a fountain against one wall. The interior of this church was remarkable. Below the gallery it was decorated in dark colors, brown and black, with a little gold, yet the gallery itself was bright, resplendent in white and primary yellows, greens, blues and reds.

It was one of those occasions when Konstanze had been able to make confession and I waited for her outside in the courtyard, by the fountain. I can remember sitting, half mesmerized by the dripping water, a little nervous in view of what I planned. She did not emerge for over half an hour and I found myself disturbed by what might be happening in the confessional. The sputter of the fountain was comforting, but only up to a point.

When she did come outside she emerged from the church shading her eyes with her hand. It was not simply the sharp sunshine.

"Do you often cry in the confessional?" I asked as I passed her a handkerchief.

There was no reply at first. She wiped her eyes, blew her nose. Held her face to the sun for its heat to remove all trace of tears. "I cry all the time. Anywhere."

I felt the urge to put my arm around her as she sobbed again. I had come across these inexplicable tears before, the kind that came racking up from deep within and which, like cancer, divided and grew, rising, boiling, escaping in helpless, unforgiving sobs. Usually I was embarrassed when a woman cried this way, but not this time.

However, as if sensing that I was about to touch her, Konstanze moved away. She looked about her and, seeing no one, went to one of the walls in the courtyard where there was some ivy hanging down. She broke off a small branch and brought it back to the fountain and handed it to me.

"Other women get flowers, Walter. I would settle for leaves, anything."

Now, forty years later, I believe I know what she meant by that statement, that plea. I think I understand women enough to be able to decode most of their cryptic conundrums. But not then. What she said totally perplexed me.

I suggested coffee and brandy as a way of relaxing us.

The walk into the center of the town cheered her, the more so when we found a café overlooking the river. Just below where we sat, the Steyr flowed into the Enns and that, in turn, would eventually become the Danube. We sat and watched as a line of swans and cygnets moved regally downstream and wondered to each other what the chances were that it was the same family that had fallen out with Dieter.

"I haven't heard from him yet," I said, conscious that talk of Konstanze's son was a good guarantee of avoiding whichever subject it was that was distressing her.

"Oh, he'll write. Don't worry. He's very responsible, very German in that way."

"Would you like more?" I asked. "Children, I mean."

She nodded vigorously.

"I'd love a daughter," I said. "And I'd like her always to remain the same age—seven or eight. No older."

"So she always thought of you as wonderful—yes?" Konstanze smiled. "You'd be a good father, Walter. But a good husband? I don't know.

Most men find it easier to be good fathers than good husbands. It's less demanding."

I felt ever so slightly scolded, but I didn't mind. "Why do you think I would make a good father?"

"You treated Dieter as an equal. That's the most important thing with a child. And you do it naturally. I had to learn. My parents never treated me as an equal: I hated it."

I found myself thinking that if I hadn't read those damn letters, I could now have asked her about her parents; she could have told me in her own words what she wanted me to know. By prying I had robbed myself of the pleasures of discovery now. It was my own fault.

A waiter brought the coffee, a brandy and some fragile-looking pastries. I offered her one and watched as she took it. She tried her coffee, then bit tentatively into the crust. She appeared to like what she tasted, for she then took a larger bite. This is what I was hoping for.

I had a question I very much wanted to ask, but I hated the idea of a rebuff. What I wanted least of all was a swift "No," the kind of response that would close the door once and for all to what I was about to propose. But, if her mouth was full, she couldn't say no right away. I would have my chance.

"Konstanze," I said as she chewed, and I tried to phrase my words and shade my voice as if what I had to say was not very important to me. "I see from the local newspaper that there is a concert on Sunday, in Salzburg. The orchestra will play Chopin, Stravinsky, Bruckner. Would you like to go with me? We could have dinner afterward, at the Sylvaner."

The swans were coming ashore a few yards downstream and she seemed engrossed by that. She took a drink of coffee, put her cup down. "Thank you, Walter, but no—not on Sunday. I can't. There's someone coming to see me."

Her reply, though delivered gently, stung me. It was the first time she had refused me anything, if you don't count my offer to help with Dieter's luggage on the day he went back to school. I felt I had mismanaged things, like a youth of eighteen who has moved too fast with his girlfriend and over-reached himself, showing his cards too early.

That night I dined in Salzburg with some English friends of Maurice's who were passing through on their way to Italy. And, though they were charming, witty company, I could not take my mind off Konstanze. They must have found me preoccupied and dull.

They had heard about my contest with Maurice in the stock market. I was able to tell them that he was far ahead at the latest count. Confederate Paper was still doing nicely, and RMC was, naturally, holding steady. They all found our contest very amusing and, looking back, that's how I see it too, but that night I was feeling quite sad and the bald figures of the stock exchange only emphasized how badly I was doing in general. I couldn't crack Konstanze and I couldn't woo her either.

Saul was growing anxious too. When I called him he said there had been a lot of activity, into and out of the Krumau warehouse, and he was worried that whatever was being shipped *out* was going to do some damage somewhere.

"Walter, I would never forgive myself if I found that people, or things, from that warehouse were being used in the conduit. Can't we make a move yet?"

"A few days, Saul. Please. Not long now, I promise."

But I couldn't hold him back for much longer. It was unfair.

It was warmer than ever when I drove out to Mondsee the next morning. I was late because I had to service the BMW. It was the kind of unseasonal heat that makes you think the weather is changing globally and permanently and that, whatever the meteorologists say, the end of the world could be a serious possibility before very long. Tiny lumps of melting roadway were picked up by the tires of the car and flung out behind me in a sand-colored gritty wake.

As usual, sleep had helped me recover some sort of equanimity, but as I entered Mondsee and drove past the jetties and docks lining the shore, it began to slither away from me again. As the car covered the short and, by now, very familiar distance between the village proper and Konstanze's house, the nervousness congealed again inside me, black and sticky, not unlike the melting tar on the roads.

At that point in our relationship, I should have known that, if I expected Konstanze to be in one frame of mind, I would almost certainly find her in the opposite one. She was firmly in control and able to dictate the mood of our meetings almost at will. And so, to my surprise, I arrived to find a table laid in the garden. The yellow gingham cloth, the one we had taken to our picnic by the Salzach, was drawn over the table, and on it were the paraphernalia of lunch: knives, forks, two wineglasses, a bas-

ket for bread, salt and pepper, a tiny vase with three or four head of
gentian.

I inspected the table before going to the door, though Konstanze
would know that I had arrived; there was no disguising the exhaust of the
BMW. As I stood admiring the table she came out of the kitchen carrying cut bread in a napkin. She gave me a broad smile.

"You're late," she said, coming very close to me. "Too late to go
anywhere for lunch." She tipped the bread into the basket. "And in any
case," she spoke as she busied herself, arranging the table, "we haven't
had a proper lunch in the last few days. It's time we did."

She pulled out one of the chairs for me to sit on. "I've managed to get
some more eggs. I'm going to give you a real Austrian omelet."

I sank into the chair in bewilderment as she vanished back into the
house. The nervousness in my stomach had all but disappeared, so warm
had Konstanze's welcome been. I noticed, on the far side of the table, on
the grass in the shade, a bottle of wine. I poured myself a glass. On some
occasions, like now, Konstanze seemed genuinely fond of me, pleased to
see me, and relaxed in my presence. But was it real? Who is more
paranoid than a love-sick interrogator who has had the tables turned on
him? It was possible to view Konstanze's behavior as a systematic alterna-
tion between blowing hot and cold. Not regular, that would be too
predictable, too easy to cope with, but systematic certainly. If our pact
had ended that day, I must admit, Konstanze would have been the
victor. And, such was her lead, such was her command of the situation, I
wouldn't have minded. It goes without saying that I had never known an
interrogation like this one. But I should also stress that, in my life before
the war and during it, I had never come across a woman even remotely
comparable to Konstanze.

The wine was fruity but with an edge to it. In those days refrigerators
were not widespread in Europe and there was no danger of wine being
served too cold, so that all the flavor is lost. I took some bread, soaked it
in my drink, and slid it into my mouth.

Konstanze reappeared, this time with Martha. The housekeeper carried two plates, with the omelets, and Konstanze held a salad bowl, large
and made of clay, and what looked like a newspaper. This she dropped
onto the grass by her chair and helped me to salad. The omelets, which
were slightly burned, crisp brown and smoky hot, were lumpy with
chunks of chicken, slices of sausage and tomato and streaked with spin-

ach. I also detected what I thought was cheese. Konstanze had gone to a lot of trouble with this meal and, such was my mood, I found even that perplexing. Why?

I had not eaten fresh eggs since Konstanze's previous omelet and this one was even better: I was silent as I munched. For me, food is almost as relaxing as sleep; I was unraveling quickly. Konstanze bent down and picked up the paper she had dropped on the grass. She passed it to me.

It was the day before's and open at an inside page. I glanced over it, eating. I could see nothing that meant anything to me and looked up at Konstanze. Using the fork she was eating with, she pointed, not at any of the local news, but at one of the advertisements. It was for the concert I had invited her to.

"But I thought you couldn't come? I told them I didn't want the tickets."

"Look again, silly," she said in mock exasperation. "It's the same orchestra, the same program, but it's a different date and a different place—Innsbruck." She took a forkful of omelet and followed it with a piece of bread, wiping her lips with her napkin. "I could go to the Innsbruck concert, if you still wanted to take me."

7

THE evening of the concert was dark, black as the stuccowork we had become so familiar with, and still unseasonally warm. It had not been easy to get tickets, but Hartt, the fixer, had somehow managed it, though it cost me close to a week's pay.

The day between our omelet lunch in the garden and the concert had been devoted to monasteries—Lochen and Strasswalchen. It had been an important day. After she had been so warm at the lunch, I was expecting Konstanze to turn cold, or distant, at any point. But, throughout, she remained relaxed, friendly, even intimate. I began to believe that she felt about me almost the same way I felt about her.

It so happened that both abbeys featured the wooden carvings of

Meinrad Guggenbichler, perhaps the most graceful and restrained Austrian sculptor. In the afternoon we stopped in Michaelbeuren for tea, or ice cream, I forget which. Afterward we strolled around the little town looking at the shops. Just as we were about to return to the car we passed an antiquities hideaway, tiny, with a small window. Inside, the shop was narrow but snaked back for as far as the eye could see in the gloom. Halfway along, to one side, was something that looked familiar. I was about to enter, but Konstanze held back.

"It's too gloomy, Walter. Let's stay here, in the sun."

I waved to the car. "Why don't you wait for me there? I don't mind the gloom. There's something I want to look at. I'll be quick and join you at the car."

The old woman who ran the shop reminded me a little of Martha. Same build, same age, same manner, like a scarecrow looking for birds to frighten. But she didn't frighten me and she didn't know what she had. I got it for a song. In fact it was so cheap that I now think it may have been stolen. She wouldn't wrap it though, saying that paper was in short supply. Yes, I thought, that's what pushes the price up, and keeps Maurice ahead. So I had to give it to Konstanze as it was.

"Walter? For me? . . . What is it?"

I could tell she was pleased. Also, that she had quite a good idea what it was. "You tell me, Konstanze. You know enough now to make an educated guess."

She held it up, turned it over, ran her fingers along the wood. "It's not a Schwanthaler, not intense enough—right?"

I nodded.

"And it can't be a Zürn—not frenzied enough."

"Correct. Well done."

What she had was a carved figure of a saint, St. Rochas, in flowing robes with a plague spot on his leg—the symbol that identified him.

"Think," I said. "How would you describe the carving style?"

She hesitated. "Well, I would say it's graceful, restrained, but . . ."

"But what?" I said.

"But it can't be by Guggenbichler—can it? They're too rare, too valuable." She searched my expression for clues.

I nodded. You can't get that kind of bargain these days. But you could then. I have a good eye and had spotted it straightaway.

The saint was about two feet high. She hugged it.

"I'm sorry it's not flowers," I said.

"Sorry?" She smiled. "Walter, this is much nicer." She paused. "Much, *much* nicer. Thank you."

I think that had we not been in the main square of Michaelbeuren, in the middle of the afternoon, Konstanze would have kissed me then. Instead, she looked at me levelly for what seemed like ages. I could make of that look what I would, she was telling me.

Physical contact would have moved us forward, of course. But, in a way, I was not sorry we didn't kiss that day. In the first place it would have been ostensibly a kiss of thanks, nothing more, and that might have made a second kiss, a proper one, harder to achieve. Second, it meant that, between us, Konstanze owed me something and I liked that. Third, it introduced a pleasant feeling of anticipation so far as our next outing, the concert, was concerned. I had deliberately suggested the concert in the first place to move things away from churches and daytime. Whatever my motives might be with Konstanze, I simply wanted to be with her, as a normal couple, enjoying a concert and dinner afterward. I would see then where, if anywhere, that led.

The gift had touched her; she held it all the way back to Mondsee and refused the opportunity to drive. She was touched, I think, in two ways. In the first place it was a religious gift and that meant a lot to her. Second, it was a gift, pure and simple. That told me something I should have thought of before. If she was so touched by a gift, it could only mean that she had not received any for quite some time. Rudolf, though he was in touch with her, was either too busy, too nervous or didn't care enough anymore to send her gifts. That is partly what the tears had been about in the courtyard at Schlierbach.

It was her response to that gift that made me believe, for the first time, that I might tempt Konstanze to America.

As we drove back that day, Konstanze fingered the plague spot on St. Rochas' leg. "You know, Walter, it's funny but Dieter has a mark on his back, to the side of his spine above the waist. And so have I. Same sort of mark, same place, more or less."

I groaned, but not out loud. I knew about that mark on Konstanze's skin. I had read about it in one of Rudolf's letters. Konstanze now *wanted* me to know intimate things about her, wanted to draw me in, to advance closer, bit by bit. Or so it appeared. Lovers getting ever closer is always a pleasure: you mustn't go too fast or too slow. But those damn letters kept getting in the way, spoiling the surprises. I was in a bind. I wouldn't have been in the delicious situation I was in but for the letters. But I still wished now that I had never read them.

I looked across at Konstanze. I had a mark on the left of my neck and I tugged at the collar of my shirt, so she could see it.

"This is *my* blemish. In America we call it a birth mark. No one's perfect—eh?"

She smiled.

When we arrived back at Mondsee that afternoon, she behaved exquisitely.

"How long will it take to drive to Innsbruck, Walter?"

"Two hours. At least."

"So, no churches tomorrow. We shall have to leave around five—yes?"

I nodded.

"And I shall need all afternoon to get ready. Can you amuse yourself during the day tomorrow?"

"I can," I said. "I don't want to, but I can."

She smiled and kissed the statue, making it clear that since Martha was hovering in the house, she couldn't kiss me. "Don't be so negative. Don't you ever enjoy anticipating things? I think that's half the fun. I shall spend most of the day slowly getting ready for the evening. There are certain things which need to be done—like ironing my dress, washing my hair—at a certain time and in a particular order. I suppose you just comb your hair and slip on your uniform and that's it. How dreary."

"Not quite," I said with a mock grumble. "It took me a week, almost, to earn the money for the tickets."

"Good," she laughed. "So you will appreciate it all the more."

I didn't go straight back to Salzburg that evening. I took a coffee in the marketplace in Mondsee and visited the church again. Then had an indifferent dinner at the hotel adjoining the café. There was something I had to do in Mondsee that could be done only in the evening.

We had spent such a lovely day together that I hated what I had to do. I parked the car out of the way in a side street in Mondsee, then walked out to the lakeshore. It was very quiet and I saw no one. More important, I was pretty sure no one saw me. Reaching the shore I turned left and walked along the road to Konstanze's house. I kept to the grass verges so no one should hear my footsteps and twice, when I saw the headlamps of cars approaching, I hid in the bushes.

When I reached Konstanze's house, I stood for a while just watching. The breeze from the lake, black and silvery behind me, pressed my hair to my head. There were lights in the house—in the sewing room and one of the upstairs rooms. It was 7:45.

I waited for half an hour. Cars passed occasionally and fish sometimes slapped the surface of the water. But otherwise there was no movement or sound.

After half an hour I slowly took off my shoes and crossed the road. I didn't open the gate; that would have been too noisy. Instead I stepped over the fence. The grass was already wet with dew and my feet were immediately drenched. No matter; I didn't want to make a sound.

I went round to the side of the house and stood as near as I could to the window of the sewing room. A noise filtered through the curtains and the glass. I edged closer. Closer still. It wasn't voices, it was music.

I couldn't see into the room, but I didn't need to. I waited outside, with wet feet, for forty, maybe fifty, minutes. Then the music stopped. A voice began to announce the end of the concert when the sound was suddenly cut off. Someone moved in the room, a single pair of feet. Then the light went out. The footsteps went upstairs, but I was already beginning my wet journey back across the lawn, over the fence and into the road.

I put on my shoes and, with my socks squelching with each step, walked as briskly as I could back to Mondsee. Konstanze had lied when she said she had someone coming to see her that night. Now I knew why.

On the day of the concert I had spent the daylight hours reconnoitering again, even farther afield. But I also took Konstanze's advice and enjoyed a leisurely bath, with a glass of wine, and looked forward to the evening.

I had no knots of nervousness as I drove to meet her. Instead, I enjoyed speculating what her dress would be like. I was excited at the prospect of seeing her in something more sophisticated, more revealing than a day dress. The way she dressed tonight, I told myself, would tell me something about the way she felt toward me. Her gown, her makeup, her hair styling would together form a code on the basis of which I might calculate my next move.

I saw Martha first and she was wearing the filthiest scowl on her gray face that I had yet seen. I should not have been surprised. Since she so venomously disapproved of our daytime jaunts, she could be expected to be more vitriolic about any evening activities. Nonetheless, she was clearly under orders to show me into the music room and to offer me a drink. She did this with the grim reluctance of a Christian in ancient Rome being asked to feed the lions. Her chore done, she scampered from the room as fast as her stumpy legs would carry her, slamming the door with an eloquent bang, as if she herself was in mortal danger from my advances.

It was the first chance I'd had to look inside the wine and music room and I wasted no time. I poked around. The piano was covered in photographs but none that were of any use. There were also the mementos we had collected—the postcards, the badge, even the feather, neatly put to one side. Wedged on the cushion on the window seat was a large pile of sheet music: Schubert, Brahms, Strauss and Bruckner, inevitably. The wine which lined two of the walls was very obviously a German as opposed to a French collection: whites easily outnumbered the reds. I quickly found what I was searching for: the section devoted to Austrian wines. There were several types: Nussberger, Grinzinger, Neuberger, Sieveringer. Sieveringer came from Kr—

Before I could take in any more, the door barged open and nearly knocked my drink from my hand.

"Did Martha give you something to drink? Walter? . . . Where are you?"

I was behind the door, trying to recover my balance.

It was a very excited Konstanze who turned to face me. Even I could see that. I could also see why she had wanted half the day to get ready. She had not wasted a minute. As I know I have said before, she looked good enough to eat.

Her hair was up, off her face. It had been washed and brushed—and brushed and brushed. It was blond in all sorts of ways: buttercup, barley, whiskey, hickory—you name it, the color was in there somewhere. Every time I looked at Konstanze's hair that night, it was ever so slightly different.

Her face had been rouged—I hadn't seen that before—but what really drew my eye was the light coating of powder that had been brushed over her cheekbones and chin. The effect of this was like that of wind on a beach; all care had been winnowed away, leaving it like porcelain.

Traveling down past her slender white throat, I came to her dress, in black lace with a scalloped neck, so perfectly arranged that it drew the eye from the curves of her shoulders into the swelling of her breasts, a purely involuntary move that would delight and disturb every man who saw her that night. She wore no jewelry but her dress was adorned with a single fold of crimson silk sashed around her waist and knotted over and draped down one side of her thigh. The dress ended well below the knee and this, together with her hair styling and powder, gave Konstanze a definite seventeenth- or eighteenth-century look. I felt complimented that she was doing this as a sort of thank you for all the instruction I had given her about that epoch in the previous days.

"Prandtauer could take a few lessons from you," I said.

She had a glass of wine in her hand and that comforted me too. It suggested she had been drinking while she was getting dressed, genuinely relaxing and not calculating, as had always been the case before. She smiled and drank from the glass now.

She turned her wrist and inspected her watch, the one ungraceful thing she was wearing. It was huge and looked to me as though it had once been the property of the German Army and had been given to her by Rudolf. "We should go?"

I nodded and set down what was left of my drink on the piano. Martha had heard our movements and she brought Konstanze's coat and that forbidding scowl into the corridor. "Good night Martha," said Konstanze. "See you in the morning."

The opera house, where the concert was being held, was a blaze of glittering white light and gold moldings worn thin with age. The lights sent long shadows across the square as people arrived. Those were the days before parking was ever a problem and so Konstanze did not have far to walk in her evening clothes. I was wearing my mess uniform that night, a warm, soft brown that emphasized the tan I was beginning to acquire from having an open car.

There was time for a drink beforehand, so while Konstanze went to check her coat and make last-minute adjustments to her hair, I found the bar. I had said I would introduce her to the delights of the martini, American-style.

The bar was in the foyer on the main level and, as she walked across it that night, well, although I am this far into my story, I savor that moment as memory number three. Apart from Martha, I had never seen

Konstanze in the company of other women, and, therefore, I had never fully realized just how sensationally beautiful she was. I saw her from across the room and realized, as I had not in the music room in Mondsee, just how close-fitting the upper bodice of her dress was. Sexy was a word we did not use then. Alluring sounds forced; ripe, a bit juvenile and pretentious; sumptuous; luscious? She was all those things and more, and every man looked at her. I had escorted many attractive women, but that evening, without a doubt, was the most exciting, the moment when I felt most proud.

I held out her drink as she approached. "If we were at a theatre in America, you would never have reached me. Three men, at least, would have left their wives for you. I feel like I'm on a honeymoon."

She laughed, pleased at the effect she had created, and tasted the drink. Immediately, her face crinkled.

"Urrgh, Walter! This tastes as though someone has been cooking crayfish in it. May I have some wine, please?"

We both laughed and I ordered her a glass of Riesling.

Although our seats were costly, they were worth it. As we sat down, I looked around; we were about five rows from the conductor. It was mainly a solid, bourgeois Austrian audience but, I guessed, far more knowledgeable about the music than an equivalent American group. One or two people nodded to Konstanze, but no one came up to us. The uniform, I concluded, probably frightened them off. In that part of the world, most people had had enough of uniforms to last them a lifetime. I gave Konstanze her program: another memento.

The lights went out and the concert started. Schubert's overture to *Rosamunde* opened the program—lively but subtle, with an insistent beat, like galloping horses. Then came Haydn's Lamentation Symphony and, after the interval, Bruckner's Seventh Symphony, the one with the very moving adagio, written immediately after Wagner's death and therefore very much affected by it. During the music I was conscious, as never before, of Konstanze's body next to mine. In the darkened theater she seemed even more desirable than in the bright sunshine. That is saying a great deal. She smelled, as ever, of the soap she used. Perfume was almost impossible to get in Austria at that time. But, just as during the day the soap seemed fresh and airy; tonight, with the powder, it seemed altogether more subtle, richer, more sophisticated.

Should I—could I—touch her? It was as easy as changing gears in the

BMW to reach across and take her hand. I made excuses to myself. It wasn't dark enough. It would embarrass her. If she refused, or in some way rebuffed me, I would be embarrassed and it would spoil the rest of the evening. The music meant too much to her, I told myself; she would not appreciate an approach in the theater. Then she would shift in her seat and almost touch me herself. Except that she never did, quite.

Anyway, I did nothing and was immensely relieved when the symphony ended. Walking down the street afterward, I lit a cigarette—a pipe was too sedate for the way I felt and, in any case, took too long to light. Konstanze chattered away about the music and how she had always felt sorry for Bruckner, despite the fact that he was, by all accounts, rather weird. "He never married, as I think I told you. And he grew to be a simple-minded old soul. He would keep falling in love with very young girls, of eighteen or nineteen even when he was ancient. He would propose to them and that, of course, made their mothers extremely angry —it made no difference that he was famous by then. Sad." She had turned to me, and the light that caught her face picked out the color in her eyes more than at any time since our first meeting. "You know what I like about Bruckner? His clumsiness. His music is clumsy in places, but that makes him more human. Whenever I listen to Bruckner, his music makes me think about men who *need* women, who are uncomfortable with them, yet can't do without them."

The Stubaier, where we ate dinner, was near the railway station and it was full of concertgoers. Those were the days when a black tie was not an unusual sight at a concert, with even the occasional opera cloak on show, and this all added to the gaiety of the evening. An old-fashioned gaiety, of course, formal in its way, that has all but disappeared now.

There was fresh saibling cooked with mushrooms on the menu, which we both decided to have, a far rarer treat then than it is now. For wine we agreed on a bottle of Grinzinger. While we waited for our food Konstanze accepted a cigarette and sat back in her chair looking at me. That moment, that evening in the Stubaier, was the peak of my contentedness. Whenever I hear other people use the word "happy" that evening flashes into my mind. I could not ever imagine, then or now, being bored by Konstanze. Nor could I imagine possessing her, as I had possessed other women. There would always be something unknowable and elusive about her. I realized that, as with a butterfly, to catch her was to destroy her, to remove the center of her. I realized, I suppose, that I had always secretly feared the type of woman Konstanze was, but that night I felt a freedom I hadn't expected. I loved it and I loved her.

I considered our pact. I cannot remember now whether I had already admitted to myself that she had won, but whether I had or not, it was true. I wouldn't force the Rudolf issue. The war was over, those other interrogators had failed. Hobel, and Eisenhower, could go to hell. Far more important, as far as I was concerned, was Konstanze herself. She seemed finally to have abandoned her suspicions and now seemed to have reached the point where she just enjoyed being with me. Eventually, and probably very soon, I thought, our relationship would become physical—perhaps that very night. Given the background against which our relationship was evolving, that was a very big step—it would change things considerably. But now that the moment seemed imminent, I felt no need to rush it. That was new for me too.

I leaned forward to pour more wine. As if she could read my mind, Konstanze said, "Tell me about America, again, Walter. I like hearing about it. Tell me about your favorite places."

I took my time.

"America is about appetites," I told her, "and I love that. There are many European jokes, carping at the American tendency to have the biggest, the best, the most extraordinary this or that, but I don't mind. In fact, I find it endearing and I think the Europeans who make those jokes miss the point of America. The thing to understand about the country is that, although it is full of Europeans, they are, in many ways, *ex*-Europeans who want to be *non*-Europeans or even *anti*-Europeans. After all, most of them left Europe for a reason and they want to keep America separate from Europe in all sorts of ways. Since, by definition, they can't honor the past in America, it makes very good sense for them to dwell on the present and the future. Hence the biggest this, the most expensive that, and so forth. So, if I may, I'll be very American and not answer your question but tell you what *I* want to tell you about America."

I took a sip of wine.

"You are going to hate this, Konstanze, but I like—I *love*—the waste."

She had looked up then, her food halfway to her mouth.

"Yes, it's true. Go into an ordinary restaurant in America—a coffee shop, I mean, not a fancy place—and order any dish. It will arrive garnished with all sorts of things—bread, lettuce, pickle, potatoes—that you didn't order. It is as much as you can do to finish your meal and clear your plate. Buy a car in Europe and, unless you are a millionaire, you will get a cramped metal box with every accessory designed to save space and cost and to avoid excess. In America the car will be twice as long as the engineering warrants and there will be far more room than you need. Instead of being designed to save money and space, the car is there to spoil you, to provide the maximum pleasure possible. The car says to you, 'Everyone can have luxuries, there's enough to go around, and plenty left over.' The car in America is not just a different machine, it's a different attitude. And it's the same with roads, beaches, beds and buildings— they are bigger, longer, above all, more *generous*.

"I admire the churches we have been visiting, not least for the fact that they represent an ideal quite different from most architecture in America. Churches here are built vertically; everyone from the architects to the congregation had their eyes on heaven. In America, outside of confined city centers, which are a special case, buildings are designed horizontally. Even skyscrapers are a series of horizontal buildings, one on top of the other. My own house is a good example; it is on one floor, but it sprawls all over the land, like a capital letter that has yet to be invented, somewhere between the *E* and the *X*. We are all very proud of having two feet firmly on the ground; so our houses must cover as much of that ground as possible."

I took my program and drew a plan of my house for Konstanze to see. She was interested but again, I noticed, more taken with my pen. I gave the drawing to her. She could keep that as a memento, if she wanted.

I continued. "Plenty has a curious effect on psychology. Strangely, it doesn't corrupt, as you might expect. At least, not in any obvious sense. Rather, it makes people naive. It is as if, not having to scramble for the basics in life—food, space, privacy, warmth—one comes to the other things less wily, less *contaminated*. One has less need of sophistication."

From the way Konstanze looked at me as I spoke, I couldn't tell whether she believed me or not. I can remember feeling a surge of affection for America and a twinge of guilt about the way I had, since leaving Fort Bragg, slipped back into many of my old European ways.

"America is a foreign country and not just because the predominant language is English. It's foreign to English speakers as well, because it isn't home to anyone. Travel around Europe—to Rome, London, Paris or Berlin. Different languages, yes, but if you know one city you know the others. The layouts will be similar; there will be a palace, a park, the railway station area will have a certain kind of feel; there will be a market, a cathedral. These are recognizable irrespective of which country you are in and which languages you speak. Not in America. Cities *feel* different, each one *is* different. Buildings are functional, not decorative or spiritual. They are there to be *pulled down* once they have served their purpose. That isn't necessarily a bad thing, quite the opposite, but as Europeans we are not used to it. We think of history as important. But America is founded on the very idea of starting over, of leaving behind a history that produced exiles, refugees, persecution and poverty.

"The buildings of America are awful to look at, but much more pleasant to be inside, compared with those in Europe. They tend to be larger, airier, warmer, lighter. It's a different world, a different psychology, a different mood. I don't think one grows to like America, not usually. Either you love it or you hate it."

"But you are an art historian, Walter. Interested in the past. What are you doing in America?"

"It's a mistake to think that historians only look back. The past is a tool to use for a better future. Sorry if that sounds pompous, but it's true."

I talked. I talked for ages. I talked through the saibling and through the second bottle of wine that I ordered. That second bottle is probably why I don't remember the details of what I talked about. But I do remember the gist.

We had finished eating. In fact, Konstanze had finished some time before—I had just caught up because I was talking so much. I lit my pipe.

Konstanze leaned forward, her elbows on the table. "I have always wanted to live by the ocean, Walter. It would be so mysterious. A lake is . . . not as romantic. You can see to the other side."

For some ridiculous reason I felt gratified by this. Her response was vague but, I felt, on the right track.

The coffee came and I asked for the bill. The cups, I remember, were a creamy yellow—her favorite color. The other concertgoers were leaving and it was getting late. It would be one in the morning before we were back at Mondsee.

"I can see to the other side of this table," I said softly. "That's far enough for me."

She smiled and moved her head a fraction in a way that touched me. She wasn't embarrassed by my compliment—rather she was gracious in accepting it. And that, I have always found, is a rare talent.

She patted her stomach. "I shan't be able to see as far as my feet if I eat like this too often. That was a lovely dinner, Walter, a lovely evening." She patted her stomach again. "You have satisfied one appetite in me but," and she looked at me levelly, "stimulated others."

We went out into the dark. In those days people seemed to travel by train an awful lot at night. In the middle of deserted towns the railway station would be brilliantly lit, alive with purpose, licensed to make noise. And so it was at Innsbruck. As we walked back to my car we could hear the bark of the platform speakers announcing deep into the night the imminent departure of a train for Munich. Steam from the trains clotted the air. In the distance, beyond the river Inn, which flowed like black blood under the railway bridge, the solitary complaining whistle of a train could be heard above the scratchy screams of shunting engines.

Away from the station Innsbruck already slept. The railway noises faded quickly, like ocean waves which fail to carry beyond the narrow strip of beach. It was too late for other restaurants and cafés, too early for tomorrow's newspaper delivery. The concert hall was closed up, like a birthday cake after the candles had been blown out.

We walked in silence, but it was an easy silence. Our two sets of footsteps, echoing off the street, proved that we were alone. My car looked very small in the square.

"I'm tired," said Konstanze, dipping into her seat. "All that wine, I suppose."

I was in no hurry to get back to Mondsee that night but the black roads were empty and we made good time, crossing and recrossing the river. I was enjoying the feel of the car and, when we reached the open road, neither of us spoke for a while. The easy silence continued until I felt a nudge on my shoulder.

It was Konstanze's head; she had fallen asleep and was leaning against me. I let it rest where it was. I could smell her powder as it rubbed off on my tunic. Not until we came to Mondsee and I had to change gears several times in rapid succession, as I negotiated the twists and curves in the village, did she wake up. She brushed back her hair. "I hope I didn't talk in my sleep."

"I wish you had," I murmured.

I pulled the car into the side of the road by the house. There was a light on in the kitchen. By the glow that came from the dashboard I could see that Konstanze was looking crossly at the house.

"Why don't we go and sit in the summerhouse for a moment?" I suggested.

She hesitated. "All right, but just for a minute. It's late."

From the balcony of the summerhouse we could see Plomberg, marked by a fragile scoop of white-yellow lights at the rim of the lake.

"I like having a view," I said, waving toward the lights. "Don't get me wrong, I love the ocean. But a lake like this takes some beating. And, right now, it's *very* romantic. Don't you think?"

Konstanze pulled her coat about her. Her dress was lace and it was still April, however unseasonably warm the weather. Nonetheless, her movement was involuntary and had to do with more than the temperature. "If you lived here a lot, Walter, you would find the lake and the mountains beyond it claustrophobic. Yes, it is beautiful. But you would be surprised to know how well one gets to know every peak, every dip in the tree line, every shade of light on the snowcaps. I even know there are sixteen lights on that string over in Plomberg. I have sat here so often and counted them. There should be eighteen, but two blew out last week and have yet to be replaced. I wish sometimes that there was a man in Plomberg who could change the mountains just like he changes the lights."

Involuntarily I counted the lights. She was, of course, right.

"All we ever get here are breezes. We are so hemmed in by the Schafberg, the Hoher Zinken and the Feuerkogel that a good, strong, *cleansing* wind cannot get through. The air is always sweet but that tends to cloy too. Everything is so tidy, so neat here, so very, very pretty. This will sound odd but, after a few years in Mondsee, you yearn for a bit of untidiness, for the occasional blot or blemish somewhere, for space and even for *ugliness*. The buildings here fit so perfectly with the landscape that when you talk of American architecture as more concerned with insides than outsides, I long to go, to see for myself what you mean. When you talk about space I think of some giant hand flattening all the mountains around here so that I can see as far as Vienna or Munich.

The countryside here has been tended by people for hundreds of years, it has had care lavished on it. I need a break from that, a bit of neglect, something that is natural and rough."

Konstanze was expressing her ambivalence, not just about Mondsee but also, I thought, about the life she was leading. There *was* a part of her that wanted to go to America, to break from the old life. It had never occurred to me before that Germans should take so personally their defeat in the war. Politicians, generals, countries lost wars. Not ordinary people. But maybe Konstanze felt that, in being married to a Nazi, however nice a man he was, she had suffered a personal loss in Germany's defeat. I don't know, for we never discussed it, not then or later. But it might well have explained her desire for change, her attraction to America. I was a catalyst, of course. But I had merely sparked something that was dormant within her. It explained why she had let our relationship continue, although she could have sent me packing at any minute.

"It's cold," she said. But it wasn't.

"Don't go. Not yet. I want to give you this." I held up my pen. I wanted her to stay, more than anything. The pen might delay her.

She looked from me to the blue thing in my hand. Then, just as she had done with the statue I had given her the day before, she took it and touched her lips to it.

"Yes," she said after a moment. "I like writing."

She turned. The breeze from the lake carried the smell of her soap, clean, sweet, anything but cloying. I wanted to drown in that smell. She was facing away, looking along the lake, to Salzburg and America.

"You know . . . I've read the letters, Konstanze. Your letters, I mean. Rudolf's. Bruno's."

In the gloom I saw her nod.

"Please look at me." Slowly, she turned back. It was too dark to be sure, but she may have been crying.

"I shouldn't have read them. I see that now. But . . . you were . . . the enemy . . . then. I didn't know . . . I *couldn't* know that—that I would ever . . . love you."

Konstanze was looking at me, but I still couldn't make out her features.

"Forgive me."

The breeze from the lake suddenly gusted into the summerhouse and we both shivered. "Come for me tomorrow, Walter. Take me some-where special. I want to forgive you. You said you love me, but maybe we are still enemies." She turned and was gone.

I waited, breathing out regularly, deliberately, to relax. I heard the latch gate open and close, then voices as she let herself into the house. Then . . . it fell silent.

I sat down, took out my pipe and involuntarily counted again the lights at Plomberg. I didn't want to go back to Salzburg, not yet. The night was warm for April, whatever Konstanze might say, and I felt closer to her in the summerhouse than I would at the hotel.

CHAPTER SEVEN

1

THE next morning I was awakened very early by the ringing of the telephone. It was Hobel's secretary, the prissy one. "The major wants you here. Now."

"Good news or bad?"

"He wants to tell you himself."

Bad.

"Now, I can't do. Twenty minutes, maybe. Half an hour, certainly."

"If I were you, I wouldn't waste time telling me what you can and can't do. I'd get on over here."

God, what a bitch! I put the phone down and skipped into my uniform as though I was frightened of Hobel. I was, I suppose, frightened of his news. And with good reason.

It was bad. I knew it was bad because, having made me rush over, he then kept me waiting in his outside office, in front of his goddamn secretary. She sat typing, putting phone calls through to Hobel while I boiled in the seat opposite her desk.

The minute I was allowed into Hobel's office I knew it was not just bad, it was catastrophic. *He was relaxed,* for christ's sake. Not smiling exactly, but there was a definite lightness to his manner.

"Thank you for coming over so quickly," he said. I think this meeting must count as my fourth most vivid memory, the oily poison which he packed into that ordinary sentence.

In front of him he had a long sheet of yellow paper. A telegram. He played with it.

"This came overnight. Bad news for you I'm afraid." He put on, or tried to, an expression of pity. But he failed.

"Two nights ago, a small force of highly trained men—fourteen of them to be precise—commandeered an eighteen-thousand-ton ship in Santander Harbor, on the Atlantic coast of Spain, in the north. The ship has disappeared but our intelligence boys believe it is bound for South America, with a precious cargo of leading Nazis. It is a German ship and the first officer and wireless officer have disappeared with it. It had refueled just before being taken and was due to leave twenty-four hours later. So inside information can be assumed. Four people, including the captain, were killed in the raid."

"Why does the intelligence branch think the ship is bound for South America? And how do they know the ship was taken by ex-Nazis or Nazi sympathizers? How do we know leading Nazis will be put aboard?"

"Nothing is certain," said Hobel as sweetly as sugar on a bad tooth. "But I spoke with our side in Spain less than an hour ago. The raiders were native German speakers and carried maps of the South Atlantic, all this according to some of the crew who were put safely ashore. Moreover, the first officer was someone called Moering, a relative of the Moering who was in charge of munitions in Hamburg. Almost certainly a Nazi sympathizer and as yet unaffected by the de-Nazification program." He paused. "There is no doubt in my mind, or the general's"—it was "the general" now, not Eisenhower—"that the ship was stolen for the purposes which the intelligence branch says. I did tell you, Wolff, that if this sort of thing were to happen, you would be taken off the case and we would play it my way. So you cannot say you have not had fair warning. As of now, your role in this investigation is finished." He drew his flat hand across his throat in a garroting movement. "Caput."

"What are your plans?" I said in as civil a tone as I could muster.

He pushed back his chair. He was Patton, or Montgomery, the wily old general confiding in a cub reporter covering his first war.

"One needs to know a little bit about human nature in this job." God, he was sickening. "You, Wolff, have been too reasonable, too civilized, too—if I may say so—European. You think you can persuade people to do things against their best interests. Well, you can't. No one can. Lieutenant Bloch had the right idea, to my way of thinking. Oh, I know you're going to bleat, and say that he failed, but look at how long he had —just a few hours. You've had weeks and have gone no further. All you have are just a few fancy theories. Fear, that's what makes people sit up and take notice, that's what they *expect* from a war, for Christ's sake. Americans, real Americans understand that. War's no different from business, for God's sake.

"First, I'm going to raid that warehouse in Krumau. Tonight, with everyone inside. *Some*thing's going on there and we're gonna find out what it is. If von Zell is there, all well and good. It will only prove you should have raided it days ago."

"And if he's not?"

"No matter. If that happens we send Lieutenant Camman to Stockerau."

"Stockerau?"

I had played into his hands. "You don't remember what's at Stockerau? I see. It's where the boy—von Zell's son—is at school."

"So?" Those knobs of nervousness were beginning to congeal again, somewhere in front of my liver and above my groin. Hobel was like some deadly upside-down alchemist, able to convert the golden feelings I had about Dieter into this base, gummy sediment in my stomach.

"We shall hold off, until tomorrow anyway, to see if von Zell is holed up at Krumau. But if he isn't I'm going to hold the boy."

"What good will that do?"

"Don't raise your voice to *me*, Lieutenant. You have precious little to show for *your* efforts. In the first place, the boy, if he is properly interrogated, at length, and by a professional, will tell us whether his father is still in touch with his mother; and, if so, where he is hiding out. But, probably more effective, we are going to release one of the Nazis captured on the Lake of Geneva—you remember the incident. He will be told that we are holding von Zell's child and he is to tell von Zell that we shall continue to hold the boy until he gives himself up. Clever, eh?"

It wasn't clever, it was wicked. "How can you hold a child like that, without good reason? It's illegal."

"Don't be silly, Wolff. We are the victors in this war. There is a military government here. We can do what we like."

"But that's the mistake the Nazis made. They thought they could disregard justice. That's why they were so reviled."

"Don't go over the top, Wolff. This is just an exception for a very special case. An important case. . . . We have an army psychologist who will say the father's continued absence is having an adverse effect on the child, that he needs to be observed by doctors."

"What if von Zell *isn't* involved in this conduit? Have you thought of that? It would be cruel to the boy to hold him. And if the father is not in charge of the underground, you are no further along."

"Yes we are. We shall know that von Zell is not the man we want, but that issue won't arise. He took the coins. If he gives himself up, he will be able to explain their disappearance at the very least."

"What if the press finds out, the Austrian or German press? You are behaving very callously, in my view. A clever editor could really go to town on this. Grown men—soldiers—picking on an eight-year-old. You could be crucified."

"Let me worry about that Wolff. We shan't take the boy until after we've raided Krumau tonight, and only then if we don't find his father there. Now, I haven't quite finished with you, not yet. My plan depends on the von Zells thinking that everything is proceeding normally. I want no suspicions aroused. So, for the next two days at least, until I tell you otherwise, I want you to behave normally. Whatever you had planned for Mrs. von Zell, do it. It goes without saying that you must *not* mention what is in the offing. More than that, she must have no inkling from your behavior that anything untoward is about to happen. She must have no chance to alert anyone at Krumau, or her boy at Stockerau. Is that clear, Wolff?"

I was appalled at what Hobel was telling me, but what could I do? He was my superior officer; I had to agree. But I didn't tell him about Sieveringer, the wine that came from Krumau and which I had found in Konstanze's house. It might be a clue and I was damned if I was going to help Hobel.

"You don't need to know any more, so you can go now. Incidentally, the art recovery unit is being closed down and you may as well clear your desk when you can. It's all over for you. Now remember, not a word, *nothing*, to Mrs. von Zell."

I returned to my office in a daze. It was not yet 8:00 A.M. and, therefore, still fairly quiet in the building. Sammy was nowhere to be seen. I slumped into my seat, my attention taken by an envelope among my mail. It was in a child's hand: Dieter's. I tore at it. As Konstanze had predicted, the boy was very responsible and rather formal. He had given some thought to his words.

Dear Professor Wolff, All the boys here, and even some of the masters, are mad with jealousy at my binoculars. Tober—he's nine, a year older than me—even said that American equipment is better than German. That made him *very* unpopular. The best thing about binoculars is that you can lend them out for chocolate or apples. Thank you very much. If you are still there in the summer may we go to the Löser again, please? As I broke my other glasses, I would like to see all the lakes through my new ones. And maybe by then I will reach the pedals on your car and can drive it properly. Yours respectfully, Dieter von Zell.

The summer holidays. Dieter didn't know what was in store for us. Whatever happened, life would be very different for all of us by the summer.

Hartt had still not arrived but I noticed a strip of yellow paper among the mail on his desk. It was the telegram he received every day from his cronies on the stock market in Wall Street. I reached across and picked it up.

Good news at last! Maurice's shares had slipped by nine points and now stood at $1,064 whereas, at long last, mine had risen, no less than fourteen cents, to $969.12. I scribbled a note on the bottom to Sammy: "Why? These things, like Hobel, are beyond me. Delighted all the same. Walter."

I didn't call Saul. I couldn't face it. He would be understanding but, at some level, he would also be very mad at me for not letting him raid Krumau sooner. I had robbed him of a clean raid, made as a result of his judgment rather than under orders from Hobel. So that took some of the shine off of his achievement. However forgiving he might be, there would be a part of him that blamed me for that.

I went out and got into my car. As I drove over the Market Bridge on my way to Mondsee, I noticed the two nuns I had seen before about to descend on the same greengrocer. They didn't pay any attention to me, but as I stopped for other traffic, I again envied them their way of life. Once I got to the village of Mondsee that morning, however, I thought it was a little early for Konstanze. Also, I had things to sort out in my mind. So instead of going straight to the house, I drove down the other side of the lake to Plomberg, where that string of lights glowed at night.

It was pretty in much the same way as Mondsee was pretty: a short stretch of boulevard with cafés at either end. Bicycles were propped against the trees and ducks and other birds outnumbered people at that hour of the day.

I took a coffee at one of the cafés and sat outside. The sun was still rather low and had not yet lifted itself over the Feuerkogel, and so the lake and Plomberg were covered with a pigeon-gray sheen, the sort of light, or half-light, that seems to encourage sound. The lake was still, but that only meant you listened more carefully to whatever noises it was making.

From where I was sitting, I could, in theory, look across to Konstanze's house. Except that the gray gloom was such that I couldn't be certain exactly which house Konstanze's was. I imagined Martha and her moving around, making breakfast, perhaps an omelet. One woman would go out to the garden—how lucky they were—and pick chives or onions. Near me some ducks were splashing and I thought of Dieter in the summerhouse and, in all probability, being as clumsy, as volcanic, as ever, wetting everyone. I smiled to myself. And I imagined Konstanze in a bathing suit, her body wet and shiny in the sun. I imagined her playing the piano, writing to Dieter late at night in the sewing room, where I had first met her. I imagined her walking into the village early on Sunday mornings so that she could prepare the church organ. I imagined her after the service, talking with the solemn priest or laughing with friends from the village. Perhaps, on those mornings, she took a coffee in the market square. Did other men in the village feel about her as I did? They must think it a bit strange that she spent so much time alone. Afterward, would she get a lift home to her house? There would be no shortage of farm workers at the church, and I smiled to myself as I pictured her aboard a tractor, standing on an axle, holding on for all she was worth. Dieter would enjoy that sort of thing far more than she would.

The sun at last climbed over the Feuerkogel. The gray haze huddled across to the other side of the lake, nearer the hills. Where I was, the yellow rays licked the pavement, warmed the paint of the small boats, green and white and black, and splashed onto the café tabletops, making the raw metal smell.

Suddenly I saw Konstanze in America. She was driving a big car across the Golden Gate Bridge and had been living in California long enough to know to have the exact toll money ready. Then she was dressed in a black lace gown, about to sit down for dinner on a paddle steamer plying the Mississippi. In no time she was standing by a bicycle on a university campus. She was waiting for me—I had been lecturing—and all my male students looked on enviously. I saw Dieter, not much older than now, fast asleep on his mother's swollen stomach. She, in turn, lay in the garden of my house, content and very pregnant.

I had never had the urge to be a father. My brother had a child, so I was an uncle, but I had few if any avuncular feelings. I wasn't sure that I felt like becoming a father then, in 1946, at least not consciously, except that I imagined Konstanze pregnant.

The thought of a life growing inside Konstanze, however, had the effect of directing my thoughts back to what Hobel had said earlier that morning. Four people had been killed in Santander. Four families bereaved, four wives or girlfriends left empty. Four women who would not get pregnant again by their chosen man. I flashed back to Konstanze. We were in America and she wasn't pregnant. We were at the top of the Empire State Building in New York. From the top, using Dieter's binoculars, we could see the fourteen lakes that surround the Löser.

I stayed in Plomberg for two, maybe three, hours. I must have drunk my weight in coffee. The sun got hotter and hotter. The village came to life around me. Men bicycled out to the fields to work, or puttered off in their boats along the shore. Women, in black or flowered frocks, shuffled by to the shops. Boys played by my car, almost, but not quite, daring to get in. The ducks and other birds washed, dipped for breakfast, stopped by the tables at the café looking for tidbits, then, as the morning sun built up its heat, they lay back to enjoy their lethargy. The rest of the village followed their example. For a whole hour I was the only one in the café.

I began to take stock of what my options were. I knew that day that I *did* have two courses of action open to me, but which to pursue was unclear. Hobel was taking things out of my hands, but I still had one day.

Part of me wanted Konstanze. Since one o'clock that morning, since we had been together in the summerhouse, I had wanted her more than any woman I had ever known. And I thought that I could have her too. I had dislodged her from Rudolf. When love has been forced into disuse by circumstances, it flowers of its own accord—elsewhere—if the opportunity arises. It happened many times in the war. And that, I think, is what had happened to Konstanze. So, yes, I could have her.

But there were those four deaths and the loss of the ship in Santander. Despite the doubts I had thrown at Hobel, it did begin to seem that some of the leading Nazis were getting away. It was within my power to stop them; it was a heavy responsibility not to. Could I make Konstanze tell me where Rudolf was? Could I use the fact that she had fallen for me, at long last, to cheat it out of her? I thought I could. I thought I knew enough about her now to produce the circumstances under which she would be unable to resist telling me.

But the war was over. Hobel might be successful with his raid on Krumau and find Rudolf there. Was it worth risking Konstanze's feeling for me, in trying to wheedle Rudolf's whereabouts from her, when I could let the major do the dirty work for me? Then I could keep her to myself. On the other hand, if I didn't try and Hobel succeeded, would that so shatter her that she wouldn't come to America with me anyway?

The sun climbed higher and higher on Plomberg. If I was going to act at all, I had to move. I returned to my car and drove south, around the bottom of the lake, coming to Konstanze's house from the opposite direction.

She seemed relieved to see me when I knocked on the door. She was dressed in a pale yellow skirt and white shirt.

"You are a little late," she said innocently. "I was worried that you wouldn't come, that you were offended by—last night."

I smiled and shook my head.

"Wait in the garden, I have something for you. It is too nice to come inside. There are some chairs around by the kitchen—and don't worry," she said, reading my thoughts, "I've sent Martha into the village. She's not here."

I went around to where the chairs had been put out and sat down. Whenever I was with Konstanze I was amazed at her ability to clear my mind for me. As of then, I knew what I was going to do.

When she appeared from out of the kitchen she was carrying a tray and on it some drinks and what looked like a letter.

She handed me a glass. In it was clear liquid, pale, the color of champagne but without the bubbles. There was a black olive in it.

"What is it?"

"An Austrian martini."

"Eh?"

She shrugged with her eyebrows. "I couldn't get any vermouth. So I used white wine. Grinzinger."

"You mean this is gin and white wine? Are you trying to kill me?"

"There's not *much* wine. And I did put an olive in it. Try it."

I smelled it first. Then took the briefest of sips. Fortunately the taste of the gin completely obliterated the flavor of the wine. "Not bad."

Konstanze seemed in a hurry that day, as if she had made up her mind. "Last night, Walter, I asked you to take me somewhere special today. Have you thought?"

She seemed eager—anxious?—to re-create the mood of the previous night. As if she, too, wanted to recapture the intimacy, the physical nearness.

"Yes," I said. "Somewhere very special."

"Where?"

"Wait."

"Yes. It's better as a mystery." She took up the letter on the tray. "This came from Dieter. Have you heard?"

I nodded, fished out my note and we exchanged pieces of paper. Dieter's letter was flattering: "The professor," he had written, "is too nice to be a soldier. But I hope he sees the buffalo in America soon. We did them the other day in geography. And they are *ever* so interesting." There were no references to his father. I was pleased but could not quite shake from my mind the feeling that this had been a calculating move on Konstanze's part. But perhaps it was just my paranoia.

"We should go," I said, giving her back her letter. "It's quite a way."

She wanted to drive and I was happy to let her. I could think better.

I told her to head east, to Linz. And that I would take over from there as our destination was secret. As she drove she talked. That day, I remember, she talked for the first time as a lover. She was full of Dieter's doings at school, she was flattering to me, she made several caustic comments about Martha and all sorts of references to America. For the first time she shut out the rest of the world; there were just the two of us, plus Dieter and, maybe, the car. It was as if she had made up her mind: she wanted me.

"Walter," she said at one point, negotiating the car through a herd of sheep crossing from one field to another. "The letters. Were they . . . did they give you pleasure?" She looked away from the road in my direction as the car—now free of the sheep—picked up speed again.

I lit two cigarettes and offered her one. "They were wonderful letters, Konstanze. Every one."

"You have stamina, I'll admit. There are a lot of them."

"I . . . I should never have even considered reading them—believe me, please. I really feel that now. But . . . once I had started . . . I couldn't stop." I tried to sound not too heavy. "I read through two entire nights without sleep. That's how good they are." I pulled on my cigarette. "That's why I was half in love with you before ever we met. Not everyone can come alive in their letters like you did. Like you do."

She drove on without speaking. Her hair was swept back by the wind we were creating. She enjoyed speed as much as Dieter, as much as Bruno.

"Bruno's accid—" I began, but she stopped me.

"Don't!" Then, more softly, "Don't."

We drove on in silence—but it was an easy peace. She wasn't angry or upset. "Today is the best yet, Walter. Don't look back."

"Don't look back." I repeated her words in my head. To think of Rudolf was looking back. Did that mean . . . ?

We came to a small lake with what to me seemed a murderously high diving board. It was much too early in the year for anyone to swim in an alpine lake, but two ducks, or birds of some sort, squatted on the board in the sun. Konstanze blared the horn of the car three or four times, trying to startle the birds.

"That's what Dieter would have done," she said, looking at me and grinning. But though the birds turned our way, they sat where they were and were soon lost to view.

"He is very lively, Dieter," I said. "I like him."

"But you are wrong. He is much more active when you are here, Walter. He has lived with women too long. He needs a father, soon."

"Soon." Now I repeated that word to myself. That was looking forward.

We had reached a stretch of unusually straight road. Konstanze looked at me, a touch of flint in her eyes—but it was a long way from the sharp shrapnel glare she had given me on the day we met.

"How brave are you, soldier?" she said mockingly. "Let's see."

And she put her foot down. Christ, did she put her foot down! In those days 60 m.p.h. was a perfectly respectable speed. She did 80. Nowadays, in European vehicles anyway, you see 140 m.p.h. on the clock, but the cars don't do anything like that. The BMW's clock only went up to 80 and Konstanze all but hit the needle.

Was I frightened? She was after all still an apprentice driver. But Konstanze was a quick learner, as I have said, so no, I wasn't scared. In fact we were both exhilarated—if silently thankful that we hadn't come across any more sheep.

Between Schwanenstadt and Lambach we passed a bank of gentian, blue as smoke, pale as dust. On impulse she pulled the car to the side of the road, got out and fell into the flowers. She lay quietly among them.

"Konstanze!" I called out, smiling. "We have a long way to go."

She did not come back empty-handed. I had never been given a flower for my buttonhole before, nor have I been given one since. That is another vivid memory.

At Linz we swapped seats. Forty minutes later, about half-past two, I nosed the BMW up the narrow main street of a tiny village about twelve or fourteen kilometers south of Linz. It was a village approached across a small but very tidy plain, with dark, spongy loam, crisscrossed with barley, potatoes and swatches of trees. Suddenly, out of nowhere, a small hill appeared and it was on this that we could see the beautiful monastery of St. Florian.

2

IT was and is, in my view, the best example of baroque architecture in the world. Better than Melk, better than Wilhering, better than Kremsmünster. It was graceful and also more feminine than the others. A large, essentially white building, the monastery was comprised of a church with

two high-domed spires, and two sets of cloisters, set around two court-
yards. The success of St. Florian, for me, was that the architects had
avoided the use of too much gold. White remained the dominant color
for the walls, the ceilings, the staircases, the fountains, even for the
stuccowork. So there was nothing forbidding about St. Florian. There
were no secrets. You felt welcome.

The one exception was the graveyard, which, for a reason I never
discovered, boasted hundreds of headstones in black, shiny marble. But
that only made the white of the monastery itself seem cleaner still.

Konstanze had been startled by her first sight of the monastery from
across the plain. She had asked me to stop the car so that she could take
in the view. The village was empty as we drove the car up the narrow
street, the only street, to the gate in the wall. All was quiet.

We entered by the Prandtauer gate. Konstanze was now able to recognize the great man's work. It was an elaborate construction, in stone, of
partially clothed figures, complicated balconies and architraves. The gate
opened into the large courtyard where, on the right, could be seen the
great staircase. Its whiteness and its grace were striking as it rose in three
regular installments with a balustrade of gleaming marble carved in
curves and curls. Yew trees and fountains of stone fish occupied the
center of the courtyard. We stood there staring at the splendor surrounding us. I could see already that Konstanze was moved.

"It's beautiful, Walter. So friendly."

"Yes. It's proportions have a lot to do with that. Compared with other
buildings, St. Florian is low and long, more like an American building
than a European one. I love it."

We mounted the great staircase, passing through some black, complicated wrought-iron gates on our way up to a light, white gallery with
white stucco everywhere and frescoes in yellow and pale green on the
ceiling. The gallery ran the entire length of one side of the courtyard
and, at the end, led to a balcony overlooking the main hall of the monastery, the Kaisersaal. Facing south, this hall was suffused in an extraordinary light, thanks to a large window made up of hundreds of tiny green-
yellow and purple patches. Even on an April day the room had the air of
a glade, deep in a forest, in autumn. It was cool, the colors suited the
silence, perfect for prayer.

St. Florian is famous for its library. It has a wonderful collection of
literature, mainly Christian, of course, but not entirely. This was one

area of religion in which I was more knowledgeable than Konstanze and I was able to introduce her to a number of Crusade stories which took her interest and to which, I knew, she would return as soon as she got the chance.

Finally, we came to the church itself. This, too, was white, except for an elaborate cornice of gold running around the entire building high, high up. The ceiling of the church, including its saucer dome, was covered in frescoes predominantly in yellow. "Rottmayr," said Konstanze, spotting his style straightaway.

The flowers on the altar were white and red and yellow, and if flowers could glow that's how these appeared. Konstanze seemed about to pray. Before she could do so, however, I said in a loud, clear voice (I no longer whispered in churches), "Turn around, look above, behind you."

She did. The enormous black gate, like the lace on the dress she had worn to the concert, stood out at the back of the nave against the natural cream of the stone. It was highlighted in gold here and there but otherwise was like an enormous cobweb woven by an inspired spider.

The whorls and flutings of the gate drew your eye upward to something even bigger and blacker: hundreds, perhaps a thousand, black pipes, in three busy clusters, running from wall to wall and almost to the roof. The organ was like an enormous black swan, not evil-looking exactly, but regal in a daunting way, its wings open in flight or to intimidate intruders.

As she moved her head up and caught sight of the organ, Konstanze gasped slightly. That was the only sound she made. She stepped off the aisle into a pew and knelt. She looked up at me. "Do you never pray, Walter?"

"I am not religious. You know that. It would be wrong."

She made a tired gesture, the way she shrugged at Dieter when he should have worked something out for himself.

"Your American poet, Auden, said that to pray is to pay attention to something or someone other than yourself. Come and kneel by me. You don't have to think about God. Just stop thinking about yourself."

I knelt. She still had the power to put me in my place in the most delicious way. No one else had ever come close.

I wanted to ask her what she was praying for, or about, but I didn't dare. *I* prayed that Hobel's plans would, in some unforeseen way, be changed totally, giving me more time. But I knew that prayer wouldn't be answered.

For a few moments we knelt silently, side by side. All of a sudden the peace of the church was splintered as the organ exploded in sound. It was as if the volcanic Dieter, grown huge, had burst into the building. The pews trembled and the floor seemed to vibrate as first one, then two, then many more deep cords cannoned around the nave, ricocheting from wall to wall to wall. A complicated mosaic of notes followed the cords as, presumably, the organ scholar warmed to his practice.

It was much cooler in the church than it was outside and that suited me, since I was often uncomfortable in the sun, especially in my uniform. I was happy to sit listening to the organ until Konstanze slipped from her knees onto the seat. The organ was much too loud for us to talk comfortably and so, after a while, I gestured for her to follow me.

At the side of the nave, hidden behind some columns, was a set of stone steps leading down to the crypt. As we descended, the sounds of the organ began to fade and we could hear our own footsteps again on the stone.

"What's down here, Walter?"

"Wait. You'll see."

The crypt was large, surprisingly so, and entirely formed out of stone. It was not well lit; there were electric lights but too few of them and, amid such shadows, all sarcophagi are apt to look forbidding. None more so than the large, lugubrious piece of stone that I eventually stopped in front of. (I was thankful I had reconnoitered here; otherwise I might never have found what I was looking for that day.) It was white, seeming to glow in the artificial light, and had deep shadows drawn along it where the stone mason had carved pronounced runnels.

Konstanze was uneasy, not afraid exactly, but puzzled and impatient to know why we had come down here.

"Go closer," I whispered. "Look at the name."

She stepped forward and gasped. "Anton Bruckner!" she read aloud. "Oh, Walter!"

"I wondered if you'd guess. He was organist here—that was his organ we were listening to upstairs. He was a sort of honorary member of the monastery and could come whenever he pleased. He often did, to play the organ and be away from Vienna, to write his symphonies and the organ music you love so much. He never married, as you know, so when he died in October 1896 it was natural for him to be buried here."

Elisabetta, the art student I had picked up on my first drive south in the BMW, had told me about Bruckner and St. Florian. She had mentioned all manner of baroque churches that night. Then I had come across the link later, in that book on baroque architecture by the English schoolmaster.

Konstanze, who had been listening to me, went forward another pace. She reached out and rested her hand on the cool tomb. She stayed like that, motionless for a moment, then turned quickly and led the way out of the crypt. As we started to climb, the sounds of the organ came back to us. She turned to me and smiled.

"I want to go to confession. Where shall I find you?"

I considered. It had been much colder in the crypt than the church proper and I felt a desire for the warmth of the fresh air. "I'll be in the graveyard, with all those black headstones. I think I saw a bench there."

"Okay," she said, with what seemed to be an American twang. I smiled as she disappeared in search of a confessional box.

I watched her retreat into the nave. She was relaxed, jaunty; suddenly she seemed very young. It had been a success bringing her to St. Florian.

I went through the black wrought-iron gate and out into the sunshine. The organ faded again but didn't quite disappear. An old brick wall ran around part of the monastery and the graveyard. Against the wall were a handful of large lean-to glass greenhouses. The vegetables and fruit inside them were being tended by two tall monks in habits that were almost as white as Bruckner's tomb. They looked up as they heard the church door close behind me but, not recognizing my face, soon went back to their work.

I walked past them into the graveyard. The graves were well tended, with the sharp green grass cut freshly and the flowers open to the sun. But what was really stunning about the area were the headstones themselves. In the sunlight the black marble glittered and rippled like the well-brushed coats of thoroughbreds in the parade ring. The gold lettering winked in the bright light and the overall effect was far from dismal.

Nonetheless, as I wandered among the headstones, I was brought down to earth. As an historian I had always had a fascination with graveyards. Being interested in ecclesiastical architecture was one excuse for this, but that wasn't the whole story. I liked looking at the names and

I was obsessed by the ages people were when they died. Presently I came across someone who had died as a child; this was a secret fear of mine, that someday I would have a child and it would die. I didn't know then how anyone could survive that. Elsewhere I found husbands and wives who had died within a year or so of each other. I was more sentimental than I let on, and I imagined these syncopated deaths were evidence that broken hearts did have the power to kill. A benevolent power, of course.

And here was a death that had occurred recently. Just a mound of earth, decked in flowers. No name, no age, no inscription from the Bible chosen by relatives.

The newness of the death reminded me of the killings in Santander. They had been German lives, but an Austrian could have been among them, even this person here.

I sat down on a bench that faced the monastery and, at this time of day, the sun also. The new grave had sobered me, reminding me of facts that Konstanze's presence drove from my head. Ironic that it should be German deaths that affected me so.

I had, until then, avoided thinking of my dilemma. But now there was no choice. There was a sense in which, whatever I did, whichever way I jumped, I was bound to fail. That was the measure of how I had mismanaged this case. For me to succeed now in a military sense, to gain the information I wanted—that my superiors wanted—would kill irrevocably what had grown between Konstanze and me. Whatever she felt for me, it did not include totally betraying Rudolf. Perhaps she would come to America and bring Dieter with her. She had no idea how long Rudolf would have to remain in hiding; technically, it could be forever, and that was hardly good for her and her son. Rudolf had put his military duty before his family life, and if I was to do the same, then I, too, would lose her. To entice her back to America I would have to give up my part in Rudolf's capture.

But if I did that, if I let Rudolf go, it was dereliction of duty, treason perhaps. No one would know, except me, but how long would I be able to stand it? I had left Germany and joined the U.S. Army to stop Nazis like Rudolf. I was trapped. I might still lose on both counts, but I couldn't win both.

I have always given the impression that I am a forthright, positive person, a man who has no doubts, who always knows his own mind. The same is true today, forty years later. Only *I* know, sadly, that at crucial moments in my life, like that afternoon in St. Florian, I make up my mind often on the spur of the moment and then live with the consequences. Are other people the same, I wonder? I had always thought, always hoped, that, when it came to the crunch, my instincts would help. No. Konstanze would come out of confession, would join me on the bench here in the graveyard. I had prepared the ground well, psychologically speaking. Though she had been clever and tough, I think I had managed things so that I could have it either way. I had a nugget of information in reserve that would, I believed, induce her to tell me where her husband was, if I used it. On the other hand, if I chose not to, and so contrived things that we embraced, or kissed, I could take her back to California. When she came, what would I do? I couldn't answer my own question.

I saw the monks by the greenhouses look up again. Someone else had come out of the church by the front door, which was not visible from where I was sitting. Konstanze?

Yes. She moved around the edge of the building and when she saw me she waved. As she came toward me, picking her way through the headstones, I could see that her step was still lively; for once confession had not brought her down.

"You were right, Walter," she said as she came close. "This place *is* special, truly wonderful." She slipped her hands into the pockets of her skirt, turned and slumped onto the bench alongside me. "All the white is so clean, so simple, so pure. That's what I prayed for—more white in the world."

"That's an odd thing to pray for."

"Not at all. There's not much point in praying in ordinary language for obvious things, is there? If you believe in a God then you must also believe that He can hear your thoughts at all times. You don't have to pray *for* something all the time. Nor do you have always to pray *to* God. You pray *with* Him. You go to prayer so that you may set aside time to do or think fresh things in a fresh way. You don't always ask for things in prayer, you know. When you knelt down in the church just now, you asked that things would work out between us. That's unfair. You have to accept responsibility for what you do. Prayer isn't a moral bank, though I know lots of people see it that way."

I was astounded at what Konstanze had said. I was much less surprised to see, behind her, beyond the headstones, beyond and above the two monks working in the greenhouses, large white clouds in the sky. The weather was beginning to break.

"How did you know what I was praying for?"

"Psychology, silly. Nothing to do with religion. There's a lot less magic in worship than you seem to think, Walter. When I pray it's like trying to hold a conversation with God. He's not a guardian or a father or a moral stockbroker. I'm not forever asking things. It may sound silly but you must try—try—to be God's companion."

"And what do you confess? What have you done, or thought, that you need to confess?"

It was a blunt, tactless question. I am ashamed and embarrassed to think of it now, but that's how it happened. I was trying to shock Konstanze into telling me her secrets.

For a long moment I thought it was a serious blunder. For she didn't reply right away. Behind her, I remember, the clouds got higher, moving above us with silent speed. Eventually, she faced me.

"You will learn, Walter, never to ask that question. In the first place, I will never tell you, but, more important, you must learn that because I have a private life it does not mean that I am hiding things from you. I don't; I never would."

I think that then, when she said that, was the moment I was more in love than I had ever imagined possible. She had said "I never would." That was worded for the future, as though she was looking forward to a time when we would be together. And she had said "never." Had I not read the letters, I would not have known how significant that word was to her. But I had, so I knew she meant it. There were all sorts of meanings, all sorts of emotions, locked into that sentence. I understood, because I had pried into her life. She knew that. She knew what she was saying. She was speaking in code, but she knew. Yet, again, the letters were being used against me, to hook me.

I noticed that the monks in the greenhouses were packing up their work things. They looked across to where we were seated and then disappeared into the cloisters. We were now quite alone, save for the sound of the organ, which could still be heard from the church, and the clouds, now closing in on the sun.

The bench was short. Konstanze and I sat close to one another, so close that I could smell her soap. Strange that I had never given her any perfume. It was scarce in Austria, but the Army could get it. Come to think of it, I had never given her any nylons or chocolate.

She looked up at the clouds and gave a sad nod. For the briefest of moments a look flashed across her face that seemed to find familiar muscles, ones that hadn't been used for years. The expression had such a familiar look about it that it must, at one time, have been very much a part of the old melancholic Konstanze; a girl who had returned then for a second, the tragic girl who wouldn't marry Bruno. I could see why men fell for Konstanze in those days: you wanted to help her, make her happy, arrange things so that she was never unhappy again.

She turned back, the sun on her pale neck. "This is my favorite place, Walter. Of all those you have shown me—the waterfalls at Krimml, that grisly glacier that Dieter loved so much, the fourteen lakes that were only twelve, all the other abbeys and churches—*this* is the jewel. How right Bruckner was to be buried here."

She stopped speaking and looked at me. Then she bit her lower lip, curling it under her top teeth, a gesture I don't think I had seen before. But that, perhaps, is memory number five: I can never see anyone bite their lip without thinking of that moment. As she did it she also lowered her eyes in an expression of tender self-doubt which, almost immediately, vanished as she looked up again, straight at me. Despite herself, she was saying she was ready. The gesture was so soft, so open, yet so vulnerable, so individual, that I was on the verge of reaching out to touch her, to brush with my thumb the lip she was biting. My mind was nearly made up. I remember thinking, Trust Konstanze to want our first kiss to be on consecrated ground.

I whispered. There was no one to hear save Konstanze and God, if there was one, but I whispered.

"Konstanze."

"Yes?" No, it wasn't a question, there should be no interrogative there. It was an affirmation. "Yes!"

"This is the monastery the gold coins were stolen from. This is where they should be returned to. They *belong* back here."

3

THE organ had stopped. Konstanze had stopped too. She was no longer the bundle of emotions, the center of life that she had been a moment before. A few strands of blond hair wafted across her face. It was the beginning of the breeze that had brought the clouds our way.

I had acted on the spur of the moment. As I had so often in my life. I sat now, waiting for Konstanze to react. She didn't. Not for a long while. Not until the first of the clouds had settled between us and the sun. Then she seemed to move but only inside. Invisibly almost, like that day in Schlierbach, by the fountain, she shuddered and a deep dry sob forced its way up her long neck and past her throat.

I whispered again. "It's true, Konstanze. The coins were kept in the library. It took the monks here three hundred and fifty years to collect them. They were taken away in 1943."

Another sob. I tried to imagine what was going on inside her head. She must have been asking herself how long I had planned this—this confrontation, how long I had had the idea to use Bruckner and St. Florian in this way to break her. Had I been calculating *all* the way? So calculating that, after a while, I could dissemble and mislead her? Had my happiness been false, my gift of the binoculars to Dieter, my behavior at the concert, all that talk of America merely a sham?

And, of course, just now, on this very bench, she had nearly betrayed her husband. She had in fact already been unfaithful in her heart. It would have been one thing to have followed that through by emigrating to America, but now . . . At least I had not kissed her, had not allowed her to kiss me. Something was salvaged. But she probably imagined that was part of my calculation too. It made her cooperation more likely.

The tears had risen now, spiking her eyelashes, glistening against her cheeks.

"I didn't know myself what I was going to do until today, until a moment ago. These past days and weeks have been wonderful for me. I am probably more in love with you than you are with me—oh yes!—I originally tried to make you interested in me, to like me and respect me. It was my only chance of finding out about Rudolf, but it soon ceased to be a duty. By the time we visited the glacier at Dachstein, I was in love with you. You think I have been calculating, but it's not true. The war has been over for a year; my wife has moved on; my close colleagues are moving on. I sometimes think I am the only one left, tidying up after the war. If we had kissed last night, after the concert, after you fell asleep on my shoulder, when we were together in the summerhouse, we wouldn't be sitting here now. I would be making plans for you to come to America."

I paused.

"But I learned this morning that, two nights ago, a German ship was hijacked in Spain. Four people were killed. Four wives or girlfriends left alone. Who knows how many children, like Dieter, left without fathers, forever? My superiors believe the ship was stolen so that it could smuggle ex-Nazis to South America and that it was all paid for out of the St. Florian gold.

"Konstanze, I left Germany *because* of the Nazis. Unfortunately for me, for us, the war is not over yet.

"I am sorry. Everything you believe that I feel, I do feel. I realized some time ago that you know where Rudolf is but it made no difference to me."

She turned to me, sharply. I nodded.

"Oh yes. Remember the night you couldn't come to the concert? You said someone was coming to visit you. I waited near your house all night. You never went out and no one came to visit you. It was a Sunday; you were listening to the radio, to the concert, just as you used to do when the war was on. It was an old habit, hard to break; Rudolf was listening, too, wasn't he? Wherever he is.

"Yes, I know about the concerts on the radio, one of your husband's secretaries told me. You don't write letters to each other anymore, that would be too dangerous. But you still have your concerts, so you are still in touch. You know where he is."

I reached across and took Konstanze's hand, only the second time that we had intentionally touched. At the same moment I leaned forward, so that I could more easily reach into my pocket. From there I took a small thick book with black covers, which I pressed into her palm.

"Konstanze, can you honestly swear on this Bible that you do not know where Rudolf is?"

I could barely get the words out. Never, not once, in all my time in the Army, had I needed to do anything as dirty, as underhanded, as shameful, as this. I can remember wondering whether, in years to come, I would regret what I was doing. That is the price you pay for being impulsive.

Konstanze looked down at the Bible in her hand. She turned it over as if it would somehow be a different book held another way. She gave me an empty stare, the abandoned gaze of the prisoner of war. A single tear clung to the bridge of her nose, as silver as the clouds that now covered the sun. Her mouth was open, its corners ɔotted with wet spittle.

A monk appeared at the edge of the graveyard. He closed the doors in the brick wall and we heard the clang of the great door to the church being forced shut. He stared hard at us before disappearing. The monastery was closing.

Konstanze got up first, still clutching the small Bible, as if it was her one contact with reality. I can remember thinking, just then, that she would never see my home, never sail the Mississippi with me, nor would we take Dieter to see the buffalo. Would she let him keep the binoculars? I doubted it.

Worse, after she had come so close to kissing me, could she ever go back to Rudolf? Would she ever tell him? Was the betrayal that I had forced out of her too damaging for her ever to recover completely? Was *I* going to feel as guilty as I did now for the rest of my life? Ironically, I thought, Konstanze had been right about one thing: my approach to interrogation was far more cruel, if less brutal, than Lieutenant Bloch's. At least he had been bluffing; I had meant everything I had said.

I put up the top of the car and we drove back to Mondsee in silence. Konstanze could not lie with a Bible in her hands so that silence said everything. She sat huddled the whole way, shriveled like someone convicted of a capital offense and on their way to begin a life sentence.

Around seven we reached the house. The wind was now of such force that, in happier times, Konstanze might have called it cleansing. I asked, "How long will it take you to contact Rudolf?"

No answer. Then: "Two days."

"Very well. I will return the day after tomorrow."

She opened the car door and hesitated as I spoke again. I whispered, like I did at first in the churches we visited. "Konstanze . . . believe me, I am very, very sorry."

She let the Bible fall to the ground and walked into the house. Her God had deserted her. In return she had abandoned him.

4

HOBEL'S raid was a fiasco. The warehouse in Krumau *was* part of the conduit—or would have been if, as I had advised, he had held off for a while. The warehouse contained a printing press and some false Vatican diplomatic papers. The renegades were to be sent south—or wherever—disguised as Vatican emissaries—clever. But Hobel didn't catch anybody worth writing home about, just a couple of Austrians who delivered things and knew nothing.

So that was something I could feel relieved about.

The next afternoon, as I was sitting in my hotel room, before I knew that Dieter was in no immediate danger, there was a loud, urgent knocking on the door of my hotel room. I opened it to find Konstanze. She was wearing a long gray coat, which I hadn't seen before, but then the weather had changed for the worse. The coat was set off by a maroon scarf. It was a very different Konstanze that I confronted from the woman who had let the Bible fall outside of her house. This one had flushed cheeks, her whole face shimmering with energy.

She swept past me into my room without waiting to be asked. She walked almost to the balcony before turning to face me. She took off her hat, shook free her hair and unbuttoned her coat.

"He never stole those coins, Walter. He never stole them."

"What?" This was unexpected and, I hate to admit it, more than a little disappointing. "We know he had them, that day in May last year. More than one witness confirms that. He was the last person to be seen—"

She cut me short. "Oh, he had them, yes. But he didn't *steal* them. He left them with the Prince Archbishop, right here in Salzburg. Rudolf is a Catholic. The coins were taken from a Catholic monastery, as you pointed out. He had to go into hiding but first he took the coins to the Prince Archbishop for safekeeping. They've been there ever since, right under your noses."

It was true. Hobel and I went to see the Prince Archbishop later that evening and there the coins were, in their original cases, all of them. The Prince Archbishop hadn't reported them, he said, for the simple fact that, in the press of events, he had forgotten about them. I believed him and so did Hobel.

But that's not what's important. What happened between Konstanze and me is what haunts me still. Konstanze, of course, was transformed. Only a day before she had nearly betrayed her husband, who was then, in her own mind, little more than a common criminal. Now she had discovered that he had acted honorably and she should never have doubted him. And, since she had not actually kissed me and committed the final betrayal, she was fast recovering her self-esteem. At the same time it became obvious that, if the coins had been with the Prince Archbishop all the time, and were still intact, they could not have been used for the political purposes Eisenhower suspected. Which meant that I had ruined what was between Konstanze and me for nothing.

Before she had left me that day, to go back to Mondsee, I had seen a new look on Konstanze's face. It was pity.

5

HOBEL was jubilant as we returned that night from the Prince Archbishop's. We had the case of coins in the car and he was imagining a lieutenant colonel's badge on his collar already. He was pretty civil to me, too, as may be imagined.

"I'm glad we didn't have to pull in the boy," he lied. "Much cleaner this way."

I said nothing. Maybe Konstanze would let Dieter keep his binoculars now, I hoped.

"How well do you know Mrs. von Zell?" asked Hobel as we swung across the Market Bridge.

"Quite well," I said evenly.

"What are the chances she will turn in her husband now?"

"Not good. Look at how protective she has been. She gave us the coins only because of the religious connection and because I specifically said I *didn't* want her husband."

He ignored this. "It would be quite a feather in our cap to have this thing completely cleared up, you know. There are just too many Nazis on the loose. Eisenhower would remember it. Do what you can, will you?"

I agreed, because I would have done anything to have a chance to see Konstanze again. So, I found myself driving out to Mondsee next morning. It had turned cold, the wind zipping through the lanes and numbing my fingers. I felt cold inside too. Konstanze would not be happy to see me. However, I had to see her again, even if it meant having to face Martha.

It did. She opened the door and looked at me with enough hatred to last me until today, forty years later. I still wince when I recall that look. Martha must be dead now for years, but, for me, her scowl lives on, feeding on my regret.

Still, she showed me inside to the sewing room. This time Konstanze was already there, needle and thread across her knee. She didn't get up.

"I was right," she breathed. "You *did* find the coins, didn't you?"

"Yes."

Her smile was radiant. "Rudi is *not* a criminal."

"Konstanze, he is still wanted. He is still a fugitive Nazi." She turned her head away from me, not wanting to hear.

"Listen to me, Konstanze," I whispered. "You have endured years of hardly ever seeing him, of writing letters and listening to concerts on the radio. As long as he is on the run, that will never change. The only way you can be together is to live secretly in South America. Do you want that? Is it worth it?"

She looked at me.

"But let's imagine that he gives himself up. What is the worst that can happen to him then? Several months—a year or two—in a camp, maybe, but at least you will know where he is *and* you will know that, at the end of his sentence, you will have him back. Dieter will have a father again, at last." I hesitated. "And then you won't have me around to pry, to read what I shouldn't read. You can have your privacy back."

I sat down and reached across to take the sewing out of her hands. She didn't look up.

"Konstanze, I can understand you being—cold with me. What I did —what happened in the graveyard—was awful, *terrible*. Already I regret it. Please believe me. You think I was calculating: I was not. But I joined the army to fight Nazis . . . not to fall in love with their wives.

"You are an extraordinary woman. Bruno knew it; Rudi knows it; and I do too, now. I have mismanaged this case from the very beginning, but I would not have missed it for anything. I am *proud* of you, Konstanze, and flattered to think that you loved—or nearly loved—me.

"When you said you would never lie to me, in the graveyard, I loved you more then than I have loved anything. But what you said meant that I couldn't lie. I have lied too much to you already.

"I wormed my way into your affections deliberately but it backfired. Christ, how it backfired! From that day Dieter broke his binoculars and we shared a brandy I have—well, you know how I have felt."

Still, she didn't look across to me. But she curled her top lip inside her teeth. "Say it, Walter, say it."

I paused. "Don't be offended, Konstanze. I'm not being blasphemous." I paused again. I remember noticing she must have washed her hair again that morning. Once more its fine edges caught the light. "I have worshiped you."

Her face softened. My insides calmed down, too.

"If you can love two people at the same time, then I will settle for being number two. Maybe sometime you will agree that you loved me a bit."

I stood up. I could smell her, watch the strands of hair play with the light. Though we were standing close, as close as we had been on the bench at St. Florian, she didn't flinch.

"Try to convince him, Konstanze, please. I'll come back in two days."

6

Hobel grunted when I reported back. He wanted to know why Konstanze was not being followed.

"If she got wind of it, it could throw the whole investigation. Don't you agree?"

He had grunted, again. Thankfully his mind was also occupied with the pullout, which was beginning in earnest. Large wooden crates had been delivered for packing our official papers, prior to shipment to Frankfurt on the first leg of their journey home. The office could be divided into those who were ecstatic about our return and those who, though they could not admit it for fear of being thought sick, had actually enjoyed the war. People who realized that they would never again have as much purpose in their lives, or as much self-respect, as the war had given them. Men and women who would never again be so happy.

So Konstanze wasn't followed and I returned alone, two days later, to Mondsee. She answered the door herself this time and suggested we go across to the summerhouse. It was still blustery but I could sense she wanted to use the place to create a mood.

She stood on the balcony of the small hut, looking at the fishermen, in almost exactly the same spot where, with luck on the night of the concert, things might have taken a different turn.

"Well?" I said.

She picked up a broken twig that, in the wind, had fallen onto the boards and threw it into the lake. "He'll do it. He'll do as you suggest. But there is a condition."

I didn't say anything.

Her voice changed to a softer tone, one that belonged to the days before St. Florian.

"You once said that . . . our days together were like a honeymoon. Yes?"

"Yes," I said, a lump in my throat. "The happiest days of my life."

She bit her lower lip, curling it under her teeth. A look that seemed to say she had been happy too.

"Now you must grant *us* a honeymoon."

I am sure I looked bewildered. I know I got a sinking feeling inside.

"You yourself said Rudi and I have been apart for too long. We shall go away tomorrow—together—and you must not follow. You or anyone else. You must promise me that. If you agree, then a week from now Rudi will give himself up, to you. Only to you. And at St. Florian.

"He knows about . . . about . . ." She never did say. "He wants to see the monastery; he wants to meet you. He will only surrender in this way, to you."

"And if I do not agree."

"Rudi will stay in hiding and you will have to arrest me for noncooperation."

We stared across the lake together, to where two boats were silhouetted against the water. The clouds were lower today; it was only a matter of time before the wind dropped and the rain started. Despite what Konstanze had said about the lack of wind hereabouts, it felt gusty to me. The lake was choppy and gray.

I wasn't sure what I disliked most, the fact that she was going away with Rudolf, to recapture whatever they had to recapture, before he gave himself up, or the fact that they might simply disappear, never to return. Part of me—the part of me that *did* love her—thought that not such a bad idea. They could smuggle themselves to South America; Rudolf would have the contacts. Dieter could join them there later. They would be happy. I would be happy for her.

I closed my eyes as if that would blot out the image in my mind of Konstanze and Rudolf together on honeymoon. Konstanze must have sensed what I was thinking about for she whispered, "Walter, please. I can't risk losing both of you in the space of just a few days. What you did was cruel. It may have been the right thing to do, but it was cruel all the same." She hesitated and I opened my eyes to look at her.

"From that afternoon when you gave me the carving, you replaced Rudi . . . it is so long since anyone gave me anything, since I was with a man—properly. The night we went to Innsbruck, to the concert, I wanted to make love to you so much. But the music, which was part of it, was also Rudi's territory. So I couldn't, not that night. That's why I wanted to go somewhere special the next day: somewhere that belonged

to just us—the two of us. But you—damaged that, in the graveyard"—
and she sighed out loud—"and now I must make the repairs. With
Rudi."

The more I thought about the honeymoon plan, the more I realized
how clever it was. The more I thought, the more I realized that I
couldn't say no. I owed her something and I had to grant her this
condition.

"Very well," I said. "A week from today, in the church of St. Florian.
At noon."

7

HOBEL thought I was mad, criminally insane, to have agreed to
the honeymoon arrangement. However, because we had received a note
from Eisenhower congratulating *us* on the recovery of the coins, and
because Hobel had already been given the nod that he *would* be promoted now, and because the pullout took up so much of his time, and
because I had presented him with a *fait accompli*, he had to accept what
I had done. He did insist, however, that we post a guard at Dieter's
school. That way, if Konstanze and Rudolf came for the boy, we could
catch them. And, if Dieter was kept safely at his school, it made it more
likely that the couple would stick to their bargain and return. I had to
admit that Hobel's plan made sense.

There was little for me to do but wait. I had few files or official papers
in Salzburg so I could not busy myself with packing. I was entitled to
leave, so I took it. I went home for the weekend to Offenbach to have a
farewell dinner with Maurice and to meet the new squirrels. We, Maurice and I, not the squirrels, dined at Gottlieb's in Frankfurt and drove
off in the BMW to Hessen and the Thuringer Wald. Maurice loved the
car, though the showery weather meant we had the top up all the time.

I did most of the talking—about Konstanze—but although Maurice
played the attentive, sympathetic friend at all times, I could not relax.
My mind was elsewhere and, quite often, I would forget the end of a

sentence before I got to it. Even in Frankfurt the signs of the grand pullout were everywhere, so that I was reminded of what I was about to lose at every turn.

Our bet still had some way to run, but it provided great interest, and some amusement, every day. Maurice's shares were down to $1,058, but RMC had been taken over by, of all things, Galaxy Studios. They had jumped four cents to $994.60. In theory I could still overtake him before the end of the academic year; even so, I awarded him the helmet.

The weekend came to a close. I wouldn't see Maurice again, not for some time anyway. We both felt sad as he came down to the car on Monday morning to see me off.

"Good luck, Maurice," I said. "I shall miss you."

"Dear boy." He took my hand. "I have something for you." It was a book, a life of Bruckner. "A memento. With love."

I drove back to Salzburg. His was the sort of gesture that made people miss the war. I like mementos too.

The next day was Tuesday, the day before Rudolf was supposed to turn himself in. It poured. I took the fast road toward Vienna, arriving at Stockerau just after lunch. I didn't spot Hobel's man though I stood outside the school in the rain for more than two hours. It was the day Dieter had said was his games afternoon, when he played goalkeeper for the soccer team. I wanted a last look at him, but maybe they didn't do games in the teeming rain, or maybe his day on the fields had changed with the new term. I was too embarrassed to go into the school and ask for him. Konstanze would not have liked that. So I never saw him.

8

IT was pouring the next day, too, silver and slate-colored streaks hitting the pavement with such ferocity that they bounced back into the air. The Goldener Hirsch had given my old room to someone else. I could hardly blame them, but my new room felt quite different and I regarded it as an omen.

Hobel insisted that I not take my own car on this last journey but that I ride in a jeep, with an armed guard, plus a backup vehicle—"in case of any funny business." No one, not even I, expected the von Zells to turn up as arranged.

Early that morning, Sammy had winked at me and shown me his slip of yellow paper. The previous day Galaxy had bought a chain of radio stations with which they could plug the records they made at RMC. My shares had jumped another five cents; at $1,026.45, I had made my first money on the stock exchange and was within $31.55 of Maurice, whose shares were "steady." But I didn't have time to call him.

The convoy, if it can be called that, left Salzburg around 9:30 A.M. and took the main road to Linz, which meant that I never had a final look at Konstanze's house in Mondsee, as I had intended.

If anything, the weather got steadily worse as we drove east. We were held up at Linz due to a damaged bridge and for a while I was worried that we would not make it to St. Florian in time. But within twenty minutes we were through the town and crossing the plain toward the white building.

It was just before a quarter to noon as we pulled up by the Prandtauer gate. The rain was slapping against the long white wall of the monastery, the grass and trees cowed by the weight of the water and the wind. I got down, motioning the others to stay where they were. I turned up my collar and hurried along by the wall into the church. As I pulled back the huge door I glimpsed, beyond the edge of the church itself, the black headstones in the graveyard, like the shiny lumps of black tar that had stuck to the wheels of my car when the weather had been so hot. When Konstanze and I had been getting to know one another.

Inside the church it was empty but unexpectedly light. I had forgotten that. I slapped at my tunic to shake off the surplus water and stepped down the aisle. It was ten to twelve.

I sat more or less where Konstanze and I had sat on our previous visit. But I didn't pray this time. What would I have prayed for? That they both came? Or that only she would come? I still didn't know. I didn't know anything. I stared toward the altar. Someone had changed the flowers, they were now yellow, Konstanze's color, that I remember. The sound of the rain could be heard against the windows, an uneven clattering. In one or two places it had forced itself inside the church, staining the walls and ceiling. I had brought with me the book Maurice had given me. I dipped into it. I had not realized what a foolish old man Bruckner had been. All those young girls he fell for who hardly knew he existed. I pitied him in the way Konstanze pitied me.

The monastery bell struck the hour. Noon to the world no longer at war but sext to the monks who still used the medieval ecclesiastical clock.

There was no sign of anyone. Despite the coolness of the church, I began to sweat. All of a sudden I realized that I was desperate for Konstanze to come. No one else. I wanted to see her again. I could not quite remember what she looked like; my mind was betraying me. The precise arrangement of her features became blurred. I wanted to see her again, had to see her again, like a man in need of a drug.

The rain was drumming against the windows, slapping against the roof. The light in the nave seemed to come from the walls rather than from outside, as if the architect had enlisted divine aid in decorating the church and the walls had absorbed light from more generous days and now gave off a glow when it was needed. I heard footsteps.

What startled me at first was that the footsteps came not from behind, as they should have done if the main door had been opened, but from the crypt. Konstanze and Rudolf must have been down there all this time, alone together, and, I suspected, praying.

I rose as they came toward me. Konstanze was dressed in her gray coat, with the maroon scarf. The man was taller than I expected and wore a long blue coat, with a belt. His hair was swept back and he had a scar on his left cheek. He carried a hat, a trilby. He stopped.

The war was over—no salutes—I shook his hand. Like his wife, he did not whisper in churches. His voice was deep, warm, a voice that was easy to like, more at home with soft vowels than hard consonants.

"Thank you for helping my wife, Professor," he said, setting his jaw to one side, just as I had seen Dieter do. "You are a better German than I."

Involuntarily I looked at Konstanze. She nodded and smiled but didn't speak. I turned back to him. "You just have time to kiss your wife good-bye, Herr Doktor. Then we must go."

I walked to the rear of the church, turning my back on them as they embraced. I couldn't look. Absently I picked up a Bible from a stack at the back of the nave and opened it at random. It was Lamentations, chapter four, first verse: "How is the gold become dim! how is the most fine gold changed!"

After a moment von Zell joined me. I looked back but Konstanze had knelt to pray. He and I went out together into the rain. We pulled our collars about us and hurried to the jeep. He climbed in but I waited. I took a small package from the front seat and, as he settled, I said to him, "Will you excuse me a moment?"

He looked at me hard, but then nodded. I returned to the church.

Konstanze was still there, kneeling. The rain pelted against the windows, like chains being unraveled from out of the heavens, rasping on the roof. I walked forward to where she was kneeling, my footsteps all but drowned by the weather outside. Without a word I placed the letters on the pew beside her. She must have heard me but she never looked up. After a moment I went back to join von Zell in the jeep for the ride back to Salzburg.

EPILOGUE

T HAT is not the end of the story, not quite. Hobel *was* promoted and for a long while after the war I used to receive a Christmas card from "Colonel Hobel." My shares eventually passed Maurice's and on May 31 that year I was worth $1,153.85 against his $1,084, though I never did get the helmet. Maurice became a professor soon after his return to Cambridge but was killed in a skiing accident in 1949 and I never saw him again. I still have the book that he gave me though I can never bring myself to read it now.

One loose end that was never tied up was that newspaper which Allie and I found on the mountain, the one from Worms with the strange advertisement circled in pencil.

Muhlman and the others were caught—eventually. They had indeed been a staging post in the underground pipeline helping renegade Nazis to freedom. I sent written evidence to the court which convicted them, so those nights on the mountain with Allie were useful as well as pleasurable. The pipeline, which Hobel and I thought ran from south Germany/Austria to Spain, in fact was shown later to run south most of the time, through Italy.

Von Zell, ironically, *had* been living under von Haltern's identity as a wine merchant, but in Bernkastel, where he and Konstanze had met and been married, staying with the host who had introduced them and devised those games. So perhaps I didn't deserve the medal I never got; the letters had contained that clue, but I never spotted it.

I sold my shares—for $1,800—after Maurice's death and never bothered with the stock market again. But Sammy Hartt went on to make more millions, naturally. I followed his career in the newspapers. He put some of his money into Israel, some into Simon Wiesenthal's research center in Vienna, the one which sought to track down renegade Nazis; and the rest he took with him to a private island he bought near Hawaii. But he became a golf fanatic so I could never bring myself to visit him, though he invited me several times. I'm hopeless at golf. He had a heart attack a few years ago and left all his money to create a Sammy Hartt Golf Classic.

The BMW went back to its rightful owner, minus the badge. I have mixed feelings, now, about open cars.

And Konstanze? I heard nothing until a few months after I had returned to America and had again taken up my post at the university. I received a letter from her early in 1947. Being a great one for anniversaries and birthdays and so forth, she had written it on New Year's Eve. I have it here, with all my other things, so I can quote it in full. It was written in English—her brand of English. She had started to learn as soon as I had left.

"Dear Walter," she had written. "Dear Walter, I do not wish to let the old year come to an end without sending you a Christian greeting and blessing. You should not really believe that I have already forgotten you because I have for so long not let you hear anything. I have by contrast often thought of you, how you might be and whether you would, on some occasions, think back to here. Now I surprise you, with my English already. Better than Dieter's, not so?

"How are you living after your long sojourn in Europe for the war? How did you adjust yourself back to your new existence? All of that I would like to know of course, very much and I would be eternally enjoyed to hear from you.

"Here with us since you left nothing changed very much in the village as well as with me personally. My husband was fourteen days after you saw him transferred to a large internment camp near Darmstadt and considering the circumstances he is in good condition. He is confident and hopes in the spring to be released. About that, Walter, you were right.

"Of the rebuilding and of the often applauded democratic liberties one does not notice very much with us. Above all, no Austrian today may have any real taste of liberty because furnitures, living quarters, our existences are desperate. We are deprived but hope for a better and happier future.

"I envy all those that have thoughts to emigrate; to judge by the letters of my husband he also plays with such ideas. I am glad that he is in the American zone which is more generous than elsewhere. Perhaps for us too the sun will shine again someday. Not so much for myself do I desire that, but for Dieter, who should have it better. Walter, he does not forget your handsome car. And I do not forget the things you gave me, the feather of the swan, the statue of the saint and the pen, with which I write this letter.

"Often do I think still of the nice hours in the spring which I spent with you. But all of this is now for the past. That I have lost you so entirely and should never see you again makes me endlessly sad. Despite all the disagreeable things and torturings that I have experienced through you, you have nevertheless become very close to me and I am still very sorry that our separation was too soon upon us. So much did I still have on my heart that I should have liked to tell you. Konstanze."

I am still unable to read that letter, after all these years, without feeling—well, without *feeling*. In fact, in normal circumstances I avoid it. If I come across the envelope, with its familiar Austrian stamp and Salzburg postmark, I push it away, bury it back in the recesses of my desk. It is too painful, still.

I am aware, of course, that at last I became a recipient of one of Konstanze's letters. It was not a love letter perhaps, not in the strict sense of the word, but close. And I was aware too that I was being put on a par with Bruno and Rudolf—at least I like to think so.

But what pains—no, saddens me most—is the letter's tone. Konstanze was saying—was she not?—that she regretted the outcome, perhaps that she regretted the choice she had made. And that a lifetime's regret is what we both gave each other as the price for our mistake.

Or perhaps she was asking to love me at a distance—through letters— as she had done with Bruno and Rudolf. Letters, it always came back to letters, the letters I should not have read but would not have missed for anything.

I don't know, for I never replied.